Battleframe

Book One of
The Mindwars

Michael Gilmour

MRG Asset Trust

PO Box 37, Dingley Village 3172,
Melbourne, Australia

michaelgilmour.com

This paperback edition 2015
Edition 1

First published by the MRG Asset Trust 2015

ISBN-13: 978-0-9942191-0-7

ISBN-10: 0994219105

Set in Garamond

Printed and bound in the USA by CreateSpace, an Amazon.com Company

Available from Amazon.com, retail outlets and other online stores.

Maps, character profiles and additional information available at
michaelgilmour.com

Table of Contents

Prelude   i

Part I Friendship   1

Chapter 1 The Past   2

Chapter 2 Freehold   7

Chapter 3 War has come   21

Chapter 4 Called in Help   27

Chapter 5 Research Ravine   31

Chapter 6 Training   37

Chapter 7 Fighting For His Life   48

Chapter 8 New Friends   54

Chapter 9 Test Pilots   61

Chapter 10 Teamwork   73

Chapter 11 Struggle   84

Chapter 12 Assault   95

Chapter 13 The Search Continues   108

Chapter 14 In the Hanger   116

Chapter 15 Bosk   123

Chapter 16 A Scourge Fist   137

Chapter 17 The End   143

Chapter 18 Concord Central Command   150

Chapter 19 Return to Freehold   156

Chapter 20 The Beginning and the End   166

Part II Revelations   171

Chapter 1 The Real World   172

Chapter 2 Deliberations 176

Chapter 3 Is this a dream? 181

Chapter 4 Plans and Gliding 186

Chapter 5 Selfia in Command 193

Chapter 6 A Father's War 200

Chapter 7 Pyro's Dance 206

Chapter 8 Out of the Frying Pan 212

Chapter 9 Fight to the Death 222

Part III For Real **229**

Chapter 1 Early Morning Rush 230

Chapter 2 Taxis and Bus Stops 235

Chapter 3 The Boardroom 241

Chapter 4 Decisions 254

Chapter 5 Goodbyes and Enemies 262

Chapter 6 Alpha Three 271

Chapter 7 Transformation 282

Chapter 8 Breakfast 289

Chapter 9 Central 294

Chapter 10 Dissention 301

Chapter 11 Water, Poison and the Barrier 306

Chapter 12 Attack! 316

Chapter 13 More to do 324

Chapter 14 The Battle in the Dome 335

Chapter 15 It is Finished 351

Glossary 362

For my wife
Who is always at my side cheering me onwards.
You're an amazing editor that always has a smile and a cup of tea.

For Timothy
Who has my back in playing games.
You're the best son that a Dad could ever wish for.

For Sarah and Elise
Both of you are incredible daughters
You challenge me to make the female heroes like you both.

For my father
Who is a man of imagination.
You continue to inspire me to new heights!

For the game players
Bosk, Elzetro, Pyro, DG and Kheldar.
Thanks for all the good times defending the universe!

Prelude

With a surge of mental energy, Wisdom energized the form of an elderly English gentleman. Gold rimmed round spectacles and a greying goatee adorned his face. A matching soft cap complimented a brown tweed jacket and pants that were reminiscent of mid twentieth century Earth, a planet that was light years away from where he now stood. For some reason he had grown quite accustomed to this shape and drew a sense of comfort from resting his hand lightly on the carved wooden walking cane at his side.

Wisdom looked around the dark alleyway created by the surrounding, soaring skyscrapers. Abandoned old wooden pallets, cardboard boxes and several small clear plastic containers littered the area, the refuse of a burgeoning civilization. High above, he could make out a small patch of blue sky, where every now and then a flitter-car would scoot into view and just as quickly vanish from sight.

Chuckling to himself as if to a jest only he could hear, Wisdom walked to the end of the alley and stepped out into a huge open square at the heart of a bustling city. He loved this place and remembered when the builders had laid the first blue paving tile that seemed to mirror the cloudless sky above. The area was so large that even with the number of workers employed it had taken them years to complete the task. Skyscrapers, of a similar size to the ones that had created the alleyway from which he had just stepped, fenced the square in on all sides. Everything was on a vast scale in the capital.

Wisdom let his gaze wander across paving to the eight large water fountains positioned equidistant from each other along the circumference of a giant circle. Each fountain represented one of Kaladon's eight continents with a single larger fountain in the middle symbolising unity. The sound of the spraying water provided a soft undercurrent of tranquillity as it gently echoed off the surrounding buildings.

Kaladon IV was the fourth planet out from a binary star system and teemed with over twelve billion inhabitants. It was the home world of the fledgling Concord of planets, and was the birthplace of a human society that had only recently developed interstellar travel.

Across from Wisdom, a teacher led a procession of primary school children towards one of the fountains. A little further away was a group of families with the adults enjoying each other's company while their children ran around like satellites orbiting a planet. Despite being in the centre of a city of forty million people, it was beautiful and peaceful.

As Wisdom wrested his hands lightly on his cane, he stopped for a minute to enjoy the warmth of the distant twin suns on his face. As he gazed upwards, the sunlight highlighted his unusually bright blue eyes. His entire ancient race had similar coloured eyes and his seemed to sparkle with eagerness behind his spectacles. It had been quite some time since the three of them had met in this fashion and only now because the plan was nearing a critical juncture.

The people going about their business subconsciously made way for Wisdom as he strolled across the blue stone pavers towards the bench directly opposite. There was a calmness and surety about him as he settled on the seat between a young man and a middle-aged woman.

The young man looked like a university student from the college on the far side of the square. His ruffled unkempt hair mirrored his rumpled pants and t-shirt that was emblazoned with the university's motto of, "Think, Plan, Act." A smudge deposited from his last meal, disrupted the final word. To their loss, many had made the mistake of judging him by his dishevelled appearance. In one hand, he held a reading tablet as he digested the latest scientific news from the inhabitants of this world.

In sharp contrast to the young man, the woman was stunning and would be a head turner at any party. Long blond hair cascaded down her back while her white blouse revealed just a little of what was discretely hidden underneath. Her fingers thrummed rhythmically on the outside of a black violin case that rested on her equally black neatly pressed slacks. On the ground beside her was a dark leather briefcase with a folded silver music stand sticking out the end.

Unnecessarily clearing his throat Wisdom asked, "So Intellect, what do you think of Kaladon?"

The young man looked up from his tablet, paused to refocus his bright blue eyes and to ponder the question for a moment. "I've been scanning the latest scientific research papers and it appears that all is in order. No one has detected our influence over the last several thousand years."

Wisdom smiled and turned towards Intellect beside him. "I didn't ask for the results of the plan. I asked what you thought of this world and its people."

"It's wonderful."

Wisdom raised his eyebrows to encourage his colleague to continue. Intellect sighed and reluctantly put his reading tablet down. "The humans here have passed through so many obstacles: war, famine, environmental problems and economic disparity to name but a few. With a little help from us they've now started colonizing the star systems in this sector."

Wisdom nodded. "And you Creativity?"

Creativity shifted on the bench so that she could get a better view of her two strange companions. Each of them indulged in energizing a form they felt the most comfortable but she always wondered why Intellect liked to wear unclean garments. Her intensely blue eyes sparkled in remembrance as she replied in a voice that was like a perfectly tuned instrument. "I played with the Kaladon orchestra and Balnarth's music brought me close to tears. The highs and the lows pulled at my heart. The way he managed to bring the audience with him on the journey was close to remarkable. The arts, education and health are everything that we could have dreamed."

Wisdom again sighed deeply, "That is good. Although young, the Concord of planets is even now beginning to glimpse the dangers that await in the galaxy."

Creativity lovingly opened her violin case and smiled as she again remembered her last performance. Concern entered her voice as she said, "Wisdom, at your request I have ensured that the discovery of nano-technology has taken place. That will surely help them."

"Yes, it will help immeasurably but there will still be much suffering," Wisdom replied.

Intellect picked up his reading tablet and then paused in deep thought. As if reaching a conclusion he looked across at his two colleagues and said, "For all their technological advances they need the others. It's only the genes combined with the technology that will give this galaxy a chance."

Removing his hat to reveal thin grey hair Wisdom mopped his brow with a handkerchief that he'd pulled from his inside jacket pocket. "The meeting will happen soon but not here. It won't be long before the Concord and the people of Earth will come face to face."

"And what of Kaladon IV?" Intellect asked.

Wisdom shook his head from side to side as if struggling with what he was about to say. "We can do nothing for them without disrupting both streams. For the sake of their development, the Concord and the people of Earth must not know of our influence yet. They will become psychologically dependent upon us and that will mean the end."

Creativity looked across at the families admiring the fountains dotted around square. The sounds of children screaming in delight as water suddenly sprayed from the sides of a pyramidal shaped sculpture cut across the general hubbub - "So this will all be gone?"

Wisdom perched his hat back on his head and replied in a sombre voice, "Yes."

Blue eyes turned to look into blue and a tear trickled down Creativity's milk white cheek, "Isn't there anything that we can do?"

The concern of eons suddenly etched across Wisdom's face, "No, they are doomed."

Part I
Friendship

Chapter 1
The Past

"Get back in here and finish those dishes young man!"

"Oh Mum. Can't I skip them just this once? I really want to build the lean-to with Dad in the woods."

Ray's mother quickly wiped her hands on her apron and glanced out the window. She squinted as she gauged how long it would be until the first sun set and the second rose above the horizon.

"Please Mum?" Ray whined.

"Oh get going you scoundrel!"

"Yeah!"

Without looking back (in case she changed her mind) the blond-haired, blue eyed ten year old rushed out through the fly wire door and slammed it behind him. The red barn was on the other side of the family's old flitter car at rest in the driveway and it did not take Ray long to reach the huge double front doors. As he pulled the left one open, he could hear his father rummaging around for what they would need for building the lean-to together in the woods.

"So your mother let you off the dishes?"

Ray pulled the door of the barn closed behind him just like his Dad taught him since he was little. "Yes sir."

A broad grin crossed his father's face. "You'd better do something special for her tomorrow. Come here son."

Ray ran to his father and felt himself immediately lifted off the ground in a bear hug. "Oh, my you're getting big and heavy."

Ray hugged his father back even harder to show off his muscles. He loved hearing his father say that he was growing up. One day he was going to be as strong as his dad and wear overalls and a checked shirt just like him. They both ended up laughing as Ray's father gave his son a little tickle under the ribs before putting him back down.

"OK, I've got the saw and the nails. What else do we need?" Ray's father said half to himself.

"A hammer! We need a hammer Dad!"

"That's right, we need a hammer."

Ray laughed at his dad for forgetting the most critical tool. After packing their things into a bag, Ray's father grabbed his rifle and they both headed out of the barn and down white fence line that separated the fields of wheat from the woods.

Behind them, Ray's mother smiled to herself as she placed another dish in the rack. Flicking a strand of hair out of her eyes, she looked lovingly at the two most important men in her life walking side by side away from the house.

After reaching the edge of the forest a few hundred metres from the house Ray's father asked, "So have you picked a place?"

Ray screwed up his face in concentration. "I think just through there looks good."

His father replied seriously, "I think that's a good choice as well. The trees are bent at just the right point to help us with the construction."

Ray clambered through the fence's crossbars while his father climbed over the top. They could still see the house not far away through the undergrowth and for the next few minutes, they cleared the area around the base of the selected tree. Ray's father bent down to check that the tree did not have any spines like many of the species in the woods.

Just after he had married Ray's mother, they had made the decision to be one of the first farming colonist of this world. The vast wheat fields helped feed the Concord's core worlds and it was not long before their little farm began to prosper. Soon after arriving, Ray was born and the planet felt more like home every day.

"Dad, what's that noise?"

"What noise son?"

Just as he asked the question Ray's father turned his attention to the sky as the screeching wail of something falling reached him. Through the brush, he watched a dark metallic pyramid slam into the ground next to their flitter car, sending a cloud of dirt into the air. The pyramid was a few feet taller than the flitter and at the apex, an energy orb began to pulse faster and faster.

In a strained voice his father said, "Son stay by my side and don't leave it. Do you understand?"

Ray knew that his dad was using his very serious voice and only replied, "Yes sir."

With his rifle in his right hand and his son's hand in his left, Ray's father abandoned all thought of the lean-to. Skirting along the edge of the woods, with tree branches whipping against them, they ran as fast as Ray could back towards the house.

With a dishtowel still in her hand, Ray's mother stepped out onto the porch to see what was making all the commotion. She had heard the awful whining sound and the thump as the object fell from the sky. A shimmering purple haze formed at five distinct points around the machine. Within the haze, sparks flashed like small lightning bolts back and forth until the vague shape of men in some sort of strange armour began to form.

She recognized those shapes and dropped her dishtowel as she fled along the porch in the direction where her husband and son had gone.

As he ran to keep up with his father, Ray watched as his mother jumped down to the ground and run towards the fence line. A brilliant beam of red light lanced out and seemed to pin her in the air mid-step. Her face contorted in agony as she collapsed to the ground. Ray watched as his father screamed in a way he had never heard before. He had seen his dad angry with him or yelling at a contractor but he had never seen his father like this.

With tears building in his eyes, Ray's father dropped to one knee and lifted his riflescope up to his eye. Ray heard the brief build-up of energy and watched in grim fascination as his father's blue beam fled the rifle's muzzle. The man that had hurt his mother dropped to the ground.

The earth in front of them suddenly erupted in a rapid series of puffs of dirt. As if in a dream, Ray watched his father tossed backwards by an invisible force and his good work shirt suddenly turn a deep crimson colour. Crawling over to his dad, he looked into vacant staring eyes.

Ray was confused and bewildered. He had never seen anything like this before. Were his mum and dad playing a new game? When was the happy part? He then looked down at his father's rifle and he knew how this game needed to end.

He had fired his father's rifle a number of times before. All children that grew up on a farm in one of the colonies learned to fire at targets with their dads. Picking up the rifle in his small hands Ray lay in the grass and looked through the telescopic sights.

He saw the ugly pale faced man with the pink eyes that had hurt his father and squeezed the trigger. The man dropped and Ray felt a little better for it. Just then, Ray's home exploded in a ball of fire and a wave of heat washed over him. Ray looked through the scope at the big bad man who had hurt his house, just as his father had taught him, and squeezed the trigger again. The big bad man fell to the ground and then stood up again and turned in Ray's direction.

The bad man smiled with sharp pointed teeth and lifted a much bigger gun toward Ray. That was when Ray's saviour arrived.

The undergrowth next to Ray suddenly parted and a man in a uniform that Ray recognized from the tridee-reels at school fired his gun at the bad man. The evil man fell backwards and did not get up anymore. This time, Ray felt even happier about that. The uniformed man rushed forward and in rapid succession fired his weapon at the remaining bad men. He then focused on the horrible black pyramid until the ball on the top stopped glowing. Ray was going to have a great story to tell his Mum and Dad at dinner that evening! Why was he crying? What was happening?

That was when he noticed the boy about his age lying beside him. He must have come with his saviour. Like him, the boy was crying. His mother had always told him to help anyone that was crying so he managed to stammer, "Hi, my name's Ray. What's your name?"

The boy looked back at him and like all brave boys quickly wiped his tears. "My name's Thomas. Hi."

"Thomas, do you want to be my friend?"

"I'd like that Ray."

By this time the man that had saved, them both returned and squatted next to them. Turning to Ray he asked, "What's your name son?"

"My mother told me not to speak to strangers. What's your name?"

"Gasp."

"That's a funny name. I guess that now I know your name then you're not a stranger. Mister, my name's Ray. I think that my Mum and Dad are hurt. Can you help them?"

"I'm sorry son, I can't help them but I think that I can help the both of you." Gasp stood up and looked down at the two boys. "Here take my hands."

Ray and Thomas looked at Gasp's smiling face and without hesitation they reached up to hold Gasp's outstretched welcoming hands. With his other hand, Ray held firmly onto his father's rifle.

Chapter 2
Freehold

Squad leader Whizzbang raised his arms for the microscopic nano-robots to generate his battleframe armour perfectly around his trim body. The familiar tingling sensation on his skin indicated that billions of nanites were feverishly converting the energy from tellurite crystals into his battleframe exoskeleton.

Whizzbang looked around the small rectangular ready room and nodded a greeting to his friend Happy sitting on the plasteel bench across from him. "I'll never get tired of this," Whizzbang said in wonder.

With several loud metallic clunks, Happy slapped the grey walls with his armoured gauntlet. It was a habit that he had developed over the years to reassure himself that everything was just fine with his equipment. "What you talking about Whizz?" he replied in his deep resonating voice.

Whizzbang flexed the soft gloves of his Raven battleframe. "Each day we put on the most sophisticated infantry combat technology that the Concord has ever developed and we treat it like were putting on a change of clothes."

As the legs of his frame materialised around him Happy stood up and stretched his dark skinned six foot five muscular body. "Frap Whizz, I leave that sort of thinking to the tech guys. You and I are battleframe pilots, designed and bred for ushering the enemies of the Concord into the afterlife."

"That's our job now Hap but what are you going to do when it's all over?"

"Seriously? The war against the Scourge has been going on for more years than I care to remember. Well before you got those streaks of grey in your hair," Happy chuckled at his own joke. "I don't imagine that either of us will be unemployed anytime soon. By the way, where's Bosk? You guys are always together."

Whizzbang stood to his feet and picked up his sniper Charged beam rifle. "I was busy last night but I think he headed down south to do some Digging."

Happy nodded and chuckled. "Your friend Bosk is one of a kind. How long you two known each other?"

"Since our parents were killed in a Scourge assault."

"Frap, we've all lost someone we love."

Whizzbang nodded in agreement while he checked his wrist computer or wrist-comp to ensure that all of his systems were nominal. "Do you think that we'll ever get off this planet and return to Kaladon?"

"Get off Alpha Three?" Happy ran his fingers through his long black dreadlocks before replying. "Frap Whizz, it almost seems like a dream. What I do know is that we need to secure the tellurite crystals for the war effort. Alpha Three's loaded with the richest veins of crystals in this sector. Without pilots defending the mining Diggers, the war would be over in a few weeks. I'm just glad the Scourge haven't figured that out yet."

Tellurite crystal is the raw material for almost all Concord technology. Molecular sized robots convert the tellurite into energy and then reconstitute the energy back into almost any substance. The crystals power everything from battleframes to household appliances. It was the most malleable source of energy ever discovered and if it is to win the war, the Concord of planets had an insatiable appetite for more of it.

Whizzbang pressed the button to login to his wrist-comp and mumbled to himself, "I've been here so long I can barely remember what the home world is like." Looking up at his friend, Whizzbang saw Happy encased in a Rook support battleframe and armed with a shoulder mounted Lightning gun. Happy energized his frame, flexed his servo-assisted legs a number of times and gave a brief noisy burst of his boot-mounted jump jets. With a rush, the smell of burning tellurite crystals from the pre-ignition systems instantly permeated throughout the ready room.

Satisfied that everything was in working order Happy loudly stomped his metal shrouded feet a couple of times on the plasteel floor grating. "Whizz, when are you going to get rid of that pea shooter and get some serious firepower like my friend Lightning here?" Happy affectionately tapped the gun mounted on his battleframe's shoulder. He looked back at his friend and the barrel of the Lightning gun immediately tracked to point at Whizzbang.

"You mean this little thing?" Whizzbang hefted his long barrelled Charge rifle in his soft-gloved hands. "Happy, if I could only zoom in close enough with my scope I could boil your brains at a few thousand meters. The problem is the target's just so small," he laughed.

Happy tapped the side of his head. "If I recall this little pea brain has managed to rescue your ass a number of times."

"I'll give you that one."

Whizzbang completed his post-frame energizing checks. As was his habit Whizzbang raised his rifle above his head and stretched his arms and back. Lowering his gun, he swung his arms from side to side to ensure that the soft Raven battleframe armour did not restrict any movement. As expected, it fitted perfectly. He loved the Raven, as it was ideal for deep enemy reconnaissance. It allowed him to be as silent as death while the Charge rifle delivered a killing blow at a long range. Each time Whizzbang piloted the Raven he was reminded of his chief instructor's mantra, "A dead enemy can't hurt you."

A battleframe was like a second skin that augmented a pilots speed and strength so that they could move quickly around the battlefield. Depending upon the battleframe, jump jets were mounted either within the boots or on the back plating to allowed short duration flight. As well as their unique weaponry, each battleframe came equipped with a number of specialist capabilities. A built-in medical unit could release a slew of nanites to repair battleframe damage or nanomeds to assist a wounded pilot. Once used, the nanites would automatically replicate themselves from tellurite crystals and within a few minutes, they could once again be available to the pilot.

The Concord had developed over twenty different battleframes, each for a specialised purpose. Some, such as the Anvil, were heavily armoured and fitted like a suit of medieval plate armour. Others, such as the Eagle Claw and Raven, were lightweight and designed for ease of movement and stealth.

Whizzbang slung his Charge rifle over his back into its harness and a sudden feeling of vertigo gripped him. He leaned against the ready room wall to steady himself. He had experienced the feeling before but it seemed to be happening more frequently over recent weeks. Just like the other times the vertigo vanished as fast as it came. What was happening? Was something wrong with him? Again, just like the previous episodes, there was no lasting, negative side effects. He would have to find the underlying cause of the problem but for now, that would have to wait.

"Haps, you Good To Go?"

Happy looked with concern at his friend. "You OK Whizz?"

"I'm fine Haps, just a bit dizzy for a second. I'm G2G - are you?"

"Maybe you should see the base doc?"

"What are you? My mother?" Whizzbang said a little irritably.

Happy raised his hands in mock surrender while at the same time his face split into a mischievous grin. "OK, OK, I'm G2G. Let's do this Whizz."

Whizzbang nodded towards his friend and then stepped out through the energy wall that separated the ready room from the cool night air. After the confines and sterile atmosphere of the ready room, the wide-open darkness of the night was a welcome relief.

Tilting his head to the side he spoke into his comnet pickup, "Freehold control, this is Whizzbang, Romeo, Oscar, Sierra, two, niner reporting."

A handler's voice crackled over his headset, "Acknowledged, Whizzbang, Romeo, Oscar, Sierra, two niner this is Freehold control."

"Freehold, is all nominal?"

"Whizzbang, we have green across the board."

"Mission?"

There was a slight pause and the sound of typing on a keyboard. "Scouting recon ten clicks around Freehold."

"Copy That Freehold."

"Freehold out."

Happy looked across at Whizzbang and said, "All green. That sounds like a good sign."

"It certainly doesn't happen very often. Let's head across the square, jump-jet up to get some height and then start our recon."

"I'm with you Whizz."

Before heading off Whizzbang pulled his Charge rifle out of its back holster and tightened his hand on the grip. Despite what central command had told him something did not feel right. He could not put his finger on it but it was like an itch that you cannot seem to scratch and it was not going away.

As they walked across the Freehold main town square, Whizzbang moved like the wind slipping between the trees in a forest, while Happy's metallic Rook boots crunched loudly against the cobblestones with each step. Despite their differences, there was an economy of movement to both their strides. A deadly grace that was mimicked by their shadows dancing in rhythm to the light cast by the large flickering flaming torch raised upon a high narrow pole in the middle of the central courtyard. The Concord raised the torch years earlier as a sign of defiance to the

Scourge and pilots now usually referred to it simply as the "Freedom Torch".

Whizzbang glanced down the hillside towards the pristine beach far below. The moonlight shimmered off the water and he could faintly hear the surf gently lapping the shore in the distance. He had spent many of his rest days soaking up the sun and swimming on that beach. Around him, grass thatched huts provided the illusion of a vacation resort. In reality, Freehold was the second largest Concord military installation on the planet.

As long as a single battleframe remained standing, Free, as it was affectionately known, would never be overrun by the Scourge. It meant too much to the men and women who fought, not for profit or fame, but for the survival of the Concord. Freehold was also where battleframe pilots could relax and have a few drinks with their squad before they once again did their combat duty.

Pilots like Whizzbang and Happy, would ensure that Alpha Three was clear of threats and then return to Freehold to relax by the bar or laze in the sunshine on the beach. The stresses and strains of thrusting themselves into harm's way and hoping that they would make it out the other side would damage any pilot's psyche without the "RnR" that Free offered.

With a puzzled look on his face Happy looked back across the courtyard towards the ready room energy wall. "Whizz, something don't...."

Whizzbang interrupted his friend with an open-handed glove signalling for silence as he took a few deep breaths to slow his beating heart. Closing his eyes Whizzbang sniffed the air a few times and then listened intently to the noises around him, soaking it all in, looking for anything that seemed out of place. After years as a battleframe pilot, he had learned the technique of fully embracing the world around him with his senses. Time after time, it had saved him and his friends from disaster.

A hammer fell from a rack with a clatter, a master technician berated an apprentice and the gentle breeze wafted the smell of tellurite jump jets from a battleframe that had passed earlier.

Whizzbang quickly categorised the sensory inputs as friend or foe as his senses continued to roam the area to the limit of their capabilities.

Opening his eyes once again Whizzbang asked, "Happy, can you feel that?"

Happy mimicked his friend's battle stance, closed his eyes and focused his hearing and smell to identify what his friend was referring. He had known Whizzbang a long time and had never regretted paying close attention to his friend's sixth sense when he felt something was not quite right.

"Yes, something doesn't feel right."

Whizzbang flicked to the local comnet and said, "Whizzbang Romeo, Oscar, Sierra, two niner to any battleframe in the Freehold area."

Static greeted his broadcast and after waiting for thirty seconds, Whizzbang repeated the message.

Happy finally opened his eyes and said unconvincingly, "Looks like no frames are in range." Whizzbang did not need to see Happy's face to know that his friend did not believe what he said any more than he did.

Whizzbang's veteran steel blue eyes looked around at the normal scene of technicians and mechanics repairing battleframe equipment, noticing every detail, missing nothing. His pupils had seen too many battles, too many friends fall and too many loved ones lost. They were the eyes of loss and the eyes of an expert of his trade.

Whizzbang was one of a handful of older pilots that got that way by keeping a trim fit body and paying attention to what he called his "sixth sense". Right now, it was tingling like crazy. Something was wrong and he could not put his finger on it.

"Happy, we need to plug directly into the scanning tower and find out what's going on. Something tells me that central has got it wrong."

Happy realised the seriousness of Whizzbang's tone and dropped immediately into the abbreviated staccato form of talking known as battlespeak, "CT," which means "Copy That" or I understand and agree.

Whizzbang took a few more steps forward and then stopped abruptly and for almost a minute stared up at the stars as if seeking an answer to his questing mind. Why did he feel something was wrong? Happy had become accustomed to his friend's odd behaviour and on more than one occasion, it was the sole reason he was still alive.

Whizzbang nodded almost politely to the symbol of liberty flickering in a gust of wind above. With a quick blast of their battleframe's jump jets, both pilots soared over to the scanning tower uplink terminal on the other side of the courtyard. As he landed, a shiver ran up Wbizzbang's spine and he felt the hair on the back of his neck stand on end – something was very wrong!

"Happy, combat ready!"

Happy instantly replied with, "G2G." He then dropped a couple of pods of specialised nanites from his battleframe that instantly commenced building two anti-personnel turrets. The short squat automated guns sat on a tripod that could clamp itself to almost any surface and at any angle. Within ten seconds, the nanites completed assembling the turrets. Each gun automatically began swinging their barrels back and forth scanning for enemies.

"Better to be safe than sorry Whizz," Happy said a bit sheepishly.

"Agreed."

Whizzbang deftly fingered his wrist-comp and tapped directly into the scanning network that provided a detailed map of the surrounding regions and revealed any enemy activity. If there were something out there then they would soon know.

"Haps, you've got to see this."

Happy turned his eyes away from the darkness to look down at Whizzbang's wrist-comp. What he saw turned his blood to ice.

The Scourge had come.

This time they were coming in a mass invasion. Other than Freehold and Concord Central Command, every sector, from the mining settlements up north to the fisheries down in the south were now dark and under the enemies control.

No one really knew who the Scourge were or where they had come from. Those sort of questions became irrelevant once a Scourge Juggernaut had you lined up in the cross hairs of its plasma launcher. Similar in form to humans they typically wore a dark grey battle armour, which had wicked short spikes at the joints and a raised collar to protect the neck.

All the Scourge Whizzbang had fought over the years had small pink beady eyes that looked like they were tiny pools of molten lava sunken into the head. Deathly white skin covered a hairless skull and sharp pointed ears were equally as pale. Scourge had longer teeth than humans and warriors would file them to points to frighten enemies. They were deadly adversaries on the battlefield and with their own variations of battleframes they became even more so.

From many encounters, Whizzbang knew that the Scourge killed and then killed some more as they revelled in the glory of combat and destruction. They never took prisoners and never surrendered. Every encounter was a fight to the bitter end with one side dead or alive.

Whizzbang looked up from his wrist-comp. It was time to put a stop to the advance or for the first time ever, Freehold would be overrun. Whizzbang had a lot of friends in Alpha Three and right now he knew that many of them would be dying.

Happy cursed between clenched teeth, "Oh frap."

"You can say that again. We need to warn Central about what we're seeing."

Whizzbang switched his communications back to the wider comnet. "Central, this is Whizzbang, Romeo, Oscar, Sierra, two, niner."

"Acknowledged, Whizzbang, Romeo, Oscar, Sierra, two, niner."

"We've tapped directly into the Freehold scanning tower and are viewing a complete Scourge invasion with only Freehold and yourselves in the green."

Whizzbang listened to the sound of the Central handler tapping on a keyboard before they spoke. "You must be mistaken as we have green across the board Whizzbang."

"Central, I'm telling you that there is something seriously wrong with the defence network."

"Negative Whizzbang. Diagnostics indicate all in the clear."

Whizzbang took a deep breath to calm himself down before asking, "Is General Frank McCleod available?"

"Pilot, as you know, the General is a busy man and is currently in conference now."

"Can you get the General online? This is important."

"No I can't. General Felesh gave specific instructions that all the Generals were not to be disturbed."

"I'm telling you! Interrupt Franky now!"

"Negative Whizzbang. Central out."

With that, the Central command handler cut the connection.

Happy said, "They weren't very helpful."

Whizzbang nodded thoughtfully. "He's just doing what he was ordered. We have some major trouble. The scan would also explain why we haven't heard any battle chatter on the comnet. With the Scourge controlling the majority of districts there wouldn't be anything stopping them from blanketing the airwaves with powerful static. What I don't understand yet is why Freehold command hasn't sounded the alarm?"

Whizzbang suddenly spun around to stare intently down the hillside and held up his hand for silence, "Did you hear that?"

Happy paused before replying, "Sure did. I think we're about to have some 'pink-eyes' come and join us."

The two pilots listened to the distinctive discordant hum of a Scourge probe further down the hillside as it made its way upwards towards the scanning tower. About the size of a pilot's torso its golden surface was shaped like a backbone with a bulbous head that was studded with instruments as well as offensive and defensive armaments. The probe hovered on a repulsor plate that caused the all familiar hum. Scourge engineers often launched probes to scan out the territory before a fist of warriors moved in.

Happy dropped his remaining two turrets and peered into the darkness towards the humming.

Whizzbang resisted the temptation to sound the alarm and alert the enemy. He pulled out his Charge rifle from its back holster, quietly laid down and peered through the light enhancing telescopic gun site. Whispering he said, "Probe target, two hundred metres directly down the hill. Wait for enemy fist."

"CT."

Whizzbang swung his scope to the side to get a better view of an alleyway between two huts. He was just about to move his rifle again when he caught site of an enemy Scout leading a small fist of Scourge warriors around the corner of a thatched hut.

Whizzbang again whispered, "Scout spotted, two Shocks and a Slayer."

"Any Jugs?"

"No Jugs."

Whizzbang could hear Happy sigh with relief across the comnet and broke into battlespeak to say, "Turrets take out probe. I'll deal with the fist. Watch my back for surprises."

"CT."

Happy had always marvelled at the absolute calm that surrounded his friend as he went about his gruesome business. He seemed to enter a zone of serenity as he focused on his work.

Whizzbang aligned the cross hairs on the enemy Scout's forehead as it waited for the rest of the fist to join him in front of a trash compactor. Whizzbang automatically adopted the training he had received twenty years earlier and relaxed his muscles by controlling his breathing. He heard his heart slowing in his inner ear as he entered his state of calm.

He was at one with his weapon.

He was at peace while delivering death.

He waited for his heart to pause.

It beat twice in rapid succession.

He pressed the firing stud.

A brilliant pulse of intense blue light leapt from the barrel of his rifle and streaked across the open ground to the Scout below. Upon striking its head, the brain matter instantly boiled to over one thousand degrees, exploding the skull outwards with a characteristic popping sound. The beam did not stop but continued unabated to burrow, claw and rip a hole the size of a man's eye in the side of the trash compactor the scout was standing in front of.

Without waiting, Whizzbang moved the cross hair to his next target and subconsciously timed the firing after his next heart beats. The first Shock trooper fell to the ground dead just as brain matter from the Scout sprayed its body.

Within the calmness of his mental zone, Whizzbang felt his heart surge as it again pushed the blood through his veins. Timing his shot to perfection, he pressed the firing stud for the third time just as Happy's turrets opened up on the probe. The final remaining enemy was a Scourge Slayer that was definitely more brawn than brains. Bewildered at the sudden loss of its comrades it stood stunned before being ushered into the next life by Whizzbang's fourth shot.

The whole engagement had taken less than ten seconds. Whizzbang scanned the area again carefully noting if there was any further enemy activity.

"Enemies?" Happy asked.

"None present."

"Why haven't the auto-alarms gone off? You'd think that this place would be crawling with Concord battleframes by now."

Whizzbang stood to his feet and walked over to the mangled Scourge probe. The turrets had done their work and riddled the casing with depleted tellurite rounds until the probe had collapsed deactivated to the ground. Whizzbang wrenched the drone's backbone from its upper casing and walked back to Happy.

"What you got that for?"

"Freehold command needs to see this. I think that it's about time everyone woke up." Whizzbang toggled his wrist-comp open once again and tapped a series of commands on the screen. The

Freehold warning sirens immediately commenced their low mournful call and the whole of settlement was floodlit by brilliant tellurite vapour lamps positioned strategically around the town atop huge poles.

Happy grunted his agreement. "That'll certainly get everyone's attention. Whizz there must be a lot of frames out there in trouble tonight. What do you think we should do?"

"I need to head down south to see if I can find Bosk and any of the others. We need to get the squads into some semblance of order so we can defend ourselves against the invasion. Can you travel to Central and warn the Generals of the attack? My guess is that like Freehold, they don't have a clue what's going on."

Happy nodded thoughtfully in agreement. "Are you sure you don't need some help?"

"I'll be fine," and then with a chuckle Whizzbang added, "How would I hide from the Scourge if you were stomping around beside me?"

Happy did not bite at the good-natured jibe, things were starting to move fast and there was too much at stake. He looked directly into his friends eyes. "You keep safe, that's a lot of black sectors that you're about to fly into Whizz."

Whizzbang did his best to put a smile on his face. "I'll be fine. My guess is that someone or something has pulled down the wider comnet so that no alarms are sounding anywhere. You just make sure that that Central stays in one piece."

"CT. I'll be seeing you Whizz."

"You too, Haps."

Whizzbang watched as Happy jump-jetted to a higher position to gain some height prior to dropping a nanite glider pad down. The nanites instantly built a launching platform and propelled Happy several hundred feet into the air for the glide to Central Command.

It was almost 1am as Whizzbang picked up the Scourge probe's spine and blasted his jump jets at maximum burn to cut across the town square and on up to the Freehold command centre. Within the next twenty-four hours, every battleframe in Alpha Three would be put to the test.

Chapter 3
War has come

From his height, Whizzbang watched as freshly awakened Concord officers disappeared through the Freehold command doorway. Even as they buttoned their dark blue shirts, tightened belts and adjusted pistol holsters Whizzbang proudly acknowledged the discipline that refused to yield to the Scourge. Dropping to the ground with a controlled burst of his jump jets, he pushed his way past the scurrying officers. The guards at the energy wall took one look at his Raven battleframe and ushered him past. The wall was less about defence and more about keeping out the elements from the delicate instruments housed in the command centre.

A buzz of activity greeted him as he stepped across the threshold and into the command centre. A bank of huge screens lined one wall and provided a snapshot of the status of each Concord district. They also displayed the readiness of the local Freehold defence grid.

Whizzbang looked up and cocked an eyebrow when he noticed there was no sign of Scourge activity on any screen. Despite being in his Raven a few officers shouldered past while avoiding the

Scourge probe's backbone in his hand. Each officer made their way to their consoles and quickly donned comnet headsets so that they were ready to receive and issue orders.

From the back of the room a voice bellowed, "Who in the frap sounded the alarm?"

Whizzbang pushed his way past a few aids and looked up towards the senior ranking officer's raised control desk. "I did sir!"

Colonel O'Brien was a typical mid-level Concord officer that had risen to his rank not because of ability but because his superior officers had died of old age. Despite the hour, he wore and impeccably pressed uniform even while his grey bushy moustache quivered in anger. Looking down at Whizzbang the Colonel bellowed, "Squad Leader Whizzbang. I should have known it would be you or one of your friends." If it was not for the fact that battleframe pilots were semi-autonomous fighting units and outside the regular chain of command he would have had been happy to throw Whizzbang in the stockade for this act of tomfoolery.

The Colonel gestured to the screens opposite him, "What in fraps name did you think you were doing sounding the alarm when the board's clear!" The Colonel continued shouting, "Is this your idea of a joke Squad Leader?"

With a clatter, Whizzbang heaved the probe remains up onto the Colonel's desk. He then assumed his more relaxed fighting stance and calmly said, "They're wrong sir."

Colonel O'Brien gave the probe a bit of a shove with a metal ruler lying on his desk. "Where in the frap did you find this?"

"About fifteen minutes ago Happy and I toasted a Scourge fist in lower Freehold just down from the scanning tower." Whizzbang indicated the probe on the Colonel's desk. "I brought this along as proof that Freehold is about to be assaulted."

"Fifteen minutes ago?" All the bluster had vanished from the Colonel's voice as he took his seat behind his command desk. "You said they're wrong? What do you mean our sensors are wrong?"

"Sir, I'm not sure why your screens are incorrect but after tapping directly into the sensor grid tower, the picture looks a little different than what your screens indicate." Flipping open his wrist-comp Whizzbang asked, "With your permission sir?"

"Yes, yes, you have my permission," Colonel O'Brien replied irritably. Reaching down into a cupboard in his desk, the Colonel pulled out a bottle of whisky and began pouring himself a glass.

Whizzbang tapped into the command centre's systems and beamed his sensor data directly to the main screens. Rather than a clear board the screens across the command centre now displayed a sea of red Scourge activity or black districts that were presumably already under the enemy's full control. Silence settled like a blanket on the officers at their consoles. Scurrying aides stopped and stared at the screens, taking in the disaster that was unfolding before their eyes.

Whizzbang watched as fear gripped the officers in the command centre like a jackal locking its jaw on its prey. They had been sitting at desks too long rather than fighting the enemy face to face. Wrestling physically with an enemy helped you recognize fear, appreciate it, control it and then use it to heighten your own senses so that you could survive another day. The men and women around him may be disciplined when all was well but this was a moment when they needed to decide how they would respond to their own fears.

Colonel O'Brien lifted his glass in a shaking hand to his mouth. He needed something, anything to calm his nerves. Displayed on the giant screens opposite was an impossibility. With only the districts of Freehold and possibly Central Command left, the Concord would lose Alpha Three to the Scourge. This would mean the end of the war as the tellurite being mined on Alpha Three would stop flowing. All these thoughts passed through the Colonel's mind as he almost whispered, "What in the frap is happening Whizz?"

Whizzbang watched the Colonel down the remaining whisky in his glass and said in his crisp squad-leader's voice so that everyone could hear, "You can't trust your screens Colonel. It appears that the Scourge has hacked the scanning network and very likely the defence grid itself. Colonel, I'd recommend getting some cables down to the scanning tower and run a bypass directly to here. Sir, we need up to date accurate information and we need it now!"

"Oh frap! I never thought I'd see this day." The Colonel absently reached for the bottle to pour himself another glass.

"Colonel, permission to speak freely?" Whizzbang said with a flat voice.

"You've never been one to hold back Squad Leader but go ahead."

"We also need to run bypass lines to the rest of the Freehold defence grid as it's very likely that it's compromised as well. We need to do this as fast as possible sir! We could be all that's left of the Concord on Alpha Three and we must hold. I've just sent Happy to Central Command to see if they're still up and running but it's unlikely that we'll be able to rely on them for any help. We need some pilots out scouting as fast as possible until we can get some more reliable intelligence."

Despite his gruff manner, Colonel O'Brien had always liked Whizzbang and his squad. They got things done. "Yes, of course, you're right Squad Leader. We never envisaged the entire defence grid going down."

"We're going to have to sort that out another time Colonel but right now we need to see to the defence of Freehold. And one more thing Colonel."

"Yes, of course…"

Officers overhearing the conversation would have been confused into thinking that Squad Leader Whizzbang was actually the superior officer. Whizzbang leaned forward and said in a much quieter voice, "Colonel, I need you. In fact, we all need you sir." Whizzbang reached over the desk and carefully took the bottle of Whisky from the Colonel's hands and passed it to an aide to take away.

The Colonel nodded his head and he smiled back at Whizzbang. Although the he may have been officious, he was no man's fool. Straightening his back, the Colonel subconsciously smoothed his moustache with his left hand as he issued the order that no member of the Concord ever thought they would hear. At the top of his voice he yelled, "Instigate general order Epsilon Nine One Three. Freehold will stand!"

The stunned silence instantly transformed into a flurry of activity as years of drills and practice runs for such an eventuality were acted upon. The survival of Freehold was at stake and it would take everyone's coordinated effort to keep it free.

Turning to Whizzbang Colonel O'Brien said, "Thank you Squad Leader. Sometimes us desk jockeys need to be reminded what taking action is all about. I give you my word that Freehold will not fall."

"That's good to hear sir." Indicating towards the Scourge controlled districts he continued, "I need to get going and find out if there are any battleframes still fighting."

"We could really use you here."

"Sir. I'm a recon and I need to do my part in another way."

"Where will you be headed?"

"South, that's where Bosk was headed and I need to find him."

Colonel O'Brien nodded as he smiled. "I'm not surprised that you'd be going after him. You two were always inseparable. Good luck Squad Leader. If your scans are right you'll be heading into some rough territory."

Memories threatened to intrude into Whizzbang's thoughts as he suddenly remembered happier times with Bosk. Times of laughter, joy and a deep friendship that had grown since the Scourge had killed both their parents. Focusing back on the Colonel he replied determinedly, "I've got to go anyway sir. I know that he'd do the same for me."

"I could order you to stay."

"You won't sir." Whizzbang pointed at the Scourge controlled areas of the map, "You know I'm best out there."

Colonel O'Brien let out a short huff. His breath momentarily flicked up his grey moustache. "You're right. Go and do what you do best Squad Leader."

Whizzbang saluted the Colonel in the Concord fashion of his right fist across his chest. He then extended his arm above his head with his pointer and middle finger pointing to the sky. "Colonel, you just keep the lights on."

As Whizzbang strode out of the command centre, he noticed that the officer's discipline was winning the battle against their fear.

Colonel O'Brien watched Whizzbang spin on his heels and head out the double doorway. That man is a born leader he thought to himself. Pushing aside such thoughts the Colonel turned to his nearest aide and said, "Patch me through to Central."

"Yes Colonel, patching through to Central."

"Central, this is Colonel O'Brien, seven, seven, four."

"Acknowledged Colonel."

"Patch me through to General Frank McCleod."

"I have strict instructions from General Felesh that while the Generals are in conference they are not to be disturbed."

Colonel O'Brien took a deep breath. "Priority override Epsilon nine, one, three."

There was a brief pause as the communications officer realised the ramifications of the order. "Patching you through to...." Suddenly a burst of static disrupted the signal and the connection with Central cut.

Colonel O'Brien turned to his aid and ordered, "Get Central back online!"

"I'm trying sir but the static is overriding everything."

The Colonel nodded his head in acknowledgement. It looked like Freehold was on its own and Central was about to have their own problems. It would not be long before the attack. Turning to the men and women around him Colonel O'Brien straightened his back and began relaying a series of orders in preparation for the defence of Freehold.

Chapter 4
Called in Help

With a flick of her head, Selfia let the wind whip her long blond hair out of her eyes. Her ponytail must have come loose again. A battleframe pilot having long hair had its drawbacks but it was her one indulgence. She thought irritably to herself, "*If General Alban could have long hair then why couldn't she?*"

Acheron glided beside her, his massive Anvil close quarters battleframe kept aloft by its larger energized wings. He saw her reaching back to try to retie her hair in mid-flight and gave a little laugh over the comnet. "You having trouble with your hair again Self?"

Selfia made a face at him. "Oh just shut up would you!"

Acheron ignored the mild reprimand. "It's been so long since we've been back in Freehold I can almost feel the back massages and sun on my face."

Selfia finally gave up in her attempt to subdue her hair. "What I need is a long hot bath."

"Need some company?"

Selfia giggled. "I might at that."

"Sorry about the honeymoon."

Selfia looked down at the wedding band on her left ring finger. The exquisitely crafted blue tellurite crystal seemed to glow in the moonlight as they sped southwards. "CT Ach. You have a lot of making up to do."

Acheron feigned mock hurt. "It wasn't my fault; Central said we had to go north to help the digging crews."

"What's that got to do with it? I'm still going to extract some retribution in the tub. I think that you owe me at least one back massage."

Acheron smiled broadly and let his eyes wander over his wife's petite body. Why was it that her Eagle-claw sniper battleframe seemed to accentuate her figure in all the right places?

They had been gliding since early evening and finally Freehold was in sight. The glow of the freedom torch stood out in the distance like a beacon of hope in the darkness. After a quick descent, they pulled up abruptly and retracted their wings to land. Selfia was in the lead and with a few quick steps she rapidly slowed her landing down.

Behind her, Acheron did the same and not surprisingly, she felt his strong arms wrap around her body. "We're here," Acheron whispered into her ear.

She let out a sigh and for a few minutes, they stood together as she snuggled further into his embrace. Turning slowly around, Selfia looked up into Acheron's eyes as she brushed a strand of his short dark hair out of his eyes. "Yes, we're here."

"Let's go and see about that tub."

Selfia put on her sternest expression. "CT Acheron. I order you to take me to the nearest tub!"

They both laughed as they headed down a stone stairway and past a number of thatched huts.

At the bottom step both Selfia's and Acheron's comnet crackled for a second and then a male voice spoke, "Selfia, Sierra, Alpha, Romeo, four, seven this is Central. Respond."

Selfia rolled her eyes towards Acheron. "Central this is Selfia, Sierra, Alpha, Romeo, four, seven."

Selfia listened to the thumping sound of a microphone passed across to another person. "Selfia, this is General Frank McLeod."

Acheron looked questioningly at Selfia. She shrugged her shoulders to the unspoken question, "What would not just any General but *the* General McLeod want to speak to them about?"

"General, it's an honour sir," she replied.

"Let's cut to the chase Lieutenant. We need both you and your partner's help and we need it now."

"Sir, we've only just landed in Freehold after our time up north."

"I am aware of that but this can't wait."

Selfia sat down on the bottom step and put her head in her hands. Acheron watched the play of emotions across his young wife's features. She was exhausted, they both were. After the tour of duty up north, it was a long trip back down to Freehold. What they needed was a hot tub and a week's rest. With a clunk of armour, he sat down beside his wife and put one arm around her comfortingly.

Selfia took a deep breath to relieve some of her pent up tension before saying, "Yes sir. What would you have us do?"

"I need you to play a little bit of guard duty for a very special battleframe pilot."

"Pardon me sir?"

"You heard me Lieutenant."

Sighing deeply Selfia replied, "Yes sir. Who is the pilot and where is he?"

"Squad leader Whizzbang. He's just left Freehold to head south towards Research Ravine."

Acheron said in surprise, "Whizzbang? Isn't he the one who rescued those pilots and diggers out of a big mess to the west of here?"

"He's the one Second Lieutenant Acheron."

"We have reason to believe that he's about to poke a stick into a hornets nest of Scourge and we need you two to ride shotgun for him."

As the senior officer, Selfia gave Acheron a little glare for interrupting and then rested her hand on his knee to temper the mild rebuke. "All due respect sir but pilots get themselves into hot water all the time. That's why we wear the frame sir."

"He's special Lieutenant."

Selfia drew a deep breath, "I'm sure that he is sir. Can't this wait until morning?"

"Lieutenant, I know that you're both newlyweds and I'm sure that you'd like to get some time alone after your mission up north. I wouldn't have called you personally if this wasn't really important. One other thing, under no circumstances are you to reveal to him that I've sent you. Is that clear?"

"Crystal clear sir."

"Hold Lieutenant!"

In the background both Selfia and Acheron listened to a muffled but frantic conversation. Through the comnet they could make out the distant sound of heavy weapons fire.

"Sir, is Central under attack?"

A strained General McLeod replied, "Yes, we are under a massive Scourge assault. It looks like this is the beginning of a complete invasion."

"We are on our way to assist."

"You have your orders Selfia. Provide all the assistance you can to Squad Leader Whizzbang."

"Why?"

"Because he's not really here..."

Selfia was about to reply when a burst of static wiped out all possible communication between her and Central Command. It was common for the Scourge to scramble the comnet during an attack and right now, their electronic counter measures were in full force.

Acheron looked over at his wife, "What did he mean that Whizzbang wasn't really here?"

"I think that he just got cut off."

Acheron nodded thoughtfully. "So what do we do now Self?"

Selfia gave a little smile and said, "We obey orders."

Chapter 5
Research Ravine

Whizzbang jump-jetted to the top of an adjacent building and dropped a bundle of nanites from a pocket in his battleframe. Their programming quickly formed a glider launch pad from the tellurite energy impregnated in the packet. The shimmering blue energy spiral would only last a few minutes before disintegrating. He oriented himself with the moon Arkona overhead and stepped onto the launcher. The wind roared in his ears as the pad instantly propelled him several hundred feet into the sky over Freehold. Upon reaching his maximum height blue glowing wings energized out the back of his Raven battleframe to allow him to glide quickly to his destination.

For the uninitiated jumping on a glider pad tends to be a moment of terror quickly followed by a series of airborne stalls and a crash through the trees below. Gliding at night is an especially dangerous activity. In the darkness, a pilot cannot see the horizon and the balance provided by their ears would often lie. Whizzbang had experienced "the leans" a number of times. Despite his ears, telling him he was flying "straight and level" he soon discovered that he was actually descending rapidly or even flipped over on his back. The instruments in his wrist-comp helped save his life a number of times but it still took careful training to overcome his natural senses.

Glancing down at his wrist-comp, Whizzbang locked in a glide angle for maximum distance and then adjusted his course southwards. After thirty seconds and confident that his flight was stabilized he pulled his rifle out of its back harness. Peering through the scope, he scanned the area near his first landing point for enemy activity.

Even from his present distance, Whizzbang could make out the walkways high above the ravine that housed the research centre. The scientists had named their facility Research Ravine after the shallow canyon that it was located. The engineers had constructed the laboratories in a "U" shape with each nestled against the rocky walls for protection from the elements. The top part of the "U" was open to the ravine that cut its way through the foothills and flowed down to the ocean in the east. As he silently glided Whizzbang dialled up the light enhancing capabilities of his scope and resumed his search along the plasteel scaffolds and stairways for enemies.

Other than the more exotic tellurite, plasteel was one of the toughest and most flexible building materials available and used extensively by both the Concord and the Scourge. It was a blending of high-tech plastics and traditional high tensile steel. Like building blocks, square, standard sized plasteel grating was commonly used to quickly construct many structures in Concord colonies.

Through his scope, Whizzbang surveyed the aftermath of a recent battle. A number of dismembered human bodies lay strewn about and even a few Scourge accompanied them. Scorch marks from blaster fire darkened the grating in places and smoke still billowed from a number of pieces of equipment

Whizzbang's diligence was finally rewarded when he picked out the shapes of a number of Scourge warriors. They were guarding the empty scanning tower emplacement in the centre of the platforms above the northern research buildings. By taking out the scanning towers and cutting off all communication, the Scourge disrupted the Concord's ability to build a solid defence.

Even at his present distance, and without the aid of his scope, Whizzbang could now make out the ghostly pale faces of the Scourge warriors in the moonlight. A brief scuffle appeared to have broken out between three of them as they fought over something. Whizzbang again brought his sniper scope to his eye. It was not a something; they were fighting over who won the prize to eat a raw human leg. Finally, a Shock trooper roared in triumph and began gorging himself on the flesh.

Whizzbang felt sick in the stomach at what he had just witnessed and lowered his rifle as he continued to glide. He personally knew a number of the scientists at the research centre and wondered if the warriors were fighting over part of one of them. They were harmless civilians studying the indigenous life forms of Alpha Three. The Scourge viewed them as nothing more than food.

Bracing himself for what he might see, Whizzbang raised his Charge riflescope to his eye and this time he entered his zone. No one had taught him about the zone, he had stumbled into the perfect snipers mindset while terrified in a battle long ago. He was alone defending a tellurite Digger mining crew against a dozen Scourge warriors. They had suddenly poured through from the other side of the scintillating pale purple Barrier on the edge of Concord controlled land. Any human caught on the other side of the Barrier died within a few seconds of exposure.

The Scourge had developed the Barrier from an energy that consumed human life force. They had then attempted to wrap the energy around the entire planet, making it their own. If it was not for the quick thinking Concord scientists at Blue Sky, they would have succeeded and Alpha Three would have been lost. The scientists built huge repulsor generators that pushed back the Barrier and made a small section of Alpha Three habitable to humans. The generators consumed vast amounts of energy and a large portion of the mined tellurite went to replenishing the repulsor reserves.

The Digger crew should not have been mining that close to the Barrier but it was often where the richest tellurite veins were located. Where there was money to be made, there would always be fools willing to take a risk to make it. In the heat of the battle, Whizzbang had discovered a place of absolute deadly calm amidst the storm around him. Over drinks, the miners later recounted how he took out the two Scourge fists without getting a scratch.

Centred in the zone Whizzbang counted the number of enemies and assessed the difficulty in retaking Research Ravine. From this high up and wearing his camouflaged Raven's armour, he was almost invisible against the black, star filled sky. Smiling to himself, he lined up a Scourge engineer between its pink glowing eyes and pressed the firing stud on his Charge rifle. The beam sliced through the air, met the target and continued out the other side. It was a spectacular shot considering he was still gliding. Even at his present distance, Whizzbang was rewarded with the sound of exploding grey matter as the brilliant blue energy beam pierced the Engineer's forehead.

A second and then a third target met the same fate as the first. Pandemonium broke out amongst the remaining Scourge as they sought out their attacker. Indiscriminate Scourge weapons fire ricocheted off metal girders and bounced off the plasteel plated roofs of the laboratories below as they sought out their attacker.

At the last second, Whizzbang retracted his wings to land just short of the edge of the ravine. From this high up it would provide an ideal sniping position on the remaining enemy below. He slowed himself down with a few quick steps, before diving to the ground for cover. Crawling along the ground to peer over the edge at the enemy he aligned his cross hairs on a Scourge slayer and fired. Not bothering to wait to see if the slayer was dead, he swung his Charge rifle into its back holster and quickly pulled out his short-barrelled grenade launcher.

While the Charge rifle requires a special sense of precision, the grenade launcher in Whizzbang's hands was more like a surgeon using a machete to perform a delicate operation. For all its lack of finesse, the grenade launcher is a forgiving weapon. All you have to do is roughly aim it in the direction of the enemy, pull the trigger and the concussive impact would do the rest. Upon detonation, thousands of tiny pieces of shrapnel would explode outwards at a ferocious velocity. The flying metal would sever exposed limbs and bore their way through everything other than the thickest and toughest armour. With six freshly launched grenades soaring through the air it was not long before he had cleared the thoroughly stunned Scourge from around the scanning tower platform.

Whizzbang holstered his launcher, jump-jetted down to the plasteel grating and landed lightly on his padded feet beside the tower's call down terminal. Scourge body parts, blood and gore splashed outwards from where the grenades had detonated. He hated the smell of Scourge blood. It had a musky sour scent to it that made him think of a rotting garbage dump. Wrinkling his nose in distaste, he stepped over the torso of the Shock trooper that had formerly won his human prize. A soft ping emitted from his wrist-comp to indicate that he was within range and connected to the tower's call-down terminal.

As long as the DNA verified as human, a battleframe's wrist-comp could interface with any Concord system. Upon connecting, Concord pilots were required to key in their personal unique code to gain access to the system or service they required. With the previous scanning tower vaporised, Whizzbang activated the call-down sequence to request a new tower from the orbiting Concord manufacturing facility.

The massive scanning towers were exceptionally sophisticated pieces of equipment that had to be manufactured in a zero-G environment. Pilots could call down replacement towers in the event that one had failed or been put out of commission by the Scourge.

Whizzbang leaned against the railing that surrounded the scanning tower platform and looked down in the courtyard below as he thought about what to do next. Everything seemed to be going to plan; fly-in, tick, kill enemy, tick, call down new tower, another tick, win sector, major tick.

Whizzbang peered down through the plasteel grating at the roofs of the research buildings that formed the "U" shape below. So far, the courtyard between them and the ravine beyond appeared to be vacant of enemies. Leaning back against the railing again, he looked upwards into the lattice of makeshift scaffolds and walkways that led up and out of the ravine. Thankfully, no enemies were present.

What concerned him was that calling down a scanning tower was a magnet for a Scourge counter attack. Looking across at the huge empty tower locking clamps, he willed the one he had just called to hurry down as fast as possible.

Cocking his head to the side to listen better Whizzbang let out a resigned sigh. He knew the tell tale distant screeching coming from the sky above. It was like fingernails dragged down a school blackboard and it quickly grew to a reverberating roar that climaxed in a cataclysmic thump, followed by a deathly silence. He wrinkled his nose in distaste at the putrid stench of sulphurous fumes now filling the air. He was well acquainted with both the sound and smell of a Scourge battle-pod.

Chapter 6
Training

Ray listened to the calm soft female voice in his earpiece say, "Breathe out, breathe in." They always used female voices for helping you to relax during an exercise. Apparently, studies had shown that it had something to do with the maternal child relationship.

Thomas lay in the grass beside him and embraced the exercise as naturally as Ray. Since the fateful day when they had first met, the two of them had become inseparable. They attended primary school together and now the Concord Recon Cadet corp.

Ray let out his breath slowly and just as slowly breathed back in again. A lot had happened in the last eight years since Gasp had rescued the two of them from the Scourge attack. They had both lost their parents in the battle for the colony. The war had made orphans of many children. As well as being their senior training officer, Gasp had become their adopted father. Although he was not Ray's natural father, Gasp was a good man and an expert at his trade. He taught his boys everything he knew about his craft and he knew a lot.

"Breathe out, breathe in."

Everything had ended the day the Scourge battle-pods had begun falling all over the colony. Through the bravery and skills of battleframe pilots like Gasp the Concord had barely managed to hold off the assault. Now both boys wanted to become pilots but only the best of the best could get through the Cadet-training program.

"Breathe out, breathe in."

Ray and Thomas trained harder than anyone else did to become the best battleframe snipers the Concord would ever see. They wanted Gasp to be proud of them but they wanted to beat each other even more. It was a friendly rivalry born in the crucible of horrific circumstances. They were brothers, constantly fighting each other but if anyone picked on either of them then they stood shoulder to shoulder. They loved each other dearly and each would never leave the other if they were in some sort of trouble.

After all these years Ray still had his father's rifle back in the barracks but now he held a military grade Charge rifle lightly in his hands. Although Gasp had encouraged Ray to enter the recon Cadet corps, the sight of his father's rifle had finally convinced him to enlist.

"Now fire between your heartbeats."

Ray had completed this drill a hundred, no, a thousand times before. He felt his heart beating slower as he regulated his breathing. It had become second nature to him. One after another, the Scourge targets down the range fell to Ray's precise shots. Each cut out was drilled through the skull by his beam of blue energy. Immediately after completing the exercise, Ray swung his scope to look at Thomas's targets. He sighed inwardly; they too had the tell tale holes drilled through their heads. Ray did not have to look across at Thomas to know that he was already scoping out his targets.

The sergeant looked across at his trainees lying on the ground with their rifles tucked into their shoulders as they fired at the targets. There was always a standout brilliant Cadet but in this intake, the senior training officer's sons were exceptional. Gasp had given him specific instructions to give both boys hell and that he did plus some. Despite his best efforts the two did not break. What frustrated him the most was the pair viewed additional punishment exercises and barracks chores as his way of helping them get better!

Walking down the line the sergeant stopped behind both Ray and Thomas. He lifted his binoculars to look down the range at their targets.

Ray sensed the sergeant behind him and since all the targets had been eliminated he pulled the charge canister out of his gun. He then turned around and sat up straight with his disabled rifle resting on crossed legs. He smiled inwardly when he noticed that he was perhaps half a second faster than Thomas.

The sergeant lowered his binoculars and looked to both Ray and Thomas as he yelled, "A perfect score yet again Cadets!"

Thomas wondered why sergeants always had to yell. It was as if their voice volume was more of a switch, on or off and not variable.

The bellowing continued. "Do you know how many people get a perfect score?"

Ray made the mistake of attempting to reply, "I'm not…."

"I wasn't asking you a question Cadet! You're a frapping whizz with the rifle. Did you know that Cadet, a whizz!"

"I was just…."

"Keep your mouth shut Cadet! You're a whizz with your rifle and bang go down the targets, one after another."

"I like…."

The edges of Thomas's mouth turned up in a little smile. Ray always made the mistake of trying to answer every question, even if they were rhetorical.

The sergeant noticed the smirk on Thomas's face and turned his attention to him. "Do you think that something's funny Cadet?"

"Sir, no sir!"

"Then why are you smiling? Do you think that it's funny seeing me ask Cadet Ray questions?"

"Well, no….."

Ignoring the reply the sergeant raised his binoculars to peer down range at Thomas's targets. "So you think you're a genius like Cadet Ray?"

"Sir, no…"

The sergeant's volume switch was still firmly in the 'on' position. "I don't think that you're a frapping genius Cadet. Nobody thinks that you're a frapping genius. So why do you think that you're a frapping genius?"

"Well, I don't…"

Thomas sighed inwardly. He had fallen for the same trick that Ray did with trying to answer the sergeant's questions. This time it was Ray's turn to let a little smirk show on his face.

As if he had eyes in the side of his head the sergeant swung immediately back to Ray. "Do you think something's funny Cadet? Both of you seem to think that you're comedians! On your feet and fall in behind me. Apparently, it's time to discuss your futures Cadets."

Ray and Thomas jumped to their feet, slung their rifles into their back holsters and clipped the energy canisters to their belts. They knew better than to delay anything with the sergeant. With the sergeants back to them, Ray looked questioningly at Thomas who replied with a shrug of his shoulders.

With a clipped precise step, they followed the sergeant up to the command deck above the shooting range. The first thing Ray noticed was there were two other men standing alongside Gasp. Each of them wore standard black Concord uniforms and had binoculars hanging from a cord around their necks.

Gasp said, "That will be all Sergeant."

"Yes sir!"

Ray held his eyes straight forward even as his peripheral vision watched the sergeant turn and leave. Gasp saw that Ray and Thomas were taking everything in, absorbing each and every detail of the moment so that they were ready for any action. He was proud of his adopted sons but this decision would not be his alone.

Colonel Greerson turned around and inspected the young men with his hawk like eyes. "So these are your boys Gasp?"

"Yes, this is Cadet Ray and Cadet Thomas."

"That' not what I meant."

"Yes, they are my sons."

The third man, Captain Eldrich, had a much softer but no less direct tone to his voice. Like a punch smothered by a pillow. He did not mess around and wanted to know whether the Cadets met the cut immediately or move onto another candidate. "How many pens are on the desk Cadet Thomas?"

Without taking his eyes off the Captain Thomas answered immediately. "Three sir. One in the holder and two lying on the desk."

"What's the nearest armed weapon to you?"

"Yours sir."

"Are you sure?"

"From here I can see that it's at full charge."

"Cadet Ray, Who am I?"

"You're a recon pilot sir. I would say Raven class."

"Why do you say that?"

"You're not heavy set and your hands are softer than a close combat pilot. There is a callous on your Charge rifle firing finger that is in the same position as mine. I would say that you've just recently returned from a mission as you haven't become relaxed enough to turn the safety on your gun."

Captain Eldrich smiled at the Cadet's replies and said nothing more. Colonel Greerson asked, "Are you a smart-alec Cadet Thomas?"

Like a knee-jerk reaction Ray immediately came to Thomas's aid to defend him against the accusation. "No he's not sir. Although we're the top of our class there is one thing that senior training officer Gasp has taught us…"

Colonel Greerson let the fact that Ray came to Thomas's defence slide. These two boys intrigued him. Their scores were off the chart and they obviously had a quick wit. "What did he teach you Cadet?"

"That we don't know everything sir. As soon as you believe you know everything then you're as good as dead."

The Colonel picked up a sheaf of papers lying on table beside him. Feigning that he was losing interest in the conversation he casually asked, "So why do you want to become a recon?"

This time Thomas answered, "So we can live sir."

Colonel Greerson had heard many different replies to this question but never the one that Thomas had just answered. "Pardon me Cadet?"

In a flat tone of voice, Ray repeated the answer, "So we can both live sir."

Colonel Greerson could not help but display his curiosity. These two seemed to behave as a team in everything that they did. Insult one and the other defends. "What do you mean by 'so you can live' Cadet?"

Ray looked the Colonel straight in the eye. "Sir, during our personal time we've been studying the war. Both Thomas and I know that the Concord must be losing."

Now both men were curious and Captain Eldrich stepped in to question again. "Why do you say that?"

"I'm eighteen years old and a fully trained recon. For the past six years I've learned all there is about the Scourge, the Concord and how to become a sniper recon. Thirty years ago I would've just been completing high school."

Eldrich subconsciously ran his hand through his dark hair. These kids were exceptional. He had never heard answers like he was hearing now. Colonel Greerson turned to Eldrich and gave a little laugh as he said, "And we thought we were being so careful with our covert training program."

The Captain ignored his superior officer's little jibe. "So why are we here Cadets?"

This time Thomas replied, "To assess our aptitude for operational duty sir."

"What do you think our response will be?"

"The Concord needs us both and in fact, all of the Cadets. You will say yes, we are ready."

Captain Eldrich continued to stare at both young men without saying anything. Everything they said was true. They did need them and the other Cadets. In fact, they needed anyone that could hold a gun. They had been losing the war for the past couple of years. Slowly but surely the Scourge had been crushing one colony after another.

Colonel Greerson had seen and heard enough. These two were both brilliant and incredibly self composed. "Do either of you have any questions?"

Ray hesitated a few seconds before asking, "What is the new technology that's just been developed?"

This time, both men immediately turned towards Gasp accusingly. In a raised deadly serious tone Colonel Greerson asked, "What have you been telling your sons Gasp? You of all people know the consequences of sharing top secret information with anyone!"

It was clear that Gasp was as confused as the two men staring at him. "I've told them nothing." He then turned to his sons and asked, "Who did you two hear this from?"

Ray quickly answered, "No one. It was obvious."

"What do you mean by obvious?"

"The Colonel and Captain told me."

Now all three men stared at Ray with an intensity that would have terrified any other Cadets. Without thinking, Thomas instinctively rested his hand on his belt knife, ready for action. What his brother had just said had set these two men completely on edge. Captain Eldrich noticed Thomas's casual movement and found his own hand straying towards his gun.

Gasp finally broke the tension and asked, "Have you spoken to either the Colonel or Captain before?"

Ray carefully watched and analysed the reactions of the men opposite him. He finally said, "No, I have never met them before..."

Captain Eldrich began to relax and he picked up the glass of water beside him. "We all know that we've never met before. For frap sake! These are a couple of Cadets in front of us! What I want to know Cadet Ray is what did we tell you and how did we?"

Ray cleared his throat and noticed that Thomas had let his hand drop to his side. "Never in the history of the Cadet core has anyone other than the commanding trainer approved a Cadet for operational duty and yet, here you two stand. You said you were assessing us, so the question I have been asking myself is, 'assessing us for what?' In our entire conversation you had a look of hope, not despair, even though I indicated that I believed the Concord was losing the war."

"*This Cadet is exceptional,*" Eldrich thought himself. "Continue," he said aloud.

"I notice from the insignia on the Colonel's uniform that he's from the Blue Sky research division and that you're from operations Captain. Since you are focused on individuals and not something broader and larger then I would guess that there is only one thing it could be."

Gasp knew how sharp his adopted sons could be but this was incredible deductions from not very much information. Colonel Greerson looked across at Gasp and asked accusingly, "Are you sure that you didn't brief the Cadets at all before today's meeting?"

"I didn't know it was going to take place until you both landed."

Greerson nodded and returned his attention back to Ray.

Ray took note of the exchange and decided to make a very educated guess. "You've developed a new type of battleframe and are looking at testing it out on younger pilots."

Greerson replied, "Not just a new battleframe but a whole new technology. It could change the outcome of the war."

"I see."

I imagine that both of them actually do see Eldrich thought to himself. "It's called tellurite energy and we need pilots that are able to take full advantage of the prototype battleframes," Colonel Greerson continued.

Thomas nodded in Eldrich's direction. "Why not Captain Eldrich?"

"Our top researcher has insisted that we have a much younger pilot. It's something about being more flexible."

Ray was really concentrating now. "You've developed another technology to keep the pilot alive."

"You worked all this out from us being here?" Captain Eldrich said incredulously.

"It all fits Captain. That's why you're both here."

For some reason Colonel Greerson liked these two young Cadets and had already decided that they would be the ideal candidates for the prototype battleframe programme. He paused for a few seconds in thought and said, "For the past ten years we've been conducting extensive research into two fields. The first was tellurite energy and the second nanotechnology. I presume that you're familiar with nanotechnology?"

"Molecular sized machines? They have always been theoretical at best."

"Not anymore. We can now build a battleframe out of raw tellurite energy from the molecular level upwards via programmable nanites. The same nanites can repair a battleframe while in combat and different programing can allow them to provide each battleframe with unique capabilities."

This was the first time that Gasp had heard what the Colonel was revealing. The ramifications stunned him. "You mean to tell me that Blue Sky has developed a self-repairing battleframe? This could change everything!"

"Correct. Professor Steinberg's team have also recently completed research into nanomeds that can be injected into the bloodstream to heal a wounded pilot. The microscopic machines work on the pilot at the cellular level and can heal anything other than absolutely critical injuries."

Although they were both remaining calm on the outside, Ray and Thomas's hearts were beating faster than ever. Ray automatically revisited his recent drill and slowed his breathing down to regain some semblance of control over his excitement. The implications of such a battleframe would be revolutionary and they were both smack bang in the middle of it! "The professor requires younger pilots, like us, to test out both the new battleframe and nanomeds?"

"That is correct Cadet."

"So have you finished your assessment?"

Colonel Greerson looked across at Captain Eldrich who nodded his head in agreement. "Yes, we are in agreement that you both would be ideal candidates."

Ray immediately answered, "I accept" and Thomas quickly added his assent as well.

"There is just one final matter."

"And that is?"

"Every pilot needs a call-sign that can be recognized by both other pilots and Concord systems for identity verification purposes. What call-sign would you like to have added to the logs?"

Ray had been thinking on this for quite some time and had always rejected every suggestion from Thomas and his other friends. He then remembered what the sergeant had said earlier that morning. He was a whizz at firing the rifle. "Sir, I would like to choose Whizzbang as my call-sign."

Colonel Greerson tapped a few commands on his wrist-comp and said, "That name is available Cadet." Speaking into his wrist-comp the Colonel said, "Whizzbang, Romeo, Oscar, Sierra, two, niner added to Concord systems control." Turning to Thomas he asked, "And you Cadet?"

Like Ray, Thomas had been thinking about what his call-sign ever since he first joined the Cadets six years earlier. He wanted something simple, straight forward and not at all grandiose. "Bosk, I'd like it to be Bosk."

The Colonel nodded. He had heard stranger call-signs before. Once again, he tapped on his wrist-comp, "Bosk is available. Concorde system control has now added Bosk, Sierra, Hotel, Echo, zero, six to the database of authorized battleframe pilots."

"My congratulations to you both. No word of this conversation is to be uttered to anyone other than the five of us. Is that clear?"

"Yes sir," both Ray and Thomas answered in unison.

All the men were now smiling as they stepped forward to shake Whizzbang and Bosk's hands in congratulations.

Captain Eldrich finally asked, "Do you have any further questions?"

"No sir."

"Gather your things and meet us at the spaceport in three hours. You are dismissed Privates Whizzbang and Bosk."

Ray and Thomas spun on their heels and strode purposefully down the steps and back to the shooting range. So many questions were running through their heads.

They had just been promoted to private!

More importantly, where did they get all of those insights? It was as if the both of them knew what the Colonel and Captain were thinking. Something more to think about...

Chapter 7
Fighting For His Life

Peering over the railing, Whizzbang looked down at the top of the battle-pod that had just landed in the central courtyard below. The energy orb perched on the apex of the dark metallic pyramid powered the pod during its rapid flight and once landed it connected through subspace to the Scourge base on the other side of Alpha Three. Each battle-pod was capable of warping in a Scourge fist every five minutes. From experience, he knew that each Scourge could be from a variety of disciplines.

On a blaze of jets, Whizzbang sped from his exposed position on the scanning tower platform across the courtyard to the roof opposite. The plasteel metal roof slanted upwards away from the courtyard and provided cover for an excellent snipers-eye view of whatever materialised around the battle-pod.

Below Whizzbang, the battle-pod hissed and billowed smoke as it spun up its energy reserves to compensate for the drain of the TransWarp. One after another, the Scourge warriors began materializing amongst a haze of blue and purple sparking energy. Within a few seconds, they took form and instantly started firing their guns indiscriminately at anything and everything. Bullets ricocheted off girders, small holes were vaporised in beams and white-hot plasma turned sections of walls into molten slag.

Whizzbang took a few slow deep breaths to calm his racing heart. He aligned the cross hairs of his Charge riflescope on the forehead of a Shock trooper. A slight pressure on his trigger finger and a deadly blue beam raced across the courtyard to strike the warrior in the chest in a pyrotechnic blaze of molten armour and burning flesh. Before the Shock trooper had hit the ground, he had shot a Scourge Slayer and ended its life in this plane of existence.

An eerie high-pitched whine intruded into his consciousness and he instinctively ducked to the right just as a red beam of super-heated energy lanced out from a Scourge Sniper on the far side of the courtyard below. The roof where he had just been lying spewed incandescent metal fragments into the air from a hole the width of his thumb. If it was not for his Raven's armour plating and reflexes honed from many such engagements then he would have taken a direct hit.

Before his counterpart reacted, Whizzbang again raised his riflescope to his eye, sighted the Sniper and depressed the trigger. The shot pierced the Sniper's ammunition re-energiser and the image in the scope flared briefly as his enemy erupted into a ball of flame. If there was one thing that he loved doing, it was taking out Scourge Snipers.

Another screeching sound entered the battlefield and was followed by yet another. The crack of gunfire could never overcome the sound generated by two more battle-pods as they came screaming down out of the sky and crashed into the courtyard below.

Whizzbang growled between clenched teeth, "*Oh frap! Let's play fair! One I can deal with but three!*" He just finished that thought when a fourth pod smacked into the ground just below his firing position. It was clear that this was not normal Scourge tactics; this was part of a grander plan, a plan that meant the eradication of humanity from Alpha Three. It was a complete invasion.

Scourge jostled each other in the courtyard below even while more continued to materialize. Rolling onto his back Whizzbang pulled out his grenade launcher. *"This will be like shooting fish in a barrel,"* he thought to himself.

Pointing the muzzle over his shoulder Whizzbang lobbed the egg-sized explosives amongst the fists of Scourge warriors. The roar of the full complement of six grenades exploding one after another was deafening.

As if in counterpoint to the grenade's bass notes, bullets pinged off the rock face above Whizzbang's head. Like a deadly symphony Scourge Sniper, energy beams joined the concerto as they zinged passed and drove neat circular holes into the plasteel roof next to him. Whizzbang clamped his teeth to stop himself from retching as the battle-pod stench combined with the sharp pungent smell of tellurite infused cordite and the particularly distinctive bloody aroma of crispy Scourge bodies.

Swallowing his bile Whizzbang grimaced and mumbled to himself, "It looks like I'm going to make it out of here alive after all."

The distinctive sound of launching plasma cut through the battle noise. Whizzbang peered through a bullet hole in the roof and confirmed his fears by looking directly at a hulking Scourge Juggernaut. Like watching a movie in slow motion, he watched in fascination as the massively armoured Scourge completely flattened a dead Shock trooper's leg under its huge metallic boot.

A little over seven feet tall, the Juggernaut behaved more like a humanoid tank than an infantryman. From experience, Whizzbang knew that over two inches of high tensile armour plating surrounded the vital organs and the limbs. The similarities between tanks and Juggernaut's did not stop with the armour. Like a tank, Juggernaut's tend to thump around the battlefield with an incredible amount of noise as servo-assisted legs lift their massive bulk and crunched everything beneath them. They carry a heavy plasma cannon that winds up like a jet engine before igniting and launching a mass that could have come from the inside of a star. Concord scientists have wondered over the years whether the canon's noise was a deliberate attempt by the Scourge to intimidate enemies, as it often worked. The worst thing about a Juggernaut is that their armour makes them hard to kill.

Whizzbang craned his neck as he watched the first plasma salvos arc through the air towards him and splash against one of the girders supporting an instrument array on the roof opposite. Plasteel instantly liquefied and streamed down in a river of metal onto the grating below. He cursed his predicament of being like a sitting duck up on the roof. The Scourge below had him pinned him down with gunfire as the Juggernaut started winding up its hellishly powerful plasma cannon for a second shot. The noise in the enclosed ravine as the beams, bullets and plasma reverberated off the rock walls was deafening.

At the last second, Whizzbang rolled to the right just as a globe of plasma struck the roof top where he had been laying. The roof instantly dissolved in the super-heated inferno and streamed like a glowing red liquid waterfall into the laboratories below. Desks, chairs and benches instantly ignited wherever it touched. One stream struck a chemical flask that exploded in an expanding sphere of flame, incinerating everything in its path. Black acrid smoke billowed from the hole in the roof caused Whizzbang's eyes to smart. Tears poured down his cheeks as he engaged his Raven's face shield. He could feel the heat of the fires ravaging the research labs below through the still intact section of roof where he was laying.

It would only be a matter of a few seconds more before the whole structure collapsed beneath him. As suddenly as a battle-pod falls from the sky, the hail of gunfire and plasma suddenly ceased pinging around him.

"Well, what the frap's happening now," Whizzbang said to himself.

Sliding on his back across to one of the few remaining support beams still able to bear his weight Whizzbang reached out for his Charge rifle lying on the roof next to him. He carefully rolled onto his chest and shimmied over to a still intact corner of the roof so that he could look down at what was happening below. Coming from the open end of the ravine was the most beautiful sight he had ever seen. Two fellow Concord battleframes were ripping into the Scourge with reckless abandon. The first was a powerful close quarter's battleframe known as an Anvil and the second an Eagle-Claw specialist sniper.

While the Scourge were concentrating completely on him, the two pilots had been attacking from the rear and had already thinned out the enemy ranks considerably.

Whizzbang watched as the Eagle-Claw removed the head from a Scourge Engineer with almost surgical precision. Unlike his beam based Charge rifle, the Eagle-Claw used depleted tellurite slugs that fired from an extra-long barrelled sniper rifle. The slugs mass and velocity punched holes through bodies or removed limbs with their enormous momentum. In the case of the Scourge Engineer, it meant that one second his head was atop its shoulders and the next it was bouncing off the ground at his comrades' feet.

"*It's time for revenge*," Whizzbang thought to himself as he lined up the Juggernaut in the middle of its back and depressed the trigger. The blue beam flashed out and burrowed ferociously against his target's back plate but went no further. Not surprisingly, the heavily armoured Scourge turned to look up with angry pink eyes just as Whizzbang fired a second shot through its temple causing the Juggernaut to drop to the ground dead. "I've got to remember to tap them in the head next time," Whizzbang murmured to himself.

Great clouds of noxious fumes continued to spew out of the research lab opposite him as chemical stores below in one of the labs ignited. The staccato sounds of gunfire were interspersed with periodic explosions and the sounds of the dying Scourge. A number of bullets and beams nicked, scorched, scarred and tore at Whizzbang's battleframe. His nanites struggled to conduct repairs to his battleframe quickly enough to overcome the damage.

In the middle of the tumult, a low rumbling roar intruded from overhead. The scanning tower had finally arrived! From high in the sky, the massive tower hurtled towards the landing platform and the huge clamps that would secure it in place. The automated guidance systems abruptly slowed the tower on a massive central under-jet that momentarily filled the central yard with a blast of smoke from spent tellurite fuel. Several manoeuvring thrusters fired until the tower correctly positioned itself. With a number of large clanks, the massive clamps on the platform locked the tower firmly in place.

While this was happening, the Anvil and Eagle-Claw continued to take apart the Scourge. From the opposite side of the courtyard, Whizzbang picked off one Scourge warrior after another. The completely exposed Scourge in the courtyard below and even the mighty Juggernauts could not stand up to the combined firepower of the battleframe pilots. Finally, the four battle-pods were quickly put out of commission and Whizzbang watched with a smirk of satisfaction as plumes of black and purple smoke poured from the their sides.

As fast as it all started, the battle finished. No quarter was asked for and no quarter was given. Each encounter with the Scourge was a fight to the end. Research Ravine was once again in Concord hands. Whizzbang forced himself to let the tension out of his muscles. He really needed a drink but first he had to say thank his new friends.

Chapter 8
New Friends

Circular energy beam holes and bullet indentations surrounded where Whizzbang had been previously laying prone on the rooftop. Over half the roof had melted and poured like a hellish ravaging river, it flowed, igniting everything it touched in the laboratories below. As he shimmied up a plasteel girder to get away from the flames, he could hear the tinkle of glass chemical flasks exploding in the inferno.

Whizzbang dropped off the girder just before it collapsed with a metallic crash into the dying research centre. The remainder of the roof that had served as his cover during the recent battle quickly followed the girder. With a short blast of his jump jets, he settled to the ground as the Anvil and Eagle-Claw walked towards him.

Whizzbang held up a hand in greeting and cheerfully said, "Thank goodness you both arrived! For a minute I thought that I was going to be eported back to Freehold."

"eported" was slang for emergency teleporting and occurred when a battleframe was so badly damaged that the pilot was seriously at risk. Eporting could trace its' roots back to the pre-space age where aircraft had black boxes to provide information to investigators about a crash.

There were two drawbacks of modern eporting. The first was that it required quite intrusive medical sensors that layered the internals of the battleframe. A pilot did not want to be eported away in the middle of a battle unless they were on the brink of death.

Pilots avoided eports at all costs because of the searing agony as they were atomised and reconstructed at the nearest Concord outpost. Assuming of course, that there was an outpost within close proximity. Veteran pilots that had experienced an eport, would do almost anything to avoid the experience again. The process was so traumatic that it even left some mentally incapable of piloting a battleframe again for the rest of their lives.

"We were just happy to help you out", the Anvil answered with a broad grin on his face. "By the way, my call-sign is 'Acheron' and this is 'Selfia'".

Whizzbang returned Acheron's smile and automatically ran his eyes over the younger man's highly armoured battle frame. Acheron carried his frame with the confidence of a pilot that had seen too many battles for his age. His broad shoulders and height were further enhanced by his massive battleframe and made him look more as if he was carved from a large block of marble. A mop of dark hair sat like a crown on his head but did not impede his alert eyes from scanning for enemies.

Despite the recent glide and fight, Selfia had managed to tame her blond recalcitrant ponytail. She was a young petite woman that moved with the easy grace and confidence of her battleframes namesake. Across her eyes, she wore a standard issue wrap-around tinted sniper's visor. This helped eliminate the brightness of energy blasts and battle related explosions which otherwise would be enhanced by her sniper scope.

Selfia smiled and gave a little girl-like giggle. "I've never seen a Raven in such a hot spot before. When the smoke cleared, I was surprised you were still in one piece. What's your call?"

Whizzbang shook both Acheron and Selfia's hand as he said, "I'm Squad Leader Whizzbang and you both were a most welcome sight. I thought that I would be eporting it out of here before you showed up. In all my years I've only done it once and the thought of going through it again makes me want to face a fist of Jugs all alone." Laughing with relief he continued, "Other than to save me, what brings you both to Research Ravine?"

At a raised eyebrow from Selfia Acheron ignored the question and instead replied, "Whizzbang, I've heard of you. The reputation of you and your squad is legendary."

"Don't believe everything you hear Acheron."

"If half of what I've heard is true then frap you've been a pain in the Scourge's backside for years now. Don't they call you the 'StarBlade'?"

"They can call me and my squad whatever they like as long as our cross-hairs are on them. Now that you mention it, I think we have notched up a few Scourge heads over the years. So where've you two come from?"

Selfia jumped into the conversation and said, "For the last six weeks we've been helping Digging crews up north. We've been working our way towards FreeHold but decided to keep on heading southwards. Acheron just loves fishing off the beaches down near the old Concord outpost."

"That would explain why I haven't seen you two around."

Acheron acted his part. "Fishing, I just love getting some of those big guys on the end of a line. I suppose it has been a while since we've been down this far south Squad Leader."

Selfia looked meaningfully at Acheron as she continued, "We were in the area when we heard the battle-pods coming down and thought we'd investigate. It was just by luck we were close enough to help out."

"Have either of you two checked your scans lately?"

Selfia looked across to Acheron, then back to Whizzbang, and said, "No, should we have?"

"Give me a second. I think you'll want to see this."

While Whizzbang was distracted with his wrist-comp Acheron silently mouthed to Selfia, "Fishing?" He knew absolutely nothing about fishing.

She replied with a smile and a shrug of her shoulders before she returned her attention back to Whizzbang.

Now that Research Ravine was once more in Concord control Whizzbang used his wrist-comp to access the scanning tower's sensor network and check out the state of affairs. Twisting his arm around so that Acheron and Selfia could view the display both of his new friends gave a stifled gasp as the map updated. Freehold still stood clear of enemy control and the Concord Central Command sector was marked as a disputed area.

Indicating Central, Acheron said, "There must be one heck of a battle taking place over there."

Whizzbang replied, "It looks that way. I hope Happy managed to get through and warn them before the action started."

"Happy?"

"A good and brave friend who pilot's a Rook."

Selfia said compassionately, "He'll be fine Whizz."

"I'm sure he will. We've been through a lot of scrapes together over the years and we've always managed to come out the other side."

With a small amount of pride, Whizzbang watched as the Research Ravine sector changed from red to green.

"What in the frap is going on?" Acheron asked.

"I'll put it to you both plain and simple. Every Concord sector from way up north to down south is now under Scourge control. You must have been just in front of the attack wave as you returned south. We're experiencing an invasion that's aimed at wiping humanity off the planet. I'm sorry Acheron but your fishing trip has just been postponed."

"You think?" Acheron said somewhat sarcastically.

Selfia said in a resolute voice, "That's not going to happen while I'm alive Whizz."

"Acheron loves fishing that much?" Whizzbang quipped.

Selfia laughed, she was starting to like this Squad Leader. Despite the dire circumstances, he was still able to tell a joke. "No he doesn't. What I meant was that together we'll stop the Scourge!"

This time it was Whizzbang's turn to laugh. "I know what you meant Selfia."

Acheron looked completely bewildered at the exchange between the two snipers and he said, "I really don't like fishing that much. Now smashing Scourge is another matter altogether."

Selfia stretched up to give her husband a kiss on the cheek. "Acheron, sometimes you just say the most beautiful things."

Whizzbang raised an eyebrow as he watched the interplay between his two new friends. "You're a couple?"

Selfia replied, "We just got married a few weeks ago."

"Congratulations."

"Thank you."

"I imagine that you haven't had time for a honeymoon?"

Acheron brow furrowed, as he replied, "No we haven't."

"I hate to say it but I don't think you're going to get one anytime soon. Sorry the Scourge spoiled your plans."

"So am I. I thought that I was going to be soaking in a hot tub about now," Selfia grumbled.

"Plenty of time for that later."

Selfia gave a resigned smile, "Given that scan I think you're right. So what's next?"

Whizzbang glanced back down at his wrist-comp. "By now Colonel O'Brien at Freehold will have seen Research Ravine come back under Concord control and with any luck he'll be sending some forces to secure the area."

"So how did the Scourge manage to break through without every alarm on the planet going off?" Selfia asked.

"I've no idea Selfia. When I was in Freehold, the entire defence grid displayed the incorrect data unless I directly tapped into a scanning tower. Right now, I'm heading south into the middle of the Scourge controlled sectors."

"You're planning on leaving then?" Selfia asked.

"I've got to. My friend Bosk is somewhere south of here and knowing him he'll be mixing it up with the Scourge and in a world of trouble," Whizzbang said with a little chuckle, "On the way I thought that I may as well try and relieve the Scourge of a few sectors in the process."

Whizzbang ran his hand thoughtfully through his short grey hair and then asked, "So what are your current orders?"

Selfia stared at the ground for a second before looking up to reply. "We're actually all out. Our orders were to guard the Digger crews and then head south for our honeymoon."

Whizzbang nodded. "Since you're out of orders, how would you like to join me for a little payback?"

Selfia looked at Acheron with a questioning expression on her face that ended with Acheron nodding. "We're both with you Whizz, so what's next?"

Whizzbang smiled with relief. He could really use their help in finding Bosk. "Thank you for your help. I think that our first task will be to free the outpost south of here so that additional launch points for a Concord counter offensive can be secured."

"I agree", said Acheron, "but there's only the three of us against all of them."

Whizzbang replied, "Acheron, I'm sure that there are others out there fighting just like us but they'll be soloing it. If we stay together we're that much stronger." Whizzbang looked up the southern ravine wall and continued, "I just hope that Bosk and my other friends are still with us."

Selfia laid her hand on Whizzbang's arm sympathetically and gave a gentle squeeze. "We all have friends out there Whizz. I'm sure that they're all still fighting."

"I just hope that in all of this mess Bosk is OK. I haven't seen him around for a few days and the last I heard he planned on doing some exploring in the hills to the south of here."

"Well, we'd better go and find him then," Acheron said matter-of-factly.

Pointing upwards Whizzbang said, "As we jump out of the ravine the outpost is just over a rise and up a little incline. The scans are saying that it's crawling with Scourge. Are you both up for another fight?" Whizzbang asked.

"Just show me the target," Selfia replied as she swung her long bolt-action sniper rifle around and into its back harness.

Acheron laughed. "I've never met a Scourge that could survive a bad case of tellurite poisoning." With that, Acheron hoisted his light mini-gun out in front of him and mimicked firing at targets.

Laughing along with his two new squad members Whizzbang answered in battlespeak by saying, "G2G?"

Both Acheron and Selfia replied simultaneously "G2G!"

Whizzbang said quietly under his breath, "Come on Bosk. Hang in there. The cavalry's on its way!"

Chapter 9
Test Pilots

"Just hold your arms in in front of you like this," Professor Steinberg said as he held his arms directly in front of him.

Both Whizzbang and Bosk mimicked the professor and held their arms forward.

Soon after their interview with Colonel Greerson and Captain Eldrich, the four of them had boarded the fast frigate *Aurora*. The Captain then laid in a course for a large, arid moon with a breathable atmosphere several systems away from the training academy. Fast frigates were completely devoid of armaments so that they could pour all of their energy into speed. The *Aurora* had legs to burn and it was not long before they arrived at their destination.

Blue Sky had excavated an entire side of a large crater and had built the most well hidden research facility in the Concord. The enormous main hanger easily housed the frigate as well as all the analytical and measurement systems that Blue Sky would require for their research.

"Good," the professor said absently as he peered over the rim of his spectacles at a monitor. His ink stained lab coat looked like it had not seen a cleaning unit in years. Mumbling to himself, he reached for one of a number of pens sticking out of his chest pocket. Pulling the lid off with his teeth, he looked around for a scrap of paper, gave up, and then jotted a series of numbers on his sleeve.

Altavia Creatlin had been the professor's research assistant for a number of years and she stepped forward to offer a notepad. Steinberg distractedly accepted the paper while he flicked a long stray lock of grey hair out of his eyes.

Bosk leaned towards Whizzbang and whispered, "What do you think of her?"

"Who?"

"Give me a break Whizz, you're not blind!"

"Oh, you mean Altavia?"

Bosk was getting a little frustrated that his best friend was not reacting. "She's got curves you could die for."

The edges of Whizzbang's mouth turned upwards in a smile. He loved teasing Bosk and over the years had become somewhat of an expert. Still holding his hands out in front of him, he let his eyes enjoy the scenery that Bosk was whispering about. "She's got the looks alright."

"Have you seen her eyes?"

"Yeah, I've never seen eyes like hers before. Have you?"

"Nope."

"They're the most vivid blue I've seen in all my life."

Altavia's long dark lustrous hair cascaded forward as she glanced down at the equations the professor was jotting down. "Professor, I think that the sigma needs to be tied to the inverse relationship with the alpha tellurite channel."

Professor Steinberg halted his scribbling and suddenly his eyes widened as he said excitedly, "Your right! It all fits together now. I've always said that the two of us make an excellent team Altavia." He shoved the pen between his teeth and busily began tapping on the keyboard in front of him while reading numbers from his calculations.

Altavia gave a little laugh that sounded like summer birds in full song. "Yes, professor. We've always made a great team."

Whizzbang turned to Bosk, "Out of your league."

"And yours."

As if she knew that they were discussing her, Altavia looked across at the two young men with a strange expression of satisfaction on her face. They both wilted under her gaze and became intensely interested in everything but her.

Professor Steinberg shuffled over to them and pulled back his lab coat sleeve to reveal a wrist-comp. "Are you both ready?" Removing his glasses, the professor started polishing the lenses on the edge of his coat, which made them even dirtier. Altavia relieved the professor of his glasses and then gave them a clean with a polishing cloth that seemed to materialize in her hand. She handed them back to the professor with a smile.

"Ahh, that's better. Thank you for that. I can read my wrist-comp now."

Bosk whispered, "Do you know what we're ready for?"

"No idea."

For the past three days, the two of them stood exactly where they presently were while the professor adjusted the host of machines surrounding them. The only difference today was that he had asked them to hold out their arms.

"Enough chattering you two." Holding his finger poised over a single blinking light on his wrist-comp the professor said dramatically, "Five, four, three, two, and one." With a flourish, he then plunged his finger down on the miniature screen.

Nothing happened.

Professor Steinberg inspected his wrist-comp and hit the blinking light on the display a few more times. "I was sure that everything was in place."

"Be patient professor. It should be starting any second now," Altavia said soothingly.

"*Who was in charge here?*" Whizzbang thought to himself. Just then, he felt a tingling in the tips of his fingers that slowly began to spread up his arms. "What's happening?"

Beside him, Bosk started squirming until Altavia said, "Stay still, everything will be fine."

Slowly but surely a weave of material began forming over every inch of their bodies. It hardened into back and chest armour even as a helmet formed around their heads. Servos, metallic braces and joint hinges magically materialized into a full exoskeleton over a perfect black mesh of cloth that was tougher than even plasteel.

Professor Steinberg stepped back to better survey his handiwork. "And so it is born."

Altavia replied, "The nanite battleframe is at long last a reality."

From behind his sealed helmet Bosk's muffled voice said, "How do you get this frapping thing off?"

Over the next several weeks, Whizzbang and Bosk had become more and more accustomed to "accepting" the battleframe as it grew around them from tellurite energy being manipulated by microscopic machines. Standing in the centre of another machine the battleframe could be reconstituted into the tellurite energy and vanish from around them.

One morning while they were waiting for another battleframe Bosk asked Whizzbang, "Aren't you getting a little bored with all this standing around?"

"More than a little. I want to see what these battleframes can really do."

Whizzbang looked around for the professor and Altavia and saw them both staring intently at a monitor behind a large console. "Professor Steinberg," he called.

The professor's startled face appeared from behind the monitor. "What is it young man?"

"Are we going to do something with these new battleframes?"

Altavia smiled sweetly at him and said, "You seem very eager Whizz. We were just checking the last of the permutations before generating a fully functional battleframe."

Bosk loved hearing Altavia's voice. He wished he could hear it all day long. "Just take your time. We'll just keep on standing here until we're needed."

Whizzbang looked in astonishment at his friend. "Out of your league Bosk."

"I can only hope."

"There's hope and a fool's hope. That girl has more brains in her little pinkie then everything sitting on top of your shoulders. In fact, the way that she sometimes looks at us scares me a little."

Bosk sighed. "I know what you mean but she's just so perfect!"

"Do you want me to pull rank on you?"

"Because you're a day older than me?"

"Yes!"

"You can try it Whizz but we're not kids anymore."

They bantered back and forth for the next few minutes to pass the time, just like when they were little kids. The friendship that had developed between them since they first met when Gasp rescued them was stronger than ever.

Altavia cleared her throat to get their attention. Disappointingly, they had somehow missed the spectacle of her catwalk like grace as she walked from her desk to stand directly in front of them. "Privates this time is going to be it. We've completed programming a fully functional battleframe. If you two are finished your discussion then we'd like to get started."

Both Whizzbang and Bosk looked a little abashed as they said, "Yes maa'm!"

Just like with the previous times a battleframe began to grow around each of them. This time the exoskeleton servos were operational and the boots came equipped with jump jets for short duration flight.

Whizzbang began to relax as the last of the external components were finished being built by the billions of machines. Suddenly he felt a needle jab into his inner thigh and probes began pushing their way into every nook and cranny of his body.

"Ouch! What the?"

Beside him, Bosk gave a little yelp as the needle struck home and the various probes pushed their way into position.

Whizzbang looked up at Altavia accusingly, "You knew that was going to happen didn't you."

Altavia smiled back at him. "I may have but it's necessary for the battleframe to know the health of the pilot."

"Why's that?"

Altavia walked over to Whizzbang and Bosk while Professor Steinberg continued monitoring the readouts on the monitors. "In the event of a pilot being near death, there's a teleportation unit built into the battleframe that will instantly transport them out of battle and back to the nearest Concord base. The probes are designed to measure the state of the pilot's health."

"Seriously?"

"Yes, I'm always serious when it comes to battleframe technology Whizzbang."

"So what's the downside?"

"I've heard that teleportation can be excruciating and may leave the pilot psychologically distressed?"

Bosk rolled his eyes. "You mean a vegetable."

"That may be an exaggeration but it could be possible."

"So what you're saying is don't get near death or you could be alive but a bit of zombie with no brain."

Altavia laughed musically. "Bosk, you're always so dramatic. It really depends upon the individual but tests have proven that the more mentally adept a person is the less they are impacted by an eport."

Whizzbang interrupted, "So what's with the needles?"

Professor Steinberg stepped into the conversation. "They're to administer the Evkon 316 pain blockers and nanomeds."

"Can you dumb it down a little professor?"

The professor ran his fingers through his thinning grey hair in concentration. "What both you pilots need to appreciate is three things. First of all, the battleframe nanites will affect repairs on the frame if it receives any damage. Secondly, Evkon 316 is the best pain blocker that the Concord has ever developed and will allow the pilot to continue to function even though his body might be under enormous duress. Thirdly, if a pilot is hurt then the nanomeds will flood into the bloodstream via the needle and heal the wound at the cellular level."

Bosk looked incredulous. "You've got to be frapping me?"

Altavia turned to Bosk, her blue eyes seemed to shine in the light of the surrounding machinery. "No he's not. Due to the shortage of veterans the battleframe has been designed to keep the pilot alive at all costs."

"Well, I'm all for that. How about you Whizz?"

Whizzbang replied absently, "Sure Bosk. So professor, this is a fully operational battleframe?" he asked as he surveyed the readouts from a number of the different systems.

"Yes, Private it is."

"Do you mind?"

Altavia gave Whizzbang one of her stunningly gorgeous smiles. "Be my guest pilot."

Whizzbang leapt into the air on servo-assisted legs and before letting gravity take hold he kicked in his jump jets. Rather than flames, an invisible force thrust him higher into the air and rocketing towards the hanger roof. Easing back on the throttle, he stopped shooting upwards and maintained a constant height.

"Hey, wait for me Whizz," Bosk excitedly said over the local comnet built into the battleframe. Looking down, Whizzbang watched as Bosk performed the same manoeuvre and settled, hovering on his jump jets next to him.

As he looked up at the two pilots, the professor asked Altavia, "Do you think that they'll remember that the jump jets are only for short duration flight?"

"I'm sure that they'll remember soon."

"That was my thoughts exactly."

Whizzbang could not help himself, he started laughing with the exhilaration and power of his battleframe. "What do you think Bosk?"

Before Bosk could speak Whizzbang's jump jets began to splutter. Like a rock, he plummeted to the floor. At the last minute, his jump jets kicked back in and he safely landed next to the two researchers.

Through his battleframes earpiece he heard Bosk exclaim, "What the frap?" Looking up, Whizzbang watched as his friend headed rapidly towards the floor and then like his own battleframe Bosk's jump jets kicked in and let him land safely.

Altavia shook her head from side to side, as she walked back to a monitor. "Remember, the jump jets are for short duration flight…"

Professor Steinberg completed her sentence as he joined his assistant, "…and they need at least three seconds to fully recharge between burns."

Whizzbang looked at the two researchers retreating to the comfort of their analysis equipment. Calling after them he said, "So what else can they do?"

The professor tore his glance away from the monitor that he was staring at, "Why don't you go and find out?"

Whizzbang looked at Bosk and they both shrugged their shoulders. After being couped up for so long it seemed odd being told that they could do whatever they liked.

Over by the professor, Altavia picked up a comset and said in her silky smooth voice, "Let me take you both through the basics."

Through the glass faceplate of his battleframe, Whizzbang watched as Bosk settled in to listen to Altavia's sweet voice. He signalled his friend to look at him and promptly rolled his eyes. Bosk blushed, found the battleframe to battleframe comms switch and said, "What hope does a guy have listening to a trainer like her?"

"I'll agree that she's a bit different from the sergeant."

"Pilots, you do realise that since I helped build the battleframes I can hear everything you are saying?"

Now it was time for both of them to blush. Finally Whizzbang managed to stutter, "Uhhh, Mam, umm, you were talking about systems?"

Altavia laughed at their embarrassment and then all researcher she instructed, "I want you to run as fast as you can out the main gateway to the outside area."

Bosk said, "We live to obey."

Both pilot's spun on their boots and ran between the rows of machinery faster than they could ever have done previously. It was not long until they had reached the gateway to the outside.

"Good timing pilots. You both seem to have a natural gift for this. I was right in choosing young men that were both adaptable physically and able to learn quickly how to handle a battleframe."

Whizzbang and Bosk stood a little taller at her encouragement as they looked out the huge force field that separated the research centre from the outside. The field kept out the elements and any light weapons fire but allowed the free passage of personnel.

The fast frigate in which they had arrived was still in a docking cradle across the other side of the facility. Whizzbang could see maintenance crews servicing the various systems in the interstellar ship.

Even in his battleframe, Whizzbang felt a tingle on his skin as he stepped through the force field and onto the enormous landing balcony constructed in the side of the crater. "Look at all those stars Bosk. Do you ever get sick of looking at them?"

The central galactic core of stars shone brightly above and illuminated the grey dusty crater floor far below. "Not a chance Whizz. Have you noticed we're a long way up the side of the crater?"

"Yes we are."

Altavia's voice sound in their earpieces. "Pilot's you are now in a perfect position to test out another of your battleframe systems. You will find that within various pouches there are packets of nanites that can provide a variety of additional functions. These systems will typically disintegrate within a few minutes as the tellurite energy is consumed. Once a packet is used they will take several minutes for the nanites to replenish them."

"That's sounds interesting," Whizzbang replied. "So which one are we after?"

"Whizzbang, pull the packet out from your left thigh pocket and then drop it on the floor."

Whizzbang did as Altavia ordered and took a step back as the miniature nanite machines went feverishly to work building what appeared to be swirling energy platform.

"This is a glider platform. It will launch you into the air and trigger winglets built into your battleframe so that you can fly quickly from one destination to another."

"So what do we do now?"

"Step onto the platform and then quickly learn how to glide."

Whizzbang looked across at Bosk dubiously. Bosk shrugged his shoulders and said, "Here goes nothing." He jumped onto the glider pad and found himself instantly propelled one hundred metres into the air. "Yeeeehaaaa!" he screamed.

Whizzbang watched as his friend reach the top of the launch and wings suddenly energized out the back of his battleframe. After struggling for a second Bosk seemed to manage to get the gliding under some control.

Whizzbang stepped onto the launcher and felt the same adrenalin rush that Bosk must have. The sides of the crater raced past him as he shot upwards towards the stars. Just as he reached the top of his arch, winglets energized out the back of his battleframe. Like Bosk, it took him a few minutes to get the act of gliding under control. The exhilaration of his first experience of actually flying would stay with him forever.

"Oh frap I love this," Whizzbang said over the comnet.

"You and me both Whizz."

Back in the research centre, Altavia watched from a monitor as her pilots glided back and forth around the crater. They landed, dropped down another packet of nanites and repeated the procedure time and time again. Smiling to herself, she sighed deeply and just enjoyed the moment.

For the next month, with the help of Professor Steinberg and Altavia, Whizzbang and Bosk learned the many systems that made up the state-of-the-art battleframe. One of the tests they conducted included Whizzbang purposefully cutting his arm with a knife. As soon as the knife scored his skin, the Evkon 316 immediately dulled the pain and he then watched as the wound was healed by the nanomeds. There was not even a scar to indicate that he had been hurt.

They tested and retested each system as the two researchers gathered data and their two young pilots learned what it meant to be the next generation of Concord battleframe pilot.

Colonel Greerson looked out his office window down to the hanger deck below. He had his back to Captain Eldrich and Altavia when he asked, "How are they going?"

Altavia answered in a matter of fact tone of voice, "They're progressing better than can be expected. Their young physiology is providing us with invaluable data on how to best program the nanomeds for a wider range of pilots."

"And what of the development of the other frames types?"

"The professor is leading a team on that task and they are making good progress."

Captain Eldrich leaned forward in his chair, "Colonel, how long do we have?"

"I'm unsure but the news isn't good. We lost another two colonies last month." Colonel Greerson leaned against the glass as if to brace himself for what he was about to say. "If we don't get these new battleframes operational within the next few weeks then there's not going to be much of a Concord left to defend."

Altavia stood up and walked over to the Colonel. He turned his red-rimmed eyes to look into her vivid blue. "They will be ready Colonel. I give you my word."

"That means a lot coming from you Altavia. Thank you."

Almost as an afterthought Greerson added, "There's one more thing. Intelligence has intercepted a Scourge communications suggesting that they are somehow aware of our developments and are hunting us down."

Captain Eldrich joined the other two by the window, "How could they know?"

"We have no idea. Maybe a leaking coms channel?"

"Unlikely, I've personally ensured that all outbound communications are routed through my office."

"Any thoughts Altavia?"

"Could there be a traitor?"

The Colonel let out a sigh. "I'm sure that we'll find out soon enough. Captain, immediately arrange the transport of any non-essential personnel off the base."

"Yes sir."

"Altavia, push those boys hard."

"We are sir."

Chapter 10
Teamwork

Arkona, Alpha Three's second moon, set below the horizon and darkness once again enveloped Research Ravine. Three sets of jump jets flared and rose up towards the scattered ruined buildings at the top of the cliff. After taking Whizzbang's advice of tapping directly into the Freehold scanning tower Colonel O'Brien had indeed seen the change in data at the research facility. He immediately sent twenty militia to dig in to defend the sector from a Scourge counter attack. Although often outclassed, the militia fought valiantly as they defended sectors as wearers of the more advanced Concord battleframes struggled elsewhere. Many brave militia men and women had died fighting impossible odds to protect loved ones from the Scourge.

"Perimeter established", crackled the militia Captain's voice over the local comnet. The extended communication network or comnet was still blanketed by Scourge electronic counter measures.

"Captain, any news from Freehold?" Whizzbang asked as he soared through the air on his jump jets.

"Thanks to your warning, Freehold is dug in and any stray squads and thumping crews have been recalled."

"That's good to hear. How about Central?"

"No news there I'm afraid. Scans indicated that the sector is still under attack so it must be one heck of a battle raging. We'd send a relieving force but we're expecting to be hammered ourselves any time now."

"CT Captain. Dig in good and tight in the ravine." Whizzbang replied as he, Selfia and Acheron touched the top of the south ridge surrounding research facility.

"Will do Squad Leader. Over and out."

Whizzbang and Selfia quickly ducked behind the safety of a pile of rocky rubble. Raising their sniper scopes, they scanned the area ahead for any sign of Scourge activity. In the meantime, Acheron hid behind the ruined wall of an abandoned house, stretched his muscles and checked that nothing had jammed his mini-gun after the previous battle.

"I see two Slayers on the right side and an Engy just coming around the back. No sign of any Jugs or Shocks", whispered Selfia.

Whizzbang replied in a hushed voice, "Check out the top ramp. Looks like one, no two Jugs and a couple of Snipes."

"Enemy sighted. Oh frap Whizz! The lower ramp has a couple of Shocks coming down it right now and I caught a glimpse of a few Engies inside. The place is crawling with Scourge and that's just what we can see!"

Whizzbang lowered his Charge rifle from his eye. "We need a plan. With so many Scourge, muscle alone is not going to be good enough. Sorry Acheron."

"No offence taken Whizz."

"Self, do you think that your jets will burn long enough for you to get up on that ledge overlooking the outpost. It would be a great spot to pick off a few of them."

Lowering the scope from her eyes Selfia's visor flicked to completely transparent mode as she blinked a few times to help them adjust from looking through the image enhancer. "I think I can make that. It'll be tricky but I'm pretty sure I'll be fine."

"Good. While you're getting into position I'll head across to the top of that big rock over on the left. We'll both have a maximum firing angle to do as much damage as possible."

Acheron looked up from inspecting his gun. "So what do you want me to do?"

Selfia looked across at her husband and smiled. "We need you to go straight up the guts. Right Whizz?"

"Exactly Self."

Now that got Acheron's attention. The words "straight" and "guts" in the same sentence was the way he liked it. "Gotcha Self but you two snipes better have my back because once I start unloading all hell's going to break loose."

"Agreed. Self, you and I have to cover Acheron but Acheron don't start firing until I give you the all clear. Self and I will try and take out as many of the Scourge as we can before you even get there."

"No problem. I'll wait but don't take too long. I want to have some fun too!"

"They'll be plenty of fun for everyone Ach." Whizzbang smiled, amused with his two new friends. It was as if they had known each other for years. "Selfia, when you see me start firing you open up as well. Got it?"

Selfia was more used to giving orders than taking them, especially from a pilot that she had only just met. The General had stressed her mission to look after Whizzbang so she smiled and replied, "Sure thing Whizz." Besides, the plan that he outlined made sense.

Whizzbang watched as Selfia and Acheron moved towards their assigned positions. Once satisfied they were in place he moved like a shadow and slipped through the undergrowth, kicked in his jump jets with a short muffled burn and quietly landed atop the boulder overlooking the outpost.

From experience, Whizzbang knew that battles are often won or lost by the side the exhibits the most patience. In numerous previous skirmishes, he had delayed the actual fighting to first assess the Scourge's strengths and weaknesses. This allowed him to calculate the most effective method of assault and help protect his own squad from any unnecessary injuries.

The number one skill that Gasp taught him as a Cadet recon was not shooting but patience. He could still recall his adopted father saying, "Wait for *the* shot not just any shot."

Gasp had an incredible reputation as a battleframe pilot. Prior to becoming the Concord's chief recon instructor, he had served in numerous campaigns. His call-sign of "Gasp", was the last sound an enemy would make if they were his target. He had drummed into his adopted son's heads "Wait for the best shot and don't ever rely on being lucky. Luck is for those who are impatient." Therefore, Whizzbang learned to become patient.

The outpost had three levels, a top, middle and ground. From their earlier reconnaissance, the Scourge infested all three tiers. Slowly and methodically breathing in and out Whizzbang began the process of slowing his heart rate down and entering the calmness of his zone. He could almost feel Selfia going through the same discipline perched on the ledge directly across from him. Likewise, down below hidden by the undergrowth he knew that Acheron would be doing the exact opposite.

Whizzbang flexed his hand a number of times to ease the tension just as his father had taught him all those years ago while shooting targets. Peering through his telescopic sights, he lined the cross hairs on the forehead of a Scourge sniper and pressed the firing trigger. The high energy beam streaked from the gun's muzzle and struck true. The sniper's head disintegrating in a mass of boiling blood and bone fragments.

Within an instant Whizzbang heard the crack of Selfia's sniper rifle and in the top right corner of his scope he witnessed the aftermath of a Juggernaut's head violently lifted from its shoulders.

"Good shot Self," Whizzbang acknowledged over the local comnet.

"Thanks Whizz, glad to oblige."

Swinging onto his next target Whizzbang waited the second it took the Charge rifle to spin up to maximum power and again pressed the trigger. This time a Scourge Engineer met the same fate as the Sniper.

Zing! A bolt of red energy lanced through the rock just next to his head. Rock and dirt exploded harmlessly around his frame. Whizzbang yelled into his comnet "Oh frap! Self, did you get a bead on the Snipe that nearly took my head off? He's somewhere at my twelve o'clock on the top level and has just ducked out of my sight."

There was a loud crack followed by a spent cartridge ejected from the chamber over the local comnet, "Got 'em Whizz. I don't think that they've noticed me as yet."

"Just keep on firing Self!" Whizzbang urgently replied as he lined up a Jug and plugged its eye with a thousand degrees of raw energy. He then quickly swung around to take out a Slayer with a tap to the chest.

Two Shocks fell almost in unison and even their mighty suits of armour were not able to withstand the onslaught of both the snipers. Less than a minute had passed and the outpost's top tier was littered with Scourge bodies.

Whizzbang thought, "*She is good, very, very good. I'm glad to have her at my back.*"

Whizzbang watched helplessly as the red beam of a Scourge Sniper round reach out from the first level ramp and upwards to Selfia's position. Selfia screamed through the localnet as pain blossomed in her shoulder. Red hot metal cauterized her skin as the thumb-sized beam flamed its way through her battleframe armour and then out through her back.

Prior to heading to their positions, the three Concord pilots agreed that both the snipers should apply their talents to the top of the outpost and then work their way down. The goal was to destroy the Scourge TransWarp on the top level as quickly as possible and prevent reinforcements from warping in.

A TransWarp is almost identical to a battle-pod in that it allows the near instantaneous transportation of Scourge warriors to its location every few minutes. Unlike a battle-pod a TransWarp can bring in up to twenty Scourge warriors at a time. After exhaustive analysis, the Concord research division had deemed that TransWarps functioned in much the same manner as eporting. Warping in reinforcements would not be good for Whizzbang's squad and especially considering there are only three of them. This meant that shutting down the TransWarp was the number one priority. However, this left a problem.

If both Whizzbang and Selfia were taking out targets on the roof then that left the ground and the first level solely to Acheron. Even though he was wearing an Anvil battleframe, how much punishment could he really take? Acheron had to keep out of the fight for as long as possible while the snipers thinned out the enemy. Trying to explain to an Anvil that they should stay out of the fight for as long as possible was educational to say the least but so far, it appeared that Acheron was listening to sound advice.

When Whizzbang saw and heard Selfia, hit by the Scourge Sniper three things happened almost instantaneously. The Sniper met a grizzly death on the receiving end of Whizzbang's energy beam, Selfia murmured that she was "OK and needed a few minutes regenerate" and Acheron began unleashing hell.

It is hard for words to describe what an enraged Anvil with Acheron's experience and audacity can inflict on an enemy. Needless to say that when a hundred rounds per minute of depleted tellurite erupted from the muzzle of his light mini-gun the Scourge had no choice but to melt before him. Armour was sliced like a hot knife through butter but unlike the surgical precision of a scalpel the mini-gun tore, wrenched and ripped. Arms, armour and unrecognisable Scourge anatomy sprayed in all directions as a bellowing, enraged Acheron became the irresistible force against a very movable object.

Acheron screamed in his berserker's battle voice, "You frapping scum! Take this and this! Do you want some more? How about a nice tellurite sandwich? Not enjoying the flavour? See if I care you frapping Scourge cowards!"

True to his word, Whizzbang protected his squad mate's back. With one carefully aimed charged shot after another he picked off Scourge soldiers that would have ravaged Acheron flanks and rear. Blood flowed down the outpost's outer ramp in a steady stream of purple as the two Concord pilots went about their profession.

Crack! Thanks to the Eagle-Claw's nanites and nanomeds, Selfia re-joined her friends in picking off targets. "You G2G Self?" Whizzbang said into the localnet over the sound of Acheron's rants.

"Yeah, I'm good to go Whizz. The little bots have me all stitched up good as new." Selfia was not exaggerating about the incredible capabilities of the nanomeds. The tiny robots flowing from her battleframe and into her bloodstream had miraculously repaired her wounded shoulder. Each damaged cell was individually repaired and those that were beyond repairing were replaced by other non-essential cells from other parts of her body. Fortunately, adequate doses of the anaesthetic, Evkon 316, were automatically administered by her battleframe to dull the considerable pain from her wound. In another five to ten minutes, the wound to her shoulder would be completely healed.

"Great, keep an eye on Acheron while I take out that TransWarp on level three."

"CT. Do your worst."

The noise below had abated a little from the tumult when Acheron had first assaulted the Scourge outpost. "*He must be running out of targets on the ground,*" Whizzbang mused as yet another yawning roar of mini-gun fire reached his ears. "*Well, maybe not quite yet,*" he chuckled to himself.

Standing to his feet, Whizzbang flipped his rifle onto his back and pulled out his favourite close quarter's weapon, the grenade launcher.

After ensuring that both Acheron and Selfia were coping with the Scourge down below Whizzbang quickly jump-jetted from his rocky aerie to the roof of the outpost. Moving quietly on his padded Raven boots he peered over the edge to the balcony below to see if there were any enemies.

A Scourge Shock trooper swung around and looked up in surprise just in time to ingest a few grenades. The explosion instantly liquefied the contents of the troopers armour prior to splattering it like a macabre piece of modern artwork across the balcony and surrounding walls.

Whizzbang ignored the purple gore and flicked his wrist to reload his launcher in preparation for any additional enemies. He dropped off the roof and with a short burst of his jump jets settled onto the balcony that spanned one entire side of the third level. Nothing else seemed to be moving on the third level. Other than the Scourge he had just killed, the combined sniper fire of both Selfia and himself had taken out the enemy.

On the far side of the room, an exit to an outside walkway was visible at the top of a short ramp. The wall along the balcony was completely missing leaving the entire third floor exposed to the elements. There would normally have been a force field in place along the open wall if the Scourge had not messed with the outpost's security protocols housed on the second level. A clutter of equipment, munitions and empty stacked crates lay scattered across the floor.

The TransWarp stood in the room's centre, a dark narrow pyramid with a control interface built into one side. It was dormant for the time being but Whizzbang knew that it was only a matter of time before it activated to bring in Scourge reinforcements.

Whizzbang cautiously moved towards the TransWarp, looking to the left and right, alert for any sign of the enemy. Every so often, he could hear the crack of Selfia's rifle as she fired at a Scourge target. Acheron had been relatively quiet the last minute.

A Scourge Slayer looked down at Whizzbang's back from its hidden position on top of a stack of crates. It relished ending this accursed pilot's life. With an almost silent shifting of its weight onto its front foot, it prepared to leap.

Whizzbang heard a faint sound behind him and instinctively dove to the floor just as the Slayer let out a primal snarl and leapt from its perch towards his him.

Surprised by Whizzbang's sudden move the Slayer stretched its arms out towards its quarry to try to prevent it from escaping. Rather than embedding the eighteen inch tellurite crystal dagger between Whizzbang's shoulders the Slayer had to be satisfied with driving it into the his upper right thigh.

Searing pain exploded in Whizzbang's leg as the dagger struck home. With a crash, the Slayer and Whizzbang sprawled across the floor, smashing into empty ammunition boxes. Whizzbang kicked out with his uninjured leg connecting his lightly armoured Raven boot with the Slayer's pale-skinned cheek. The quick move caused the Slayer to lose its grip on the dagger and allowed Whizzbang a second to glance down at his wound. The perfectly polished razor sharp blade cut through his thinly armoured battleframe and he watched with grim fascination at the point appearing out the front of his leg.

The moment the dagger struck home counter reagents flooded Whizzbang's body from his battleframe in the event the Slayer had used a toxic coating on the blade. Evkon 316 swirled through his body and within his bloodstream millions of nano-sized micro-machines flowed into action to begin healing the wound. While the nanomeds stemmed the blood loss, nanites began the work of repairing the Raven.

Behind Whizzbang the Slayer scrambled to its feet, flailing wildly against a stack of crates as it stood up. Purple blood poured from a fresh gash in the side of its face. Its pink beady eyes seemed to flare in rage as it charged forward.

Still lying on his back Whizzbang fired his jump jets and scooted across the floor to flee his attacker and buy himself some time. The pain from additional pressure on his leg was almost unbearable. Crates caught in his jet blast disintegrated in a flurry of wooden shards that rained down on the Scourge charging after him. Thankfully, his helmet protected his head as he ploughed through a neatly stacked array of ammunition boxes, sending them in all directions. He finally slammed into the far wall. The Slayer still came onwards crashing through the destruction of Whizzbang's passage.

Whizzbang twisted around and grasped the dagger hilt with his right hand to pull it free. Even the anaesthetic could not entirely mask the shock and he screamed through gritted teeth as he wrenched the blade out of his leg.

Whizzbang's servo enhanced battleframe automatically braced the temporary weakness in his left leg as he pulled himself to his feet. The Slayer was almost upon him by now.

Kicking in his jets, Whizzbang shot towards the high ceiling and hovered while he lobbed a couple of grenades onto the Slayer below. Though tough, the slayers body is no match for the explosive power of a grenade. The resulting incandescent fireball created by the explosive impacts of rapidly fired tellurite infused grenades engulfed the Slayer until it was nothing but black charcoal.

With his jump jets exhausted and requiring time to recharge Whizzbang settled to the floor and collapsed against the wall. Taking deep controlled breaths, he waited thirty seconds to give the nanomeds time to deal with the worst of his wound. He had lost a lot of blood but thankfully, his arteries remained intact. It would not be long before his bone marrow began producing more red blood cells, spurred on by the nanomeds.

Unless he did something immediately, lethargy would kick in soon and he would be a sitting duck for any Scourge still roaming the area. Whizzbang wrinkled his nose as pulled out a replenishment syrup from a side pocket and with one gulp sucked down the highly processed disgusting cocktail that would provide his body the necessary nutrients to speed up the healing. "*Why couldn't they do something about the smell and the flavour?*" he thought to himself as he limped over to the TransWarp.

For a piece of tech that could summon more Scourge from who knows where, the TransWarp was not really a big or complicated device. Standing about eight feet tall, it had what looked like a crown of metal plates that ended in sharp points at their apex.

Whizzbang bent over the control panel and instantly felt like he was falling through the air from some great height. Not like gliding but plummeting to his death. He gritted his teeth until the sensation passed. The moments of vertigo were coming more regularly but they seemed to go away after a few seconds. This one was no exception.

Take a deep calming breath he again looked closely at the TransWarp control panel and then extended his arm towards it. Two universal interface-connecting plugs automatically extended themselves from his battleframe and inserted into the TransWarp's input socket. Whizzbang watched on his wrist-comp, numbers and symbols flash by as his battleframe began hacking the TransWarp's on-board systems until, with a cheerful beep, he knew that he had access.

The TransWarp interface offered two options, "Summon" or "Self-destruct". Whizzbang selected the latter and to avoid the blast he hastily retreated around the corner to the ramp leading to the middle outpost level.

It was then that he came face to face with a pink-eyed Juggernaut.

Chapter 11
Struggle

Whizzbang knew his doom was all but certain and felt a strange slowness of time as it trickled through his hourglass. In the twinkling of an eye memories flooded through his cerebral cortex of past achievements, lessons learned and most of all regrets. His first day at sniper school, his first kiss and his first kill all blurred together. They cascaded one upon another until the memories began colliding into a kaleidoscope of images so bewildering that his body reacted by instinct. Fight or flight?

In what appeared to be slow motion the Juggernaut lifted its plasma canon and levelled it at Whizzbang's chest, ready to end his life. Flight!

Whizzbang kicked his jump jets to maximum thrust at the same time the ignition sequence in the plasma canon ignited the lethal molten projectile. Unexpectedly the Jug's arm and plasma canon was violently wrenched around by some unseen force causing its point blank shot to miss. As he blasted into the air Scourge blood sprayed across Whizzbang's legs from the Juggernaut's wide-open astonished maw.

"I've got your back," Selfia's voice crackled over the comnet.

The mixture of relief at being alive combined with Selfia's simple statement was almost overwhelming. From one hyper-charged adrenaline, enhanced second to the next, Whizzbang realised that he lived to fight another day. Subject to the hellish energies produced by a direct plasma canon erruption there was a good chance that the eport systems would fail in his battleframe. That end could have been his permanent game over.

"Thanks Self," Whizzbang replied as he tempered the jump jet thrust to settle back down to the top level of the outpost. "I thought I was done for."

"Just returning the favour Whizz. All's clear on the ramp to mid-level."

"Acheron is everything good down below?" asked Whizzbang.

"All Scourge accounted for. I'm heading up the ramp to the second level. Meet you in the middle."

"CT, meet you at mid Acheron. Self, can you come and give us a hand?"

"CT Whizz. See you in five."

Whizzbang watched as Selfia gently glided down beside him on flaming jets. As with him, the nanomeds seemed to have done their work and healed her wounds.

"All set?" Whizzbang asked.

Rather than being in any sort of discomfort Selfia appeared angry. In answer to his question, she deftly flipped her sniper rifle into its back holster and pulled out her close quarter's assault rifle. "Let's kill those frapping Scourge!"

Other than a lone Scourge Engineer who was trying to engage the outpost's automated defences by hacking the central comptroller, the outpost's mid-level was almost disappointingly absent of enemies. With a brief blaze of gunfire, Acheron dispatched the Engineer as it tried to hide behind a control panel. He then put out of commission a couple of golden Scourge drones by the time Whizzbang and Selfia made it to the control room.

"Alright, that was exciting!" exclaimed Acheron with a beaming smile on his face.

Like a cloud about to rain on a parade Selfia said, "It's OK for you to say that Ach! You've got to take more care of yourself! Haven't you noticed that the frapping Scourge are getting smarter every day? Did you even notice the number of Scourge that Whizz and I were taking out while protecting your frapping backside?" By this time Selfia's voice had reached a crescendo. "Did you? Well, did you? What would have happened if I'd missed one Ach? Would you be smiling then? Protecting both you and Whizz kept me busier than ever!"

Acheron held up his hands in surrender and said in a more subdued voice, "I'm sorry Selfia. I just got so mad when I thought that frapping sniper had you."

"It nearly did have me you big lunk! My armour took a pounding that will take a complete overhaul to completely repair."

"You're G2G now though aren't you Self?"

"Yeah, I'm G2G. Now get over here."

With that, Selfia reached up and grabbed Acheron's chin in her soft Eagle-claw gloved hand. She stood on tippy-toes and gave a small blast of her jets so that she could plant a kiss firmly on his lips. Quickly recovering from his surprise Acheron lifted Selfia off her feet and returned the kiss with equal fervour.

Selfia beamed up at him but said with a stern voice, "Now don't you do that again Ach. No berserking." Then she kissed Acheron again, just a little more gently but just as passionately.

Whizzbang stared at his feet and said, "Hey guys, can't we leave that for Freehold?"

"Sorry Whizz, I'd thought that I'd lost her."

"And I thought that I'd lost him."

"CT. Let's leave playing lovers until later, we've still got to engage the towers defences and call in the militia before heading out to find Bosk." Whizzbang typed the authorization code into his wrist-comp to get access to the outpost's comptroller and auto-connect him to the internal outpost systems.

"Sure Whizz. No need to get shirty. Self and I have only been married a few weeks and we've never managed to get a honeymoon yet," Acheron replied defensively.

Whizzbang sighed, "I'm not shirty Ach. I see you two and I'm really happy for you. I really am. I just feel that there's something different about the Scourge we've been fighting. At times it seems like they're smarter or something. I picture my friends out there fighting for their lives and for the survival of everyone on this world. I've got to find them so that we can get some semblance of a plan together."

"You're right Whizz," Selfia said, "We'll help you find them."

"Thanks Selfia. I appreciate you both helping me out. I really mean that."

Whizzbang's wrist-comp made the familiar cheerful ping of an authorized connection. While he was distracted, Selfia looked across at Acheron and raised one eyebrow questioningly. Acheron replied with a nod and a smile. They may have been ordered to guard Whizzbang but now they were coming together as a squad.

"OK, let's see what we've got here," Whizzbang said as he stared at the giant monitor in front of him. Logging into a Concord battle net system that is half-hacked by Scourge Engineers is not particularly difficult when you are in a battleframe, but sometimes they left little surprises that could be unpleasant.

"Thank goodness the Scourge Engies didn't have time to leave any code hacks. That's good for us. I'll just reboot the system and help will be on the way," mumbled Whizzbang more to himself.

"It looks like that's got it. We just need to wait a couple of minutes for the defence net to reboot and we can call it done and dusted," Whizzbang said, with a flourish, he toggled the activation key on his wrist-comp.

Just then the whine of multiple battle-pods reverberated through the outpost.

"We've got company!" yelled Acheron over the noise.

"*How did they know and react so fast?*" Whizzbang thought.

For some strange reason, despite all of the technical innovations by the Concord "Blue Sky" research team, they still had never managed to reduce the three minutes it took to reboot an outpost's comptroller to activate the defence grid. Surprisingly, the Scourge seemed to immediately know when an outpost returned to Concord hands and launch a counter-offensive.

Crunch, crunch, crunch. The three Scourge battle-pods slammed into the ground around the outpost, sending sprays of dust and rock in all directions. The gyrating energy orb atop each sparked, flamed and pulsed as the warp connections routed through subspace to the Scourge base.

"Acheron, can you hold the east ramp?" Whizzbang yelled over the noise.

"I'm onto it Whizz."

"Selfia, let's you and I hold the west."

Selfia nodded in agreement.

Defending the two ramps that lead up from the ground into the outpost was their best chance against whatever materialised out of the three battle-pods. With any luck, they could hold the Scourge off from the control room and deny enemy Engineers the chance to re-hack the outpost defence network.

Through gritted teeth, Whizzbang said to Selfia, "Don't fire yet. Wait until they appear and then send everything you've got."

"CT Whizz." Selfia reached into a pocket in her battleframe and pulled out a flat round metallic object that rested in the palm of her hand. Gauging the weight she said, "I'll throw my deployable mine as soon as they begin materializing."

"Good idea."

"You G2G Ach?" Whizzbang yelled across to his new friend guarding the opposite ramp as he kept an eye on the battle-pods energy cycle.

"G2G Whizz. I'll unleash hell on those frapping monsters as soon as they stick their stinking noses out."

Whizzbang said to Selfia beside him, "He's one of a kind isn't he."

She immediately smiled at the comment. "Of course he is. He's my husband and yes, he's one of a kind."

A faint deep purple sparking appeared at five distinct points around the battle-pod that Selfia and Whizzbang were keeping an eye on. The sparking grew more aggressive by the second and began to take the shape of five Scourge Juggernaut battleframes.

"We've got five Jug's here Ach!" Whizzbang yelled.

"A few Slayers and a couple of Engies here."

"Open fire!" Whizzbang screamed as he launched his first of six grenades into the startled Juggernauts. Simultaneously Selfia hurled her deployable mine into the midst of the Scourge and pressed the remote trigger switch. KABOOM! The combined impact of the mine and grenades going off shook the foundations of the outpost to its core. That was nothing compared to what the combined explosive force did to the Scourge below.

Arms, legs, heads, plasma canons and chest plates soared into the air and away from the epicentre of the blasts. Whereas in the past the arms and legs were connected by bone and sinew this time they flew both separately and freely amidst the purple mist from Scourge blood that slowly settled over the surrounding area. A hole in the ground was all that remained of the drop-pod. Above all the devastation was the low groaning of Acheron's mini-gun spewing its deadly contents onto the still materialising Scourge on his side below.

It was not long before two of the battle-pods were ruined husks with black acrid smoke billowing out of their sides as the delicate internals were violently wrenched apart. The trio needed to reload and as if on cue, the remaining Scourge from the battle-pods attacked.

Three Shock troopers charged around the corner with guns blazing as they ran up the ramp towards Whizzbang and Selfia. In front of them, a Scourge drone dropped a barrage of sparks and smoke making it almost impossible to see targets.

Whizzbang's battleframe was constantly "pinging" with the sound of the Shock trooper's small arms fire. "Selfia, we're not in an Anvil battleframe, we can't take much more of this punishment. Time to move."

"CT Whizz!"

"Selfia, get back into the control room and take a position at the top of the central ramp. I'll buy you sometime." Whizzbang said urgently over the sounds of the battle.

"CT Whizz. Moving now."

That's when Whizzbang noticed that the methodical whine of the mini-gun was silent.

"Nooooo!" Selfia cried out in anguish. All thoughts of the plan to hold the central ramp fled from her mind as she sprinted across the control room with jump jet assisted speed. Acheron lay on his back and a weak voice sounded over the comnet, "Medic, I need a medic…"

Defending the ramp by himself Acheron knew that he had taken a lot of damage and his battleframe was in tatters. Although the Evkon 316 stopped the worst of the pain, the number of holes in his armour seeping blood was not a good sign. His nanites and nanomeds had overloaded and commenced an auto recharge sequence. This was the stage immediately before an eport. He desperately needed help from either Whizzbang or Selfia.

"Oh frap!" Whizzbang cursed. He had managed to down one of the Shock troopers but the other two were still charging up the ramp. Ducking back inside the control room gave him a moments respite from the hail of bullets and with a blast of his jets he launched himself for the central ramp. While flying through the air he twisted around and fired a couple of grenades in the direction where he and Selfia had been defending. Two satisfying thumps greeted his ears as bits of Shock trooper sprayed into the control room.

Speeding across the large control room Selfia yelled across the comnet over the detonation of Whizzbang's grenades. "Don't you eport Ach!" Selfia knew that many pilots were changed by the trauma of an eport and whatever happened she loved Acheron just the way he was.

Selfia skidded to a halt beside Acheron and immediately extended her battleframe's emergency nanomed tube out of the back of the armour in her forearm. She then quickly inserted it into a small socket in Acheron's chest armour. A flush of fresh nanomeds and nanites gushed across the battleframe connection slamming into Acheron's now exhausted semi-dormant micro-machines. It was like a high-tech version of jumpstarting a flittercar but in this case, it was a billion mini-jumpstarts all at once.

The connection auto-terminated before too many of Selfia's nano-machines overloaded the now active ones in Acheron's body and in his battleframe. Acheron's eyes flew open just as first one and then another red beam of a Scourge Sniper fire burrowed into the wall above Selfia's head.

"Whizz, we need some help here!" yelled Selfia. It would be at least another fifteen seconds before Acheron could start moving and those sniper rounds were too close for comfort.

"CT Self. I'm on it"

Whizzbang lobbed a couple of grenades at the entrance behind him just in case any Scourge had any thoughts of following. He raced up the inside central ramp to the one connecting both the outside walkway linking the second and third levels. As he ran, he slammed his grenade launcher into its hip holster and pulled out his Charge rifle.

Reaching the ramp, he peered through the scope and murmured to himself, "Where are you?" Quickly panning in the direction the beams had come from he caught the glint of metal armour. "Gotcha you frapping monster!"

Whizzbang pressed the firing stud ended the Scourge Sniper's life. The second sniper revealed his position with another shot towards Selfia and Acheron.

Selfia yelled again, "Whizz!" through his comnet earpiece just as he fired at the Scourge Sniper. Like everything else, that is elevated instantly to one thousand degrees centigrade the Scourge died.

"All clear Self. I got him. How are you guys going?"

"G2G Whizz," came Acheron's strained voice via the comnet.

"Like fun you are! You're to stay right here until the meds fix you up," Selfia ordered.

"Yes Mum," Acheron replied attempting a cheeky grin.

"Hey guys. I hate to break this up but we have the third battle-pod to deal with out there and I know that there is at least an Engie to take out", said Whizzbang.

"Let me deal with this!" said Selfia as she got to her feet and pulled out her assault rifle.

It goes without saying, that the Scourge Engineer died and the third battle-pod was quickly vanquished. Hell hath no fury like a woman scorned. That is when the three minutes clocked up and the outpost defences came online.

General Grendig, supreme commander of all Scourge forces on Alpha Three leaned forward on his command throne. He revelled in the feeling of power that he always experienced as he looked out from his position in the middle of the massive dome. From here in the centre of his fortress, he planned and plotted the downfall of the human habitations on the other side of the planet. Below his dais, in expanding rings around him, officers tapped at consoles while they grunted orders to fists and strike leaders all across the planet. Each of them was busy unfolding their part in the plan for the extermination of the humans on the planet.

Grendig indulged in a parody of a smile that revealed a mouthful of sharpened pointed teeth and two longer fangs. His pink eyes were in sharp contrast to his deathly pale skin and missed nothing as they scanned the reports pouring in on two of the three huge screens suspended from the ceiling of the dome opposite him. Today was turning out better than he could have hoped.

Surprisingly, the spy had done a remarkable job with the accursed Concord defence network. The plan was on schedule and losses were within acceptable parameters. Despite the natural viciousness of his race, this put him in a good mood. Absently he reached down with his right hand to a bucket beside him and pulled out a human arm, puncturing it with his sharpened nails. He noted that blood still flowed freely so it was fresh from a recent battle. Still reading the reports, he nonchalantly began ripping the flesh from the arm, savouring every morsel. *"There was nothing quite like devouring ones enemies,"* he thought.

The new off-world troops made the plan of eradicating the humans from this world possible. They had arrived in stealth a few weeks ago by entering from the far side of Alpha Three and using the planet itself as cover from the orbiting Concord space station. Once landed, the troops immediately started training and becoming acclimatized to the gravity and atmosphere. The General had waited a long time for reinforcements on this backwater of a planet and a second detachment would be arriving within another few weeks.

With the successful conquering of this world, he could begin to contemplate the next stage in his ascendancy up the Scourge command structure. He was sure that it would take an assassination or two but that was no matter to him. If those above were too weak to realize his threat then they did not deserve to rule.

Flicking a switch on his left armrest, he brought up a map of Alpha Three on the far left screen. Other than the Concord Central command and the baneful Freehold, all the sectors were a glorious vivid red. Looking at the readouts, he was confident that the Concord command sector would soon fall. Glancing at the invasion plan timer on the right screen he again smiled in anticipation as the battle for Freehold would be commencing shortly. He looked forward to pulling that so called "Freedom Torch" down himself!

A morsel of meat became stuck between two of his fangs so with a quick wrench he ripped off one of the human fingers and used it like a toothpick to extricate it. Looking back up at the map one of the sectors due south of Freehold changed from red to green. It was most likely a glitch in the system as the vast amounts of data was collected, collated and summarized before him. He would have that officer's head on a spike on the outer wall for that failure!

It never occurred to the General that the information was correct, the master plan wasn't infallible and overwhelmingly superior numbers of troops was not a guarantee of victory.

Chapter 12
Assault

Whizzbang raised his Charge riflescope to his eye and adjusted the magnification to zoom in on Altavia finishing a conversation with Professor Steinberg. *"The woman certainly had all the right curves,"* he thought to himself.

Annoyed at himself for getting distracted, he dialled back the settings on the scope and scanned around the hanger bay. It was an amazing feat of engineering for Blue Sky to cut the huge area out of the moon's bedrock. He zoomed in on the gigantic plasteel beams that arced overhead and supported the roof over a hundred meters off the floor. "Bosk, you're going to just love the scope on the new rifle."

Bosk still held his arms out for the nanites to complete the building of his Raven battleframe. "I'll be with you in a second Whizz."

Altavia strode up to Whizzbang, her hips just swaying in just the right way to enhance her femininity. "So you like your new toy?"

Whizzbang lowered the scope from his eye and cleared his throat before speaking. "Yes, like the battleframe, it's magnificent."

"I personally oversaw the design of the energy transfer system. It's a generation ahead of anything currently available," Altavia answered with just a hint of pride.

"I haven't fired it yet so I wouldn't know."

Whizzbang thought, *"Why was it that he always became so nervous around this woman? There seemed to be something about her that was downright unnerving."*

"Hey, Altavia," Bosk interrupted, "Did you really develop this rifle?"

Altavia blessed Bosk with a smile. "Not all of it. As I was saying to Whizzbang, just the energy transfer system."

Bosk returned the smile with one of his own. "Don't be so modest, that's the core of the whole weapon."

Whizzbang said, "Come on Bosk, let's head down to the test firing range."

"Good idea," Bosk replied as he swung the rifle up into its back harness.

High overhead a low moaning siren began winding up. A voice over a loud speaker blasted, "Incoming Scourge assault. This is not a drill. Incoming Scourge assault imminent. I repeat, this is not a drill."

A look of intense concentration crossed Altavia's features as she listened to the announcement. "You two wait here. I'll go and find out what this is about."

Both Whizzbang and Bosk ignored her last remark and followed her to the nearest terminal. Professor Steinberg appeared from behind a rack of equipment and quickly headed towards them. After working with him for the past several months, his dishevelled appearance and smudged spectacles were now a common sight for both pilots.

Altavia pointed a perfectly manicured fingernail to an image on the monitor. "I don't know how they found us so fast but it looks like we have a Scourge cruiser dropping out of subspace just outside the gravity well of the moon and planet. It will only be a few minutes before they get here."

The professor became flustered at the news and stumbled over his words as he asked, "Wha,…what should we do? We have technology here that the Scourge could only dream about. How are we going to save it?"

Altavia's voice took on a timbre that neither of the two pilots had heard before. It commanded and expected instant obedience. "Professor, send all of the data that we have on the battleframes back to Blue Sky on Kaladon. Do it quickly!"

"Yes, yes, of course Altavia."

Whizzbang lifted his Charge rifle out of its harness and checked the power levels. Thankfully, they were fully charged. "Won't the signal be intercepted?"

"We'll have to risk that."

"How long will it take to send all the data?"

"At least ten minutes."

Whizzbang glanced down at the monitor. "We don't have ten minutes."

Altavia looked the two pilots up and down in their new battleframes. "You and Bosk will have to hold them off. There will be a lot of them though."

Bosk quipped, "That'll mean we won't be able to miss."

Altavia ignored Bosk's comment. "The professor and I will get as many people as we can into the frigate. My guess is that Captain Eldrich will already be prepping it for launch." Altavia paused as she thought through the ramifications of what she was about to ask. "Whizzbang, Bosk, we're going to need as much time as you can give us."

Whizzbang nodded. "Understood. Come on Bosk, we have some work to do."

"Got it."

Whizzbang and Bosk kicked in their jump jets and side-slipped to increase their speed along the main throughway that ran down the centre of the hanger. Technicians and other research staff jumped out of their way as they raced past. Glancing over his shoulder Whizzbang watched both Altavia and the professor feverishly working at their consoles.

As they neared the outside energy wall Whizzbang shutdown his jets and ran a few servo enhanced steps to slow down. Colonel Greerson and Captain Eldrich were both running towards them, obviously intent on reaching the professor.

"Colonel Greerson sir," Whizzbang said.

Relief passed across the Colonel's face as he said, "It's good to see you both in uniform."

"Thank you sir."

Whizzbang related what Altavia and Professor Steinberg were doing further back in the hanger.

The Colonel and Captain quickly absorbed the implications of the information. Colonel Greerson looked Whizzbang and then Bosk in the eye, "It looks like you're about to be the first line of defence for the base."

Whizzbang nodded in acknowledgement.

"Once we heard that the Scourge were hunting for us we thankfully evacuated most of the teams here to other Blue Sky facilities. There's only a skeleton staff left. Both you and Bosk need to stop the enemy outside the hanger while the Captain and I coordinate the evacuation of the remaining personnel."

"Yes sir."

Even through the energy wall Whizzbang could hear the sound of multiple battle-pods screaming towards the crater. He hated that noise. It was as if someone was dragging their fingernails down an old blackboard and it grated on every fibre of his being. He had been dreaming of a chance for revenge ever since the death of his parents at the family farm but he just did not expect it was going to be today.

Whizzbang turned to leave and felt the Colonel's hand on his arm. "Son, be careful out there. This isn't a game. You too Bosk. Stay frosty and stay calm."

Whizzbang replied, "Take care of everyone here Colonel. Bosk and I will do our part. Good-bye."

"No good-byes, see you later Private."

Whizzbang and Bosk once again kicked in their now recharged jump jets and passed through the energy wall separating the hanger from the outside. The screeching noise of battle-pods plummeting to the ground competed with the automated warning message in their earpieces. It looked like there was going to be a lot of enemy and pretty soon.

Bosk pointed out the dark shape of a Scourge cruiser in the night sky as it occluded the stars behind it. "You think they'd just blow us to pieces from up top."

"Not likely. I think that they're after some of the technology being developed here."

"That makes sense."

"Bosk I'm getting sick of that alarm. Switching to local three three seven."

"Switching to local three three seven." Bosk adjusted the frequency to one that just he and Whizzbang could communicate. "I thought that you'd never suggest going local Whizz. That automated alarm sounded like the navigation unit in my flitter-car."

Despite their dire circumstances, Whizzbang gave a little chuckle. "You know I think you're right. The voice even has that same sense of urgency when you're the one driving."

"Eh, that's not fair. I'm a good driver."

"If we get through this then you can show me how good you are. Anyway, back to business, suggestions?"

"We could stay here and shoot down at them."

"No, we'd get picked off. How about behind those rocks we found on one of our glides on the far side of the crater?"

"Not a bad idea. We'd have a clear view of the entrance and provide incentive for the Scourge to attack us rather than the base."

"Done."

"One of these days I wish that you'd take my sarcasm a little more seriously."

"If we get through today then I promise that I will."

"Done!"

Whizzbang dropped a packet of nanites down and the now familiar glider launch platform took shape. It was only a short glide to the other side of the crater so they both sprung their wings open before the top of the arc and pointed their noses to their destination.

Below them huge puffs of dust flew in all directions as one battle-pod after another slammed into the crater floor. In another few seconds, the Scourge warriors would start warping in.

"Bosk, did you see how many of them there are?"

"Too much dust."

"I didn't see either."

At the last second, they both retracted their wings and scurried behind the shelter of a boulder perched precariously half way up the crater. Around them, rocks the size of small flitter-cars lay half embedded in the dirt and dust of the steep sloping crater wall.

Whizzbang pointed as he said urgently, "Bosk, take up position here and I'll take cover behind that rock over there. It will give them two targets rather than one."

"Got it. Whizz?"

"Yep?"

"Take care of yourself."

"You too."

Whizzbang jump-jetted the twenty feet across to his position. From their spots, both pilots had an excellent view of the hanger entrance to pick off targets attempting to climb up the crater wall and invade the research facility. Now that the dust had settled, they also had a clear line of site to the dozen battle-pods spinning up their power orbs.

Purple dancing sparks began coalescing at more and more distinct points as Scourge warriors warped down from the cruiser above. A crackle of angry electricity reached Whizzbang's ears as the warriors forms began to take shape. It had been years since he had seen the Scourge warp in at the farm and the intensity of the sound caught him by surprise.

Sighting a warrior taking shape in his scope he said, "Bosk, remember the drill. On four."

"CT Whizz."

"Breathe in. Breathe out. Breathe in. Breathe out. Fire."

Two blue beams raced down into the crater and ended the life of two Slayers just as they emerged from warping in.

"Breathe in. Breathe out. Breathe in. Breathe out. Fire."

The four-count drill provided time for the Charge rifle to build up energy for another shot while helping provide a routine to assist the sniper's aim. Two more targets died as the blue beams zinged down.

This time Bosk did the count, "Breathe in. Breathe out. Breathe in. Breathe out. Die."

Down in the crater over fifty enemy warriors had completed the warp-in. Recognising that they were under attack, fist leaders organized a response to the pilot's attack. In the space of a few more heartbeats, two enemy snipers died before they had a chance to fire.

Shock troopers laid down a withering covering fire with their rapid automatic assault rifles. Before he could take a hit, Whizzbang ducked his head behind the safety of the boulder and then crawled along the ground to its left side. Peering around the edge, he spied a few warriors making their way up the far side of the crater. "Bosk, we've got some problems towards the hanger."

"Sighted."

They were now out of sync with their firing ritual. Each of them, aimed, fired and killed two more warriors before they had to seek safety behind their boulders.

Bosk suddenly yelled, "Oh frap!"

Whizzbang heard the whumps of four plasma launchers flinging their deadly superheated contents heavenward. The trajectories of the glowing pulsing energy balls placed their impact zone at Bosk's position.

"Bosk, get over here now!"

"I'm on my way."

Bosk blasted his jump jets at maximum power to shoot across the distance between him and his friend. Such was his unexpected speed that the enemy below did not have time to pick him off as he entered the open. His jump jets did unleash a small avalanche of loose dust and dirt that rolled down the side of the crater.

Behind him, the four balls of plasma splattered across the front, side and back of his boulder. Where the plasma touched, the stone simply vanished in a hiss of steam and ionized gas.

Bosk dove head first behind the temporary safety of Whizzbang's position. "Good to see you again."

"You to Whizz. We didn't expect a few Jugs did we?"

"Nope."

"So much for the two target theory."

"How much time do you think we have?" Whizzbang asked.

"About twenty seconds until the next launch and then we're in for it. Any ideas?"

Whizzbang looked around for some sort of inspiration and then smiled. "I think that I may have just come up with one but it will need the both of us."

"I need you to brace yourself with your servos against the crater wall and begin firing your jump jets on maximum burn at the base of my boulder."

"You've got to be kidding me?"

"No I'm not."

Suddenly Bosk got the idea and smiled back at his life-long friend. "I got it."

Both of them lent against the crater wall and fired their jump jets at full burn. Loose dirt and small rocks created a cloud of debris around them as their jets dug out a growing sized hole around the boulder. Their battleframes easily withstood the punishment that they were dishing out and their servos took the majority of the strain.

Down in the crater the Scourge warriors whooped as they thought that the cloud of dust had to signify the death of the pilots. A Strike Leader directed a fist up the slope to confirm the kills while the remainder of the warriors formed up as they waited for the next warp-in.

Straining with the effort of controlling the jump-jet blast Whizzbang said, "OK, I think that will do it. Give it all you've got at the top of the boulder."

"CT," Bosk panted with exertion.

Whizzbang hoped that they had done enough to destabilize the rock and that the combined impact of their jump jets and gravity would do the rest. The boulder started leaning outwards. It was going to work!

"Nearly there Bosk!"

Suddenly both their jump jets cut out.

Whizzbang toggled his jets a number of times in desperation, "Oh frap! They need time to recharge!"

"They had to pick now to cut out? You got to be kidding me!" Bosk complained.

The sudden cessation of the noise from their jump jets made the whumps further down in the crater all the louder. Four balls of plasma commenced their deadly arc towards them.

Just when they thought things could not get worse the boulder began to slide back towards them and the hole they had just made.

"We've got to get out of here!" Whizzbang yelled.

Bosk did not even wait to reply as he leapt to his feet and started running on power-assisted legs. Whizzbang was not far behind but risked a glance over his shoulder to see the bottom of the boulder break loose from where they had undermined it. Slowly the rock began its deadly fall down the side of the crater, picking up momentum and other boulders along the way.

"Run! We've just lost our cover!"

The approaching Scourge fist were further up the slope and quickly jumped out of the way of the tumbling boulders heading to the crater floor below. As he ran, Whizzbang watched as dirt kicked up by gunfire beside him.

Behind them, the four plasma globes slammed into the ground where both the pilots had been only moments earlier. Rather than splashing and dissolving solid rock, the plasma slammed into loose stones, dirt and dust. The resulting explosion as the smaller objects instantly turned to gas sent a concussive shockwave outwards.

Whizzbang felt himself picked up and hurled through the air while Bosk only just managed to keep his feet. The Scourge fist had managed to escape the majority of the explosion by diving behind a large boulder that had not joined the avalanche that was now hurtling towards the battle-pods. The explosion did dislodge several additional boulders that were now joining the fray roaring down the slope.

Bosk quickly took stock of his position of relative safety behind another large rock that seemed was more firmly bedded into the side of the crater. He looked back down the slope and saw Whizzbang face down in the dirt and dust with his leg at an odd angle. Thankfully, he still seemed to be breathing. "Whizz! Get up Whizz!"

A Shock trooper stood to its feet, dirt falling off its armour, and smiled as he spied Whizzbang lying prone up the slope. Raising his automatic rifle he let loose one round before falling to the ground dead.

"That's right you frapping monster. Not all of us are down!" Bosk yelled in challenge.

Upon seeing the wall of tumbling rock heading towards them the panic stricken Scourge warriors broke formation and started running in all directions. The avalanche continued to grow and gain momentum until it finally crashed headlong into the fleeing warriors. Battle-pods toppled over and were crushed by tons of rock and dirt. Scourge warriors flew through the air under the avalanche's assault and buried under the rushing tide of rubble. A few warriors managed to escape the destruction by scrambling up the far crater wall just below the hanger. When the dust settled, two battle-pods remained visible, leaning over at a precarious angle with muted energy orbs blinking forlornly. Purple sparks formed shapes half embedded within the debris and the warriors warping in died as they materialised.

Bosk slid down the slope to his unconscious friend, being careful not to dislodge another avalanche of small stones. A ruby red Scourge sniper beam just missed his head as he stumbled forward. Taking quick aim, he silenced the enemy sniper forever.

The three warriors left in the Scourge fist stepped out from their cover and fired up the slope. A number of shots pinged off Bosk's new battleframe and jerked him around with their momentum.

"Come on Whizz!"

Within Whizzbang's body, a billion tiny machines were feverishly working to heal his leg by straightening it out and reconstructing the shattered bone. The Evkon 316 painkillers blocked the majority of the pain and the bump on his head that had knocked him out did the rest.

Bosk turned around and fired again, just missing an enemy engineer. Bullets ripped and tore at the dirt around him. As he protected Whizzbang's body with his own his battleframe came under constant assault. Turning around he again fired and this time cut the engineer cleanly through the neck, sending a shower of blood over the two remaining warriors.

"Here goes nothing," he mumbled to himself.

Grabbing Whizzbang under the arms Bosk fired his now recharged jump jets to drag them both up the slope and to the safety of another rock. Behind him the two Scourge screamed obscenities in their language even as they kept on firing.

"Same to you!" Bosk yelled back. He did not know what the warriors were saying but presumed that it was not very pleasant. He finally reached the relative safety of the rock just as his jump jets again cut out.

Turning to the still unconscious Whizzbang he said, "I'll be back in a second. There's just something that I've got to do first."

He returned two shots and thirty seconds later said, "Just tidied up a couple of loose ends." Looking with concern Bosk choked out, "Time to wake up now."

Whizzbang felt like he was floating in a perfect bed surrounded by cotton wool. It was so nice here. So comfortable and inviting. If it was not for the incessant noise.

"Whizz! Whizzbang! It's time to get up now."

That sounds like Bosk's voice. I wonder if he would like to stay here with me?

"Whizz! Wake up! It's action time!"

Like a computer slowly rebooting, Whizzbang's brain began to piece together the events of the last few minutes. The boulder, the run, the explosion and then darkness. I'm in my battleframe! Whizzbang's eyes flew open and he instinctively reached behind for his rifle. "Bosk! What happened?"

Bosk smiled with relief. "You took a bump to the head and it looks like your right leg got a little mangled."

Bosk looked down at Whizzbang's now straight leg. "While I'll be frapped."

"What is it?"

"It looks like the little meds have performed some emergency surgery on your leg while you've been out cold."

"What's happened to the Scourge?"

"Can you sit up?"

In answer, Whizzbang rolled onto his front and crawled out from behind the rock. There was a lot of dust still in the air but it was clear that all the battle-pods and the majority of warriors had now been decommissioned. On the far side of the crater, half a dozen surviving warriors were pulling themselves up over the hanger bay ledge.

Whizzbang sighted a Slayer and pressed his firing button. With a distant scream, the Scourge fell to his death below. In the meantime, Bosk drilled a shock trooper through the back of the head. Before they could again fire, the Scourge passed through the energy shield and into the research facility.

"C'mon Bosk, we've got to get across there."

"What about your leg?"

"Feels as good as new."

"Liar."

"It'll be fine once I get into the air. What do you think those warriors will do to all those people without battleframes?"

In answer, Bosk tossed a bundle of glider-programmed nanites down next to them.

Whizzbang stood tenderly to his feet and tested out his right leg. It was still weak but he could not afford to wait for the nanomeds to finish their work. Gritting his teeth, he stepped onto the shimmering glider pad and despite the Evkon 316 screamed in pain as he re-broke his leg under the force of the upward thrust.

In the air, Bosk reached out a reassuring hand to his friend. "You'll be fine Whizz, you just need to give the meds a few minutes."

The wind whistled past them as they steepened their angle of attack towards the hanger entrance. "We don't have that sort of time Bosk."

They both knew that unless he landed just right with all of his weight on his left leg then it was likely that Whizzbang would break his leg again on landing.

Chapter 13
The Search Continues

The warm northerly breeze flowed through the Barrier, subtly warping the surface and setting off a ripple of purple sparks across its surface. The Scourge designed Barrier was initially meant to cover the whole of Alpha Three. The Concord had managed to push it back in a small area so that they could continue mining the precious tellurite crystals. Far below, creatures within the Barrier fought and squabbled over scraps of food but such things were of no matter to the wind as it passed by.

With an almost imperceptible tug, the breeze broke free of the Barrier to flow down into a valley where humans had previously built a tower. The communication aerials arrayed around the top swayed gently in its passing and it made a strange moaning sound as it wound its way through metal girders to the other side of the structure. Down below, automated tellurite mining machines, known as Diggers, lay scattered around the tower. Some still gushed smoke from their sides, the results of a recent battle.

Continuing its journey southward, the wind broke through a narrow pass. The wind carried the smell of cauterised flesh, both human and Scourge, as it passed a battle over Belver's outpost perched on the edge of a cliff. Stray bullets punctured the breeze a number of times until it was too far out of range of those fighting and dying below.

Picked up in a thermal along the cliff edge the wind headed directly southwards over a vast green and purple forest. If it had taken notice, it could have seen fully-fledged battles and small skirmishes all the way to Freehold. The small settlement anchored the humans far below to the remnants of their world but the wind ignored them all and continued on its journey unconcerned.

Flowing through Freehold, an element of peace seemed to have settled over this part of Alpha Three. Either that or the bloody combat had moved on elsewhere. Going past Research Ravine the wind gained momentum as it rose up a small rise to where a lone figure stood atop an outpost staring towards the south. The wind ruffled the man's short greying hair and then disappeared upwards in an eddy that is common in that part of the world.

Whizzbang absently rubbed his left eye to help remove some stray dust that a gust of wind had just blown in his eye. He again tried his comnet, "Whizzbang, Romeo, Oscar, Siera, two, niner calling Bosk, you read? Over." Since the Scourge had launched a full-out invasion against Alpha Three the ether had been blanketed with electronic counter-measures. This wiped out both the wider comnet and reduced the localised comnet to a few hundred meters. By standing on the roof of the outpost, Whizzbang hoped to extend the reach of his communicator. His friend Bosk was somewhere south and had disappeared at the beginning of the Scourge assault.

"Whizzbang, Romeo, Oscar, Sierra, two, niner calling Bosk. You read? Over." Whizzbang repeated the message.

Whizzbang's new squad mates, Selfia and Acheron, appeared over the edge of the outpost's roof and with a quick blast of their jump jets settled softly next to Whizzbang. "It's OK Whizz." Selfia said with a concerned voice, "We heard your broadcasts over the local. I'm sure that Bosk and your other friends are OK."

Whizzbang sighed, "Thanks Self. With the invasion, the whole of Alpha Three's in turmoil and I feel like we're the fish in the barrel that the frapping Scourge are shooting at. I know that we'll find Bosk but I just want to do it before he's spread over the landscape. How you going Ach?"

It was just over an hour since Acheron nearly found himself eported. Selfia's quick decision to do an emergency nanomed transfusion to her husband's battleframe had saved him from the trauma. Acheron complained, "Other than having to suck in three pouches of nutritional syrup I'm feeling pretty good. That stuff is horrible! You'd think that they could somehow make it taste a little better."

"I know what you mean but at least it keeps you alive."

"I'm wondering what would be worse."

Selfia gave her husband an elbow in the ribs.

"Go easy Self, I'm still healing up."

Selfia smiled sweetly as she said, "I was just checking to see if you were better yet darling." She then elbowed Acheron a second time for good measure. "Feeling better yet?"

"Whoa! I give up."

"So stop complaining and pull yourself together you big lunk."

"Will do Lieutenant," Acheron replied sheepishly.

Ignoring the friendly banter Whizzbang pointed off into the distance and said, "I've been scoping out the area around the Terrarium and it looks like there's a lot of gun fire over there. Feel like a glide and shoot?"

Acheron's face spread into a big grin, "I've always wanted to take a look at that massive glass dome. Just point the way Whizz."

Selfia gave her characteristic little giggle. "It would be great to check out all the plants and relieve a few Scourge of their lives. I'm G2G Whizz."

Whizzbang suddenly held up his finger to indicate silence. Tilting his head to the side to speak into the comnet he said, "CT Captain. Ensure that you secure the surrounding perimeter from any Scourge that we may have missed."

There was a gap of silence while the Captain replied before Whizzbang said, "We're on the roof now and leaving in a few minutes."

Turning back to Acheron and Selfia, Whizzbang relayed the conversation. "The militia Captain will be here in a couple of minutes and he said that it's fine for us to move out."

Both Selfia and Acheron nodded in understanding.

Whizzbang pulled out a packet of nanites from his battleframe to build a glider jump pad. "I'm so glad that I met you two when I did. I don't think I could've made it without you."

Selfia smiled as she mumbled to herself, "You would have found a way Whizz."

It was not long before the nanites had completed manipulating the tellurite crystals to form the glider launch pad. Whizzbang set the directional waypoint on his wrist-comp map to point to the Terrarium and then stepped onto the glider pad.

Whizzbang loved flying and most of all he always got a thrill when he stepped onto a glider pad and experienced five G's of vertical force. At the peak of the arc, his battleframe's wings energised and he took a second to glance over his shoulder to ensure that Selfia and Acheron were on his six, directly behind him. The three of them soared silently over the lush green forest below towards the Terrarium. Even from their current distance, they could hear the faint crack of weapons fire.

As he glided, Whizzbang peered through his Charge riflescope to get a better appraisal of the situation. Scourge warriors were directing their gunfire predominantly towards the top of a large rock face overlooking the massive plexiglass dome of the Terrarium. Massive hexagonal glass sheets the size of a man slotted into a plasteel frame and formed the outer skin of the Terrarium. As he glided, the morning sun reflected in bright flashes off the flat plexiglass hexagons. Every now and then, Whizzbang watched as a Charge rifle beam reached out and "melted" a Scourge warrior. Despite the obvious skill of the Concord Raven, it was evident that the pinned down shooter would not last much longer.

Whizzbang spoke into his comnet pickup, "Whizzbang, Romeo, Oscar, Sierra, two, niner to Concord Raven at Terrarium.

Three inbounds to your north will be at your position in one minute."

"Whizz is that you! Frap am I glad to hear your voice!"

Whizzbang grinned. He'd finally found Bosk! Trust him to get into a mess with two Scourge fists.

The wind whistled about his battleframe as Whizzbang steepened his glide angle downwards towards the Terrarium facility and his friend. Acheron and Selfia followed close behind and he chuckled to himself as Acheron let out a little "YeeeHaaaa!" over the comnet. Acheron's enthusiasm was contagious and it was not long before they were all yelling a chorus of "YeeeHaaa's".

Whizzbang levelled his Charge rifle's scope to his eye and peered at the melee in the distance rushing towards him. Controlling his glide angle while scoping out an incoming battle is more art than science. The subtleties of a slight wind shift required him to make corresponding small changes in his position relative to his battleframe's tiny energised winglets. Moving the Charge rifle's scope to his eye, changed the position of his centre of gravity and required an almost super-natural gliding ability to compensate for the weight of the rifle barrel now sticking a long way out the front. In addition, the visual cues of the surroundings were now irrelevant since he was staring through the scope. Without a sixth sense for his glide angle he could easily end up stalled with his nose to the sky or racing towards the ground. In the end both options usually finished in a grizzly death.

Whizzbang was more at home in the air than on the ground and it was not long before a Scourge Juggernaut was in his crosshairs. A slight pressing of the firing trigger resulted in the Juggernaut's head spreading a highly volatized purple spray over the other Scourge firing up at Bosk. Although Selfia was not as accurate as Whizzbang in the air, a solitary boom of a sniper rifle behind him let him know that she was making the most of their inbound flight time.

Just before Whizzbang de-energised his winglets, a Scourge Slayer met a similar fate to the Juggernaut. With a few short breaking steps, he landed on the roof of the ready room directly opposite the Terrarium and then immediately rolled onto his stomach. Selfia and Acheron followed closely behind him. Directly across from them was the empty scanning tower landing clamps. Just before they had arrived, the tower was vaporised so that Concord communications remained disrupted.

The three of them lay flat on the roof to remain out of sight of the Scourge below and carefully checked out the composition of the enemy firing up at Bosk. Like Research Ravine, the scanning tower platform was constructed entirely from standard issue Concord plasteel grating. Stairways descended at both the south and north side of the upper tower deck to the ground below where the majority of the Scourge were now positioned.

Leaning over the edge of the roof, Whizzbang peered through the grating at the Scourge scurrying around wondering what had killed a couple of their comrades. It would not be long before one of the enemy on the upper deck next to the tower clamps decided to investigate the roof the three of them were using as cover. That is when all hell would start heading their way.

Ducking back out of sight Whizzbang whispered into the local comnet, "Bosk, how goes it up there?"

A panting, strained voice responded, "Not so good. My battleframe's got more holes in it than a block of cheese and my nanites are working over-time to repair the damage. I could really use a minute or two to get a bit of self-maintenance happening."

"CT Bosk. Hang in there."

"Doing my best."

Acheron slid along on his stomach to lie next to Whizzbang. He peeked over the roof edge at the Scourge below and asked, "Plan?"

Indicating the direction of the Scourge, Whizzbang replied, "First we've got to clear the few Scourge out of the high ground around the tower platform and second deal with those two battle-pods and the enemy below. Self, you take position up here on the roof and snipe a few. I'll stay with you until the upper deck is cleared and then jump across to the Terrarium roof on the other side. Ach, you smash them on the deck below and then head down the northern stairs to create a three way kill zone," ordered Whizzbang.

"CT Whizz," Selfia said as she took up position and began getting a bead on a Shock.

Acheron looked down at the group of Scourge milling around the tower platform who were clearly agitated about what had recently killed their two companions. Smiling, Acheron glance back at Selfia and silently mouthed, "I love you" just as he dropped off the roof onto the deck below.

"Bosk, you sit tight while we create mayhem," Whizzbang stated as he lined up a Scourge Engineer in his sites.

"CT Whizz. I'll remain behind cover," Bosk replied.

Another spent cartridge ejected from Selfia's bolt-action rifle and fell onto the roof beside her. It landed with a metallic clank as it bounced off her growing collection of empty shell cases. A faint thin trail of blue smoke rose from the spent ammunition just as another crack of the rifle delivered its deadly contents in the direction of the now thoroughly confused Scourge.

Lying prone on the roof beside Selfia, Whizzbang waited for his Charge rifle to power up to maximum before pressing the firing stud. The beam of super-heated energy sped through the air cutting first one Scourge and then bored its way through the enemy behind as well. One of the nice things about a Charge rifle beam is that it tended to keep going when only obstructed by flesh.

Selfia glanced at Whizzbang, raised an eyebrow and said with a cheeky smirk on her face, "No need to show off Whizz."

"Two's always better than one Self."

Acheron grunted in acknowledgement across the comnet as he opened up fire on the remaining Scourge warriors. They scattered to the left and right in an effort to dodge the torrent of bullets heading in their direction. Despite their desire to avoid being riddled with holes Acheron picked each and every Scourge off and was as subtle as a surgeon doing a brain operation with a chainsaw. He was good at his job, in fact very good. It was not long before he cleared the upper deck of enemies and was ready to play his part in stage two of Whizzbang's plan.

Whizzbang kicked his jump jets into action and scooted across to the Terrarium roof opposite Selfia. Acheron jumped down the stairs three at a time. On his way down, he smashed a humming Scourge golden drone with his armoured fist and pumped a few rounds into it for good measure.

The Scourge on the ground around the battle-pods that had been previously focusing their fire on Bosk, had now managed to regroup. An Engineer launched a second drone to attack Bosk's position with the obvious intention of finishing him off. Two Shock troopers directed their attention towards Selfia's rooftop position while two Juggernauts sent blasts of plasma at Whizzbang as he jump jetted across to his new vantage point. A couple of snipers began to take an interest in Selfia but she was already safely lying flat on the roof to avoid the fire already directed towards her. Selfia involuntarily pressed her face into the roof as a ruby red high energy beam zinged over her head and burrowed into the rock behind her.

Three Slayers raced up the path and around the corner to face a smiling Acheron who braced himself as he gently squeezed his gun's trigger.

As Whizzbang can testify, Slayers can be annoying combatants, especially for a sniper when they are concentrating on targets through their scope. Before they know it, a Slayer can plunge eighteen inches of polished tellurite crystal into their backs, and the sniper finds they have been eported back to a Concord stronghold.

The Slayers charging around the corner did not face a sniper, but Acheron who stopped them dead in their tracks. They literally shuddered to a halt. Not because they were hopelessly outmatched but rather because the thousands of rounds of depleted tellurite pouring from Acheron's small mini-gun had severed their legs from their bodies. The stunned looks on their faces were almost comical if it was not for the fact that the three Slayers became six gently twitching body parts.

Chapter 14
In the Hanger

"Come on professor! It's time to go!" Altavia yelled across at him.

"I'm nearly done Altavia. Just a few minutes more."

What is going on out in the crater Altavia thought to herself. She had tried to contact Whizzbang and Bosk on the comnet but not surprisingly, they had switched channels. She cursed the fact that she could not use her unique abilities as Creativity as it would reveal herself to the ultimate enemy. Typing faster than was humanly possible Altavia finished her part of the programming scripts that would send all of the research back to Kaladon.

The professor looked more haggard than usual. He had hardly slept the last few months and there was only so much that stimulants could do before they took their toll.

The voice in Altavia's earpiece suddenly changed its' message to, "Scourge have entered the building." Bosk and Whizzbang must have failed.

"Professor, we need to leave now!"

Professor Steinberg tapped the keyboard a few more times and looked up at Altavia. "It's done." That simple statement summarized his life's work. "I hope the Scourge cruiser doesn't intercept the signal but it can't be helped now," he stated flatly.

"It will be fine professor." She loved this man, like a mother loves a son.

Opening a drawer in her desk Altavia reached in a pulled out a small laser pistol. It may not do much against a warrior's armour but it may be helpful in distracting them.

Taking the professor by the arm, she guided him to the main throughway. It was the quickest way to the frigate but it was also the most exposed.

Before entering the throughway she whispered, "Stay here professor."

Ducking down Altavia slowly looked around the corner and to the energy wall in the distance. Everything looked clear. It usually did until an enemy appeared.

"Come on," she whispered.

They quietly creeped past racks of equipment, computers and machines as fast as the older professor could move. Altavia kept her eyes roving and searching forward for the Scourge that had entered the base. They finally made it to the edge of the research zone and she paused to let the professor catch his breath.

A burst of automatic gunfire suddenly echoed off the high hanger roof. Signalling for the professor to wait where he was Altavia poked her head around a large computer rack to look at the frigate. Four enemy warriors had just gunned down a technician that had tried to make a run for the stairway leading up into the ship. His body now lay sprawled on the hanger floor in a pool of his own blood.

Altavia needed a plan and one that did not involve both the professor and her dead. "Professor, I need you to hide between these two racks of computers and when the Scourge are gone board the frigate as fast as you can."

"What about you?"

Altavia gave one of her most becoming smiles. "With any luck, I'll be shortly behind you."

"Altavia."

"Yes professor."

"Be careful."

"Of course professor. Just remember to head to the frigate as soon as they're past."

The professor nodded. He had an inkling of what she was going to do and knew that they may not see each other again. If he was a young man then it would be her in hiding and him defending.

Altavia pulled out her laser pistol, took aim and fired at a compressed air bottle lying on the floor in the hanger directly opposite the fast frigate. With a sound like a clap of thunder, the pressurized oxygen instantly exploded outwards. Pieces of the metal bottle flew outwards in all directions and some even managed to hit the roof high above.

The Scourge instantly spun around and started running towards the explosion. Altavia stepped out and fired her pistol at a Shock trooper. The beam did nothing to its armour but the shot did attract its attention. *"Time to run,"* Altavia said to herself as she turned and ran back down the main thoroughfare and past the racks of equipment.

Behind her, she could hear the hard metallic boots of the Scourge hotly in pursuit.

Colonel Greerson watched Altavia's brave act from a doorway that lead from the facilities offices and into the hanger near the frigate. Behind him, trailing up a corridor, were a half a dozen terrified administrative clerks and secretaries.

Just as the last of the Scourge chased Altavia, he whispered back down the corridor, "OK everyone. Now's our chance. Go as quickly as you can and get into the ship!"

The fast frigate was built for speed and had no offensive armaments. Once moving, nothing could catch it but the Colonel would have given anything for a heavy laser battery mounted on the side right now.

As he glided through the air, Whizzbang brought the scope up to his eye to view what was taking place within the hanger. He saw the flash of the laser pistol and the compressed air bottle explode. He then watched as the four warriors began to chase after the person that had caused the diversion. Swinging back to the frigate he watched a group of people led by the Colonel up the stairway and into the ship.

"Did you see all that Bosk?"

Bosk lowered his rifle. "The person that created the diversion is either incredibly brave or incredibly stupid."

"Or both."

"Yes, or both. They're not going to stand a chance against the Scourge warriors."

As the wind whistled past him, Whizzbang raised his scope to his eye again. He nearly stalled in the air when he saw the professor shambling towards the frigate. "Bosk, I know who created the diversion."

"Who?"

"Altavia."

"What?" Bosk replied incredulously.

"I just saw the professor heading across the hanger bay. She would never have left his side unless she didn't have a choice."

"We need to hit the energy wall high and keep on gliding into the building. It's the only way that we'll catch them."

"Agreed."

"Your legs going to hurt."

"I know but we don't have any choice."

Altavia ran as far as she dared down the central thoroughfare before turning down a side corridor between two long storage racks stacked eight feet high. It was only a matter of time before the Scourge overtook her in their own powered armour. With that time, her goal was to get them as far as possible away from the professor.

A rapid sequence of bangs erupted behind Altavia as the Shock trooper let loose a spray of bullets. The bullets tore and ripped their way through several rows of computer servers, shattering circuit boards and power supplies alike. Sparks and smoke immediately erupted from the electronics spraying the surrounding equipment in hot metal fragments.

Altavia's heart was beating faster than it ever had in her life. Adrenalin coursed through her blood stream. *"So this was what it was like for battleframe pilots,"* she absently mused? The terror was strangely intoxicating and she finally understood why some men and women put themselves repeatedly into danger.

Altavia knew she needed to hide. Anywhere a heat source could mask her body's own infrared signature. She presumed that the Scourge battleframes could see in that spectrum as well as in ultraviolet and the normal visible light frequencies. What she needed was a fire.

Still running, she fired indiscriminately at one piece of equipment after another. The sound attracted the Scourge and she could hear them coming all the faster in her direction. *"Something had to burn!"* she thought in frustration. And then, something did.

It took Altavia a millisecond to realise that she was in the research sector that was developing a miniaturized tellurite reactor. Her shot must have pierced the power core of a prototype unit as the resulting explosion was nothing short of spectacular. Like a hammer, striking an anvil the shockwave hit her in the chest and slammed her against a box filled with spare parts. The explosion was not large but the long corridor of equipment filled racks had focused the energy straight towards her. Lying sprawled on the floor, she was only dimly aware that a number of her ribs and left ankle were broken.

Whizzbang and Bosk penetrated the energy wall and looked down as the Colonel lead the stream of administrative staff into the frigate. Gliding towards the central thoroughfare, they spotted two Scourge running away from them.

"Bosk, I've got the left one."

"CT."

As one, two blue beams shot out and pierced the back of each Scourge's neck, a spray of purple blood and the two warriors dropped to the ground dead.

"Two to go."

"Whizz, I've got one but the other has disappeared down a rack of equipment."

Bosk fired and the Engineer died.

By now, the racks of equipment raced past them on the left and right as they lost altitude. Bosk looked across at his friend.

Rather than risk slowing down with a few quick steps on his partially healed leg Whizzbang skidded along the main thoroughfare on his chest. The screech of his battleframe on the plasteel floor reverberated off the roof high above. As he slowly stopped, he rested his damaged leg on his good one to help protect it and provide some level of support. Bosk sprinted past him and suddenly dashed between two long racks of machine parts.

"Bosk, do you have him?"

"I just saw a Shock move up ahead…."

Bosk only had a second to watch the shockwave of an explosion race towards him. The foundations of the facility seemed to rock back and forth and then the wave hit with a mighty boom. One minute he was running forward and the next he was thrown back out into the thoroughfare. His battleframe protected him from any serious injury.

Being further away from the explosion all Whizzbang felt was a rush of wind across his face. "What the frap was that?"

Bosk picked himself up off the floor and said, "It looks like Altavia set off some explosive device. How's the leg?"

Whizzbang gingerly stood to his feet and tested his right leg. The nanomeds had not had sufficient time to heal the fracture but they were now well on their way. "I'll manage. Let's go find Altavia."

Bosk ran back down between the racks of equipment that he was just unceremoniously ejected from. Whizzbang hobbled after him by placing more of his weight on his left leg and letting the battleframe's exoskeleton help brace the broken limb.

Bosk again ran ahead and provided a running report via the comnet, "Frap that was quite a boomer. Look how some of these heavy racks have been pushed back."

"Any sign of Altavia or the Shock?"

"Not as yet."

Chapter 15
Bosk

Laying prone on a massive rock looming over the Terrarium, Bosk kept his head down and out of sight while his battleframe's nanites went about their busy repair work. A rising hum of a golden Scourge drone dropping in behind him alerted him to his danger. The sound always preceded a drone self-detonation that scattered shrapnel in all directions.

"Frapping nasty little smart bomb aren't you," Bosk said to himself. Rolling onto his back, he pulled his Charge rifle out and pumped a couple of quick shots into the drone that fatally stopped the destruction sequence.

Now that the drone lay smouldering at his feet, Bosk did a quick inventory of his battleframe. Although not perfect, Whizzbang and his squad had bought him enough time to partially self-regenerate.

A grim smile spread across his face as he mumbled, "Time for some frapping payback!"

"Hey Whizz I'm G2G. Engaging enemy snipers now," he announced via the local comnet.

As he jump jetted across to his new position, Whizzbang twisted in the air to let an eruption of deadly plasma launched by one of the Juggernaut's shoot by. He could feel the heat radiated by the plasma as he weaved out of its path. Once landed on the plexiglass Terrarium roof, he ducked down and replied, "CT Bosk. Self, you stay down. Help's on its way."

Selfia replied, "CT Whizz" and quickly followed up with "Oh frap!" as another ruby sniper beam missed her head by inches. Scrambling further back along the roof she yelled, "Frap Bosk, show me how good you are and be fast about it!"

Through his scope, Bosk watched as the Scourge Sniper's rifle tip glow as it built-up energy prior to firing. He had the enemy within his cross hairs and pressed his firing stud a few milliseconds before the other Sniper could shoot. The result was one dead Scourge Sniper and one alive Selfia.

"One down, one to go!" Bosk said as he swung around to the second sniper's position just in time to see the impact of Whizzbang's Charge rifle beam render the warrior permanently inoperative. Without stopping to think, he pulled his scope around to centre the crosshairs on one of the Shock troopers and pressed the trigger. Two Charge rifle beams, one from Bosk and the other from Whizzbang, pierced the trooper. The resulting explosion of armour and flesh cascaded around the still living Shock trooper. It then also experienced the simultaneous effect of two super-heated blue energy beams through its body. Not surprisingly, the second Shock trooper also exploded into its constituent parts.

Whizzbang smiled as he said, "Beat you to the target Bosk!"

Bosk laughed in relief. "Whizz, you've really got to get a better hobby than splattering Scourge!"

They had both been trading jibes for so many years that the two of them were accustomed to the banter in the middle of a battle. Bosk briefly raised his head from his Charge riflescope and suddenly screamed over the comnet, "Whizz look out!"

From his many years of fighting alongside Bosk, Whizzbang knew that when Bosk screamed a warning, you did not try to work out why. If you valued your life, you just reacted. Even though he was lying on his front on one of the hexagonal glass Terrarium windows Whizzbang, instantly fired maximum thrust on his jump jets. The instantaneous kinetic energy rocketed him forwards off the roof and in an arc towards the ground beneath the scanning tower platform. It also sent him towards the two startled waiting Juggernauts.

Just as Whizzbang fled from his perch, the two molten balls of plasma launched a few seconds earlier completed their high trajectory arc. With a crash, they slammed into the plexiglass roof of the Terrarium right where he had just been lying.

The deafening roar from the detonation of the super-heated plasma against the cool plexiglass generated a concussive shockwave traveling outwards from the epicentre of the explosion. Razor sharp shards of plexiglass, some several feet long, propelled outward in all directions. The spraying glass instantly shredded the plants in that corner of the Terrarium, imbedded themselves in the scanning tower grating and some were even later found on the beach far to the east. The hi-tensile plasteel girders that supported that corner of the enormous Terrarium buckled under the impact. Far away in FreeHold, battleframe pilots looked up from working on the defences as the sound from the detonation and ricocheting glass fragments passed over them.

Rather than stopping to fight the two Juggernauts intent on his destruction, Whizzbang kept his jump jets at maximum blast and twisted so that his armour bore much of the impact as he shot along the ground. Dirt flew in all directions and he ploughed a dead straight furrow that would have made his farming father proud. If it were not for the collision at the base a sixty-foot high solid granite cliff face he would have kept on going. Other than feeling a little groggy, he felt quite protected in his battleframe and surprisingly unhurt from his impromptu farming activity.

The Juggernauts that Whizzbang had raced past were not so lucky. Both of them had half a dozen long plexiglass spears impaling their bodies. One of them was hit with such force, that the glass spear had lifted its body off the ground as it arrowed into the dirt. It looked more like a grotesque broken statue raised up on high. Purple blood dripped down the sides of the glass and soaked the ground around both bodies.

Whizzbang groggily turned over in his furrow just to see one and then the other Juggernaut's body violently shake under the impact of a shot from Selfia. Looking down from her rooftop sniper nest she said over the comnet, "Better to be safe than sorry with those brutes."

Still feeling a little light-head Whizzbang replied, "CT Self. I would've done it myself if I could just focus my eyes a little better. In some ways, if they could survive all those glass spears going through their bodies then they'd almost deserve to live. Almost…."

"Not by a long-shot. When I see a Scourge I see a target."

"CT Self."

While Selfia ensured the two Juggernauts were completely dead, Acheron literally tore his way through the remaining Scourge Engineers and with Bosk's help, silenced the two drop pods.

"Whizz, you finished being a farmer?" Whizzbang heard Bosk chuckle in his earpiece.

Whizzbang stood to his feet and a pile of dirt fell from the many crevices that made up the exoskeleton of his battleframe. He gently shook his head from side to side to test if everything was in still in place. "I'm done with being a farmer Bosk, although I feel like I've just been through a meat grinder."

Acheron doubled over laughing. "I've never seen anything like it. I hear your friend Bosk give a warning and the next thing I see is a massive explosion followed by you getting the frap out of there. I just wished I'd captured the faces of those two Jugs on an imager! I've never seen a Scourge look stunned before but when you raced straight at them and right on past they looked hilarious!"

By now, Acheron was in full flight recounting the story and his face mimicked the Juggernaut's stunned expressions. With his arms imitating a massive explosion he continued, "That was when the plasma discharges smashed into plexiglass roof. Kaboom! After all these years, you'd think that they'd learn that plasma and plexiglass just don't mix. What do you get when you add plasma and plexiglass?"

As Bosk looked at the Juggernaut's impaled on the glass shards, he could not resist yelling down to Acheron, "Statues?"

Acheron pointed up at Bosk, "Exactly! You're the winner my friend."

Whizzbang smiled at the joke. It was good to hear his friends having fun with one another. Only minutes earlier each of them were fighting for their lives and it was only by chance that the explosion did not seriously injure any of them. Laughter was always a good medicine.

Whizzbang looked up at the bright purple Scourge blood that decorated one of the plexiglass wall panels of the Terrarium like some grotesque mural. *"Will the fighting and death ever end?"* he thought.

The stench of battle was still evident in the air as Bosk drifted down from his rocky perch and finally settled next to Whizzbang with a brief controlled flare of his jets. Selfia and Acheron quickly followed him to stand beside Whizzbang. Whizzbang turned to his life-long friend and embraced him in the way that spoke of the depth of their friendship.

Bosk was a few inches shorter than Whizzbang's five foot eleven and had black hair, a solid build and a perpetual broad grin on his face. Through the years, the two adopted brothers had become inseparable as they fought side by side on a huge range of battlefields.

As he hugged his brother, Whizzbang's voice cracked, "Bosk, I thought I'd lost you."

Bosk returned the embrace even tighter and stumbling over his words as the impact of the moment hit him. He quietly replied, "Whizz, I knew you'd find me."

Half embarrassed, the two stepped away from each other and Whizzbang quickly wiped the corners of his eyes, leaving streaks in the dirt already smeared on his face.

Once again, Bosk's easy smile lit up his face as he said, "Hey Whizz, glad to see my warning about those Jugs wasn't too late and that you're still in one piece."

Now that he was more composed, Whizzbang said with a cheeky smirk, "I should thank you for that Bosk but if there's a next time don't cut it so fine."

Bosk gave a brief chuckle. "Where would the fun in that be? Seeing you blast off horizontally and plough a furrow will always be one of those special moments in my life." Looking over at Acheron and Selfia, Bosk asked, "Whizz, are you going to introduce me to your friends?"

"Of course!" Whizzbang did the customary introductions, "Bosk, this is Ach and Self, Ach and Self, this is my best friend Bosk."

Bosk extended his hand first to Acheron and then Selfia. "Great to meet you. I thought that I was a goner until you all showed up."

Acheron enthusiastically shook Bosk's hand and replied, "At long last we get a chance to meet you Bosk. This is the third Scourge skirmish that Whizz, Self and I have had in the last few hours trying to find you."

"I'm really happy that we've found you in one piece," Selfia said, "The whole of Alpha Three is in complete turmoil with this latest Scourge push."

Whizzbang nodded in acknowledgement. "So what happened to you Bosk? The last time we spoke I thought we'd be catching up at Folly's bar in FreeHold."

"Frap Whizz, I could really use that drink right now. For the past eight hours, I've been running from the Scourge as far south as Fisherman's Bend through to Rock Wall and now here at Terrarium.

After leaving you in FreeHold, I decided to head out and do some quick solo Digging, to get enough tellurite for some new equipment to upgrade my jets. The Concord may be good but it still costs tellurite to maintain your frame. Besides, we all need to make sure that the Concord research team at Blue Sky are funded to invent stuff before the Scourge develop them."

Bosk paused for a minute as he recollected, "Where was I? That's right, I was minding my own business, bagging a few Spyderlynx that I could sell later on. You know those coffee table sized critters with the dark outer shells. The ones that look more like a giant spider crossed with a crab. Anyway, suddenly, all hell seemed to break loose. Two fists of Scourge zeroed in on my position and after a short but brutal discussion I only just managed to send my Digger back to the orbital station in one piece and get the frap out of there.

After running for frap knows how long and dodging or hiding from one patrol after another I ended up at the top end of the beach due east of here. You know the one Whizz. It's just north of that Concord outpost where we used to do sniping practice when we first arrived on Alpha Three. The crazy thing is that I've been regularly checking my scanner on my wrist-comp but everything must be frapped up as I'm not getting a thing. Either that or the whole networked is frapped."

Whizzbang interrupted Bosk. "It's not the network alone. Right now, every sector is under a massive Scourge assault. When I first entered Freehold with Happy I just knew something was wrong and like you, I checked my wrist-comp. It was all clear until I patched directly into a tower." Whizzbang placed his hand on Bosk's shoulder and said, "Bosk, other than Freehold and Central Command the entire network was red with Scourge or not responding at all. The network isn't frapped, it's just not there anymore!"

"Oh frap! Oh frap! Oh frap!" Bosk said with rising tension in his voice.

"Bosk do you know where the others are?" Whizzbang asked.

"The last I heard, Elzetro, Pyro, Kheldar and DG were planning on having a party with a few friends on top of that big rock overlooking Freehold. With any luck they've managed to make it through this whole mess."

"That sounds like them. I just hope that they're still up there." Whizzbang smiled warmly. "Frap I'm glad to have you with us Bosk. It's only been a few hours since Freehold, but I feel like Self, Ach and I have lived a life-time. We managed to get the scanning tower up and going in Research Ravine. We also retook control of the outpost just north of there."

Turning to all three of his friends Whizzbang said, "OK I hate to be the bearer of bad news but we have to call down a new scanning tower from the orbital station right away. Without it, we won't be able to get an accurate picture of what's going on. As we've already found out, the network's frapped up and we need to patch directly into a tower to find out what's really going on."

They all knew what that meant. Calling down a scanning tower was like inviting the Scourge into your living room for a cup of tea with a few cakes on the side. It was a magnet to all enemy in the area to drop in a few battle-pods and immediately shutdown the tower. It was also a message that there were active Concord battleframes, which meant the Scourge, would come in mass and they would come in hard.

Selfia, Acheron and Bosk looked at each other and then at Whizzbang. Finally, Acheron said in his deep gravelly voice, "CT Whizz, you point the way and we'll follow," this was quickly followed by nods from his two other friends.

"Before calling down the tower we need a plan. But first I need to change my clothes" Whizzbang said with a thoughtful smile on his face. "Bosk, do you know if the Scourge had time to take out the battleframe console?"

"Not that I'm aware of. I think they were more intent on killing me at the time."

"We're all happy that you didn't oblige them," Selfia said.

Bosk put on a dumb sounding voice and said, "Well, I do my best Mam."

Ignoring the friendly banter Whizzbang strode over to the building where Selfia had positioned herself on the roof for sniping. He sighed with relief when he saw that the battleframe terminal was undamaged. Pressing the power button on the side, it hummed into life and presented him with only a few battleframes from its limited memory capacity. The Terrarium terminal was much smaller than the one in the ready room at Freehold. Toggling through the list of available frames, he selected the "Rook". It was Happy's favourite and Whizzbang knew that it was the most suitable for what they were about to do.

A marvel of technological simplicity the battleframe terminal was the culmination of hundreds of years of Concord technological endeavours. It was regarded as one of the greatest innovations ever developed by Professor Steinberg's team at Blue Sky. It combined breakthroughs in malleable energy and molecular computing to build battleframes from raw tellurite energy.

Unlike other forms of energy, such as electricity, tellurite based energy could be manipulated in many different ways, hence the scientific field of malleable energy. For example, tellurite energy could be transformed into physical objects and this gave Professor Steinberg's team an idea.

By creating battleframes out of tellurite energy, the process could be reversed and the majority of the energy recycled. The biggest limitation was the computing power used to manipulate the individual atoms to convert the tellurite energy crystals into something as complex as a battleframe. With the birth of massively parallel high speed, molecular computers, battleframe terminals, like the one Whizzbang now stood in front, were a programmer's thoughts away from reality.

When Whizzbang selected "Rook" from the battleframe console, in a matter of seconds the nanites that built his Raven frame began decomposing it around him and converting it back into tellurite energy. The recycled energy was then reconverted again back into a Rook battleframe by the trillions of programmable nanites embedded into the energy stream. Like in the Freehold ready room, all Whizzbang had to do was accept the miracle of the nanites and hold out his arms so that the new frame battleframe could form around him.

Whizzbang stepped away from the battleframe console and tested the lightning gun on a block of plasteel setup in the corner for that purpose. After assuring himself that all of the specialized capabilities of the frame were functioning, he headed back to the rest of the squad. Strange that in a matter of so few hours he had come to view the other pilot's as his squad and he as their Squad Leader.

Turning to Acheron, Whizzbang said, "Ach, let's setup a perimeter around the tower emplacement clamps. I'll drop a few turrets down that will help discourage any Scourge that try to attack the new tower."

"CT Whizz."

Whizzbang pulled three specialist nanite pods from within his battleframe and tossed them on the plasteel grating next to the scanning tower locking clamps. Within a few moments, the nanites began forming the familiar shapes of three single barrelled light infantry gun emplacements. When completed they stood about two feet high on a tripod stand. The business end of the gun began swivelling back and forth to automatically scan the surrounding area for enemies.

"Whizz, what do you want us to do?" Bosk gestured to Selfia and himself.

"Hmmm….. Self, you can get back on the roof where you were before but this time if you're pinned down crawl out the back and jump-jet to the rock where Bosk was previously. Bosk, you can set yourself up on the flat part of the Terrarium roof next to where I was blown off. With Ach and me on the deck and you two higher up I think that between the four of us we'll have a clear kill zone around the tower. Any questions or thoughts?"

"Only one" said Bosk.

"Go on."

"Can you give me a little bit more warning than I gave you if a couple of Jugs get a bead on me?" Bosk said with a laugh.

Whizzbang rolled his eyes heavenward. With mock sincerity he said, "What have you got against farming Bosk?"

All four of them laughed nervously at the joke to relieve some of the stress before entering battle. The fact was that calling down a scanning tower was dangerous in the good times let alone when the whole planet in the midst of a Scourge invasion. They were lucky at Research Ravine, but this distance out from Freehold there would be more Scourge patrols attracted by the commotion, let alone battle-pods.

With the plan set and all of them in position, Whizzbang linked his battleframe's wrist-comp input to the tower's landing platform interface. His forearm wrist-comp screen changed from red to green indicating that the necessary call down codes integrated into his battleframe had been accepted by the Concord satellite station high overhead. The weightless environment of space allowed the nanites to manufacture large sophisticated pieces of machinery such as scanning towers and diggers.

"Stay frosty everyone. We've just become a Scourge magnet!" Whizzbang whispered into the comnet.

Whizzbang quickly dropped his the nanite packet that built his one heavy turret pointing along the catwalk towards the building where Selfia was perched.

Birds chirped happily in the trees around them and the wind gently swayed the branches while the warm tropical sun warmed the back of Whizzbang's hand. It was such a peaceful, tranquil scene. It was like the calm before a storm, the eye of a hurricane or the sound of soldiers softly praying to their God to keep them alive.

It was then that the far off whine of four battle-pods intruded in the tranquil Terrarium scene. The noise normally generated fear in Scourge enemies, but in the case of Whizzbang's squad each of them were veterans and at home in the confusion and terror of battle. While the birds fled with the wind, his squad calmly and patiently waited. They knew the drill and they had survived innumerable skirmishes with battle-pods before. More importantly, despite their short time together, they had confidence in each other and their Squad Leader. Where he would go, they would follow, even if that meant into the enigmatic

Barrier itself. Therefore, they waited for the hurricane to arrive in force and the storm to bring them into their own form of tranquillity, battle.

It was at this critical time that Whizzbang felt another wave of vertigo wash over him. It was if the world suddenly compressed and then expanded to its correct dimensions.

"Hey guys did you feel something strange just then?" he squawked over the local comnet.

His question went unanswered as three of the four battle-pods thudded violently into the ground below Acheron and him. Fine dirt and small rocks created a grey mist as they sprayed into the air. The fourth slammed with a metallic crunch into the wide southern hi-tensile plasteel stairway leading up to the tower. With a wrench of screaming plasteel, the stairway buckled under the strain that shook the tower platform to its core. Standing next to the clamps, Whizzbang and Acheron staggered back and forth like drunks until the platform stopped swaying. With a hiss and a billow of smoke, the battle-pods established a subspace connection to their base and Scourge began materialising in a shower of sparks at five points per battle-pod.

"Oh frap, there's so many of them!" cried Selfia into the comnet.

"It'll just mean we can't miss," Whizzbang said reassuringly. "Pick your targets carefully everyone."

Selfia quickly assessed where the largest concentration of rapidly forming figures and launched her deployable mine into their midst and yelled across the comnet, "Deployable mine away."

Whizzbang and Bosk had their grenade launchers at the ready so they could hit as many of the Scourge as possible in the shortest amount of time.

Many people mistakenly assume that battle-pods actually contain the Scourge warriors. This is not the case. Similar to a radio receiver, a battle-pod provides a subspace teleportation bridge between a Scourge base and where they land. Concord scientists have surmised that within the Barrier, launchers must exist that fire battle-pods to any location on the planet. Due to the Barrier's effect on human physiology, this only remains a theory

Just as the first group of Scourge were nearly materialized from within their flashing hazy mauve storm Whizzbang issued the order, "Launch!"

Three sets of grenades simultaneously soared into the air and a second set quickly followed. The huge concussive force of the first three tellurite infused grenades ripped through the Scourge ranks. Laying on the roof, Selfia's sniper visor automatically shielded her eyes from the flashes by flicking to its maximum setting. All she could now see were the outlines of materialising Scourge falling to the ground dead and those that remained standing after the first round of grenades quickly falling to the second.

Selfia triggered her deployable mine and was rewarded with the screams of still more wounded and dying. Smoke and the sounds of slaughter filled the air but still more shapes continued to form up until the grenade launchers ran out of ammunition.

"OK squad, here we go. Now the fun begins!" yelled Whizzbang through his comnet over the sounds of the explosions.

The turrets surrounding the scanning tower hummed into life and happily chirped their deadly contents at the materialising Scourge on the stairs leading up to the scanning tower emplacement. Over the comnet Whizzbang heard his heavy turret upgrade itself from a single to a double barrelled weapon as the built in artificial intelligence analysed the enemy actions and instructed the nano-machines to add the new capability. The Concord only recently developed smart weapons like the heavy turret and they often made the difference between winning and losing an engagement.

In a crackle of energy, Whizzbang fired his lightning gun at a Scourge Engineer running up the stairs and enveloped it in a field of high voltage electricity that paralysed and stopped its heart. Arching its back in agony the Engineer opened its mouth in a silent scream and collapsed dead with a clang onto the metallic stair grating.

Acheron, with his usual lack of finesse, turned his light min-gun onto the battle-pod on the stairs until it exploded and vanished into oblivion. Bosk picked off one enemy after another while Selfia reciprocated from her perch at the opposite side of the kill-zone.

All was going to plan as the four fighters extracted their toll on the enemy below and that was when something strange happened. Honed reflexes from countless encounters with the enemy was all that saved Whizzbang from the enemy sniper. He caught the glow of the sniper barrel out of the corner of his eye and immediately dove for cover behind one of the massive scanning tower clamps. Rather than cutting him in half the ruby red beam nicked his upper arm, burning through his battleframe and into his still smouldering skin.

"Oh frap!" squeezed past Whizzbang's lips just as he saw Bosk puncture the sniper in the side of the head with his Charge rifle beam. The nanomeds in his battleframe kicked in to deal with the wound just as they sorted out all of his other injuries over the years. Despite the pain killing nanomeds, his arm still felt like it was on fire.

Whizzbang stood to his feet and thought to himself, "*Come on meds, get a move on!*"

Chapter 16
A Scourge Fist

As Acheron put the final battle-pod out of commission, Whizzbang said over the diminishing sounds of battle, "Guys, watch out. That sniper wasn't from one of battle-pods. It had to be a scout from a roving band of Scourge zeroing in on our position."

"CT Whizz." Bosk answered.

"Selfia, get higher now," Whizzbang ordered.

Whizzbang watched as Selfia jump-jetted up to the huge boulder above her previous position.

"See anything Self?" Whizzbang asked.

Selfia yelled across the comnet, "Guys, we've got company and a lot of it! Look to the north-east and arriving in, maybe, two minutes."

"Oh frap! I'm in the wrong frame," Whizzbang said to himself as he sprinted down to the battleframe console and keyed in to select his Raven. Unusually, his arm where the sniper had nicked him was still hurting. *"Come on meds, do your stuff and get me back together!"* he thought.

While Whizzbang was charging off to change his battleframe, Bosk shimmied along one of the twisted Terrarium girders and laid prone along to get a steadier shot at the incoming enemy.

The sound of descending thrusters on full burn thundered from on high as the scanning tower plummeted towards its landing clamps. The deafening roar of the main under-jet blanketed the area while the higher pitched whine of the four manoeuvring jets auto-aligning the base of the tower with the huge docking clamps.

As Whizzbang keyed in the codes at the battleframe console for his Raven, he heard Selfia's rifle begin its deadly song in counterpoint to Bosk's high-pitched zing. It took all of sixty seconds to change frames and have him standing on the platform next to Acheron.

"Situation?" he asked.

"Both Self and Bosk are trading shots with a few Scourge Snipers. It seems that the majority of the enemy is using the covering fire so they can move forward. Whizz, I've never seen the Scourge behave like this before."

"I agree, something's changing and it's not in our favour. Let's see if I can alter the odds a little before the close quarters fighting starts."

Whizzbang knelt down on one knee and balanced the barrel of his Charge rifle on the railing that surrounded the tower platform. Sighting a Scourge Sniper in the cross-hairs he press the trigger but this time rather than the typical explosion of purple flesh the Scourge Sniper took the shot in the chest and then ducked behind a boulder.

"Self, Bosk we've got to hit them in the head. It looks like these frapping Scourge are tougher than we're used to." Whizzbang said over the comnet.

Normally, such a statement would be met with bewilderment as hitting a moving target perfectly in the head each and every time was nearly impossible but Selfia and Bosk simply replied, "CT Whizz".

A sudden spray of sparks danced like chaotic fireworks at the end of the girder where Bosk was perched as a ruby red sniper beam struck the steel and instantly vaporised a fair chunk of it. Bosk ducked his head and began inching his way back towards the intact side of Terrarium building.

"Don't worry Bosk, I've got 'em," Selfia said as she gently squeezed her trigger. The three-inch slug of depleted tellurite leapt from her rifle barrel and sped across the space towards the Scourge Sniper's head.

"Thanks Self," Bosk said as he inched his way back into position.

Whizzbang peered through his scope just in time to see the glow of a Scourge Sniper gun barrel signalling an imminent shot. "Down Ach!" he yelled as he grabbed his friends arm to drag him to the deck. The shot was wide but not by much and the energy was dissipated as it struck the outer shielding of the scanning tower without much effect.

"Guys, they're nearly here," Acheron yelled over the gunfire as he clambered back to his feet and heaved his light mini-gun into position.

Laying prone on the deck Whizzbang sighted the Sniper that had just taken a shot at him. The scorch mark on its chest told him that he had shot this one earlier. Taking a number of long slow breaths, he pressed the firing stud and the blue beam cleanly punctured the Sniper's head.

"Are all the Snipes accounted for?" Whizzbang asked.

"All done" answered Selfia.

"We've got about twenty seconds to deal with the rest of them or at least soften them up for Acheron," Whizzbang said just as gunfire began pinging around his position.

The three Concord snipers played their deadly symphony of zing and bang across the dozen elite Scourge coming up the hill. Juggernauts, Shock troopers, Slayers, Engineers all fell, and the few that remained were cut-down in the crescendo of Acheron's mini-gun. After the ungodly and terrifying music had stopped echoing off the surrounding hills an eerie silence beset the four Concord pilots as they surveyed the carnage that their symphony had wrought.

Arms were ripped from sockets, heads splayed open, torsos missing legs and small wounds in the chest belied the fact that the Scourge no longer had a back. Whizzbang, Selfia and Bosk were stunned at the carnage that they had inflicted on the enemy. There were no groans from wounded coming from the field in front of them as each enemy was dead.

"Well, that was kind of...," Bosk trailed off.

Over the comnet came the sounds of Selfia uncontrollably retching as the impact of the last few minutes hit her. Acheron kicked in his jets and soared up to comfort his wife on the rock high above.

Whizzbang pulled out his earpiece to give Acheron and Selfia some privacy. He glanced up at Bosk straddling the girder and noticed that he had done the same. Suddenly the world seemed to compress and then expand as he experienced the same strange sense of vertigo that he felt just before the battle. He lost his balance and fell to the deck with a metallic clunk next to the tower.

"What was that?" Whizzbang exclaimed as he slowly regained his feet. Looking over at his friend, he saw Bosk giving the girder a bear hug and that his eyes were squeezed shut. "Did you feel that?" he yelled over to Bosk.

"What in the frap was that? Is it finished?" Bosk replied with a strained voice.

"I have no idea. I experienced the same thing..."

"...just before the battle?" Bosk finished Whizzbang's sentence.

Whizzbang nodded and said with a concerned voice, "Something's happening and we need to find out what it is."

Acheron and Selfia jump jetted down to the plasteel tower deck next to Whizzbang just as Bosk kicked in his jets and glided across from the Terrarium roof.

Looking across at Whizzbang and Bosk Acheron asked, "What's going on with you two?"

Resting a hand on Selfia's shoulder Whizzbang asked, "Self, you OK?"

Selfia gave a weak smile, "I'll be OK Whizz, thanks for asking."

"Not a problem," Whizzbang replied compassionately before turning to Acheron. "Bosk and I were just talking about it. There's something really strange happening."

"I felt like I was being squeezed through a tube of toothpaste and then spurted out into the basin," Bosk said as he mimicked squirting toothpaste.

Whizzbang said, "We'll have to sort that toothpaste issue later. Now that the tower is up and running we need to find out how bad it is out there and see if Concord command is still in one piece. If they are, it would be good to find out whether anyone else has experienced what we all just felt."

Whizzbang thumbed his wrist-comp to tap directly into the wider comnet and displayed a map of Alpha Three with the current state of affairs. As well as Freehold, Research Ravine and the Terrarium it was clear that there were aggressive counter attacks going on all over the map with the Scourge slowly being pushed back. Central Command, Belver's Pass and even Fisherman's Bend were already back under Concord control.

Peering over Whizzbang's shoulder Bosk let out a slow whistle and said, "Now that's more like it. It looks like we're sending them back into the Barrier."

Selfia said, "Yes we are pushing them back, but look at the concentration of battleframes around Freehold. There must have been a huge battle and a lot of pilots eported back to safety. They're going to be in a bad way for a long time as they pull themselves together."

Whizzbang nodded to Selfia in agreement.

Bosk said, "It must be a mess in Freehold right now."

Whizzbang said, "As long as it keeps on standing."

"Can you check and see if the others are within comnet contact Whizz?" asked Bosk.

Whizzbang selected a different option on his wrist-comp that allowed him to see a list of his friends. "It looks like they're all at Freehold Bosk. Let me try and get in contact with Pyro."

Strangely, Whizzbang's upper arm was still hurting from the wound he received from the Scourge Sniper earlier. The nanomeds would normally have healed such a superficial wound by now. He involuntarily grimaced as he tapped on the screen to select a different mode and bring up Pyro's face.

Whizzbang spoke towards his comp, "Hey, Pyro you copy?" Static emitted from his forearm comp. "Hey, Pyro you there?" he again asked.

Suddenly his wrist-comp erupted loudly into life, "Due to recent Scourge activity this transmission has been intercepted and blocked by Concord central command."

With a concerned look on his face Acheron said, "Well I've never heard that message before."

"It must have been worse than we thought Ach," Whizzbang replied. "Let me try and get in contact with someone from Central Command."

Chapter 17
The End

Altavia dragged her battered body across the cold floor, leaving a smear of blood to mark her passage. Each breath was agony as the fractured ribs bit into her left lung. Propping herself up against a shredded box relieved some of the pain from breathing.

"*My hair must be a complete mess,*" she thought to herself. This was quickly followed by, "*What strange thoughts you have when your body is about to die.*"

Slowly turning her head, she could see the Scourge Shock trooper laying on its back about twenty feet away. It would seem that the detonation came just in time. At least it was dead. Her head was pounding from the effort of remaining upright and she could feel her own blood soaking through her undergarments. This energised body must be experiencing damage that she could not see or feel without using mental power.

"*If only Intellect could see the mess I'm in now.*"

Altavia turned her head suddenly to look back at the Shock trooper. Did she just see it move?

A strange, very human, sense of frustration washed over her as she watched the hulking Scourge haul itself to its feet. She could not risk revealing herself to the ultimate enemy by mentally eliminating the Shock trooper. She would have to let her energised body die.

Her mission to pass on the nano-technology to the Concord had been a success. The micro-machines would just need the right genetic encoding to complete thousands of years of work. Resigned to her fate, Altavia Createlin closed her blue eyes in anticipation of her inevitable passing.

Bosk raced around a large multi-spectral analyser that was leaning precariously on its side against another box after being tossed away from the epicentre of the explosion. The analyser's screen was completely shattered and glass crunched under his metal boot as he ran past. With a quick blast of his jump jets, he skated over an upturned computer rack that was blocking his path.

Running around the corner Bosk finally came in sight of the final Scourge just as it let fire a triple burst at an unseen target. He quickly raised his Charge rifle to his shoulder and fired. With a crash of armour, the Scourge collapsed to the floor revealing Altavia's beautiful but now disfigured body. Her usually straight perfectly groomed hair was a mess and half draped across her blood-splattered face. The Scourge's attack on her unprotected body had completely shattered her chest and red blood sprayed the surroundings in testament to the violence.

Bosk walked past the warrior and then staggered forward towards Altavia. "No, no, no," was all he could say as tears streamed down his face.

Ripping off a cloth covering an upturned machine Bosk knelt down beside Altavia and gently, almost lovingly wiped her face clean with one corner and covered her mangled body with the rest. It was then that he heard Whizzbang's urgent voice across the comnet, "Bosk, Bosk, Bosk! Are you there Bosk?"

Choking past a sob Bosk replied, "Whizz, Altavia's dead. I didn't get here in time."

There was a long pause before Whizzbang replied, "I'm nearly with you."

Bosk first noticed his friend when Whizzbang knelt beside him and placed one arm on his shoulders. Altavia almost appeared asleep lying against the box with her eyes closed. He half expected to see her eyes open and give one of those stunningly beautiful smiles that she frequently bestowed. However, she was still, unmoving and dead. How many would have to die before they stopped the Scourge? He quickly wiped away a tear that came unbidden with the back of his Raven glove. Now was not the time for mourning. There was still a Scourge cruiser high above and they need to leave if Altavia's sacrifice was not to be in vain.

"Bosk, we have to go."

"I know but I'm not leaving her here."

"We'll both carry her."

They carefully lifted Altavia's body and wrapped the remaining material around her. With Bosk at one end and Whizzbang at the other, they carried her back towards the frigate as if she was in a hammock between them.

Colonel Greerson greeted them sympathetically at the top of the stairs leading into the frigate. "Captain Eldrich heard everything over the comnet as he prepped for launch. Altavia was an amazing person."

Both Whizzbang and Bosk nodded sombrely.

"You can rest her body in the last seat up the back."

Whizzbang and Bosk carried Altavia to the seat and Greerson said, "Here, let me give you a hand," as he unbuckled and then refastened the safety belt around Altavia's body.

Whizzbang said gratefully, "Thank-you Colonel. Do you know where the professor is? He'll want to know."

"He's in the upper deck but right now we've got bigger things to worry about. Although this ship's fast, it's not going to be fast enough to escape the moons gravity without getting picked off by the cruiser up top."

"Do we have any weapons?"

"She was built for speed not offense. There isn't enough to light a cigar. We didn't think the Scourge would be this bold or even find us."

Bosk said, "No offense Colonel but they have and we need to get out of here before they decide to blow us to bits from orbit. It's only a matter of time before they notice that Whizz and I took out their ground forces."

"You took them all out?" the Colonel asked incredulously.

"All of them."

Colonel Greerson touched the comnet at his ear, "Captain we've got to go and go now."

The crisp Captain's voice replied, "CT Colonel. Closing all hatches. Firing manoeuvring thrusters."

The outside door slowly closed and a low rumble filled the cabin. A little jerk indicated that they were now rising above the docking cradle in the hanger.

"I think that we'd better get settled in as it's likely to be a rough ride."

They belted themselves into three seats facing each other. "Colonel, did we get everyone?" Whizzbang asked.

"Yes, all personnel managed to get on-board. Thanks to both your efforts."

Leaning forward, Whizzbang looked out a small round window just as they passed through the energy wall. So much had happened in such a short amount of time. "Colonel, how are we going to get past the cruiser?"

"I really don't know what Captain Eldrich has in mind."

Still staring out the portal Whizzbang looked up into the night sky and watched three distinct flashes appear from where he had previously seen the Scourge cruiser. "We're in for it now. I just saw the cruiser launch three missiles in our direction."

Bosk leaned over Whizzbang to get a better view. "I think they'll hit us in about ten seconds. By the way, how's the leg?"

Whizzbang flexed his right leg a number of times and said, "It's as good as new."

Sweat beaded and rolled down Colonel Greerson's temples. These boys really were the cream of the crop. They discussed their potential deaths with a calmness that was completely mystifying.

"Any second now," Bosk said.

Whizzbang looked across at the Colonel's worried face. "Sir, it will be better if you tightly hold your arm-rests."

Powered only on its manoeuvring under-jets the back of the sleek fast frigate left the edge of the hanger bay. The tail dropped suddenly and with precise control, Captain Eldrich fired the main thrusters in a minimal burn.

Within the cabin, everything suddenly turned ninety degrees. The safety harnesses slung over their shoulders tightened and kept Whizzbang and Bosk from falling onto the Colonel. Cabin equipment not already secured fell to the back of the spaceship with a crash.

Whizzbang glanced at his wrist-comp and counted aloud, "Five, four, three, two, now!"

Within the cockpit, Captain Eldrich slammed the thrust levers to maximum burn a fraction of a second before the missiles struck the crater. The three simultaneous explosions completely collapsed the craters walls and vaporised the research facility. A massive plume of dust and rock soared several thousand feet into the air in a great mushroom cloud.

Within the cabin, the instantaneous acceleration of the main engines made breathing almost impossible. The addition of the concussive force of the missiles shock wave sent the fast frigate forward at an unspeakable velocity. Its teardrop shape tore through the moon's atmosphere and the friction of the air against the outer hull caused the reinforced plating to glow a malevolent red.

Every bone in Whizzbang's body shook violently under the stress of the forces. He managed to shift his head to look across at Bosk who widened his eyes to indicate that was a little too close. Whizzbang replied with a barely perceptible nod of his head. Any greater movement than that would cause his head to roll to the side with the additional weight of the acceleration. All at once, the shaking stopped and they were hurtling through space with the moon rapidly receding behind them.

Bosk sighed with relief. "That was a little too close."

"What happened?" Colonel Greerson asked.

Whizzbang replied, "Once the missiles were launched the Captain knew that he was given an opportunity for us to escape."

The Colonel wore a mask of confusion as he asked, "What do you mean?"

"Rather than taking the more traditional and much slower route of leaving the atmosphere he flipped us onto our main engines and waited for the missiles. At the last second, he shot us out of the crater and then rode the shockwave from the explosion to add to our already rapidly growing velocity. The flash of the explosions would have also disguised our ascent. The cruiser would need to react instantly to respond to the completely unorthodox manoeuvre."

"When did you work this all out?"

"As soon as we started moving."

"How so?"

"The Captain could have left the crater at maximum burn but he didn't. He manoeuvred slowly to make sure the Scourge cruiser had an easy target. In fact, he made us irresistible. He wanted those missiles firing down at us. They not only provided an escape route but also destroyed the research facility."

Colonel Greerson nodded his head thoughtfully. These two were very special. The professor had been right in suggesting that they find some young, highly intelligent Cadets to test the nanomeds and nanite battleframes. Or was it Altavia who came up with the idea? He involuntarily looked over at her enshrouded body strapped into her seat. Sadly, it really did not matter now.

In the cockpit, Captain Eldrich plotted a course for Kaladon and flipped in the inter-spatial drive. Outside the ship, the stars vanished and replaced by roiling clouds of orange and black gas. After checking the readouts from the automatic pilot he closed his eyes and let some of the tension slip away. Against the odds, they made it.

Chapter 18
Concord Central Command

Whizzbang spoke clearly and concisely into the direction of his wrist-comp, "Concord Central, Whizzbang Romeo Oscar Sierra Two Niner request."

Whizzbang used the call-sign and identification code that Colonel Greerson had provided all those years ago when he and Bosk were selected to test the first battleframes. When initially engaging Central Command it was mandatory that a pilot use battlespeak to reduce the possibilities for misunderstandings in the heat of combat.

The reply from Concord command came crisply through, "Concord Central acknowledge Whizzbang, Romeo Oscar Sierra Two Niner."

"Request status update on Scourge activity in vicinity of Terrarium."

"Did you say Terrarium?"

"Affirm Terrarium."

Whizzbang listened to several thumps as the microphone was grabbed from the communications handler. A strong confident voice then said, "Whizz, its Franky here. Was it you guys that got the tower back up at Terrarium just now?"

Whizzbang had met General Franky a number of times at Concord Central and he had always seemed to be a no nonsense General who could twist you into a pretzel if you got on his wrong side. Luckily, after a few drinks at the officers club they had both hit it off and developed a solid mutual respect for each other.

"Affirm Franky. It's good to hear your voice. We've been to hell and back this past day."

"CT Whizz. We were caught with our pants well and truly around our ankles this time. We'd thought that Terrarium was lost for good. I don't need to ask now how you managed it but let me send a team to relieve you so that you can hike it back to central for a debrief."

"Thanks for that General but we need to stop into Freehold for a few friends first."

There was a slight pause in the communication before Franky said, "Whizz, cancel Freehold, need a face to face asap."

Whizzbang grimaced and replied, "Sorry General, no can do. We will make all haste Central via Freehold."

Again, there was a pause before the reply, "Roger that Whizz, see you when you arrive but make it snappy. Central out."

The four veterans looked at each other with concern etched on their faces. Something was wrong, very wrong for Central Command to 'request' a personal visit.

Bosk broke the silence and said, "Whizz, what in the frap is going on?"

Whizzbang flexed his still throbbing arm and said, "I have absolutely no idea."

Selfia noticed Whizzbang stretching his arm and said, "Everything OK Whizz?"

"Not really. Something's changed. I've seen a lot of combat Self and suffered my fair share of scrapes, even an eport but that last near miss from the Sniper that grazed my arm is killing me. After every other battle, the meds have fixed me up and I was G2G but this time my arm feels like it's still on fire. Have any of you felt the same?"

Bosk immediately jumped in and began complaining about his various aches, cuts and bruises. Acheron discretely raised a questioning eyebrow in Selfia's direction. She briefly shook her head in the negative before Whizzbang and Bosk noticed anything.

Whizzbang held up his hand and said, "Hold on a minute. Let's take a look at this in a little more controlled fashion. I'll tell you my symptoms and you let me know if yours are the same. OK, immediately after being wounded I felt the nanomeds kick in to fix me up," Whizzbang stated with a matter of fact voice.

There were three nods from each of the squad members.

Whizzbang began peeling back his frame to show his wounds and said, "When I look at where I was shot it looks perfectly healed with not a mark."

Each of the others did the same as Whizzbang showing nothing but beautifully smooth skin where previously there had been shrapnel burns and other typical minor combat injuries.

"Despite the nanomeds appearing to have done their job in patching us up, my injuries feel as if they're still there."

Once again, there were nods of understanding from Whizzbang's companions.

Marking his points with his fingers Whizzbang continued, "So let's think about this for a minute. Each of us has injuries that look like they've healed but not properly. The Scourge in that last fight seemed smarter than ever. We have the 'toothpaste' squeezing syndrome and Central wants us to hike it asap."

Bosk said, "That seems to summarise things pretty well Whizz."

"Come to think of it, things only seem to change after we experience that sense of vertigo Bosk. Things seem to be changing and then going back to normal on an increasingly regular basis. I had Slayer knife embedded in my thigh and it feels just fine but my arm is killing me."

Bosk replied, "Really? A Slayer knife? You'll have to tell me that story sometime." Bosk paused in thought before continuing, "Whizz, there's definitely something going on but I don't think that we're going to find out about it here. What I do know is that we need to get to Freehold, spin up some refining and get our frames seen to. I don't know about you guys but my equipment's almost being held together with force of will alone. We can't defend ourselves if we run out of tellurite and our gear lets us down."

"CT Bosk. We've all seen better days. So the decision stands that when relief arrives we head back to Free and then onwards to Central."

While they waited for the relief to arrive Whizzbang regularly checked his wrist-comp scans to get an update on what was happening in the various districts. It was clear that there was horrendous fighting up north with some areas swapping control a number of times. A few hours after speaking with Franky, Selfia spotted a number of battleframes gliding in from the north through her scope.

Whizzbang put his hand up to shield the glare of the bright late afternoon cloudy sky. "I know that frame. I'd recognize it anywhere," he said.

"Who is it?" Selfia asked.

"A good friend that I wasn't sure I'd see again."

Whizzbang cocked his head to the side to speak into his comnet pickup, "Happy, boy am I glad to see you."

The airwaves crackled for a second and then Happy's deep voice broke through, "Whizz, you still alive? I thought I'd never see you again after I left you in Freehold."

"It looks like we're both hard to kill targets Haps."

Happy and the other four battleframes in the relieving force arrowed towards the scanning tower deck and Whizzbang's squad. At the last instant, they de-energised their wings and with a few short steps were standing opposite Whizzbang.

Walking up to Whizzbang in his familiar Rook battleframe, Happy's dark face split into his characteristic wide smile as he extended his hand warmly and said, "Hey Whizz it looks like you've had some fun here. I just wish that we'd been invited to the party a bit earlier."

Whizzbang returned the handshake vigorously. "We could have used some extra guns. I must admit that during this past day we've had more than our fair share of action."

"I can see that" Happy said as he looked across to the mangled corner of the Terrarium and the field covered in Scourge bodies.

"So how's Central going? Did they make it through in one piece?"

"Central was hit and hit bad Whizz. Just as we saw at Freehold, something went crazy with the defence grid. They had no idea that the attack was coming. If it wasn't for a brilliant defence by General Bardon on the ground and General Alban in the air, Central would have fallen. Franky acted as supreme commander and co-ordinated those two while General Felesh was out in the field somewhere doing what intelligence Generals do. It's all a bit above my pay grade but what I do know is that Central did not fall."

"That's a relief. I'm not sure what we would have done without them. Have you heard anything from Freehold?"

"No I haven't. In fact, on the way inbound to here I experienced a lot of Scourge static so something must be building in that area."

Whizzbang nodded in concern, "Did you see anything from the air?"

Happy shook his head, "No we didn't. Nothing's on the comnet either although I still wouldn't trust it unless I was plugged directly into a scanning tower. Anyway, we may as well get this over and done with then Whizz."

Happy straightened up and formally said, "I relieve you of your position at Terrarium."

"I so stand relieved."

"OK, that's done. Before you head back to wherever you're going can you give me any intel on how the Scourge attacked?" asked Happy.

Whizzbang related the experience of the fight at Terrarium, leaving nothing out that could help Happy's squad in the event of a Scourge counter attack.

"So you've found that they're getting smarter as well Whizz."

"Frap yes Haps. I can't put my finger on anything specifically it's just that the Scourge seem to be getting harder to kill each battle. It could be that we're now on the receiving end of Elite Scourge units."

Bosk strode up to both Happy and Whizzbang and said, "I hate to interrupt you guys but Whizz, it's a long glide back to Freehold and I'm parched."

Happy burst out laughing and said, "The same old Bosk. It's good to see that some things never change. Both you and I need to sort out who can actually win that drinking contest Bosk."

"What contest? It won't be a contest Haps, I'll see you under the table any day. Besides, don't you owe me for that round of drinks the other night?" Bosk replied with a broad grin.

Happy lightly cuffed Bosk on the back of the head. "I thought that your payment was for the previous week?"

"What previous week?"

"C'mon Bosk. Remember the big dance party outside the bar?"

Laughing Bosk said, "I think that I'd prefer to forget that one. My head still hurts from it. OK, let's call it even," and then more sombrely he said, "If we get through this Haps I'll buy you a drink anytime."

"Me too Bosk."

Whizz watched on for a minute at the good natured discussion and then raising his voice slightly so that he could be heard by the relieving squad, "Keep frosty and your eyes wide open," and then to Happy, "Keep safe my friend."

"You too Whizz." Happy turned to Whizzbang's squad. "Fly high and fly safe."

Chapter 19
Return to Freehold

As Whizzbang kicked in his jump jets to fly up to the rock above the Terrarium he glanced down at Happy positioning his squad into a defensive perimeter around the scanning tower. *"He'll be fine,"* he thought to himself.

Once he reached the top of the rock, Whizzbang took a minute to take in the view all the way down to the ocean. Selfia, Acheron and Bosk joined alongside him beside the glider launcher he had just dropped.

Whizzbang said simply, "It's a beautiful view."

Selfia answered, "I sometimes forget to stop take the time just to look how stunning Alpha Three is."

Acheron grunted in agreement beside her.

Bosk said, "I agree that's it's a great view but right now a glass of just about anything at Folly's would be even more beautiful."

The three other pilots laughed and Whizzbang said, "You got that right Bosk."

The sun was setting and it would not be long until it was dark so without another word Whizzbang stepped onto the spinning platform, shot into the air and headed northwards towards

Freehold. It was going to take one more glide from the outpost that they had recently liberated to reach Freehold but with any luck they should be catching up with the others within the next hour. Looking down at the jungle far below, Whizzbang reflected that it all appeared so quiet and peaceful, a sharp contrast to the mayhem earlier in the day.

After landing at the outpost, Whizzbang greeted the militia Captain who expressed concern that he had been unable to contact Freehold for the past eight hours. With that ominous news, the four of them quickly re-launched for the final leg of their journey. From their altitude, they could see the signs of a recent large battle in the terrain below. Scorch marks, burned trees, ruined piles where buildings once stood and abandoned damaged equipment littered the landscape far below.

Over the noise of the wind, whistling around their frames Bosk said, "And I thought that we had it bad."

Acheron replied, "The battle's always worse on other side of the fence."

"You can see that the combat went right up to the very edges of Freehold from up here," Selfia joined in.

With a concerned voice and a furrowed brow Whizzbang said, "It was a big one all right. We must have been fighting the edge of the main force all the way to the Terrarium."

"Look at the size of that burnt out artillery piece!" exclaimed Bosk.

The remnants of a huge black canon jutted out of the sand on the southern outskirts of the town. Rather than a traditional barrel, the Scourge artillery piece tapered to a jagged point from which it would launch massive balls of plasma at its target. Whizzbang coughed and his eyes watered as the stench of melted war machinery and spent munitions rose up towards them as they passed overhead.

"I've heard about those big Scourge guns but I've never seen one," replied Acheron.

Wiping his eyes to clear his vision Whizzbang ordered, "Form up on my wing. We're nearly there"

The three squad members pulled in beside Whizzbang to form a V-formation. As the steps rising to the top levels of Freehold rushed towards them, Whizzbang's squad de-energised their wings at the last second and gently touched down. In unison, they kicked in their jets to head for the tellurite nano-printers and repairs.

Reaching the top level the noise from the crowds of battleframe pilots was deafening. Drills whined as technicians serviced frames for minor repairs, jump jets screamed overhead and mechanics yelled at apprentices to move faster. Compared to the stillness and serenity of when he had first materialised almost a day ago it was now a seething mass of confusion and chaos as people raced back and forth on errands of the utmost urgency. Crowds of desperate pilots jostled and pushed each other as they tried to exert their influence to be the next to use the nano-printers.

The nano-printers were overloaded with 'top priority' requests for urgent battleframe and weapon components that the built in nanites, technicians or mechanics could not easily repair. A battleframe just did not have sufficient computing power to control the nanites to repair all its components. A tellurite shortage made it completely impossible to manufacture complete battleframes.

Pilots demanded everything from new gun barrels through to ammo clips and energisers. They were all short on even the most basic of commodities. The nearest battleframe terminals was surrounded by pilots that had just been in combat as half of them had severe structural damage to their exoskeletons and a number of them no longer had their armour or jump jets operating. If they had the tellurite then their own battleframe nanites may have been able to conduct some of the repairs. However, the battleframes had seen such intense combat that they were completed depleted of tellurite energy.

As they pushed their way through the surging mass of humanity and battleframes, Whizzbang's squad reached the top of the stairs leading down to the courtyard holding the liberty torch. Rather than blazing in the darkness as a symbol of freedom the torch, now appeared to be almost feeble. Any light from its flickering flame cast chaotic shifting shadows that danced in a manner that added a sense of foreboding to the unfolding scene below.

"Oh my gosh..." Selfia trailed off.

The three of them stared at the sight before them and stopped dead, unable to move as the enormity of the disaster struck them with full force.

Bosk quietly said, "I don't think I need that drink anymore."

While the upper deck was a complete mess of confusion, nothing could prepare Whizzbang and his squad for the site of the courtyard below. Lying in row after row were bodies. Some with sheets pulled up over their heads and many without, one mangled corpse after another, all laying perfectly still. Some were burned beyond recognition while others were missing limbs, torsos or just stared with wide open accusing eyes at nothing in particular.

The stench of death amply combined with the groans of the dying lying on stretchers at the far end of the paved open area. Despite the best available pain meds, wounded bodies twitched feebly in a futile attempt to remind themselves they were still alive. Moans, screams and retching came from broken bodies all across the courtyard as once proud members of the Concord came face to face with their own mortality.

A number of pilots were lying with their backs propped up against the wall staring vacantly into space. Their bodies were intact but their minds were continuing to suffer the aftereffects of an eport. Whizzbang watched in compassion as a tear trickled down the cheek of a pilot on the far left while the pilot next to him mumbled nonsense words to himself.

A trail of fresh red blood smeared the ground beside an abandoned body. Blood flowed freely in rivulets across the paving and a spray from a severed artery decorated a wall in crimson. Feeling sick to the core of his being, Whizzbang thought that he had recognised a few of the battleframe pilot's colours on a number of the dead. They were his friends and now they were gone.

"Oh please no…" Whizzbang muttered as he thumbed the local comnet channel. High-strung voices swamped the channel; crying out for medics, demanding repairs, requesting assistance and even a scream followed by the screech of an eport. All the voices sounded desperate. All the voices were terrified. The comnet mirrored the chaos surrounding him and the sensory overload was almost overwhelming.

Whizzbang selected the local comnet to filter out all but his friends and with a trembling voice said, "Whizzbang calling Pyro, Kheldar, DG or Elzetro"

Nothing but static greeted his request so again he said, "Whizzbang calling Pyro, Kheldar, DG or Elzetro. Come on guys, are you there?"

Bosk reached over, put a hand on Whizzbang's shoulder and said softly, "They'll be OK. We'd know it if they were gone."

Just then a burst of static erupted in Whizzbang's earpiece followed by a relieved voice, "Whizz is that you?"

Whizzbang's eyes welled up with tears and a lump caught in his throat as he said, "Pyro! Pyro, son, are you OK?"

"Dad, its sure good to hear your voice. I wasn't sure if you'd made it," an equally distraught Pyro answered.

Bosk jumped in and with a trembling voice asked, "Is Elzetro with you?"

"Hey Uncle Bosk it's great to hear you! Yes, Elzetro is with me although his comnet is out and he's in the middle of fixing it. Hang on a second," Pyro replied.

"Dad, Dad is that really you?" a relieved voice came over the comnet.

"Elzetro, it's really me son," replied Bosk jubilantly.

Selfia and Acheron looked from Whizzbang to Bosk and then back to each other. They now understood why their two friends had to get back to Freehold so urgently and were prepared to defy Concord Central. Their two sons were here and in the middle of the fighting.

Pyro's voice came across the comnet again, "We've got Kheldar and DG with us as well. We're all pretty beat up but nothing's broken."

"Pyro, where are you guys?" asked Whizzbang

"You know the big chunk of rock behind Freehold? We've been camped out on top while we sorted out what the heck was going on Dad. We all could really use some maintenance on our frames but Elzetro has fixed everything that has caused any serious problems. Dad, Elzetro may be an apprentice mechanic but he really knows his stuff."

"Good to hear son. He's always been a lot cleverer than many people give him credit for. What do you need?"

Pyro passed on a list of items that would really help them out in getting properly operational.

Whizzbang said, "CT Pyro. We'll see if we can get the spare parts printed off and head on up. It may take a little while as it's absolute bedlam down here. Whatever you do sit tight and don't move."

"CT Dad, see you soon."

Whizzbang looked up into Bosk's eyes that mirrored his own relief that their sons and friends were alive. While life continued, there would always be hope. So in the midst of the chaos, death and dying Whizzbang, Bosk and their new friends did what they did best. They brought hope and order to those around them.

Pushing their way through the stench of sweating bodies and cauterised flesh the four hardened veterans reached the central battleframe terminal at the top of the stairs. That is when Whizzbang did the unthinkable. Bending down he wrapped his armoured hand around the terminal's massive power adaptor and yanked it from its receptacle. The lights on the console faded to blackness as its pleasant hum spun down and fell silent. His action received everyone's instant attention and most of it was not very good.

"What in the frap do you think you're doing?" yelled a voice from the hulking Rex frame who had just been disconnected from the terminal. The stench of his breath was second only to the noxious fumes from the cigar hanging out of his mouth.

The press of the crowd surged forward, pushing the four of them back against the console and leading the charge was the growling Rex. A few frames suggested tossing them over the top and down the stairs and there were nods of agreement from others in the crowd. Things were on the verge of getting out of hand and a riot was likely.

In his deepest, loudest military parade voice Whizzbang yelled authoritatively, "Halt!" It did help that at that precise moment Bosk decided to emphasize the command by pointing his Charge rifle into the air and letting off a burst.

The crowd and even the Rex paused and that was the only hesitation that Whizzbang needed, "Pilots, technicians, mechanics and medics of the Concord, I'm Squad Leader Whizzbang. Some of you know me and given time, there are others I'm looking forward to getting to know."

Taking a deep breath Whizzbang continued pushing his voice out over the crowd. "My squad and I have just returned from fighting Scourge as far south as the Terrarium. All the sectors between here and there are now back into Concord hands." Glancing across at Acheron and Selfia he continued, "I've been rescued by new friends" and indicating Bosk, "and rescued my oldest friend. In all that time I wondered if my son was alive and tonight I have heard his voice over the local!"

"My brothers, my sisters, my friends, in order to stand against the Scourge we need to stand as one family, one body, united together. Fighting over resources just allows the enemy to have a victory when they've had none!"

Pointing at the grizzly scene of the bodies lying on the paving below Whizzbang continued in a more tempered voice, "What would they say of our conduct now? What would they think if they saw us fighting one another when we should be protecting each other? What would the fallen say to you if they knew that you squabbled like Spyderlynx over their corpses? What would the wounded say to you when they find out that that they've bled in vain?"

"Have you checked your wrist-comp lately? Your brothers and sisters are still eporting into Freehold or dying in the dirt and mud of Alpha Three on the end of a Scourge blaster."

One at a time and then in groups, Concord personnel hung their heads in shame as Whizzbang's words struck home. In the midst of the chaos, they had forgotten who they were and in the desperation of the moment, they needed someone to awaken them from their stupor.

Planting his finger on the Rex's chest Whizzbang yelled, "Pilot, what's your call-sign?"

"Tiny, sir," came the answer in a gravelly voice that sounded more like rock than human.

While indicating Selfia and Acheron Whizzbang put his face right up to Tiny's and yelled at the top of his voice, "Tiny, I need you to work with Selfia and Acheron! Can I count on your support Tiny?"

Years of training kicked in and Tiny replied, "Yes sir!"

"Acheron and Selfia, I need you to triage which frames can be made whole and which ones will require more extensive work. Divide the frames between the garages, technicians, mechanics and nano-printers. Tiny, you are to ensure that ONLY, and I repeat for all, that ONLY those tagged battleframes for a resource can get access to that resource. Is this clear Tiny?"

Tiny straightened to his full six foot nine inches, looked straight ahead and yelled, "Yes sir! Smash anything that doesn't behave sir!"

Whizzbang smiled, "Yes, you do that Tiny!"

Speaking now to the silent mass of people around him Whizzbang projected his parade voice once again, "I want all frames backed out of this area and on the double! We need operational battleframes and ideally squads on the perimeter NOW! If you're capable of holding a pea shooter I want you to let Bosk know." Whizzbang pointed to Bosk, who was still holding his Charge rifle above his headed, cocked and ready for action.

"If you cannot fight then you can do something that's just as important." Indicating the corpses crowding the courtyard around the liberty torch Whizzbang said softly, "Your brothers and sisters need you to put them to rest. They've fought their last fight and the most honourable thing that we can do for them is to lay them to rest, deep in the sand at the far end of Freehold beach. Point their feet in the direction of the sunrise and a new day."

Once again, Whizzbang increased his volume and fervour as he looked into the eyes of every filthy battle weary face, "Today, with a surprise attack, the Scourge have bloodied us but they have awakened something far stronger than they could have imagined! They've awoken the blood that runs in all our veins, the blood of brothers and sisters united in a common purpose, a common Concord!"

With a look of defiance and determination, Whizzbang thrust his fist into the air and yelled, "We are the Concord!" The sudden twinge of pain from his wound caught him by surprise but he kept a brave face and once again pumped his arm upwards and yelled, "We are the Concord!"

Cheers broke out from the crowd as they took up the chant of "Concord! Concord! Concord!" Whizzbang and the mass of battleframes and other personnel around him pumped their fists into the air. No one knows who started it but it was not long before "Whizzbang!" replaced "Concord!" and as the throng honoured the pilot who reminded them of their heritage. Men and women who fight to defend their land from an insidious invader, that is both remorseless and unrelenting.

While the crowd continued to chant his name, Whizzbang stepped down from where he was perched and said to Bosk, "There's been a change in plans."

"You think?" Bosk replied incredulously.

"We're going to need some help. Can you call the guys down from up top to give us a hand? On second thought, leave Kheldar and DG on the mountain to immediately report any Scourge activity that they see." Grimly smiling, Whizzbang added, "Also, tell them it's not time for a dance party just yet."

"Good idea. After your little speech, I figure we're all going to be working double time to get things back together. Don't forget that Concord central want you for a face-to-face."

Rolling his eyes heavenward Whizzbang muttered through clenched teeth, "I haven't forgotten but it looks like they've forgotten about Freehold. Somebody had to do something."

Bosk nodded his head, "I agree, Freehold is the bridge between north and south Alpha Three, and it has to hold. Enough chatting, I'd better get to work." With that, Bosk disappeared into the crowd to take a prominent position so that he could do his bit to bring some order to the chaos.

Whizzbang thought to himself, "*What they really needed was some tellurite. Without it they wouldn't last long.*"

Far to the north, a lone Scourge strike leader turned towards the sudden tumult arising from Freehold and snarled back a challenge to the darkness around him, "Humans, why do you fight? In the end you will all die!"

Chapter 20
The Beginning
and the End

Whizzbang smiled as he looked across the main Freehold plaza and saw his close-knit squad go to work. After a warm greeting, Bosk had conscripted their sons, Pyro and Elzetro, to help organise a defence of the settlement in the event of another Scourge attack. Tiny helped Selfia and Acheron triage battleframes that suffered extensive damage versus those that could be readied and sent back into the field as soon as possible. The most difficult task was to inform the pilots of some of the more damaged battleframes that they would have to sit tight and let others get access to the nano-printers and technicians.

When they had first arrived in Freehold the population was in a state of panic with fear gripping the hearts of even the most tested veterans. Now there was order. Purposeful actions, according to a plan, now supplanted the frantic chaos of a few hours earlier. Courage replaced fear, resolve overcame defeat and the previous sense of pointlessness was no longer evident in the faces of those around him.

It was not long until Whizzbang found out why he was now informally in charge of Freehold. During the initial Scourge assault, an artillery barrage had accurately targeted and taken out the entire Freehold Concord command staff. As a battleframe Squad Leader, he was the highest ranking officer still alive. For safety sake the command centre would often move locations and for it to be picked off so easily indicated only one possibility. There was a traitor in their midst. Colonel O'Brien and the rest of the officers coordinating the Freehold defence had paid the ultimate price for treachery.

The Colonel may have been officious and a stickler for the rules but he was also an officer of the Concord and deserved respect and remembrance. Whizzbang bowed his head before the smouldering ruined structure of the former command centre and said a prayer for those lost. There would be no bodies to bury as the massive plasma discharge had eagerly devoured everything in its path. Whizzbang reminded himself that there would always be memories. Taking a deep breath, he spun around and walked back to the central Freehold courtyard.

There was a lot to do and even more to think about if they were to survive this disaster. When he had given his speech, earlier that night Whizzbang had unknowingly filled the vacuum left by the previous leaders and had become the default Freehold Commander.

It just so happened that Whizzbang and his squad were the right people at the right time. They provided some semblance of hope to those in desperate need. Naturally, each of them were heroes in the making, forged by the circumstances thrust upon them.

Moving through the crowd Whizzbang gave a smile and a word of encouragement here and a pat on the back there. He even shared a hug and shed a few tears with those who had lost loved ones in the recent Scourge assault. He was every inch the Commander, restoring morale everywhere he went.

Before sunrise, Whizzbang and those that could be spared from the immediate Freehold defence headed to the far end of the beach to say their last good-byes to lost friends. Crews dug graves well above the high tide mark and the fallen were lain with a light white cloth covering their bodies. Their toes all pointed to where the sun was about to rise above the ocean in the east.

In place of a gravestone, each gravesite had a short stake driven into the ground. As people came to pay their respects, they hung keepsakes on the rough wood in remembrance of good times with friends who were now enjoying eternal sleep.

It wasn't lost on those gathered in the early morning that the two hundred and thirty-nine bodies looked like a line of sunbathers soaking up some rays before going for a cooling swim. A few chuckles could be heard which helped alleviate the corporate feeling of grief as one person after another pointed it out. Maybe, Paradise would be like enjoying a long overdue holiday.

Standing on the sand below the graves Whizzbang turned towards the ocean just as the suns first rays appeared above the horizon. It had been a long night and after the battles of the day before his very bones seemed to be weary.

The gentle breeze brought the smell of fresh salty air. Whizzbang closed his eyes and took a few slow deep breaths to help remind himself that at this moment, there was still some peace and tranquillity in the world. Strange that the last gift of the dead was a small respite from all the terror and destruction.

Opening his eyes Whizzbang looked down at several hundred expectant faces staring up at him. Like a Juggernaut's plasma canon the burden of leadership suddenly hit him as he realised that these people were looking to him to say something, anything that would strengthen the tenuous thread of hope that their courage hung by. It had been thirty hours since he first arrived and what he really wanted was time to find out why his arm still hurt so badly, followed by several hours of shut-eye. Like many things, they would both have to wait until later.

Looking back at them, tears welling in his eyes, he stammered, "I didn't know most of these brave souls, but I can see that hanging from every stake are memories of good times with those that did."

Looking over his shoulder at the graves he continued, "Raven, Rex, Anvil, Rook, Eagle, whatever their battleframe they all fought so that we could live and defend this land from the enemy at our gates. The question they are asking from the grave is, 'What are we going to do with their sacrifice?'"

Turning his back on the crowd below him Whizzbang faced the line of graves, dropped to one knee and bowed his head. Behind him, he could hear those assembled do likewise and then with a firm resolute voice said, "While there is yet breath in me I will not let this land fall to the Scourge. I will not see Freehold fall! I swear this by the sacrifice that you have made for us all."

Slowly standing to his feet Whizzbang turned to face those assembled as they also rose to theirs. He squinted his eyes and looked at the sun rising above the horizon as it began the new day in its journey across the sky. The yellow rays had a purple tinge from shining through the Barrier before illuminating the beach and the lost pilot's graves.

In the age old Concord salute to fallen comrades Whizzbang clenched his right fist and slapped it against the left side of his chest, and then arm outstretched, pointed his middle and pointer finger straight up to the sky. The two fingers indicated that no member of the Concord would ever be alone, even in the journey into the next life. His arm still ached but it was worth the additional pain to honour the fallen. Just then a lone seagull cawed high overhead as if to signal the end of the ceremony and the assembled gathering drifted slowly back to Freehold. Silently, those assigned filled in the graves.

Climbing the steps from the beach up to the Freedom Torch Whizzbang noted the purposeful activity all across the settlement. As he passed he nodded encouragement to technicians, mechanics and pilots. Their faces, though grim had the glimmer of hope in their eyes. Nano-printers hummed with newly infused tellurite from Diggers deployed within the Freehold district during the night. *"That was good news,"* he thought to himself.

Fresh, new battleframe components materialised on the various nano-workbenches, ready to be rushed to mechanics and technicians for the replacement of damaged parts. They were still short the tellurite to manufacture complete frames and would have to make do with the parts.

Bosk strode up to Whizzbang and said, "How'd it go?"

"As good as can be expected. A lot of friends died yesterday and there's still a lot unaccounted for."

Bosk nodded solemnly in agreement. "I've had the two boys, I mean, our two young men coordinating with several squads of frames, running patrols both to the south and north. Kheldar and DG are keeping their eyes open up top, but to be fair, their itching to get some payback rather than being on nanny duty."

Whizzbang sighed, "They'll be plenty of time for that by the time this is over. Hang on, did you hear that?"

"I heard nothing."

Whizzbang cocked his head to the side, "Bosk, I've got to go. Sorry, I know we're in the middle of a big one here. Esther is calling." Speaking into his comnet Whizzbang said, "Sorry guys, I've got to cut out now. Hopefully I'll see you online later. Pyro, Mum's calling, we've got to go now. It's dinner time."

"Oh come on Dad! It's just starting to get really interesting!"

"We can't hang around any longer otherwise she'll have our heads!"

"Sure thing. Cheers Elzetro. Hey, Kheldar and DG. Thanks for the dance party earlier!"

The sound of laughter erupted across the local and Kheldar said, "Anytime Pyro. Guys, DG and I are going to call it quits as well. Let's see if we can get together tomorrow."

Bosk looked across at his friend and watched him vanish just before he quit as well.

Part II
Revelations

Chapter 1
The Real World

Russell, alias Whizzbang, removed the virtual reality screen assembly from his head and placed it on the desk in front of him. He had a smile a mile wide on his face. His heart was still pounding from the experience. Wow, what a session! For a game still in beta test, "Scourge Wars" was like nothing he had ever experienced before. It was so real, so engaging! The graphics and sound made it feel like he had actually been on Alpha Three.

For the past thirty-five years, Russell had been playing computer games. Starting on clunky text adventures right through to the latest releases that could only run on high-end graphics gear. He even did a stint as a games programmer, but soon discovered that designing games and business models for them, was much more interesting than searching a few thousand lines of code for a semicolon or some other error.

Russell turned across to his son James and said, "So what did you think of that session of "Scourge Wars" Pyro?"

James finished hanging up his VR gear on a stand in front him and turned to his father. There was a broad smile on his face as he said, "It was amazing! I think this time was the best we've ever played!"

James was twenty years old and had grown up on his father's healthy diet of games. Just shy of six feet, short brown hair and a ready smile made him the attraction for girls at any party. It also helped that James worked out regularly with both weights and a jogging regime that put his father to shame. His easygoing manner and bright sparkling mischievous blue eyes ensured that he was never short of friends, either his or his father's.

One time James had accompanied Russell on a work trip to help man a booth for his father's business at a trade fair in Los Angeles. It was not long before he became the hit of the conference and made such a positive impression that people still talked about him a couple of years later.

Russell flexed his neck and said, "We'd better see what your mother's prepared for dinner. Whatever it is, it smells outstanding!"

James' sniffed the air expectantly, "Smells like chili garlic lamb with noodles."

Russell pushed his chair back from the desk, stood to his feet and stretched up to the ceiling to loosen his muscles up a bit. It was then that he let out a yell as he grabbed his upper left arm. "What the!!!" he managed to say between clenched teeth. At his father's pained voice James instinctively leapt to his feet to support him.

The door to the study flew open and Russell's wife, Esther, burst in with a concerned look on her face. "You OK Russ, I heard you from the kitchen."

Esther's lustrous brown hair had a few lighter highlights and the cut revealed her neck at the back while remaining longer on the sides. She had a figure to die for and stunningly gorgeous brown green eyes that Russell repeatedly got lost in. In her mid-forties, she had not lost any of her enthusiasm for life and currently had an apron around her waist over blue jeans.

As James guided his father to a chair Russell winced, "I think I'm OK but my arm feels like it's on fire."

"Here, let me take a look at that," Esther said with a note of authority in her voice. Many years earlier, she had trained as a nurse and all the members of the family were used to the efficient manner she would deal with any ailment.

Russell carefully unbuttoned his shirt and with his wife's help pulled his arms out of the sleeves. Bending down to look carefully at his arm Esther asked, "Russell, what have you been doing?"

"What do you mean?"

"You've got what looks like a third degree burn along the back of your upper arm."

Russell twisted his head around to try to look at the wound and gave a momentary gasp as the skin in his arm tightened. The red, blistered welt was a little over a pencil in width and about ten centimetres long.

Esther shook her head from side to side, "It looks like you've leaned against a heater for a few minutes. Are you sure you don't know what caused this?"

"I have no idea." Russell replied flatly.

Esther gave him one of those, you are not telling me everything looks and said, "Wait here and I'll go and get some burn cream."

Esther closed the door behind her and James looked up at his father and whispered, "Dad, that's exactly where the Scourge Sniper hit you in Scourge Wars."

"I know son."

"What's going on Dad?"

"I have no idea but I do know that I haven't been lying against any heaters lately."

Just then, the phone on the cluttered desk next to his computer rang. Reaching his right arm across his body Russell hit the hands free button and said, "Russ here."

Bosk or Mihaly in the non-game world's strong voice came over the speaker, "Hi Russ, have you experienced anything strange after leaving the game this evening?"

"What do you mean?"

"I feel like I've been peppered with holes. I've got bruises all over my body about the size of twenty cent pieces." Mihaly took a deep breath and continued, "Nothing serious but I'm aching all over. It's like I've been in a warzone. Marie's just got home and is wondering what the heck I've been up to."

"Remember in the game I was hit by a Scourge sniper in the arm and it just kept on aching and aching."

"Yep, you complained about that a number of times."

"I've got a third degree burn in that exact same spot on my arm and it's fair to say that it hurts a lot. Esther's just gone to get some burn cream now for it."

"Is James OK?"

James jumped in and said, "Yeah, I'm fine Uncle Mihaly. How's Alex?"

Although they were not related in any way both Russell and Mihaly had known each other since primary school and so it was only natural that their sons used "uncle" when addressing them.

"He's fine thank goodness. Not a mark on him."

Russell sighed deeply and said, "That's good to hear." Just then, Esther came through the door armed with the tube of burn cream.

Russell spoke towards the phone and said, "Mihaly, can you and Marie come over after dinner? I think that we need to talk."

Esther looked at her husband quizzically.

Hang on, after a few seconds Mihaly replied, "Sure thing, see you guys in about an hour."

"See you then. Bye"

Whizzbang pushed the hang-up button and looked up at his wife.

With her best bedside manner, Esther smiled grimly and said, "Russ, this is going to hurt but once it's applied it will help numb the pain and speed up the healing."

He sometimes hated that his wife always told him the truth. In times like this, a lie would have been much easier to accept. True to her word, applying the burn cream caused him to squeeze his eyes shut with pain. After a few minutes, the pain subsided and his arm felt much better than before, courtesy of the wonders of modern anaesthetics.

Chapter 2
Deliberations

Russell donned a clean shirt and quickly finished his dinner. There was a knock at the front door and Mihaly, Marie and Alex arrived, armed with some of their favourite apple cider.

The two father's had been through a lot together over the years and were about as close as friends could possibly be. Mihaly was about six inches shorter than Russell and had short-cropped black hair that was silvering as much as his friend's. His parents were Hungarian born and had moved to Melbourne, Australia just after World War II as a part of the many southern Europeans that escaped the devastation of Europe at that time.

Russell and Mihaly had been playing games together since they were in their early teens and this developed into a love for computers. After a stint in the Royal Australian Air Force as a fighter pilot Cadet, Mihaly decided to follow his desire to work in the computer industry. For the past seven years, he had been working with Russell managing Internet domain names.

Marie was about the same height as Esther and her stunning straight red hair nearly reached her shoulders. For as long as Russell had known her, she had worn delicately framed glasses.

Her quick and ready wit revealed a razor sharp mind that Russell had verbally fenced with many times over drinks. A primary school teacher by profession, Marie's love for her students was only dwarfed by her love of Mihaly and their two children.

The two couples had been best of friends for more years than they cared to remember. After initial greetings, they all adjourned to the comfort of the soft brown leather couches in the lounge room. Russell poured a round of drinks and set them out on coasters on the wooden coffee table.

They quickly dispensed with further pleasantries to start unravelling what had happened while playing the game. During the discussion, Mihaly showed a number of his bruises and Russell lifted the bandage Esther had applied to his burn. Their two sons looked on with thoughtful expressions but said nothing.

Russell looked across at his best friends and said, "Something's going on Mihaly. How could it be that we both received actual injuries from a game? Remember when we were playing, I kept complaining about a problem with my arm? It must have been because I was actually hurt."

Mihaly looked thoughtful as he stared intently into his glass. "I really don't know how all of this is possible. We also need to consider the fact that you two boys," turning to both James and Alex, "seem to be fine."

"Did either of you experience any strange sensations while playing?" Russell asked.

The two boys looked at each other and then back to their parents, when James said, "The lag did seemed to be especially bad this time. It was almost like the game was constantly surging."

With a smile on his face Alex said, "There was that moment when that girl began dancing with us during the party."

"Get serious Alex," interjected Marie.

"Hey Mum, she was spectacularly good looking!"

James laughed and added, "You know you're right Alex, she was good looking! The only problem is that the she is probably a he, and about two hundred kilograms!"

Before the mothers could begin dressing down their two sons on the proper way to treat a girl, virtual or otherwise, Russell said, "I felt that strange surging as well. From the first moment I arrived in Freehold. It didn't happen all the time but it seemed to get progressively worse." He turned to speak directly to Mihaly. "In fact, it seemed to get really bad when I arrived at the Terrarium to rescue you. As we discussed in the game, it felt like the whole world was compressing and then expanding. It was a really strange feeling but I put it down to the take-out that we'd had for lunch."

"Come to think of it I felt the same thing from the moment that I first stepped into the game," Mihaly said.

Russell turned to the two boys, "Did either of you feel anything like that?"

A look of concentration crossed James's face as he said, "I wasn't going to mention it because I thought it was nothing. Dad, remember when we first met at Freehold? I felt like I was suddenly falling. You know when you're flying in an aeroplane and your stomach ends up in your throat after hitting an air pocket. It only lasted a few seconds so I thought nothing of it."

Alex looked back from James to both their fathers, "Like James, I wasn't going to make a big deal of it, but I did feel something when you both arrived in Freehold. It was only for a few seconds and I didn't think of it again."

Esther had remained silent as she listened to each of the boys share their thoughts, finally she said, "So let me understand this. Each of you experienced something you've never felt before while playing a game and this has resulted in both Mihaly and Russ getting hurt. The solution seems pretty simple to me, stop playing the game!"

Russell placed his handed gently on Esther's knee and said, "You're right of course. We could stop playing 'Scourge Wars', but I for one, need to find out what happened to us. It must be some new technology that induces a psychosomatic physical response in the player."

Esther turned to her husband and said with just a hint of sarcasm in her voice, "Spoken like a true consultant Russ." Looking at the four men she continued, "Seriously guys, you have no idea what is going on and don't pretend that you do."

Marie joined in and said, "I agree with Esther. You have to stop playing, whatever it's called. It's just too risky. We don't know what's going on but I do know that you all could be seriously hurt by that thing."

Russell nodded his head and smiled warmly as he said to both Esther and Marie, "You're both right of course, it's a dangerous game and I have no intention of getting burned again but..."

Esther interrupted, "Russ why is there always a *but* with you? Can't you just leave it be?"

Marie rolled her eyes. Over the thirty plus years she had known Russell she'd heard that *but* numerous times before. It always meant something bad was about to happen and would somehow involve Mihaly.

Russell raised his voice to be heard above his wife's objections, "As I was saying. I need to find out what has happened to me. What about you Mihaly? How about you James and Alex? Aren't you curious about what happened to you?"

The three other males in the room looked at each other and then back to Russell. Mihaly then hesitantly said, "Russ, I know this may sound crazy but we seemed to be really there, on Alpha Three. If this is really the case then we were making a difference and for some reason those people needed us. I don't know how it happened or why it happened to us but for me I need to get to the bottom of it."

Marie sighed in exasperation as she exclaimed, "Men!"

By this time, Esther had had enough of the conversation and said, "Mihaly, can you hear yourself? You're talking about a game. Alpha Three, or whatever it's called, is inside a computer. It only exists in the mind of a bunch of programmers in Los Angeles."

Russell looked thoughtfully over at Mihaly and Mihaly back at him before saying, "You're right Esther. We need to go to Los Angeles."

"What?" Esther asked in amazement.

"You heard me. We need to go to LA and speak with the guys at Blue Sky Studios."

And so it went on, hour after hour, as the two couples and their sons discussed the strange unfolding of events into the late hours of the evening. At one point, they even called both Kheldar and DG to find out if they had experienced anything similar to themselves. Both of them had not received any physical evidence like Russell and Mihaly but they had felt that strange compression and release sensation.

After their friends had left, Russell and Esther said goodnight to their son. While they cleaned up, they chatted about their girls, Michelle and Rose, schooling, the business and other more mundane matters. It was all so normal, something they had done many times before, but this time it was so false.

Finally, when they were in bed with the light off Esther leaned over and gave Russell a kiss good night. Whispering, she said, "I love you."

"I love you too."

"Russ, do what you think's best."

With that, Russell closed his eyes with a sense of peace and drifted off to sleep.

Chapter 3
Is this a dream?

Whizzbang looked up as a huge hand engulfed his and hauled him to his feet. A half-familiar ugly face seemed to rush towards him as Tiny rumbled in his gravelly voice, "What are ya doing down there Whizz?"

Whizzbang shook his head from side to side to help recover from his momentary vertigo. The last thing he remembered was saying goodnight to Esther, so this was either a dream or somehow he'd been ported back to Alpha Three. He looked around at the open Freehold plaza with its cobblestoned paving and the freedom torch towering in the middle of the courtyard. He ignored Tiny's question and said authoritatively, "Report soldier."

Tiny took a half smoked cigar from between his lips and responded with his deep reverberating voice, "Since last night we've managed to get twenty-four frames operational sir. The nano-printers are still short on tellurite but we've got a couple of squads of Diggers to the north, just outside Free, to see what they can mine out. The scouts have reported no contact with the enemy and the lookouts up on the rock above haven't seen anything either."

"*Twenty-four frames! That's not going to be enough!*" Whizzbang thought to himself. He looked up at the sun and saw that it was halfway across the sky. I've been away for about eight hours he thought. That's about the same amount of time as I was back home.

"Tiny, can you point me in the direction of Bosk?"

Pointing through an archway leading out of the plaza Tiny said, "Sure, for the last fifteen minutes he's been working with the scouting teams just where the parts vendors have set up shop."

"Thanks for that" Whizzbang replied and almost as an afterthought said, "It's good to see you soldier."

A broad smile split Tiny's face in two, revealing a number of broken teeth. He straightened his back, saluted by raising his right pointer and index finger to his temple and then sweeping them forward by pivoting from his elbow. "Yes sir!" he said in his very best soldier's voice.

Whizzbang returned the salute, turned and jump-jetted up the steps in the direction that Tiny had last seen Bosk. Cocking his head to the side, he spoke into his Raven's local comnet pickup, "Bosk, you copy?"

Bosk quickly replied, "Heh Whizz, you back here again as well. It seems like we don't have to play anymore to be sucked back to Alpha Three. So much for our girls telling us to leave well and good alone."

Whizzbang rounded the corner and spotted his friend, just as he stepped away from speaking with a squad of five pilots. Whizzbang settled gently to the ground next to Bosk. "So this isn't a dream then?"

"Doesn't look like it Whizz. Put it this way, when was the last time you had a vaguely intelligent conversation with me in a dream?"

"Good point. Who else is here?"

"No idea, let's find out"

Bosk tilted his head to speak into his comnet, "Bosk and Whizz calling, Kheldar, DG, Pyro and Elzetro." Leaning towards Whizzbang he asked, "Who were those other two you were with again?"

"Acheron and Selfia"

"Also, add Acheron and Selfia to the previous list. All identified pilots, reply."

Suddenly the local comnet was awash with familiar voices. Above the clamour Whizzbang heard his son say, "Dad is that you and Bosky?"

Motioning to get Bosk's attention Whizzbang said, "Call them all in, we need a serious talk."

While Bosk arranged for the pilots to come in Whizzbang tuned into a private comnet channel and said, "Yes it is son. Bosk is calling all of you in, so get to my location ASAP."

Pyro slipped straight back into battlespeak and replied "CT Dad, your position in five."

Whizzbang watched the familiar scarred battleframes jump jet, run and bound towards Bosk and him. Each one had their own style but all of them exhibited a deadly grace and an economy of movement that betrayed their elite competency. Looking up he saw Pyro bearing down towards him in a steep glide, pull up and then do a leisurely aerial circuit of Freehold.

"Thanks for the overhead Pyro," Bosk said into his comnet.

"CT Bosk, just taking a last check for Scourge. All clear, we are G2G."

Pyro broke out of his circuit and headed down to his father and uncle just as Kheldar and DG arrived with Selfia and Acheron not far behind.

"It's good to see you guys!" Whizzbang exclaimed over the sound of breaking jump jets and screeching massive plasteel shod boots on stone pavers.

Giving hugs in a battleframe really was not possible so each of them gave the same salute to each other that Tiny had given Whizzbang earlier. It seemed appropriate for such an occasion.

"So my friends, by now you've probably worked out that playing 'Scourge Wars' isn't just a game," Whizzbang said in a matter of fact tone of voice. "So let's hear where everyone's really from," he continued.

Kheldar spoke first while he raised his hand towards the others, "San Francisco here Whizz."

"Los Angeles," piped in DG.

"We're both from London," replied Acheron as he indicated Selfia.

Whizzbang cocked an eyebrow towards Selfia in surprise and then continued the introductions, "Everyone, this is my son Pyro and my best friend Bosk. We're from Melbourne Australia."

Bosk turned towards Pyro and asked, "Where's Elzetro? I thought that he was with you up top."

Pyro spared a glance skyward and replied, "He wanted to do a high altitude circuit and the last I heard he thought that he saw something south-west of Free, so he used some of his extra height to glide closer to check it out."

Bosk held up his hand to stop any further discussion and spoke into his comnet, "Bosk to Elzetro, come in Elzetro."

Other than static, the comnet was devoid of a reply to Bosk's call. This time it was a father's voice calling a son across the comnet, "Bosk to Elzetro. Are you there son?"

Whizzbang moved to stand next to his friend, while the seconds ticked by waiting for some sort of reply. Whizzbang could see the stress play itself out across Bosk's face. The normally smiling carefree eyes betrayed the inner anguish and turmoil as Bosk again called, "Son, are you there?"

The constant monotone noise of static again greeted them all across the comnet and it appeared as if the whole of Freehold was holding its breath. Suddenly there was a greater volume of noise followed by, "Dad, it's me!"

The relief was short-lived as Elzetro's stressed high-pitched voice again sounded over the comnet, "Dad, I'm coming in hot! I've got a damaged winglet that's been punctured by sniper fire!

I've been trying to call you for the last couple of minutes but the Scourge are blanketing the area with interference again."

Chapter 4
Plans and Gliding

The blaring of the Freehold Scourge attack-warning siren sounded. It was immediately followed by a burst of local comnet battlespeak from outlying squads that were on scouting duty. Battleframes all around Freehold froze whatever they were doing as they mentally zeroed in on what was important for their specific duties amongst all the comnet chatter.

Looking across at his friends Whizzbang took charge and said, "Guys, the reunion's going to have to wait. It looks like we've some uninvited guests heading our way. Bosk, you, Pyro, Kheldar and DG make sure that Elzetro receives some covering fire as he comes in. He may crash short of Free and your job is to make sure that he gets to safety in one piece."

Bosk did not need any further instructions and neither did any of the others. In a single uniform motion and a roar of jump jets, the four battleframes leapt into the air to get some height so that they could glide to Elzetro's rescue.

Whizzbang signalled to both Selfia and Acheron to follow him as he spoke into the private comnet channel and said, "Whizzbang for Tiny."

Tiny's gruff voice instantly responded, "Tiny here, awaiting instructions."

"We've got company heading our way. How many frames are ready and active in Free right now?"

"We've got fifteen within Free and twelve as a ready reserve to the outlying squads"

"Tiny, have the northern Digging teams checked in as yet?"

"No, they haven't as yet." There was a slight pause and Whizzbang could hear Tiny typing on his wrist-comp. "Whizz. Squad three is long overdue."

Just as he rounded the corner and passed through the archway into the plaza Whizzbang said, "I thought that would be the case. Whose squad was Digging?"

"I think that was Gardner's."

"CT."

With Selfia and Acheron hot on his tail Whizzbang jump jetted down the steps to where Tiny was waiting. Not taking the time to do a more controlled burst from his jets Whizzbang let his servos take the impact as he landed in front of Tiny and his cloud of cigar smoke. Behind Tiny, the newly repaired Freehold ready reserve battleframes that were not on other duties scrambled into position.

Selfia's face was a mask of concern as she said, "Commander, both Acheron and I need to speak to you."

"Selfia, not now."

"It's important."

"As important as the safety of Elzetro and everyone in Freehold."

"No sir."

"Then it will have to wait."

Speaking now to Tiny, Selfia and Acheron Whizzbang said, "I think that Elzetro stumbled across the main Scourge attack force to the south, but from experience, Scourge tactics have always been to attack from two places at once to throw us off our guard. The first will be a feint while the second will be like a hammer fall. My guess is the feint was disrupted by the unexpected arrival of our Digging squads so soon after the recent Freehold assault, and the second by Elzetro's curiosity."

A smile spread across his face as he leaned in to his three friends conspiratorially, "Are you interested in some payback?"

Selfia was the first to speak, "It's been long overdue."

Acheron quickly followed with, "I've been meaning to further test the effects of a few tellurite rounds on Scourge anatomy."

He spat his old cigar from his mouth, and as if by magic, a new freshly lit one materialised in its place. Tiny's voice rumbled, "Time for a new cigar." He then emphasized this plain statement by smashing his Rex's enormous armoured right fist into his left armoured palm.

Whizzbang expected no less enthusiasm from the three battleframes before him. "I need you three to head north with the Freehold reserve to where those thumping squads were mining and get them out of there. My guess is they have been calling for help but like what happened to Elzetro the static has been too strong to get through. With any luck you should have overwhelming odds to deal with the feint."

Whizzbang pressed a few commands on his wrist-comp to bring up a map of the area. Pointing to a position on the map he said, "Next I want you to high tail it back to this position due south of Freehold and above Research Ravine." Pointing again to various locations on his map, Whizzbang continued, "Given Elzetro's last call, the Scourge should be coming up the hillside next to this abandoned village."

Whizzbang looked up from the map. "I need you, the Digging squads and the Free reserve to come over the top of the hill from Research Ravine and give the Scourge a little surprise."

Selfia leaned in to get a better look at the map and said, "While all this is happening, what are you going to be doing Whizz?"

"I will join the squad heading to help Elzetro and going to meet the major Scourge force. Our job will be to delay them as long as possible, until you get into position. If you can, let me know once you're good over the local comnet."

With a puzzled look on his face Acheron said, "So let me get this straight Whizz. You, Bosk, your two sons and a couple of friends are going to delay a hundred or so deadly Scourge veterans. Is that right?"

Slapping Ach on the back of his frame, Whizzbang gave a little chuckle and said, "You've got it in a nutshell Ach, so make sure you don't take too long."

Whizzbang raised his voice for the benefit of everyone in the plaza area. "Your Squad Leaders will brief you with the details of your mission, but I want you to know that I'm confident that each of you will perform your duty with all the zeal and energy that a Concord battleframe pilot can muster. Once this is over I look forward to seeing you at the bar for a round on me."

Whizzbang could hear a few laughs at the last comment and saw many more nods of agreement that they would make sure that he made good on his offer of a round of drinks. It was good seeing them so positive after the recent disaster. He knew that by the end of the day it was likely that a number of frames would be eporting back to Free, and a few may not even make it that far.

Standing with his back completely straight he first saluted his three newly appointed Squad Leaders and then the rest of the battleframes in the plaza. With the clunking of armour the battleframes responded in unison with the salute that would normally be given to those that had passed into the next life. Two fingers slapped armoured chests and then pointed skywards that told Whizzbang he would never be alone.

Whizzbang humbly accepted the honour and stood at attention for another few seconds before wheeling and kicking his jump jets to life to head in the direction of his friends.

Whizzbang left with Selfia's words ringing across the local comnet, "G2G Whizzbang. We'll see you asap."

Elzetro struggled to keep the glider wings activated with a few electro-mechanical hacks that he had developed over the last month from playing "Scourge Wars". He was a natural mechanic, but even for him it was a feat of genius to keep in the air while repairing a critical system. Sweat poured off his face as he simultaneous adjusted inputs to the power relays and dodged Scourge Sniper fire.

Looking back over his shoulder, he could see squads of Scourge moving forward out of the cover of the undergrowth. They poured out like ants from a disturbed nest onto the rocky terrain at the base of the hill. For the past minute, he had been trying to adjust his angle of attack to stretch his glide so that he could soar over the hill without stalling. The distant glow of a sniper barrel told him that he had better abruptly shift his direction to the right or risk being pinned mid-air on a beam of molten energy. The zing of the Sniper beam passed through the space he had just vacated, but the sudden wrenching on the glider's control surfaces, created a number of additional urgent problems for him to address.

As he continued down his glide slope, it became evident that the constant dodging of both Juggernaut plasma discharges and Sniper fire, that he did not have enough height to get all the way back to Freehold. His left winglet was leaking tellurite gas like a sieve, which meant that he really could not risk stretching the glide any further without risking a mid-air explosion. It was a miracle that he was in the air at all.

Hoping beyond hope that he was again out of range of the Scourge jamming signals Elzetro broadcast on the local comnet, "Hey Dad, Bosky, are you there?"

An instant later Bosk replied, "Elzetro, Bosk here, son."

Relief passed through him like a soothing salve as he heard his father's voice. "Dad, I can't stay in the air any longer and I'm not going to get over that hill a click south-south west of Freehold."

Bosk's voice tinged with worry, "CT Elzetro, hang in there the cavalry's on its way. Just do your best to keep heading home."

"CT Dad. I'll be heading in with at least eight Scourge fists on my tail plus more on the way."

"CT Elzetro."

A few seconds later, the left winglet finally gave out. Unlike physical wings that would buckle or rip from an airframe, a battleframe's wings were pure energy. When Elzetro's wing stopped functioning, one minute it was working and the next it vanished. The resulting lift from the right wing without the corresponding balancing lift from the left instantly spun Elzetro in the air and slammed him into the ground on his back. As he hit, dirt and rocks sprayed up all around him. Luckily, with the upward slope of the hill working to his advantage the fall was only about ten feet and his battleframe easily absorbed the impact.

Kicking his servos into action Elzetro leapt out of his impromptu foxhole just as a Scourge sniper beam bore into the earth with a steaming hiss where he had been laying. Glancing back at the enemy below Elzetro viewed two new Snipers bursting out from the jungle undergrowth. They immediately crouched down and lined him up for the kill. At the last possible instant, he kicked in his jump jets to scoot into the air and accelerate forward up the hill. The two ruby red energy beams slammed into the ground to either side of him, showering him with shattered rocks that pinged off his battleframe as he raced up the hillside.

Elzetro allowed himself a brief smile. He was just about out of the frying pan, and hoped he was not into the fire.

His hover-jump up the hill, however brief, finished with the last sputter of his energy drained jets. They would require at least fifteen seconds to recharge. Settling to the ground in a running motion Elzetro's servo assisted legs kept him moving upwards. It felt like the tallest hill in the world but he was almost at the top.

His left leg suddenly gave out and a searing pain enveloped him as he plunged head first onto the ground. The sniper shot had taken him where his calf muscle was enshrouded by his battle armour. Steam and molten metal jetted and burbled out of either end of a pencil wide hole that went through his entire leg. The intensity of the pain continued to escalate as the liquid metal met muscle and bone. It only slightly cooled itself in his quickly cauterising blood.

In his fog of pain, Elzetro crawled his way behind the cover of a small rock. It was agony and the rock seemed so far away. Down below two of the Scourge Snipers were getting ready to fire again.

The comnet crackled with Elzetro's pained voice, "Are you there Dad?"

"I'm coming as fast as I can son."

"I've been hit and I think this is it. I love you Dad. Tell Mum that I did a good job. Arrrrrr….it hurts so bad! Where are those frapping meds!" Elzetro's pain broadcast across the comnet and the normally noisy airwaves suddenly went silent.

Tears streamed down Bosk's face as he pushed his battleframe to the limit to reach his son.

Chapter 5
Selfia in Command

Selfia resorted to hand battle signals to both Tiny and Acheron. One of the reconnaissance Raven's in her squad had reported there were four Scourge fists up ahead along the trail. The hand signals were a standard part of pilot training and used when there was a possibility that even the local comnet was being eavesdropped by the enemy.

For the past twenty minutes, the three Concord squads had rapidly deployed to the north of Freehold in the hunt for the Scourge patrols that had disrupted the various tellurite Digging operations. They needed that tellurite more than ever if they were to survive the next few days. Each of them had assumed their roles as Squad Leaders with four battleframes plus themselves in each. With both Tiny and Acheron more suited to smashing enemies with their fists rather than using their brains, Selfia had naturally assumed the role of squad group leader. No one disagreed that she was the brains and they were the brawn.

Selfia hand signalled for Tiny to hide his squad on the opposite side of the path that the Scourge were about to come down. Both Acheron and her squads remained hidden where they were as the guttural sounds of Scourge speech bit its way through the air towards them from around a corner in the trail.

Selfia swung her rifle off her back and peered through the scope at the oncoming Scourge fists while signalling to the others the number of Scourge moving down the path. "No wonder the thumping crews had bugged out." she thought, "There were close to twenty Scourge marching down the path." She indulged herself in a small smile, "...and towards her ambush".

Kneeling down behind a large rock, Acheron raised an eyebrow when he saw Selfia's hand signal indicate the number of enemies moving towards them. *"All the more to smash,"* he thought to himself.

Other than the crunch of metal shod boots on gravel, all was silent. The local indigenous wildlife had fled either on wing or into secluded burrows, in anticipation of the impending violence. The air almost crackled with tension as the dark armoured, pink eyed warriors moved towards the apex of the trap.

Unexpectedly the lead Scourge Engineer stopped and began sniffing the air, while he looked from side to side. Holding his hand out palm upwards, he uttered a few unintelligible commands and a golden drone began to shimmer and take shape above the tips of his outstretched fingers.

Selfia sighed and said under her breath, "That does it."

She aligned her cross hairs upon the Engineer's forehead and pulled the trigger. One-minute the Scourge's head was on his shoulders and the next it was flying off the path into the rocks beyond. Since the drone was only half materialised it rapidly disintegrated into its component atoms as the Engineer's body fell to the ground dead.

Selfia's impromptu signal unleashed an avalanche of pent up loss, anguish and fury as the Concord pilots took out their retribution upon the Scourge in full force. As the trap sprung shut, the initial barrage violently wrenched apart over half of the Scourge warriors. The intense emotional distress that many of the pilots experienced during the recent battle to save Freehold was carried on every beam, bullet and rocket.

With a roar that would rival even a Juggernaut, Tiny bellowed various obscenities about the Scourge's mothers, as he jetted into the air and landed with a thump into the middle of the path. His mighty chain gun let out a low groan as it disgorged its contents towards one enemy after another.

Acheron had the same stupid grin on his face he always got when he was in battle. He was an intensely focused berserker, which made him one of the most impressive Concord pilots ever to don a battleframe. A torrent of depleted tellurite greeted a Sniper that tried to slink into the undergrowth, tossing it head over heels a number of times until it did not even twitch.

The Scourge were not cowards and they were not stupid. They realised that they were doomed and fought with the recklessness of a rat in a trap, which knows that unless it chews its own leg off it will never be free. Three Juggernauts managed to fire a broadside of plasma at two of Acheron's squad but a quick thinking Concord Rook engineer rapidly deployed a shield, which took the brunt of the attack. Plasma cascaded over the force field in a bright pyrotechnic display and slid to the ground with a bubbling hiss.

A couple of Scourge Shock troopers focused their fire on a Concord Recon in Tiny's squad that shredded the pilot's chest plate. Luckily, a Concord Medic battleframe leapt in and instantly administered booster nanomeds and nanites into both the damaged battleframe and pilot while the two Shock troopers met their maker courtesy of one of Tiny's onslaughts.

The battle was quickly over and it was not long before the last sounds of gunfire could be heard echoing off the surrounding hillsides. Selfia jump-jetted down to her squad to ensure there were not any serious injuries. Incredibly, all her squad members were completely unscathed.

Tilting her head towards her comnet microphone she said, "Squads, report in!"

"We're G2G here Self," Acheron quickly replied.

This was immediately followed by Tiny's deep baritone voice, "Same here, we're G2G as well."

Selfia sighed in relief. Twenty battle hardened Scourge taken out in a few minutes and not an eport or serious problem amongst any of the frames. That was more than she could possibly have hoped.

"Acheron, Tiny, have your squads form up behind me and send your Recons to scout out our flanks just in case we've missed any Scourge friends. We've got to…"

A voice burst over the comnet, interrupting Selfia's order, "Digger crew ready for orders."

"Selfia, Sierra, Alpha, Romeo, four, seven. Who is speaking?" Selfia stated in a level voice.

"Umm, ahh, Gardner, five, five, five, five," replied the deceptively calm voice.

Selfia's brow furrowed, they were unusual call-sign numbers. No time to worry about that now. She glanced at the friend or foe indicator on her wrist-comp and saw with relief that it still flashed green. This meant that Gardner checked out for both voice and digital identity. In the early days of the Alpha Three war, many frames lost their lives to ambushes that were instigated by false Scourge broadcasts. Since then the Blue Sky research team developed a system where every Concord battleframe had an encoded digital under-signal that automatically broadcast when they engaged the comnet. This signal combined with the voice identity check allowed other battleframes to know they were not speaking to a potential Scourge trap. The result was many Scourge ambushing teams ambushed themselves.

"State your position Gardner," Selfia asked.

"We're about half a click north of you and inbound."

Selfia turned to look northward for sign of Gardner as she said, "Who are you speaking for?"

Gardner's voice seemed to be a lot firmer now as his battle training kicked in, "There's six of us here from the digging crews sent out last night. The Scourge swept in here a few hours after we started mining and after a short skirmish we sent our Diggers skyward and high-tailed it out of there. Ever since then we've been trying to get back to Free without tripping over our 'old friends'.

The noise of your little battle and the fact that the static in the comnet had stopped caught our attention."

The digging crews were often some of the toughest most resourceful battleframe pilots in the Concord. They had to be, as they often deliberately placed themselves in harm's way, to mine precious resources and tellurite for a little profit. Diggers were similar to giant drills that extracted resources from the ground and could be called down from the Concord orbiting satellite to any location on Alpha Three. When a Digger commenced mining, the vibrations attracted every creature or Scourge within a click. The principle job of a digging crew was not to operate the fully automated Digger, but to protect it from attack.

Selfia smiled as she said, "CT Gardner. It's good to hear that you guys are all in one piece. I'd appreciate you making it quick as we're on a strict time frame here."

"CT Selfia. See you in thirty seconds."

Placing her scope to her eye Selfia again scanned to the north looking for signs of Gardner and his team as they jump jetted towards her squads. Eight hundred meters away three indigenous Spyderlynx sunned their dark hard outer bodies on a large boulder. Other than the giant crustaceans, there was not any sign of life.

From directly behind her and only about ten meters away Selfia heard, "Hi there."

Selfia instinctively spun and dropped to one knee with her rifle up and ready. Gardner stepped out from behind a rock with his hands held out so she could see them. The soft gloves of his Recon battleframe clearly did not hold any weapons.

"Oh frap! Don't you ever do that to me again Gardner!" she yelled across at him.

Despite his size, Acheron could move with incredible speed and it seemed that he almost materialised beside Selfia when Gardner raised his arms in the universal sign that he meant no harm and said, "Whoa there big fella!"

Then speaking to Selfia he continued, "My team and I had to make sure that it was really you and not some Scourge trap. Frap,

I know all about the sub-signal verification Blue Sky mumbo jumbo. Let me tell you, that when you've been out digging as long as me, there's nothing like checking out a person's skin and eye colour. If you know what I mean."

Selfia lowered her rifle as five more battleframes stepped out from behind various boulders down the path. "CT Gardner but don't ever do that again. I could have blown your head off."

Gardner shrugged and replied, "It's not by chance that we were able to avoid the Scourge patrols you know. Me and my boys know a thing or two about keeping hidden, and doin' sneaky kinds of things."

"While you were sneaking around did you happen to see any more Scourge in the area?"

Gardner smiled and replied, "Only the odd Sniper, scouting ahead of that main group that you put an end to. Me and the boys took care of them. It was that big group of fists that you took out that gave us the willies."

"CT Gardner. I presume that you're the Squad Leader?"

Gardner nodded.

Selfia looked Gardner dead in the eye and said, "Gardner, we've got to get back to just west of Research Ravine and fast. Commander Whizzbang is depending on us, and we have to move double time, if he and a few of his friends are going to make it. You probably haven't heard yet, but a massive number of Scourge are coming through there with the goal of over running Freehold. I need a straight answer. Is your squad fit for duty?"

Indicating his digging squad by pointing with his thumb over his left shoulder, Gardner returned Selfia's stare and replied, "Look, I really don't care for what rank you are Self. Me and my boys have been digging tellurite or running half the night from Scourge patrols." Gardner turned his head to the side and spat out a big wad of chewing tobacco before continuing, "Despite being as tired as all hell we've still got enough gas in the tank for some payback."

"I was hoping that you were going to say that. I need you and your boys to run a scouting screen in front of us. We've got a few Raven's out on the flanks but you'd be mighty handy out front."

Gardner glanced at both Acheron and then said to Tiny, "So you following her?"

Tiny took a long pull on his cigar and breathed out a waft of blue smoke as he calmly rumbled, "Gardner, I know we've split a few pints and a few heads over the years but she's the brains of this outfit. Do you see any of that Scourge squad that's been harassing you alive?"

Gardner grunted in acknowledgement, "CT Tiny." Turning again to Selfia he made a perfunctory salute and said, "Me and the boys are yours to command little Miss Selfia."

Selfia accepted the casual salute with good grace, and said in a voice that carried to the gathered troops around her, "As you all know, the Scourge are about to make a second massive assault on Freehold and all that's between them and our friends and families are six battleframes. I've fought with Commander Whizzbang and Bosk and they're good, very good at killing Scourge, but they're fighting against overwhelming odds and they need our help! We must make for Research Ravine with all haste; the fate of Alpha Three depends on us!"

Selfia turned towards where Gardner had been standing to find that he was gone. He and his squad were already scouting a way ahead for the battleframes to follow. She then turned to both Tiny and Acheron and said, "We're not going to let Whizz and the others down. We've got to push our squads hard and push them fast. Move out!"

Chapter 6
A Father's War

Soaring on the air currents high above the countryside, a lone hawk searched the landscape below for any sign of prey. The instincts of a mother, seeking to find sustenance for its surviving half-starved chick back in its nest, drove it back and forth across the landscape, ignoring its own gnawing gut. A mouse or even a rat would have been a welcome respite for mother and chick but nothing moved below since the world had changed. The hawk extended its wings further to catch an updraft as it searched. Questing and forever looking down for the slightest hint of movement, that would suggest a potential quarry was about to make a quick dash from the safety of its burrow.

Other than a brief gust of wind, that created a swirl of dust nothing of interest moved in the land between the abandoned man-village nestled against the mountains and the two-legged settlement in the cul-de-sac at the end of the ravine. The bird searched the top of a hill that lay between the new and the old two-legs nesting grounds. Then it continued looking southwards down the hillside and on towards the jungle at its base. The lush green foliage sharply contrasted against the randomly strewn rubble that was sadly devoid of any life; not a blade of grass, a shrub or even a rodent could be spied on that hillside.

The hawk remembered seeing, from its lofty position high above the terrain below, flashes of lightning. The sound of thunder and terrifying fire raining down on the hillside time and time again. It was not all bad for sometimes, after such events, the two-legs stopped scurrying back and forth, and this provided a great feast. The meat was not as good as a tasty mouse, but there were never any complaints from the chick in the nest.

Looking more closely, the hawk spied a two-leg. With wings pulled tight, she rapidly descended towards the top of the hill. These strange two-legs had become more common of recent days, and she had learned to avoid them as unnatural clumsy flyers, that typically did not appreciate the joy of being one with the wind. As if confirming her suspicions the two-leg crashed into the ground, flailed around like a newborn hatchling until it began an awkward run up the hillside. A bright red flash streaked across the land from below, clipping the two-leg in the lower leg, and it stumbled and fell onto the ground in a cloud of dust.

It looked like the time of lightning and peals of thunder had returned. This would mean meat for her chick and herself in plenty. Salivating at the thought, the bird spiralled downwards towards the fallen two-leg that was now screaming out in pain.

She should have remembered. Maybe her hunger drove her onwards or the demands of her chick. From her meagre experience, she should have remembered that the purple skinned two-legs, boiling out of the jungle like angry Spyderlynx, were very different from the others. At first glance, they all looked the same to her. She should have remembered that the purple ones took joy in killing her lifelong mate with their red light, as bright as the sun. She should have remembered but now it was too late. As she hovered above the two-leg on the hillside she did not even have the time to register surprise when a red needle beam of energy pierced her heart. Her last dying thought was regret that her chick would now die because its mother forgot.

Panting heavily from his exertions, Bosk was the first member of the squad to reach the top of the hill and look down the bare slope to the jungle below. He watched as a ruby beam lance out and rather than strike his son it strangely punched through a bird in mid-air and burst it into a cloud of charred feathers. The distraction of the bird had likely saved his sons life.

In a single fluid motion, Bosk whipped his Charge rifle out of his back holster and dropped to the ground as he brought the scope up to his eye. He looked at his son lying behind the scant cover of a small rock on the hillside, screaming with the primal desperation of a wounded trapped animal. For Elzetro to live or at the best suffer the trauma of an eport, Bosk would have to be faster and more accurate than he had ever been in his life.

"Frap! I must save my son!" he thought to himself.

In the space of a couple of heartbeats, Bosk identified the key Scourge Sniper targets, lined up the first and pressed the trigger. The blue beam of incandescent energy leapt from the muzzle of his Charge rifle and instantly traversed the distance between it and the Scourge's forehead. Unlike Selfia's bolt-action rifle, his Charge rifle drilled a neat hole about an inch across. Matter directly impacted by the beam vanished in a cloud of super-heated gas while any surrounding material instantly liquefied.

The Scourge's skull held together for a brief second and then vapourised in Bosk's superheated needle of energy. He did not take any notice any of this as he was concentrating with such a ferocious intensity that he paid no heed to the bead of sweat that trickled down the side of his forehead. Timing the shot between heartbeats, he lined up his barrel on the next target and fired.

The vein on the side of his temple pulsed with the blood rushing from each pump of his heart. Like a strange galloping horse, Bosk tuned his inner ear to his internal beating drum, timed his shot and fired again. The training back in Cadet School flowed through his veins and combined with more than twenty years of experience. Less than five seconds had passed and three enemy bodies were in the process of collapsing to the ground.

Through the cold methodical Raven's ritual of his Concord training, a thought broke through to the surface, *"Get up son!"*

Again, Bosk listened to his heart so that he could more accurately fire his rifle in between the beats. Thump, thump. Fire. Thump, thump. Fire. Two heads snapped off enemy shoulders in the space of four heartbeats. He knew that he was pushing the recharging rate of his rifle but decided to risk firing shots that were not a maximum charge anyway.

Ruby lasers raced instantly up the hill towards Elzetro missing him by mere inches. Like a plasma welding torch they clawed at the ground and punched boiling holes in the rocks around him. What seemed like hours, was only seconds and the nanomeds in Elzetro's battleframe flooded his wound and eased some of the pain. At the same time, the battleframe nanites began repairing the hole drilled through the plate armour covering his calf muscle. Without his battleframe and nanomeds Elzetro would have permanently lost his leg. Crawling on all fours, he began to move up the hill. A singular thought raced through his mind, *"Dad, I'm coming!"*

Thump, thump. Fire. Thump, thump. Fire. *"There's too many of them!"* Bosk's mind cried out in desperation.

By this time, rapid assault rifle fire began pinging the rocks around Elzetro and Bosk as Scourge Shock troopers sprayed covering fire up the slope. A few rounds gave a metallic ding as they bounced off Elzetro's back armour. An enemy sniper round tore a hole through a rock just in front of Bosk's position and with a crack the escaping superheated gases split the stone neatly in two.

Bosk was frantic. *"Son, move faster!"*

Bosk ignored all the fire and noise around him even as a few machine gun rounds pinged loudly off his own shoulder armour. Thump, thump. Fire. Thump, thump. Fire. It was almost a routine now but the stress was showing on his face as he blinked away another trickle of sweat that made its way into his eye. Thump, thump. Fire. Thump, thump. Fire.

He was the dealer of death to those that would harm his son. The best training in the Concord was being hyper-focused by a parent's instinct to protect their child. Bosk became something almost supernatural as bolt after bolt of energy leaped from his Charge rifle to disable, maim, slice and tear at those that would try to harm his son.

"Elzetro, keep moving!"

Scourge gunfire rained all around Elzetro. Bullets thudded deep bass notes into the earth in symphonic counter point to the high-pitched pings when they bounced off his back armour. The kinetic energy induced by each impact threatened to push his face back into the earth and render him completely helpless. Elzetro kept crawling towards his father, one foot and hand after another he kept moving towards the safety of the other side of the hillside.

"Dad, I'm coming!"

A squad of three Scourge Slayers with their wicked sharpened teeth barred, raced up the left side of the hill and began cutting back across towards Elzetro as he stumbled his way towards his father. Thump, thump. Fire. Thump, thump. Fire. Thump, thump. Fire. Three shots.

Three bodies.

Ignoring the twitching remains of the Slayers through his scope, Bosk swung his rifle back around to the main body of Scourge. More enemies rushed out from under the trees even while others began climbing the hillside.

Elzetro had spent months studying manuals to become a masterclass battleframe mechanic and he personally knew his own Rook frame from the inside out. Despite his injuries, he was certain that his frame's nanites had managed to repair the connecting systems to his left-boot jump jet. Without both jets operating in tandem a controlled burst could end up with him flopping over the battle field like a rag doll and even possibly dump him down amongst the Scourge.

"Move son! You need to move faster!"

Looking up towards his father's position Elzetro watched him firing one beam after another and never at the same target. It was not necessary. He knew that his father was shooting first at the targets that could reach his position quickest as he crawled his way forward.

"I will get to you Dad!"

Filled with a sense of pride for his father's prowess Elzetro risked firing his jump jets. The rapid acceleration threatened to break his leg in half but miraculously the newly formed armour, bone and sinew held together. Sensing the increased stress on his body, his battleframe automatically injected a cocktail of new counter pain meds that suddenly made the world a much happier place as he raced up to the crest of the slope. Bullets that had previously been bouncing off his battleframe now passed through empty space where he had been only moments ago. He had made it to the other side and temporary safety!

A bellow of malevolent rage rolled like thunder up the hill from a hundred warriors denied their quarry. Like a rushing tide, the mass of Scourge began running towards the hills crest.

"Elzetro was safe!"

As relief for his son's survival swept over him, Bosk looked down at the mass of Scourge coming up the hill. He now fired into the host almost indiscriminately to cause as much chaos as possible. He had never seen so many Scourge in one place before. The most important thing was that his son was safe, at least for the moment.

Chapter 7
Pyro's Dance

Bosk spared a glance up from his scope to see three squat automated turrets materialise out of the air around him. Once in place they immediately began firing at the Scourge climbing the hillside. Piloting his Rook Engineering battleframe DG dropped a health and ammo supply station just behind Bosk on their side of the hill and spoke the clipped staccato of abbreviated Concord battlespeak, "Bosk, supply, six o'clock"

DG's instructions drilled their way into Bosk's consciousness and he rolled backwards towards the supply station just as Kheldar arrived flushing the area around the squad with a massive dose of nanomeds from his Concord BioTech battleframe. The instant health infusion blasted the fatigue of rescuing his son away and he turned towards Elzetro to see the last vestiges of the hole in his armour close over. Sadly, due to the Scourge racing towards them their greetings had to be short.

Turning to Elzetro, Bosk said in battlespeak, "Status"

"G2G"

Bosk and Elzetro smiled back at each other for a second and then went straight back to their grizzly work.

Pyro's battleframe had a significantly slower glide speed than the rest of the squad with the result he was the last man to arrive over Bosk's position. From his vantage point above the battlefield he surveyed Bosk's handiwork with his Charge rifle and saw the huge number of Scourge racing up the hillside towards his squad-mates' position. Rather than joining the others and providing a single position for the Scourge to focus their fire, Pyro decided to do something eminently more dangerous. He would become the second front.

Diving earthwards Pyro pulled in his wings at the last minute, lightly touch down, and then fully introduce himself to the Scourge below. In some ways, introductions were unnecessary because many of the Scourge had heard of Whizzbang's son, while others would never need introducing to anyone else in this life again. Seeing Pyro in action was like watching a ballet dancer leaping, rolling and pirouetting through the air. While a dancer wore a leotard, Pyro wore over half a ton of Concord Dreadnaught battleframe armour and carried a super-heavy chain gun that fully communicated his intentions.

The Blue Sky research team designed the super-heavy chain gun to fire a thousand rounds of depleted tellurite every minute. Despite their every effort, they had never managed to resolve the Newtonian problem: "For every action there is an equal and opposite reaction." Put simply, when first fired, the initial chain gun prototypes dislocated the shoulders of the firer and shoved his back through the testing range door behind him.

Thinking out of the box, the researchers did not solve the gun's recoil problems, they just made the Dreadnaught battleframe massive enough to take the punishment. They massively increased the armour and structural reinforcement, which meant the size of the leg servos, and jump jets, had to compensate for the additional weight. For most pilots this meant a huge reduction in speed and mobility, which essentially turned them into a lumbering gun emplacement. However, as has been suggested, Pyro was not like other pilots.

When he commenced his non-verbal communication with the Scourge below, it was in a language that both sides clearly understood and did not require translating. His chain gun did not rudely thunder its introductions to a fist of five Scourge Slayers, but rather it gently purred like a kitten as it sliced each of them cleanly in half. The seething mass of Scourge received Pyro's message and roared in defiance back at him, even as they continued racing up the hill with all their weapons blazing.

That was when Pyro began to dance. Dodging bullets to the left and then to the right he kicked in his jump jets and half a ton of reinforced battleframe soared into the air. Rather than brace for the gun's recoil he took advantage of the kinetic energy induced by the bullets as it shunted him across the battlefield and away from his friends. In their bloodlust, the Scourge did not realise that they had split into two large groups: The first continued to focus their fire upon Bosk and the rest of the Earthmen. The second group threw everything they had at the "StarBlade's" son leaping about in front of them. The Scourge had given Whizzbang the name "StarBlade" but unknown to them, the StarBlade was not a single person but a squad. Now he had the Scourge's attention, Pyro's challenge was to remain alive.

Scourge bodies lay twitching on the ground in his wake as Pyro lightly landed atop a massive boulder balanced on the crest of the hill. He was three hundred meters away from the others and could see that he had bought them enough time to regroup. Gulping in a lung full of air, bullets once zinged around him. In his dance across the battlefield, his frame had taken an awful pounding with the repairing nanites no longer able to keep up with the damage.

Pyro sighed, it looked as if he was about to experience his first eport. Like his father, he believed that while there was life there was hope and he chose to never give up. It was time to move and move fast and so Pyro kicked in his jets.

Down the slope, a lone Scourge Sniper sited Pyro and pulled the trigger just as his target spun and fired its jump jets. Rather than boring a hole through Pyro's chest the laser burrowed its way through the weakened thigh plating and on out the other side.

"Oh frap, I'm hit," Pyro spluttered across the comnet.

The time that Pyro had bought the rest of the squad had given Kheldar in his BioTech battleframe the time to deal out huge doses of repairing nanites to Bosk, Elzetro and DG. While this was happening, DG deployed one heavy and five anti-personnel auto turrets to do as much damage as possible to the Scourge that were now only twenty meters from the hill's crest.

Pyro soared through the air on his jets even while he felt waves of intense, overwhelming pain in his upper left leg wash over him with each beat of his heart. If it was not for the structural integrity of the Dreadnaught's frame, his weakened leg would have given way and he would have been flipping his way down the other side of the hill on blasted jets.

Pyro glanced down at his leg as he flew through the air and watched with grim detached fascination at the trail of blood pouring from the wound wafting down towards the Scourge below. Thankfully, the pain was rapidly decreasing as his battleframe's medical systems injected swarms of nanomeds to heal the wound while providing a huge dose of Evkon 316 to relieve the pain. The downside of the pain relief was that, for a few crucial seconds, he felt like he was outside his own body as it soared in a straight line over the battlefield. His deadly darting dance ceased and made him an ideal target for the Scourge below. Thankfully, his battleframe automatically adjusted to support his weakened leg and relieve some of the stress.

Down on the ground the Scourge Sniper said uttered a few curses. Having missed the kill shot and he followed the target through his scope. With a rictus smile, his finger tightened on the trigger.

As he glided towards his friends, Whizzbang peered through his Charge riflescope and watched his son's incredibly brave act of putting himself in harm's way. A slight twitch of his energised wings was the only indication that he felt anything as he watched the ruby beam of death slam through Pyro's leg. Whizzbang was in the zone.

The zone was the personification of brutal calmness. It was the essence of being focused with a singular purpose. Every sense hyper-aware and time itself seems to slow as the acceleration of thought becomes ideas and ideas become actions. You can feel the wind moving the hairs on the back of your hand, smell an enemy from a hundred meters away and hear a heart beating around a corner. Being in the zone is what helped Whizzbang and his squad earn the Scourge name "StarBlade".

The Scourge sniper did not stand a chance. The flash of blue light from Whizzbang's Charge rifle streaked past Pyro and penetrated the Sniper's neck, gushing purple blood in all directions. A Shock Trooper met a similar fate just as Whizzbang folded his wings, kicked his jets and reached out to grab Pyro and drag him back down on the far side of the hill to temporary safety. They both hit the ground on their backs and rolled a few times to a stop. A flight instructor had once told Whizzbang, "Any landing you can walk away from is a good landing." This was a good one.

Speaking calmly from within the serenity of the zone, Whizzbang used battlespeak, "Whizzbang to Bosk. Will retrieve Pyro. Retreat, southern building, abandoned village."

Bosk glanced around at DG, Kheldar and Elzetro, who upon hearing the order were already laying down covering fire to guard the quick retreat. He spoke into the comnet, "CT Whizzbang, southern house stat."

Whizzbang knew that he had at the most three seconds before the first wave of Scourge crossed the crest of the hill. They had to move fast and move now. He quickly inspected Pyro's wound and saw that the nanomeds were doing their miraculous work and the armour hole it slowly closing over courtesy of the nanites. A similar healing would be happening to Pyro's leg.

Floating in the emotionless void of the zone he asked, "Pyro, you GTG?"

Pyro's eyes flickered open and his infectious smile split across his face as he said, "Dad, I'm G2G."

Whizzbang looked into Pyro's eyes, studying every feature from within the serenity of the zone. He noted the pulse on his son's temple, viewed the capillaries that paraded across his eye for signs of stress and even listened to the air as it filled Pyro's lungs. Whizzbang thought, "*Yes, he's G2G*"

Whizzbang said, "Pyro, destination southern building village."

"CT Whizz," Pyro replied as he gingerly got to his feet.

Chapter 8
Out of the Frying Pan

Whizzbang dropped a glider pad and indicated for Pyro to go first. Rather than jumping upwards, Pyro propelled himself horizontally so that he remained out of sight of the Scourge just now coming towards the top of the hill. Unlike his son, Whizzbang jumped straight upwards into the air and in one smooth motion, he shouldered his Charge rifle and pulled out his grenade launcher. Lobbing explosive shells along the top of the ridge, he created a smoke screen to help disguise the retreat. Before he lost all his height, Whizzbang turned back down the hillside and glided only a few feet off the ground all the way to the abandoned house.

The house would have been two stories high but was now missing its roof and part of its second story walls. The surrounding debris suggested that it had once formed a section of a crumbling barricade during a previous battle.

The village must have been beautiful once, with its sandstone buildings and spectacular views overlooking the valley up towards Freehold and the ocean to the east. Repeated Scourge incursions and firefights had now turned it into a perpetually smouldering ruin. Even as he arrowed towards the house's open doorway Whizzbang sighed and thought, *"How were they going to get out of this one?"*

Retracting his wings at the last second, he skidded into the house and nearly collided into Bosk in his haste. Panting with exersion he quickly asked, "Report."

Bosk understood that Whizzbang had entered battlespeak and replied similarly, "All frames G2G. DG and Elzetro, turrets strategic locations, second floor. Kheldar, eyes on Scourge."

Whizzbang turned his head on the side to speak more clearly into his comnet, "Kheldar, enemy numbers, type, position."

"Over one hundred Scourge, all types present, stopped on hilltop" Kheldar clipped back.

Bosk sighed in relief and said under his breath, "Frap, I'm glad they've stopped."

Whizzbang turned to Bosk and said, "We must get the Scourge off the top of the hill!"

"What the?"

"Selfia, Acheron and Tiny won't surprise them from Research Ravine if they have the high ground."

"Oh frap!" was Bosk's only reply.

Kheldar's voice cracked over the comnet again, "Scourge porting in artillery."

Now it was Whizzbang's turn to say, "Oh frap!"

Not trusting the half-destroyed stairs Whizzbang jump jetted up to Kheldar's position on the second level. Bosk and Pyro quickly followed. Kheldar pointed up the hill and said, "You can see the tip of the artillery piece forming just to the right of that big boulder.

"CT Kheldar," Whizzbang said as he pulled his Charge rifle out of its shoulder harness and put the riflescope to his eye. He then dialled in maximum magnification to better look at the enemy's position. Sure enough, the Scourge had brought with them a portable TransWarp to teleport in the massive artillery pieces and reinforcements. Once the warping was complete, Whizzbang and his squad would be the first targets. They would not stand a chance.

Dropping back to the urgency of battlespeak Whizzbang turned to Bosk and ordered, "Defend position!" He then pointed to himself and said, "I'll, destroy TransWarp and get Scourge attention!"

Bosk's eyes widened in surprise and he grabbed Whizzbang's arm to stop his friend. Whizzbang turned and forced out a smile. "Bosk, I'll be fine. Someone has to do it. Just keep the door open when I return."

"We'll be ready" Bosk replied sincerely.

Pyro looked at both his father and uncle which a quizzical look on his face. "What's going on Dad?" he asked.

Whizzbang stepped over to his son and embraced him as well as he could in their armour. He whispered, "There's something that I've got to do." Just do what uncle Bosk says and get ready for my return."

Releasing the hug Pyro looked across at this father and said, "Dad?"

With a slight watering of his eyes and catch in his throat Whizzbang smiled and whispered, "Got to go son."

Pyro watched as his father disappeared upwards through the broken roof of the house on flaming jets. He wondered if it was going to be the last time that he saw him. Bosk laid his hand on Pyro's back and said compassionately, "Pyro, if there is one thing that I know about your dad and that he's a survivor. He'll be back. In the meantime, let's get to work. We've got to make this place as defensible as possible."

Whizzbang shot upwards out of the second story of the derelict house with the determination of a battleframe pilot that knew the lives of his squad depended upon his next moves. He had to shut down the TransWarp to stop the artillery from materializing as well as enrage the Scourge so that they would leave the vantage point of the hill. This would then give Selfia and the Freehold reserve the surprise they would need to slam into the right flank and rear of the enemy.

Whizzbang continued to climb by jump jetting from one rocky outcrop to another until he deemed he was high enough to drop down a glider pad. Stepping onto the whirling platform it thrust him vertically into the air and within a few seconds he was high above the landscape looking across at the hillside with the two huge Scourge artillery pieces slowly materialising and becoming more solid every second. It would only be a minute or so and they would be able to fire.

One of the great things about gliding was that it was silent; the downside was you were always losing altitude. Luckily, the Scourge were more concerned about "The StarBlade" down the bottom of the hill and it did not occur to them to look upwards. As he peered through the scope at the TransWarp, Whizzbang thought, "*Why do targets always look so frapping small?*"

Whizzbang knew that he had to wait until the last minute to take his shot so that the full power of his Charge rifle could penetrate the TransWarp's outer casing. The further away the shot the less the intensity of the beam.

A Scourge Sniper watched a flickering shadow travelling over the ground and glanced upwards with curiosity. Its cry of alarm ended in a stifled gurgle as Whizzbang's blue Charge rifle beam punched through its neck. Their fallen comrade and flash of blue light still alerted the rest of the Scourge warriors that they were under attack.

Whizzbang angled further downwards to increase his speed while simultaneously aiming at the TransWarp swinging wildly in his sniper scope. A plasma discharge from a Juggernaut's cannon missed by mere inches and he felt the heat as it passed by his right wing. Bullets raked the sky around him and a few pinged off his armour but his increased speed made him a difficult target to hit as he erratically darted one way and then another in an effort to elude those below. This increased the chance of missing his shot but at least he had a chance. Dead he would have none.

Perspiration poured off his face but once again, Whizzbang found himself in the serenity of the zone. His muscles automatically twitched so that he dodged bullets, his peripheral vision picked out Scourge Snipers that were beginning to get a bead on him and he automatically took evasive action, all the while he zeroed in on the TransWarp.

Down at the house Bosk watched his friend's glide through his scope. He had always known that Whizzbang was good at gliding but now he truly understood just how good he was in the air. He winced as another bolt of plasma passed through a spot just vacated by his friend. It was terrifying, awe inspiring and riveting watching Whizzbang do the impossible. All the while, the clock kept ticking as he continued to lose height.

"Pyro, your father is amazing. I've never seen anything like it," Bosk said in an awed voice while never taking his eye away from the scope. He did not need to see Pyro straighten up as only a proud son could do. Bosk knew in his heart that he had said the right thing. *That young man is going to go places,"* he thought to himself.

The artillery was now almost completely materialised. Whizzbang suddenly pulled up so abruptly that he nearly stalled his wings. The air instantly filled with Scourge weapons fire. The sudden change in his trajectory was all that saved him. With the split second of respite, he carefully aimed at the TransWarp and pressed the firing stud. The blue energy beam leaped from his gun muzzle like some joyous stallion finally let lose in a pasture full of mares.

Within the zone, Whizzbang knew that the shot was perfect. True to his premonition it slammed into the side of the TransWarp, spewing metal fragments in all directions as it flayed open the machine and ravaged its insides. Below him, Whizzbang heard a cry of dismay from the Scourge as the TransWarp's control panel spluttered and winked out. With the receiving TransWarp destroyed, the nearly solid Scourge artillery slowly vanished in the void of subspace.

Without the proper controls governing the TransWarp, its internal tellurite reactor suddenly sprang free from its artificial constraints. With a screeching and wrenching of metal, it went rapidly critical. Like a miniature volcano, the TransWarp erupted upwards and outwards with the simultaneous explosive force of five hundred tellurite infused grenades.

Scourge dove to the left and right to get out of the way of the molten rock and metal fragments flying in all directions. Several caught the full force of the detonation and shattered fist sized shards of plasteel punched through Scourge armour and out the other side leaving a path of death in their wake. All thought of the StarBlade up above was momentarily forgotten in the ensuing confusion.

Thankfully, Whizzbang had sped past the crippled TransWarp and out of range of the exploding reactor. He used the remainder of his height to reach the large boulder that his son Pyro had been standing on recently on the crest of the hill.

De-energising his wings, he slowed his speed with a few quick steps and spun around to survey his handiwork. A small crater with smoke billowing out of it now replaced the TransWarp. Perhaps twenty to thirty Scourge found themselves caught in the blast and the remainder were obviously dazed from the explosive shockwave. Warriors lay moaning on the ground, holding their heads in their clawed hands, obviously in pain. Purple blood oozed from ruptured eardrums caused by the rapid compression of the air as it instantaneously vacated the centre of the explosion. Twisted bodies entwined themselves within mangled machinery in a grotesque parody of creatures from a bygone age.

A barest flicker of a smile intruded into the zone. Now that the artillery was out of commission and at least a quarter of the Scourge incapable of resistance, it was on to stage two of his plan. Looking down at the Scourge, he watched as warriors slowly regain their feet. A number of officers even began to bark out orders to regroup. Whizzbang knew that he had to get the Scourge off that hilltop.

Down below in the house, with the only scope in the group, Bosk continued to relay to the other members of the squad what was happening. Other than a loud bang, the TransWarp explosion was welcome but it did not have any impact upon the squad. Speaking across the local comnet he stated flatly, "Gentlemen, get ready, I believe that it's about to be our turn."

Up on his boulder Whizzbang did the oddest thing. He danced. It was not a dance of death but a dance born out of the joy of still being alive. It was also a dance aimed at taunting the Scourge not more than three hundred meters away.

A Juggernaut was the first to see Whizzbang dancing and his bright pink eyes nearly exploded out of his head with anger. The StarBlade had the audacity to attack them single-handed and then dance afterwards! Like ripples formed by a stone cast into a pond, one Scourge after another turned their heads towards Whizzbang as he danced on the top of the boulder. A powder keg of rage exploded through the Scourge as they screamed their defiance at this mere human. Shouting obscenities in their unspeakable language, they swung their multitude of weapons towards him.

Whizzbang watched bullets from a Shock trooper ricochet off his boulder. He was confident that he now had the Scourge's attention. "Time to go!" he murmured to himself.

Rather than drop a glider pad, Whizzbang triggered his wings and leapt off the boulder. The move caught the Scourge by surprise and he left bullets zinging around the rock in his wake. Racing down the hillside, he gained as much gliding speed as possible by skimming just a few feet off the ground. The now thoroughly berserk Scourge abandoned the hilltop and chased after him as he streaked towards the house and the temporary safety of his friends.

Broadcasting over the local Whizzbang said, "Bosk, mission accomplished, inbound."

"CT, enemy following" replied Bosk.

Once again, Whizzbang sped towards the open doorway. At the last instant, he de-energised his wings and took the few quick steps to slow himself down. Suddenly, massive armoured arms enveloped him as Pyro wrapped him in a half ton bear hug. The zone shattered around him as Whizzbang fervently returned the hug with all the love that a father could have for his son.

Tears of joy streaked down Pyro's face as he said with a trembling voice, "Bosk told us all what you were doing. I'm so proud of you Dad but don't try anything like that without me again!"

Whizzbang let his son go and looked Pyro in the eye as he said with a voice full of emotion and love, "I never want to have to do it again either! I wish we had more time but they're on the way. I love you son, never forget that."

Both father and son smiled at each other and with a quick nod, jump jetted up to where Bosk and the others were watching the Scourge pouring down the hillside towards them. Whizzbang reached out for the calmness of the zone as he settled in next to Bosk. If he was to die today then he could think of no better people to die with – but he would rather live!

Both Bosk and Whizzbang started firing their rifles at the same time. Like two percussionists in an orchestra their timing between heartbeats was impeccable and their aim precise. Despite losing half a dozen of their comrades within the first fifteen seconds, the Scourge still came on.

Elzetro and DG's turrets added their unique high-pitched repeated racket to the deathly masterpiece played by the two Ravens. By now the Scourge had begun returning fire and Kheldar watched as three Juggernaut plasma discharges arced high overhead towards the house. With a controlled voice into the comnet he said, "Inbound plasma. Elzetro shields."

"CT Kheldar."

At the last possible instant, Elzetro energised a temporary shield around all of them, which stopped the first two plasma discharges and greatly reduced the effectiveness of the third. Deep within the zone and lining up yet another Scourge in his cross hairs Whizzbang was only dimly aware of a burning sensation in his foot that was quickly replaced by what felt like a cool salve. The plasma had hit his foot armour and thankfully, Kheldar had deployed a healing zone to nullify its effect.

Ducking from behind a broken wall Pyro unleashed the fury of his mighty cannon at a squad of three Scourge Shock troopers. The stream of bullets sprayed across the ground and bit into armour and flesh as he quickly panned the gun across them and then ducked back out of sight.

Downstairs, DG caught a Scourge Slayer trying to run through the open doorway with a blast of his Lightning gun. Shocking high-energy electricity enveloped the Slayer, paralysing it and finally bursting its heart in a terrifying display.

DG dropped a heavy turret imprint just inside the doorway and the tellurite molecules immediately coalesced in the shape of the automated gun emplacement. The nanites continued to work on the single barrel and it was not long before two long gun barrels were thudding away at the Scourge outside.

A squad of three Shock troopers and a Scourge Engineer managed to clamber onto the roof of an adjoining ruined house. Initially, they began firing indiscriminately through the window opening leading into the area occupied by Whizzbang's squad. They then changed tactics to fire at the dilapidated wall. Bullet holes appeared along the wall and a spray of brick shards and mortar filled the second level with a choking dust.

Kheldar slid along the floor on his stomach to what remained of the window, glancing up every so often at the tottering wall above. Raising his Bio Rifle to the window he pulled the trigger and let off a triple thwump, thwump thwump of bioenergy in the vague direction of the enemy opposite.

"Kheldar, coming," Pyro shouted through the tumult.

"CT, Pyro"

Pyro risked becoming a Scourge target and blasted upwards on his huge jets. Poking his head above the wall, he let his cannon communicate directly with the Scourge on the roof opposite. The discussion was abrupt and verged on the point of being rude, but it would not be necessary to repeat it. Just as quickly, as he rose Pyro cut his jets to drop back to the others with a thud that shook the dilapidated building.

The noise of the gunfire was now more akin to a heavy metal rock concert gone mad than the previous symphony. Whizzbang yelled into the comnet to get above the noise, "Status update!"

"Pyro, G2G!"

"Bosk, G2G!"

"Elzetro, G2G"

"Kheldar…"

Whizzbang's forehead furrowed into a frown, he turned his head just in time to see Kheldar dematerialising. "Kheldar, DG gone," he informed the others.

"eport?" Bosk asked as he picked off one of the Juggernaut's that had fired earlier.

"No, they woke up."

Chapter 9
Fight to the Death

Dropping out of battlespeak Whizzbang said, "DG and Kheldar are from the USA and it's now their morning. It looks like they woke up and are now back home."

The simultaneous reply from the three other pilots was, "Oh frap!"

Whizzbang did not respond to the exclaimation, what more could he say? Instead, he focused on trying to keep them alive. "Elzetro, two turrets pointing down the stairs, stat! Need ammo and nanomed station."

Elzetro responded straightaway by placing a couple of light turret nano-imprints at the top of the stairs. He then recharged the energy on the heavy turret that DG had positioned earlier and dropped an ammo and nanomed station behind Bosk and Whizzbang. They were going to need it.

"Whizz, need help now Pyro!" came Whizzbang's cry over the comnet.

"CT!"

Pyro dashed across to his father and uncle. Bullets and beams flew in all directions ripping and tearing apart what was left of the walls. There were too many Scourge and without DG and Kheldar, the situation was next to hopeless.

Selfia was the first to jump jet up from the Research Ravine facility and look down the hillside. True to his word, Gardner and his squad cleared the way for the main force to quick march their way to the spot designated by Whizzbang. They were all tired and in good spirits but what she saw below took her breath away.

Tiny, Acheron and Gardner ran to reach her side and after taking a long pull on his cigar Tiny summed up what they were all thinking, "Oh frap!"

Scourge bodies littered the landscape with a concentration at the top of the hill. Down near the remnants of a ruined building a firefight of such ferocity was taking place that the very ether seemed to boil with weapons fire. Selfia quickly scanned the battlefield looking for any Concord battleframes and exclaimed in amazement, "They're still alive!"

Turning to Acheron and Tiny she ordered in clipped battlespeak, "Full assault, middle, execute now!"

"Gardner, left flank! Squad, right!"

Twenty pilots swung their battleframes into motion as a cohesive fighting force. They were the penultimate of thousands of years of technological advances in infantry warfare. Anvil, Rex and other heavily armoured frames raced quickly down the slope side jetting a few feet off the ground to better increase their speed. Those with longer-range rifles dropped to the ground and began selecting targets. There were less than forty Scourge attacking the building with over one hundred bodies, cast around the battlefield.

Pyro looked aghast at his father's shredded battleframe. Armour was literally falling off as more and more bullets and beams tore, gouged and ripped at it. He energised his temporary hardened armour and scrambled over to let it take the brunt of the damage. The kinetic energy of the bullets smashing into the shield nearly lifted him off the ground. The respite would only last a few seconds but maybe it was enough time for his father to claw his way across the floor to the supply station that Elzetro had dropped.

Blood seeped from a number of wounds and poured like a river from others where Whizzbang's flesh had been all that had stopped bullet and beam. The zone was all that kept him alive. A lucky shot from a Scourge Sniper had severed his emergency eport device in half so leaving by that method was out of the question. The zone helped him focus his remaining strength to drag himself across the few feet to the supply station, raise his hand and drop it on the hope of renewed life.

Like an electric pulse a wave of nanomeds surged through him, blocking out the pain and repairing his shredded body. Nanites, went to work on his battleframe, mending the many holes and mangled armour. All too soon, the supply station was exhausted.

Whizzbang looked back at his son and instinctively held up a warning hand as two plasma discharges slammed into Pyro's failing shield and tossed him like a rag doll across the floor to the other side of the building. Whizzbang looked across at Bosk who had blood pouring from a gash on his forehead and multiple other wounds were seeping more blood across the floor. He was lying flat on his back now and had pulled his grenade launcher out to lob shells down on the enemy. Whizzbang had not heard Elzetro's turrets for a while but every now and again, he heard the crackle of a Lightning gun.

"What great boys! No, young men. They are the best!"

Suddenly two things happened that caught Whizzbang completely by surprise. The first was the number of bullets flying around them decreased dramatically. The second was not so pleasant. With a groan of agony, the structural integrity of the house gave way.

Walls and floor had more holes than Swiss cheese and they finally crumbled into sandstone and mortar dust. Great beams of wood splintered in a gut wrenching shattering crack as the house died. Whizzbang sadly looked back at his stunned son crumpled on the floor opposite him. *"Was this how it was going to end?" he thought.*

Elzetro's poked his head up into the second level and with a dazed expression on his face he looked across to his father just as the stairs began collapsing behind him. His face suddenly changed to one of astonishment as eighteen inches of tellurite blade from the Scourge Slayer behind him ripped through his shoulder. Elzetro just had the final presence of mind to kick his jets to full burn so that he left his assailant behind in the crumbling building. Flipping end over end he crashed in a pile of dust and blood next to Pyro.

The front wall gave way first, tilting the second floor forward towards the Scourge hordes below. Pyro and Elzetro's slid across the floor and crashed into their fathers in a mess of entwined arms and legs. The outer wall, which they had been using as cover, collapsed and tipped outwards in a crash of broken masonry. Like milk poured from a jug, the four pilots toppled onto the ground within meters of the nearest Scourge.

Bullets, beams and plasma ricocheted in all directions, but instead of it being predominantly red, it was now blue. Whizzbang lay on his back amongst his friends when the sneering evil face of a Scourge Juggernaut lurched into view and a wicked smile spread across its face. Whizzbang had just enough presence of mind left to raise his grenade launcher, shove the end into the Juggernauts maw and pull the trigger. The constrained explosion vaporised the monster's head and a sea of purple blood rained down upon them all.

Selfia watched the house collapse through her scope and saw four, barely recognisable Concord battleframes unceremoniously tipped out of the dying structure. The Scourge were completely surprised at the appearance of her forces and the superior Concord battleframe pilots plied their trade to great affect.

As Selfia picked off targets, she was aware of Tiny and Acheron smashing the centre of the Scourge lines with reckless abandon. Gardner and his squad were like a group of master class surgeons, darting in for a quick kill and ducking back out of the fray to safety. They repeated their tactic over and over.

Looking up from her scope Selfia watched Acheron soar across the field on a flare of jump jets to rescue a sorely pressed Concord Rook pilot from harm. Guns rattled, beams burned and specialist frame capabilities flared like a solar flare where they could do the most harm or protect the most friends.

Finally, it was over and the echo of the last gunshot bounced off the surrounding hills. Selfia stood to her feet and jump jetted down the hill to see if her friends were alive.

"Status?" she inquired over the comnet.

"Acheron G2G, one frame eported."

"Tiny G2G, two frames eported."

"Gardner and squad G2G."

Selfia thought to herself, "Her own squad was G2G. Three pilots! Frap! That was a terrible loss when so few were operational but it was better than she expected."

"Gardner, perimeter, two hundred meters. Kill anything that moves," Selfia ordered.

"Tiny, Acheron perimeter twenty meters. Likewise."

Selfia and two other pilots pulled away a number of Scourge bodies and rubble from around Whizzbang and his unconscious squad. They were a jumble of bodies and limbs. Without moving her friends for fear of causing further injury, Selfia quickly assessed their vitals to confirm that each was barely alive. A mixture of dust, congealed human red and Scourge purple blood caked all four pilots. Each frame had received incredible punishment and was now a poor excuse for elite Concord technology. It was clear that the nanites were completely dormant, exhausted of energy after healing the pilots and their frames. All of them had parts with non-existent armour and in some places, she could see gaping holes with vicious wounds.

Still in the emergency of battlespeak Selfia said, "Medic, stat"

A healing BioTech frame dropped a green tinged regeneration zone around Whizzbang's squad and flooded the area with nanomeds and nanites. Four pairs of eyes sprung widely open and four mouths gasped for air with the shock of the regeneration.

Bosk's voice drifted out from beneath his squad members, "Frap! Can you please get your backside off my face! Whizz, if you so much as think of letting off some gas I'll finish the job the Scourge started!"

Whizzbang extended his hand weakly towards Selfia, "It's good to see you Self. It seems that rescuing me has become quite a habit of yours."

Selfia laughed with relief. "Let's stay clear of making it a habit Whizz," she said as she grabbed his hand and hauled him to his feet. With a smile on her face she continued, "I can't believe what you and your squad accomplished."

"Eh, it's me down here!" Bosk said good-naturedly. The medic helped Bosk to his feet and scanned him with his wrist-comp for any injuries not addressed by the first regeneration.

Both Elzetro and Pyro sat up and propped up their feet wearily on a couple of dead Scourge Juggernauts. Elzetro's wound from the Slayer's knife had closed over without a scar. Other than a receding headache and a multitude of cuts and bruises, Pyro was in reasonable shape.

Pyro turned to Elzetro and said, "Look at those two old timers eh Zeet."

Elzetro chuckled as he said, "Yep, they're our Dads and boy can they fight."

Pyro smiled back and said, "They're our Dads alright."

After ensuring that there was not anything more seriously wrong with any of Whizzbang's squad Selfia reported to Whizzbang on her mission while she watched the miracle of tellurite based nanite technology repair her friends and their battleframes.

"Self, I just noticed a major change?"

"What are you talking about?"

"We didn't go through the compression this time."

With that last statement, Whizzbang woke up

Part III
For Real

Chapter 1
Early Morning Rush

Sitting bolt upright in bed Russell cried out in sudden pain. It was still dark outside and glancing at the clock radio it was 4:30am. His face was a bath of perspiration and his pyjamas were soaked in perspiration.

"Russ, you all right? What's the matter?" Esther said sleepily as she fumbled with the bedside lamp switch. With a click, the lamp flooded the room with a soft light and she looked over at her husband. "Russ! What happened? What's going on?"

A lattice of scars and bruises cover Russell's sweaty body. He also now had a swollen left cheek that was fast becoming purple.

Russell thought, *"Blasted nanomeds didn't finish their work and it looks like I've translated some of the injuries back here."* To Esther he said flatly, "I ache all over but I'm fine Honey. We need to talk, but first I need you to check up on James, while I give Marie and Mihaly a call."

"Russ, its 4:30am!" Esther said in a surprised tone of voice.

"Trust me when I say they'll be awake."

Esther quickly donned her dressing gown and headed up to check on James. Russ reached across for the phone just as it began to ring. Picking it up he said, "Mihaly it's me."

Mihaly replied, "What in the hell just happened Russ? Marie's having kittens!"

"Have you checked up on Alex?"

"I sent Marie off to see if he's OK so that I could give you a call."

"Same here with Esther. It looks like they can pull us into Alpha Three when we go to sleep."

"Tell me something I don't know Russ!"

"The girls aren't going to like this, but if we don't find out what's going on, then at some point we may not come back."

"Agreed. I was wondering if we were going to make it through that last battle."

"You and me both. Mihaly, we need to go to Blue Sky Studios in LA and get to the bottom of this before we have another episode."

"You're kidding me aren't you?"

"No I'm not"

Just then, Esther returned to the bedroom with James in tow. Like his father, he was battered and bruised from head to toe. He had a slight limp caused by a red burn on his left thigh and his eyes had dark rings under them from exhaustion.

Russell looked up at his son, smiled warmly, and quickly winced due to his swollen cheek. Esther disappeared into the bathroom and Russell could hear her rummaging around for the burn cream. It seemed like only a moment ago that she had rubbed the same cream on his own arm. Russell caught James' attention and mouthed the words, "It doesn't hurt too much, just a lot!" James rolled his eyes heavenward and went to his mum to receive her ministrations.

Continuing his conversation with Mihaly, Russell said, "I'm going to drop a note in the support forum and try and call them but we've got to leave now. We can't afford to go to sleep again.

From our last business trip I believe that flight QF93 leaves at 10am."

Mihaly's tone was deadly serious as he said, "That's right. This is for real isn't it?"

"It's as real as it ever gets. While I'm trying to contact Blue Sky, can you see if Kheldar and DG can meet us in Los Angeles? Whatever you do, tell them they can't go to sleep. See you at my place in a couple of hours."

"CT. Bye."

"See ya soon," Russell hung up the phone, donned his dressing gown and headed to the study. After buying their flight tickets, he keyed in the address for the game's support forum.

While he thought about what to write, in the other room, he could hear James arguing with his mother about how hard she was pressing on his burn. Sighing, he rubbed his temples to help relieve some of the stress and tension. Who would have thought that having fun with a game would lead to this?

Hunching over his keyboard Russell was just about to start a new thread in the forum when he felt Esther's hands gently massaging his neck and shoulders. Bending her mouth near his ear Esther whispered, "Don't worry, you'll get to the bottom of it. I know you will."

Slowly turning his desk chair around Russell wrapped his arms around her waist and rested his head against her chest. Esther gently stroked his head, each one almost magically taking the tension away.

Russell tilted his head to look up into her eyes and said, "I don't know what to do or say."

"You'll think of something, you always do."

Pulling gently away, Russell stared lovingly into Esther's eyes. "Thank you, Honey. You always seem to know what to say to keep me going."

"Whatever happens, you look after them Russ. Promise me you'll keep the boys safe."

"I'll do my best."

232

Lost in each other's eyes, the sum over two and half decades of marriage communicated the love they felt for each other. That look said much more than words could ever have conveyed. Finally, Esther gave a small brave smile and said, "I'll go and pack your things and see what our son's got together."

"Thanks again Honey"

Esther stopped at the study door and said, "Remember, you promised and I know you always keep your promises."

The confidence that Esther encouraged in him firmly placed the responsibility of everyone on his shoulders. He could take it, but only because she believed in him.

Turning back to his computer he began to type in the new thread.

> *"Hi all, a group of us have just had an unusual experience while playing Scourge Wars. We felt like we were actually on Alpha Three fighting the Scourge. Has anyone else experienced anything out of the ordinary?"*

Russell paused for a second to consider whether he should mention their experienced in the game while they were asleep. He decided to keep the message sussinct and pressed the "Post" button. He then scanned the forum for Tony who worked as a Blue Sky Community coordinator and known affectionately online as "thaman". After finding him, Russell opened up the "Personal Message" system and typed.

> *Hi Tony, a group of us were playing Scourge Wars last night and we've had some hard to believe experiences. After playing, each of us has actually experienced similar hurts to what we experienced in the game. Not only that, we are all absolutely convinced that we were somehow actually transported to the real Alpha Three. What's going on????*
>
> *We are travelling from Australia and will be at your offices within twenty-four hours to get to the bottom of this. We need answers!*

Regards,
Russell

Russell reviewed his message, clicked the "Send" button and sat back with his eyes closed to think everything through.

Chapter 2
Taxis and Bus Stops

A couple of hours later Mihaly arrived with Alex and Marie in tow. After an emotional good-bye, the boys and their fathers climbed into the waiting taxi and raced to the airport. The plane boarded at 9am and it was not long before they were airborne and on their fourteen hour journey to Los Angeles.

Just before leaving, Esther had thrust a small slip of paper into Russell's hand. Slipping it out of his pocket Russell unfolded it and read, "I believe in you." Smiling he returned it to his pocket, settled back in his seat and dreamed of his wife massaging his shoulders.

With a start, Russell's eyes flew open as the plane's intercom blared with the Captain's voice, "Ladies and gentlemen I hope that you have had an enjoyable and relaxing flight. We are presently thirty minutes from Los Angeles international airport…"

He had fallen asleep and nothing happened this time! Looking across at Bosk and their sons, they were still sleeping soundly. What could he expect? They were all exhausted after the battle and their bodies needed time to recuperate. Why didn't they go to Alpha Three this time? More questions that demanded answers.

The plane landed at 7am Pacific Time and after clearing customs the four jumped into a cab to immediately head to the Blue Sky Studios offices in Orange County. While on the way, Russell pulled his laptop out and linked it to his phone to check for any messages from either Blue Sky or other game players.

The thread he started was full of the usual garbage comments, pictures of cats and complaints about programming bugs.

Bosk asked, "Anything?"

Scanning through the forum posts Russel said, "No one's even hinted that Scourge Wars is anything more than just a game."

"Tony say anything?"

"Hang on, let me check." Russell brought up his personal message folder and found a reply from "thaman". He read it out aloud.

> Hi Whizzbang,
> I'd love to catch up with you while you're in Los Angeles, but sadly its company policy not to meet with any game players. I hope that you enjoy the next patch update that's coming out next week.
> Tony

"You've got to be kidding me," said an exasperated Mihaly. "Do they actually think that we'd come all this way for nothing?"

Russell thought for a moment as he listened to the thumps of the joins in the concrete freeway roll under the taxi's tires. "I think we should go anyway. Do you boys think we should stop trying to find the answers to what we experienced because of Tony's message?"

"No way!" Alex jumped in, "I nearly died on that hillside."

"So did I!" James added. "And we all have the scars to prove that there's something not right."

Bosk nodded and glanced down at his vibrating smart phone, 'DG and Kheldar just texted. They're going to meet us at Blue Sky in about thirty minutes."

With a cheeky grin on his face James said, "At least we've got the old squad together. Nothing can stop us now!"

The mid-morning sun shone pleasantly in the Californian sky, cutting through the brown smog for which Los Angeles was infamous. A gentle breeze blew past the five-story glass office building and rippled the carefully manicured lawn to either side of the entrance pathway in its passing.

Sitting at a bus stop in front of the building, a solitary, elderly gentleman thoughtfully stroked the stubble of his aging beard with one hand while his other rested lightly on the walking cane in his lap. A dark blue and white checked shirt complimented his brown tweed pants with a matching jacket. A navy blue tie completed the ensemble and made him look like the perfect elderly grandfather. The thick black framed glasses that seemed to come from some bygone era further enhanced this impression. Behind the glasses, spectacularly azure blue eyes gazed at the world with a sense of secret mirth at a joke that only he understood.

A young man skateboarded toward the bus stop while he balanced a pile of books under each arm and a pack on his back. He wore faded threadbare blue jeans and a T-shirt that looked like he had worn it the previous day and possibly the night before as well. Despite his dishevelled appearance, the spectacles sitting across the bridge of his nose were the very latest fashion statement for students of southern California, but they did nothing to hide his incredibly blue eyes.

A woman headed towards the bus stop from the opposite direction to the student. She carried a violin case swinging by her side in one hand and in the other a briefcase with a folded music stand sticking out one end. Her black pants, white blouse and neatly pressed jacket complimented her long blond hair. She seemed to be savouring every step as she walked purposefully towards the bus stop. Her amazingly blue eyes darted back and forth, missing nothing along the journey.

The grandfatherly old man acknowledged the student and the musician with a nod as they arrived and took their seats. Taking a deep breath he said, "It's good to feel the sun on my face again."

The student replied to the elderly man, "Wisdom, it is a wondrous simple thing feeling the rays of the spectrum upon the epidermal layers of this covering."

The musician gave a chuckle, "Intellect, why can't you relax with the science lesson and enjoy the moment? Don't you get a sense of wonder at vibrating the very air with your vocal chords rather than using thought?"

Intellect replied with just a hint of mock hurt in his voice to the musician, "But Creativity, I am having fun. It's just my sort of fun." Taking out one of the books from the stack beside him he said, "Can you believe this? They haven't realised the true nature of light yet and are still debating the particle and wave theories!"

Wisdom smiled at the comment. "Intellect, are they ready? Are the probabilities aligned?"

"I have checked and rechecked the permutations and all is as it should be." When Intellect indicated that he had double-checked "something", it was a foregone conclusion that "something" would come to pass.

Wisdom's eons of age seemed to suddenly rest upon his shoulder as he spoke again, "The plan has been in process for over fifty thousand years and it comes down to a yellow taxi delivering one group of individuals to another."

The fact that Creativity chose this time to interject, indicated the gravity of the situation about to take place. "Over the years we have seen failures but the Earth's genetic bloodlines have been preserved. Do you sense if any of them suspect our manipulations?"

"Both the humans from the Concord and Earth are unaware of our existence," Intellect replied as he casually flipped open another book.

With a click of a latch, Creativity opened her violin case to peer lovingly at the instrument. "If they were, it could have seriously damaged the development of both strains. Despite all our care, only one branch on Earth is still viable and the other necessary."

In a husky elderly voice Wisdom replied, "That is well. The time is not yet right for them to know of us. Does Russell suspect who is in this building?"

"He has his suspicions but they are still at the subconscious level," Intellect said.

"And what of the team from Blue Sky?"

"They have been more focused on their mission and this has blinded them to all else."

Creativity absently plucked at the strings on the exposed violin and asked, "What of Kaladon IV? Is there still nothing that can save them?"

Wisdom paused as he remembered the central square and the children enjoying the sunshine before replying. "Nothing can be done. We can't disrupt all that has been accomplished."

Creativity nodded soberly. "I understand but..."

Wisdom placed his arm around Creativity to pull her close and empathise in her loss. "Creativity, there can be no buts."

"I understand but my time seeding the nanite and nanomed technology as Altavia brought me close to the Concord."

Like a father consoling a child, Wisdom absently stroked Creativity's long hair. "You did a masterful job on that assignment and even your death at the hands of the Scourge fitted into the plan."

Creativity sat up and replied, "Thank-you Wisdom. That was the most difficult assignment that I've ever had to undertake."

Wisdom cocked one curious eyebrow behind his spectacles and asked, "Why was that?"

"Because I felt the love of those around me and I wanted to do almost anything to protect them."

Wisdom nodded sagely. "Love is a strong emotion and one that will hopefully drive the heart of the plan."

Intellect flicked his eyes up from his book and with a tinge of excitement in his voice said, "The taxi comes." He then closed the book and with the others, sat expectantly waiting for eons of planning to come to fruition and a yellow taxi door opened to the future.

Chapter 3
The Boardroom

Mark Anders, chief executive officer of Blue Sky Studios balanced his coffee mug in one hand and a notepad in the other as he pushed open the fourth floor boardroom door with his backside. The mid-morning sun streamed in through a wall of windows opposite, providing a view along the main boulevard to a solitary bus stop. The long dark wooden board table sat imposingly in the middle of the room. Twenty high backed, black leather chairs with solid armrests, surrounded the table providing a very corporate feel for such a creative enterprise. His community management team filled the three chairs down the far end and it was clear from their faces that something was not right.

As his Commander entered, Matt looked up from reading a bundle of papers in his hands and hastily tapped the page edges on the table to get them into some semblance of order. Matt's round face sported a full beard and a ready smile that disguised a cunning intelligence that had helped elevate him to the rank of major. However, today he looked distracted and perturbed.

Mark's, rectangular framed glasses did not hide the dark rings under his eyes from lack of sleep. He had been working too hard again. As he walked up he raised an eyebrow at Tony and was about to reprimand him, when Tony quickly removed his feet from the boardroom table. He sat up straight, like some chagrined primary school student.

"Lapses in discipline caused by exhaustion," Mark thought. *"They all needed some time to rest and recharge but that wasn't likely to happen any time soon."*

Mark tiredly took a chair facing the three opposite and said, "OK, report."

Matt cleared his throat and then said, "Well, sir…errrrr…"

"Well what Major?"

"Subject Romeo, Oscar, Sierra, two, Niner is, well, errrrr…, on his way," Matt managed to stammer out.

In a rush, Mark leapt to his feet pushing the high backed chair against the wall behind him with a clunk. Staring Matt straight in the eye and with rising tension in his voice, Mark exclaimed, "Frap! What do you mean he's on his way?"

"Tony received a message from him that he was on his way."

"From Australia? I thought one of the reasons why we picked him was because he was on the other side of this frapping world?"

"Well, errrrrrr…, yes but we didn't expect him to go to the expense of travelling here."

"Tony, when did you find out he was coming?"

"Yesterday morning sir."

Tilting his head back in exasperation Mark swore, "Oh frap! At what point did you three think that it was worthwhile that I be informed that Whizzbang was on his way?" Mark's voice reached the crescendo of his parade ground volume for which he was famous. "You frapping incompetent idiots!"

Tony made the mistake of trying to put up some sort of defence, and said, "We responded as we always have and told him that it was company policy to not meet with players."

"Frap! Tony should know better than to quote policy. This is Whizzbang we're talking about! Not just another game player!"

Tony wilted a little under Mark's verbal tirade, regrouped and mumbled, "What's so special about him?"

Matt glared across at Tony, while Frank sat in silence looking more like a monk contemplating the mysteries of the universe than an enlisted man berated by his commanding officer. Ignoring the three of them, Mark slowly resumed his seat. "Oh frap. Oh frap. Oh frap. What are we going to do?" he murmured to himself as he stared absently out the window at the three people waiting for a bus.

Tony had never seen Mark like this before. He became suddenly very interested in stroking his short-cropped goatee with one hand while he rearranged his baseball cap with the other. This subconscious habit enhanced his comedic appearance as part of his online persona. Right now, it only made him look even more apprehensive.

Coming out of his reverie Frank leaned forward in his seat and spoke for the first time. "Sir, we have to tell him the truth."

Mark spun his chair to face Frank, "What? Tell him the truth? Are you crazy?"

"We've got no choice. Like you said, it's Whizzbang, not to mention Bosk and the others."

Mark leaned his elbows on the table and brought his fingers together in a steeple with his pointers just touching his lips. It helped him think. Too much depended upon this mission. Despite all of their research and innovations, the war was nearly lost and the fate of the entire Concord hung in the balance. Even the near miraculous nano-technology developed by Professor Steinberg's team thirty years ago only delayed the inevitable. Right now, they needed a miracle. They desperately needed something or someone that would dramatically tip the balance in their favour. What they sorely needed were heroes.

Frank cleared his throat and interrupted Mark's contemplation. "Ever since Whizzbang was geno-tagged and we pushed his consciousness out of the game and into the real Alpha Three he and his squad have had a dramatic impact on the war effort. Think of it, the Terrarium's been retaken, Free's defence reorganised and six of them took out over one hundred Scourge single handed! We need these guys!"

Tony added, "Sir, I get on really well with Whizzbang. When we met recently at a games conference in Melbourne, I made sure that we really appreciated him. After a few beers, he was like clay in my hands. Let me talk with him."

"Whizzbang didn't drink the beer Tony," Matt said flatly, "but we did make a positive impression."

Tony turned towards Matt with a puzzled expression and asked, "Really? He didn't drink beer? He's Australian isn't he?"

Mark slammed his hand onto the dark red timber tabletop, "That's one of the reasons why he's the best! He's so sure of himself that he's able to say no to a beer when his entire culture says 'yes'! Frank is right, we need him in Alpha Three and we need him in actual. The trick is how do we convince him?"

Matt said, "I think Frank's right. We need to lay all the cards on the table and tell him the truth."

Mark gave a stressed laugh and mimicked an introduction, "Hi Russ, good to meet you and your team. I hope you enjoyed playing Scourge Wars. By the way, via the game we've now geno-tagged your genetic code so that we can drag your consciousness at any time into the real Alpha Three. I know that this puts you and your friends at a severe risk and that we didn't ask for your permission but hey, we're desperate. I hope that you don't mind but would you like to take a little interstellar journey? You can trust us…"

Frank reiterated to Mark, "Sir, we have to tell him the truth. They all have to know what the stakes are and why they've been fighting."

"The truth? Frank, we stole the man's consciousness and put his son and friends at risk!"

Tony had a little twinkle in his eye as he said, "I think we're missing something really important here. Remember the last time we dragged him into Alpha Three. He and his friends knew they were being manipulated. That's why they're here. Despite what we did, they fought the Scourge like no one else can or ever has. That's even with the time delay of sending their consciousness through subspace."

Matt continued from where Tony left off, "That's right! The reason why they're here is to find out what's going on. They're not trying to run away. Mark, these guys have been to hell and back already. They've been ripped out of their own world, fighting aliens, and they're here because they're curious!"

"So what you three are suggesting is that we're dealing with a group of people that aren't afraid and just want answers to questions?"

From three mouths came the loud reply, "Yes!"

Mark looked a little bewildered as he said, "What are they made of? They've faced horrors and death and they're just curious. We need these guys!"

Russell paid the taxi driver while the others retrieved the bags from the trunk. There was not much to get out of the back, as they were all travelling with only carry-on luggage.

"Where'd Kheldar and DG say they'd meet us?" Russell asked Mihaly.

"Just inside the lobby."

Picking his bags up off the sidewalk Russell glanced over to see three people staring at him from the bus stop down the road. "Did you see those guys at the bus stop?" he asked Mihaly.

"Yeah, it's California. They're probably just a bunch of weirdoes watching a few foreigners get out of a taxi."

Russell laughed. After all the stress and strain of the recent days, it was a good sound. "You're probably right."

The four of them pulled and carried their luggage up the path towards the imposing black glass building of the Blue Sky Studios headquarters. Upon stepping through the sliding glass, doors Russell heard a voice in a strong American accent to his left say, "Well you guys took your sweet time getting here!"

Smiling widely Russell walked up to his friend John and said, "So how are you going Kheldar?"

Shaking Russell's hand vigorously John replied, "I'm sure glad to see you guys."

"So am I," DG said as he walked over to the group from the direction of the washrooms.

Because they had been playing together for so long, introductions were almost unnecessary, although it was the first time Mihaly and their sons had actually met John and Mike.

Laughing John said, "Pyro, I've got to say that you do a great party dance, particularly with...," as he feigned mock forgetfulness, "...what was her name again?"

Pyro's face went red with embarrassment. "Wouldn't you like to know, Kheldar?"

"Hey!" John feigned being hurt, "I'm a married man. None of that for me thanks." Getting a bit more serious he continued, "Russ, trust me when I say we were as surprised as you must have been, when we vanished from the battle and woke up in our beds."

Mike nodded in agreement. "The last thing I remember was dropping a few turrets down and poof I was in bed lying with the covers pulled up under my chin. It was crazy."

"Selfia, Acheron and Tiny arrived just in a nick of time to save us. If it wasn't for them I think we would have each suffered at least an eport or more likely worse."

"Oh man, that's not good."

"That's one of the reasons why we're here." Russell lifted the bandage on his arm to show John and Mike his wound, "Each of us has had a physical reaction to the game. We need to know how and why this was done." Dropping the bandage back into place he continued, "We also need to know how we were transported back to Alpha Three when we were asleep. Speaking of which how are you two going?"

Mike answered, "I haven't slept a wink in the last twenty-four hours. It's the wonders of energy drinks combined with coffee and then more energy drinks."

"You're telling me DG. I haven't had a wink in over two days," John replied.

Bosk whispered conspiratorially, "I hate to break up the reunion but there's someone coming over towards us."

246

A slim young woman twenty-two years old with long blond hair in high heels walked directly up to them from the other end of the lobby. She was stunning in her navy blue skirt and matching jacket.

John leaned across to whisper in James' ear, "Put your tongue back in your mouth."

Alex gave a little snigger and John said, "You too, Elzetro."

Standing before them the young woman put out her hand and in a friendly welcoming voice said, "Hello, you must be Russell and Mihaly. My name's Crystal." Turning to the others, she greeted each of them by name, shook their hands, and then continued speaking as if everything was completely normal, "Mark and the others have been expecting you and are waiting in the boardroom. If you would like to follow me please."

Picking up their belongings Russell and the others looked at each other questioningly. Then they shrugged their shoulders and followed Crystal to the elevators.

Russell asked, "Crystal, how long have you been working at Blue Sky?"

Crystal replied in her clear eloquent voice, "Ever since I first arrived."

"What do you mean by that?"

The elevator arrived and Crystal pushed the fourth floor button and pressed her pass-key against a metal plate as they all squeezed in. "Arrived from where? I can detect an odd accent. What country are you from?"

Crystal gave a little laugh and replied, "You could say that."

Russell looked questioningly across at Mihaly, who's face mirrored his own question.

The elevator gave a momentary whirring of its motors and a few moments later the doors slid open revealing a hive of activity. Technicians and engineers were running this way and that while others were staring at control screens filled with numbers and gauges. In the centre of the chaos was a room-sized black box with what looked like hoses and wire sprouting in complete disorder out of it. Every now and then, a jet of steam would suddenly burst with a hiss from an overhead pipe dousing the box in a cloud of white vapour.

"This way please," Crystal instructed formally.

Russell and the others mutely followed Crystal to the right and through a door into a more conventional modern office area. They passed about thirty cubicles equipped with desks, chairs and computers before coming to a door marked with a sign that read, "Boardroom."

Crystal turned and said sweetly but firmly, "Here you are gentlemen. Please go on in and if there is anything that I can get for you, don't hesitate to ask. Anyone will know how to reach me."

Before Russell could say anything Crystal walked off in her very formal manner and disappeared behind a grey office partition down the narrow hallway from where they had just come.

Russell turned the handle on the boardroom door and gave it a gentle shove while he and the others juggled in with their luggage. At the far end of the large boardroom table, four smiling faces beamed up at them.

Tony jumped out of his seat with a broad smile on his face. "Hey Russ! It's great to see you again. It's been a while since the games conference in Melbourne my friend." As he reached for Russell's luggage he continued, "Here, let me help you with that."

"Thanks Tony, it's been a long flight."

After they had all taken their seats and the introductions were completed, Russell could not help stifling a yawn. The long journey, combined with the high backed, black leather chairs made things just a little too comfortable.

Tony continued the friendly banter. "Russ, I'm really sorry about the email reply. It's company policy not to allow anyone to our offices."

Russell let out a sigh. He hated jetlag. It had been a long day and it was only the morning. "Don't worry about it Tony. We're all here now."

Mark sized up the men opposite him and then asked Russell, "Tired?"

Russell nodded. "Although we slept on the plane it's never proper rest and before that, well, that's a subject for our discussions."

"So how can we help you?" Mark asked. "You guys seem to have travelled a long way to talk with us face to face."

Russell gripped the armrests of his chair a little tighter before saying, "You can start by telling us who you really are. Not your cover stories but your real stories."

Mark arced one eyebrow up at the accusation. He was not used to accusations about anything and it set his teeth a little on edge. Staring straight at Russell he said, "So who do you think we are?"

Before Russell could answer James interrupted, "I know who you are." This time it was Russell's turn to be a little surprised. James continued, "You're from the Concord. My guess is you're at least at the Commander level to be running an outfit like this. The question I have is why get us involved."

At that point Alex jumped in, "I think we were meant to see that machine out there when we came in. There is one thing I have learned from playing Scourge Wars and that's, power systems. Until the last few days I used to think it was all in my imagination but coming in here I saw the real thing with my own eyes."

Both Russell and Mihaly smiled as their sons verbalised what they were all thinking. Russell said, "You let us see that device and you're planning on telling us everything aren't you."

Frank looked across at Mark, "I told you these guys were smart."

Mark wrapped his fingers on the table a few times in deep thought and finally he seemed to come to a decision. "My name is Commander Mark Anders of the Concord Research Division Blue Sky and you're right young man." Indicating James, "These gentlemen report to me." Smiling now at Alex, "I was wondering what you'd make of the one and only interstellar TransWarp."

Alex laughed aloud and said, "I knew it! I can spot Concord technology a mile away!"

"Alex, well done but shhhhh," whispered his father.

John leaned across to Mike and said, "Man are we in for it now."

Mike replied under his breath, "I don't think we've seen anything yet."

Commander Anders assumed his authority like an old, well-loved coat, "Yes, we're not of this world but our genetic code is almost the same as yours. Some of our best scientists have even suggested that we have similar ancestry. After being on Earth for the past few years I do know we have very similar values as you."

For someone who was addressing the first alien any Earthling had encountered Russell spoke with a very calm voice, "So let me ask you your question. Why are we here?"

The Commander looked back at Russell and tilted his head in acknowledgement of the mild riposte. "Now that's a long story but...," he checked his watch, "I think we have time for a little history lesson."

"About one hundred years ago a young engineering student on our home world of Kaladon IV discovered a new substance that he later named tellurite. Tellurite became a foundation stone for a myriad of future technologies. To put it in context, tellurite is as important as the invention of the wheel or writing. It was an amazing moment in our history and it completely transformed Concord society. You know tellurite from the Scourge Wars but this was the real thing.

The Concord saw explosive technological growth and wonders became commonplace. About twenty years after the discovery, a culmination of multiple scientific breakthroughs allowed us to build the *Byron*, our first tellurite powered interstellar vessel and named after the scientist Byron Blake who discovered tellurite.

It was a golden age for the Concord. We constructed greater numbers of exploration vessels, planted colonies, and eliminated many of the ailments that currently afflict your own planet. We revelled in our youthful pride. Frap! Even the stars weren't beyond our grasp!

In all, we'd managed to colonise around forty-three worlds and not once did we encounter another sentient being. That all changed around thirty-five of your years ago, when the exploration vessel, *Kerwin,* headed into uncharted space and was never heard from again. In all our years of voyaging it was the first time that a vessel had vanished. The leadership at that time put it down to 'lost – unknown cause' and we continued on our merry way.

Several years later, the *Albion,* encountered a ship in the beta quadrant that was completely alien to us. The crew immediately sent a subspace signal back to Kaladon to fully document and record the first contact. Think of it as a video being sent back of the first time we'd met another space faring race."

Mark took a moment to look forlornly at his empty coffee mug. He continued the story while he got up from his seat and poured a glass of water from the pitcher on a side table by the door.

"The *Albion* broadcast welcoming messages on all frequencies and the response was silence until the ship was within a couple of kilometres. We later knew that the strange ship was closing within range so that it couldn't miss. The rest is history. The Scourge vessel opened its gun ports and blew the *Albion* out of the ether. There was nothing left of her or the crew other than the subspace signal of the first firing salvo tearing the ship apart."

Russell looked at the three other Concord men and he could see the impact Mark's story had on them. Staring at the table Matt mumbled, "My father was Captain of the *Albion.* It was his first command. I remember him kissing my mother and I goodbye the morning he set off for his six-week tour. He was so excited and told me that one day I would captain my own ship."

Mark resumed his seat and continued his tale, "We've been fighting ever since that first encounter. We retrofitted our vessels with defensive and offensive capabilities as quickly as possible. Despite our best efforts, slowly but surely we lost one colony after another. Procyon, Religus and Sendranon fell in quick succession. My younger brother died at the battle of Althanus. He managed to save his crew but at the cost of his own life. Everyone around this table has lost someone in the war.

We only have a handful of worlds left and we're desperately short of tellurite. Without tellurite, the war will be over and the slaughter would begin. It was only by chance that we stumbled upon Alpha Three. You see, the planet is rich in tellurite and rare minerals that would potentially give us the resources to drive the Scourge back.

The Scourge Wars game roughly reflected our own history and as you're aware our first warship from Alpha Three was the *Dreadlight*. According to the game, during its maiden voyage it crashed back into Alpha Three and brought with it the accursed Barrier. What you don't know is the *Dreadlight* was attacked as it was just leaving the atmosphere where its shielding and manoeuvring capabilities were compromised.

The Scourge had managed to find Alpha Three and as well as downing the *Dreadlight* they were the ones that brought the Barrier to prevent us from getting access to the bulk of the tellurite reserves. What they didn't expect was that Concord researchers would develop a means to push back the Barrier with modified repulsor beams. We then sent in pilots to secure the beachhead at Freehold."

Russell settled further back in his chair. "Mark, is the Barrier really as deadly as it is in the game?"

Mark ignored Russell's lack of not addressing him by his rank and replied, "Yes, nothing human survives in the Barrier. It's an energy field that appears to mess with the chemistry of the brain and cause death within about ten seconds."

Russell nodded thoughtfully and was about to ask another question when Mike leaned forward and asked one of his own. "So how did you find Earth?"

"Mike, you need to appreciate that we are fighting for the survival of our entire species. The only reason we were out this far on the edge of the galaxy was that we were trying to find a world safe from the war. It was only by coincidence that the same ship that discovered Alpha Three also discovered Earth in the very next system it surveyed. We're currently only four point three light years away from Alpha Three. In fact, I believe that Alpha Three is in what you call the Alpha Centauri system."

Mihaly leaned back in his chair and subconsciously slipped into Scourge Wars speak, "Oh frap! The Scourge are our next door neighbours!"

Chapter 4
Decisions

Russell stared at the ceiling while letting out a slow whistle. "So it's only a matter of time before they find Earth. So why'd you do this whole Scourge Wars game charade?"

Mark replied, "That was a stroke of creative genius borne out of necessity. Russell, as I said before we're losing the war. A brilliant young researcher, Oscar Intellius, suggested to Professor Steinberg that the Earth would be an ideal recruiting ground for battleframe pilots.

"Is that the same Steinberg from the game?"

"No, it was his son. The whole back story from the game is actually derived from real events though."

"Ray and Thomas were real?"

Matt interrupted. "Yes. They're regarded as heroes for what they did."

Mihaly said, "But they were us in the game."

Matt replied, "To make the game more engaging we changed the names of the characters to your own. The characters themselves were the first real battleframe pilots."

Whizzbang asked Matt, "How about Altavia? Was she real and did she die?"

"Yes and yes. History tells us that Altavia was gorgeous and amazingly intelligent but the one thing everyone remembers about her was her blue eyes. We represented that in the game as best we could."

James leaned over to Alex, "I think they did too good a job on her."

Alex sniggered, "Seems to me the art department managed to get all her curves in the right spots."

Russell glared at the two boys before asking Mark, "So we've essentially been playing the history of the Concord."

"Yes. We wanted you to experience our history not just learn about it." Mark's voice took on a heightened level of intensity as he leaned forward in his seat. "Russell, we're desperate for battleframe pilots and the people of Earth still believe they're the only sentient race in the galaxy. Could you imagine trying to convince your governments that the Scourge are real? It would take years of negotiations with an uncertain outcome and we just don't have the time."

Russell nodded in understanding.

"The Scourge Wars game was devised to find the best potential candidates for recruitment. The problem is the last Scourge push, where we nearly lost Freehold, made us desperate, and forced us to accelerate the program. Each of you were identified as the best of the best and so we geno-tagged you."

"Geno-tagged?" asked Russell.

Tony entered the discussion and said, "Geno-tagging is a very new technology where we tag an individual's genetic markers via the game. We can then TransWarp their consciousness into a real battleframe and build a facsimile of the pilot from malleable energy. There's a lot of technology involved that I don't really understand, but it allowed us to send all your minds to Alpha Three to help stop the latest Scourge attacks."

Russell said, "So that explains why we sometimes felt like we were being squeezed out of a tube of toothpaste. I presume that you can then grab us whenever we're asleep?"

"Yes, once geno-tagged we don't have to wait for you to play the game anymore. You just need to be completely relaxed or asleep."

"Let me guess for a moment Tony. If we happen to be travelling quickly, say in a plane, then you can't reach us. Is that right?"

"Yes, that's why we couldn't grab you when you were flying here from Australia."

"So Mark, was the whole back story in the game for Whizzbang real?"

Mark was a little surprised by the question. "It's a little of all three of us. Tony lost his parents in a colony attack and Gasp is his real adopted father."

"I'm sorry for your loss Tony."

"It was a long time ago Russell." Chuckling to himself he continued, "I just wish that I was as smart as the eighteen year old Whizzbang that was being assessed."

"Don't we all." Russell stifled a yawn. "So all of the background stories for our game characters are from the lives of real people?"

Mark sombrely replied, "Every one of them."

"So why did the Scourge appear to be getting smarter?"

"That's an easy one to answer. As we tested potential game pilots we had to ramp up the difficulty level until we finally risked sending their consciousness to Alpha Three."

Russell nodded in understanding, "Is that when we had a feeling of vertigo in our last session?"

"Both yes and no. As Tony said, geno-tagging is a very new technology and the squeezing effect occurred when we had a disruption in the subspace signal that sent your consciousness across the light years. If we didn't have a problem with the signal you wouldn't have noticed that you were on Alpha Three."

"Mark, one of the reasons why we're here is because we were noticing."

"I think we were more than just noticing," Bosk interjected.

Mark smiled at the obvious fact. "It's clear that we naively thought that you wouldn't notice," he said.

Russell asked, "So why don't you send more of these facsimile battleframes to Alpha Three?"

"We'd like to but as you've already experienced, there appear to be some downsides."

"And they are?"

Mark hesitated uncertainly before making the decision to continue, "Other than the technical issues, the biggest problem is that the pilot's still receive injuries and potentially death."

Silence filled the room and the atmosphere instantly became frosty. They were all aware of being hurt while playing the game but none of them had considered death as a possibility. Russell's cold blue eyes pinned Mark to his chair and with a voice like a cracking whip asked, "Are you telling us that you put all of our lives at risk?"

Mark hung his head in embarrassment and answered, "Yes we did."

"What gave you the right to do this!"

Mark snapped his head back up to glare back at Russell, "Desperation! We had nowhere else to turn to!" He took a couple of deep breaths to calm himself down and then implored, "Whizz, I mean Russell, we're almost all that's left of our entire civilisation and then we discovered all of you. I know there's no excuse for what we did…"

Ever the peacemaker, Mike leaned forward in his chair and interrupted, "Russ, I know what they did was wrong but we probably would've done the same thing in their circumstances. We're all still here aren't we?"

"Yes Mike, we're still alive."

Frank said contritely, "Russ, we're all sorry for what we did. As the Commander said, it was inexcusable. We should have been up front with you from the beginning." His apology and soothing words acted like a healing balm, releasing the tension in the room.

He then looked at each of the men opposite him, "Please accept our apology for what we did."

Russell's initial anger at the revelation of their danger began to subside as he considered Mark and Frank's words. Despite his trepidations, he found himself beginning to like the four Concord men. Assuming what they said was true, they struck him as honest men thrust into an impossible situation. He leaned back thoughtfully in his chair, was just about to ask another question, and then changed his mind.

Frank studied Russell and the others. Their reaction so far and ability to cope with meeting aliens from another planet, that had effectively hijacked them, was incredible. Most people would have been a blubbering mess by now. "*Frap we've done the wrong thing by these men,*" he thought dejectedly.

Mark said, "We all agree with what Frank just said. As the commanding officer of this mission, please accept the apology of the Concord. What we did was wrong." He paused to gauge the effect of the apology before continuing, "Russ, without Alpha Three's tellurite reserves the last remaining worlds don't stand a chance. You and your team have already bought us some time against the current invasion." Looking across at each member of Russell's squad Mark's voice cracked as he pleaded, "We need your help."

Russell leaned forward onto the table, the weight of Mark's words resting heavily on his shoulders. "Mark, I appreciate that the Concord is in desperate circumstances but I'm sure that you'd agree that we need to do what is best for our own world and families."

"Of course," Mark replied sombrely. He was about to say something else but thought better of it. These men needed some time to digest what they had only just learned.

Russell placed his head in his hands as he absently stared down at the table. The table's fine red stained wooden grain weaved in and out in ever expanding circular patterns that seemed to reflect the intricacies of his own thoughts.

A strained silence descended upon the room as each person retreated into their own thoughts on the decision at hand. Unbeknown to Russell, the fate of the entire galaxy depended upon what he would decide. Several minutes went by as he contemplated all the possible options. Wearily he looked up and met Mihaly's eyes. Years of friendship and trust conveyed exactly what each other was thinking. Mihaly give a small nod of his head and that simple exchange was all that Russell needed to know that he had his friend's full support.

Finally, Russell asked, "What do you think they'll say?" It was not necessary to articulate that he was talking about both their wives and daughters.

Mihaly responded with a wan smile, "Russ, by the sounds of it they're going to be the least of our problems."

"I know," Russell replied in voice full of concern.

Mark nervously looked across at each of his men. He subtly shook his head in the negative when it looked like Tony was about to say something. So much depended on these Earthmen and yet he needed to let them make their own decision.

Russell breathed in deeply and slowly let his breath out to help calm the chaotic thoughts racing through his mind. Finally, as if a switch flicked to a new position he reached an internal decision point. Turning to Mark he asked, "That box we saw with all of the tubes sticking out of it is a way for us to get to Alpha Three. Isn't it?"

Mark carefully worded his reply so as not to accidently dissuade the men opposite from helping them. "Yes, it's been powering up over the last twenty-three days and it should be ready in about six more. It takes a lot of energy to send something four point three light years to Alpha Three."

James looked across at his father and asked, "Dad, are you thinking what I think you're thinking?"

"As Mark outlined, we don't actually have a choice," Russell answered with a grim smile, "The Scourge are next door and it's only a matter of time before they discover Earth."

"What about Mum and the girls? They're not going to like this."

Russell grimaced, "I know," and then looking across at Mark he said, "We'll let them know when it's safe and maybe then they can come and join us."

Across the other side of the table, Mark nodded slowly in tacit agreement that he would do whatever he could to reunite their families. Mark cleared his voice of the tension of the last few minutes and said, "There is something else that you should know. Warping four point three light years to Alpha Three is likely to be an uncomfortable experience."

"What do you mean?"

"I've heard that it's like an eport but for a lot longer."

"Since we've never actually experienced an eport before I'll work under the assumption that we'll cope."

This time it was Mark that looked thoughtful before he said, "An interesting thing is that I think that you may be right. When we geno-tagged you, we were able to process your genetic make-up. It appears that each of you have some unusual and extremely rare markers."

"What do you mean?"

"The genetic markers are similar to those found in pilots that are able to mentally withstand the rigours of an eport. There's only been a handful of pilots in the whole of the Concord that exhibited this trait."

"Is what you're saying is that we're one of the few groups that could possibly make the journey?"

"That's exactly what I'm saying." Mark indicated the other members of his team, "Any of us wouldn't survive the trip but each of you most certainly can."

"That's good to hear."

Mark pondered aloud, "It's almost like you've each been pre-selected for this task." Chuckling at the absurdity of his own thinking, he said, "Never mind, that was a stupid thing to say."

Mark Anders never realised just how close he came to unlocking one of the greatest secrets of the galaxy.

Russell said, "Mark, can we have some time to ourselves?"

"Of course."

Mark signalled to the other Concord members and he followed them out of the room. Over the next hour the Earthmen debated the pros and cons of what they were about to get themselves into. Each member was given the opportunity to gracefully back-out. Finally, Russell called Mark and the Concord team back into the boardroom and said, "We're in."

Mark held out his hand and said, "Welcome to the Concord Whizzbang."

"And so it is done," Wisdom spoke out aloud.

Creativity stared upwards towards the sun, "Yes, but it's just the beginning"

"When you were Altavia, all those years ago, the Concord didn't need much of a push did they?" Intellect asked Creativity.

Creativity's faced blossomed into a smile as she said, "When I energised Altavia's form I nudged Professor Steinberg's research here and there. At the time, the Concord was desperately searching for fresh ideas. The Earthmen and the Concord are the only hope for the innumerable civilisations across the galaxy. Without them, system after system will succumb to the enemy and fall into chaos." She bent down to make sure that her violin and music stand were secure in their cases before continuing, "When will we reveal ourselves to them?"

Wisdom put his hand to his chin in imitation of someone pondering thoughtfully. "Not for some time yet. As you know, they have a few surprises awaiting them in Alpha Three that they have to sort through first." He then stood and looked back up at the boardroom windows. "I don't know about you but I think that I'm going to miss the bus and take a walk in the sunshine."

Intellect and Creativity looked at each other and nodded. With that, the odd companions shuffled, skateboarded and walked down the boulevard with a feeling that the plans of thousands of years were firmly set in motion.

Chapter 5
Goodbyes and Enemies

After speaking to their wives, both Russell and Mihaly's families boarded the next plane to Los Angeles to join their husbands and fathers. Although there were many tears shed there was also a sense of resignation that they were all fighting for the sake of humanity. The husbands and sons on Alpha Three and the wives and daughters back on Earth.

The following six days passed in a blur of being briefed on Concord technology and getting to know the Blue Sky team. Overall, Whizzbang was impressed with the discipline and openness of each operative.

During one of their many discussions with Mark and the senior staff, they decided that it would be best to retain their game persona once they arrived on Alpha Three. Since they had all been geno-tagged the Concord personnel stationed on Alpha Three all knew them as Whizzbang and Bosk and not Russell and Mihaly.

The night before he left, Russell and Esther said goodnight to their girls and then retired to bed in the adjoining hotel room.

Russell could not help wondering if it was the last time he would say goodnight to Rose and Michelle. Both girls were in their late teens and old enough to understand their father's decision to go to Alpha Three but it didn't mean that they liked it. The tears flowed and the hugs seemed especially tight. He was so proud of the both of them. When he looked into their blue eyes, he felt both their pride and hurt reflected towards him.

After climbing into bed Esther lay with her head propped up on her pillow. "Russ, tell me you're going to be coming back."

Russell turned on his side to look into Esther's eyes. "Honey, I promise that I'll come back. Nothing will keep away from you."

"I really mean it Russ."

"So do I."

Determination gave way to raw emotion as Esther stammered, "I don't know what I'd do without you."

Russell slid across the bed and embraced his wife as they had done a thousand times before. He bent his head and kissed her hair as she snuggled in closer towards him. He loved her more than life itself. If he did not firmly believe he had to go to save his family then he would remain behind. He could feel her ragged breathing as she sobbed and it was not long before he felt her tears on his chest.

Russell's own eyes welled up as the reality of leaving Esther and his girls behind began to hit him. He took a deep swallow to help calm his voice before saying bravely, "Esther, everything will be OK. I'll be back before you know it."

Before he could wipe his eyes, Esther tilted her head to look up to see a tear roll down his cheek. She knew that this was as hard for him as it was for her. "I'm going to miss you and James so much."

"We're going to miss you too. I promise that we'll keep an eye on each other."

"I know you will."

"Honey, can I ask you to do something for us?"

Esther leaned over for a tissue as she regained a semblance of control over herself. It was a testament to her resilience and strength of character that she was able to focus on the task at hand so quickly. She wiped her eyes dry and with a puzzled look on her face said, "Of course. What do you want me to do?"

"I need you to stay with the Blue Sky team here. Can you do that?"

"Sure, the girls and I will meet with them each day."

"No, not just meet with them."

Now she was getting curious. "What do you mean?"

"I need the three of you to learn everything that you can about them and how their technology works. I know that this is a big ask but I'm sure that the girls will help out a lot."

"Why do you want us to do this?"

Russell released his wife from his embrace so that he could better see the reaction on her face. "If what Mark and the rest of the Blue Sky team say is true then Alpha Three is only a tiny side battle in a much larger war. How long do you think it will take for the Scourge to discover Earth?"

Esther paused for before continuing, "Oh… It won't take them long," she said with sudden understanding at what Russell was driving at.

"While we're gone you and Marie will have to prepare our girls as fast as you can."

"I understand," Esther answered thoughtfully.

Russell absently ran his fingers through his wife's hair. "I've already spoken with Mihaly and he's going to talk with Marie tonight."

"I'll get us all studying as soon as you leave in the morning."

Russell smiled at his wife.

"What is it?" she asked.

"You're an amazing woman."

Esther batted her eyelids provocatively and coyly said, "Why do you say that?"

Russell reached behind him to turn off the light as he said, "I think we've had about enough talking for now."

Despite the dire circumstances, Esther gave a little giggle as she felt Russell's hands lovingly reach across towards her.

The next day and their wives and girls said their good-byes over a lengthy breakfast. The previous evening they had unanimously elected not to attend the interstellar eport just in case they saw their loved ones go through something they did not want to see.

Before he boarded the van to take them to Blue Sky Russell turned to Esther and said, "I'll see you later."

Esther returned a reassuring smile and said, "I know."

After a short drive to the Blue Sky offices, the van door opened and revealed a smiling Crystal who said, "It's so good to see you all again."

James could not help himself and replied, "It's always good to see you Crystal," as he took in her very feminine charms.

Beside him Alex mumbled, "Calm down James, she's way out of your league."

James smiled at Alex and whispered, "Nothing wrong with aiming high."

Russell stepped in between the two young men and said, "That's enough you two."

Crystal ignored the byplay and once again as the consummate professional, she escorted them all to the room housing the interstellar TransWarp machine. Each of the men was wearing a set of grey Concord overalls and a pair of sturdy boots designed to withstand the rigors of the eport. Mark and the majority of the Concord staff stationed in Los Angeles were waiting for them to arrive.

Mark stepped forward and formally saluted the Earthmen. "Don't forget that when you get to Freehold you can use your wrist-comp to communicate to here. Sending and receiving a few bytes of traffic is possible as long as there is an active scanning tower nearby."

Russell was efficient as ever and replied, "CT Commander."

Tony, Adam and Frank approached, shook the Earthmen's hands and wished them well. When Tony came before Russell he said, "I knew you'd come through for us Whizz." He then embraced Russell in a bear hug and whispered, "Get those frapping Scourge for my family's sake." Releasing his hold, he stepped back a little embarrassed by the display of affection.

"Tony, don't worry. We'll do our best for us all."

"Thanks Whizz."

Mark opened the door to the TransWarp and ushered them all inside. Despite the myriad of hoses, wires and other strange apparatus sticking out of the interstellar TransWarp on the outside the inside was plain, almost boring.

Mark looked through the doorway at the six of them standing in the centre of the room. So much hinged on these six men. He hoped they had the strength to carry the hope of the Concord on their shoulders. Pushing aside his concerns, he smiled encouragingly at each of them and said, "Gentlemen, good luck," and with a sense of finality, Mark closed the door.

The Earthmen found themselves standing in a plain unfurnished room about the size of typical bedroom. The walls, ceiling and floor were all the same featureless grey. They could not hear any sounds from outside and their own voices sounded dull and lifeless.

"OK, this is a bit of an anticlimax," Pyro stated flatly.

Elzetro looked around at the blank wall and said, "You're telling me."

"Be quiet you two," Whizzbang whispered in a hushed voice as he held up his fingers and began counting down on them. "OK, get ready!"

General Grendig thrummed his right claw irritably on the metallic armrest of his high backed throne. The raised throne sat upon a dais in the middle of the Scourge Alpha Three command dome. It contained a series of dials and switches to activate various functions that the General required. Flicking one of those switches the General flipped to a fresh screen as he surveyed the results from the recent setbacks. Data flooded onto the left of the three massive displays suspended from the dome over forty feet above and in front of him. From these three screens, the General viewed the dispositions of individual fists, groups of fists known as strikes and could even launch battle-pods into the accursed human sanctuary inside Alpha Three.

Despite the best sound proofing available the nearby twenty story high Barrier generators sent pulsing sound waves through the control room infrastructure. Normally the presence of the Barrier would assuage the General's dark demeanour. However, as he watched the losses continue to increase he let out a low growl and hammered a communication stud on the control board in front of him. Things were not going to the plan.

A pale skinned, pink-eyed face materialised onto the huge right hand screen. The twin crossed swords insignia on his shoulders indicated a strike leader, the commander of one hundred and twenty warriors. Upon recognising who had called him the strike leader visibly quailed and said with an almost panic-stricken voice, "General!"

"Report!" yelled Grendig through snarling teeth that in the Scourge tradition were carefully sharpened to fine points. All the better to rip out an enemy's throat if your blaster fails.

"I don't know how to explain it my Lord..." mumbled the underling.

Grendig's eyes narrowed, "I said, report!"

"The StarBlade Lord General! The StarBlade attacked our forces and ruthlessly slaughtered them all."

"I can see that on my display you miserable excuse for one of the blessed!" The General let out a low growl in the back of his throat. "Do you think that I am unaware of the disaster that you have been overseeing?"

Upon viewing the intensity of the General's piercing eyes the strike leader panicked and resorted to the tried and tested Scourge solution in such circumstances, he lied. Suggesting just a hint of a smile the strike leader steadied himself. "General, the StarBlade ambushed us with over three hundred battleframes. Our warriors fought bravely but sadly they will be dining with their blood kin in the great halls this evening." Feeling more at ease as the lie took shape, the strike leader continued, "Due to my superior abilities and intellect I escaped the StarBlade's trap to bring this report to your greatness."

Grendig looked across to the left screen. Where only forty-eight hours earlier the board had red dots indicating Scourge warriors congregating for the final assault on the human settlement of Freehold, now there was none. Other than the forces within the command dome and a few scattered remnants, the Scourge forces on Alpha Three had suffered multiple defeats where there should have been victories.

Shifting his gaze from the map of Alpha Three back to the strike leader, Grendig said almost casually, "Your services are no longer required." He then pressed another stud on his console that activated a dormant 'friend' and watched, with almost eager anticipation, as the strike leader began to scream and claw at his face. His sharpened nails stripped great swaths of flesh from his sunken cheeks before he collapsed to the ground, twitching and convulsing uncontrollably. Death finally took hold and all was still except for a white grub that devouring the strike leaders pink eye, from the inside out. With the underling already forgotten the General indulged himself in a rare smile, after feasting, the little one would grow to become a large Barrier-born Spyderlynx.

Turning back to the problem at hand Grendig mulled over what he had learned. It was obvious that the incompetent strike leader was lying and that it was more likely that two hundred and not three hundred battleframes had attacked his forces. Who was this StarBlade? Since he had returned, there was one set back after another. The plan was in tatters! The General was just about to order a minion to bring a cup of blood wine, when the central monitor sprung to life.

He had only ever seen the middle screen activate once, when he was first instructed to conquer Alpha Three and enslave the surviving population. Now it was the General's turn to be nervous.

The indistinct fuzzy shape in the monitor was all that materialised of his superior. Although the video was purposefully distorted, the audio was crystal clear and crackled liked a lightning bolt across the central command dome. "General, report!"

General Grendig swallowed slowly and replied, "We have pushed the Concord to a small patch of Alpha Three. Their defeat is now certain my Lord."

"Why is it that you claim to have nearly subdued this world and yet the forces at your disposal are greatly diminished?"

The General took another swallow and felt the burning of stomach acid rising in his throat. "We are dispatching forces from the command dome now to complete the task."

"Your conclusion that the Concord is near defeat is based upon conjecture and hearsay, not fact!"

"Yes, my Lord."

With a snarl of derision the disembodied voice blasted out, "You will only speak when you have facts!"

"Yes, my Lord."

"Keep your troops at the command dome and prepare for an attack."

This time the General's turn to be shocked, "An *attack* my Lord? We are within a fortress in the middle of the great Barrier." Then with disdain in his voice he said, "No human can reach us here."

The voice took on an air of malevolence as it boomed, "General, you are wrong! You will be attacked and it will be soon! Do as I command!"

General Grendig bowed his head and replied, "My purpose is to obey."

The connection snapped shut and thirty light years away Zechlan, a green skinned, white haired humanoid sat in a dome similar to Grendig's and looked for the first time in his long life, worried. It was clear that a new player had emerged in the war and was turning the odds in the Concord's favour. He was certain that the fool Grendig would be attacked but he had to make certain that his hunch was correct. Punching a stud on his command desk, he opened up a one way communication screen into the

General's command dome so that he could observe what transpired while he remained hidden.

Zechlan face broke into an evil smile and one inch sharpened incisors revealed themselves. He wondered if it was time for the General to develop an itchy eye.

Chapter 6
Alpha Three

A typical eport lasts only for a few seconds and tears at the very heart and soul of a battleframe pilot. It is so traumatic that some pilots never recover from the experience. What Mark did not tell the Earthmen, was this was the first time the interstellar TransWarp had transported anything bigger than a mouse.

Rather than lasting a couple of seconds, Whizzbang and his squad experienced the most horrendous, terrifying pain inflicting teleportation for a full forty-one seconds. There were not any swirling clouds or following a tube like in a science fiction novel – they saw nothing and felt like a hundred knives were slicing the skin from their flesh. The agony was unlike anything either of them had experienced before or wanted to experience ever again. Later, Kheldar would say his major car accident, that put him in hospital for two months, was a walk in the park compared to the experience.

Nevertheless, the Earthmen endured the experience. They had the mental drive and fortitude to hang-on and push through the rigours of the interstellar TransWarp.

Mark also did not share with them the fact that the TransWarp would place them within two hundred metres of the Freehold scanning tower, horizontally and vertically! When they materialised on Alpha Three, it was by sheer luck that they appeared on the top of the giant rock behind Freehold. They could very well have been dropped above the courtyard with the Freedom Flame and plummet to their deaths or worse still, materialise in the middle of the rock itself!

The teleportation finally finished and the six travellers unceremoniously crashed to the ground next to the lookout tent above Freehold. The tent was not big but it did provide some cover for scouts. Panting and sweating profusely Bosk asked no one in particular, "OK, if you have the energy, put your hand up if you want to do that again."

Still lying on the ground Russell shook his head from side to side to make sure his brains were still intact. He seemed to be doing that a lot lately. "There's not a chance I'm having the girls go through that."

DG slowly got to his feet, staggered a few steps and then steadied himself by leaning against the side of the tent, "Hey guys, do you feel the difference?"

"Hang on while I shove my brains back into my head DG," Pyro replied, as he laid sprawled upon the ground. He finally got his elbow propped up under him and replied, "DG, I do feel the difference. It's not like before at all. This feels real!"

"That's because it is real," a gravelly bass voice said from the other side of the lookout tent. Tiny's face appeared from the far side of the tent, surrounded in a cloud of blue cigar smoke. "It's good to see you again Whizz," he said as a big grin split his face in two and revealed his trademark shattered teeth.

Whizzbang gritted his teeth, stood up unsteadily and said, "Tiny! It's great to see you too! What are you doing up here?"

"After you all decided to leave us at the end of the battle on the hill, Selfia coordinated Acheron, Gardner and I into squads to run patrols on the perimeter. I assigned myself up here and the rest of my squad is down near the beach doing lookout duty."

"I knew she had it in her to get things under control!"

Tiny swiped at a passing fly with his armoured fist and said, "Can I just say you're all looking terrible and a little naked without your battleframes."

Whizzbang had always enjoyed Tiny's down to earth way of saying things just straight. He smiled and replied, "We've been through the equivalent of a forty one second eport. You'll have to excuse us but I'm just happy no one is drooling out the side of their mouth." Looking across at Kheldar, Whizzbang asked, "Kheldar, you OK?"

Kheldar replied with an effort, "Yeah I'm OK. Pyro, I won't be doing any partying for a while. I feel like I've the worst hang-over ever!"

"Don't worry Kheldar, I'm not dancing with anyone!" Pyro answered as he slowly gained his feet.

Whizzbang laughed, "I think that you need some of the good liquid medicine served a Folly's Kheldar." Turning back to Tiny he asked, "So what's been going on since we left?"

Tiny took another long pull on his cigar and slowly exhaled a trail of pungent blue smoke. "After you left we scoured the battlefield for tellurite and spare parts. Selfia ordered your cyber-frames moved into the main courtyard until you returned. She was certain you'd be back."

"It's fair to say that the Blue Sky team on our home world of Earth made it a compelling proposition."

"By the way, we called them cyber-frame because they had some hi-tech gizmo that allowed you to control them from where you come from."

"Didn't people notice that we looked a little different?"

"Whizz, over the years I've seen all sorts of crazy stuff dreamed up by Blue Sky. It's real strange looking at you all in the flesh though. The exact replica of you they materialised from malleable energy was pretty good. Unless you looked close, no one would have noticed that you were energised. Besides, most of the time you had your face shields down or it was at night." Tiny took another long pull on his cigar before letting out a long stream of blue smoke. "I must admit that even for Blue Sky this was one out of the box. What counted for me was that it was obvious that a real person was piloting the battleframe and that always gets my respect."

"You're a good man Tiny."

Tiny revealed his shattered teeth in a smile that seemed to light up his face. "Don't spread that around Whizz or I'll lose my reputation as a rabble rouser."

Whizzbang winked and said, "You're secret's safe with me."

"Now that you're here in person you won't know yourselves when you finally get dressed with some good armour around you."

"Tiny, you have no idea how much I'm looking forward to getting into my Raven." Before continuing, Whizzbang took a moment to gaze across at the spectacular vista and Freehold far below. "I can't believe that I'm actually on another world. For the whole of my life I've wanted to go into space and now we're all farther than any Earthmen have ever been before." Coming out of his distracted ramblings, he reached up and patted Tiny's armoured arm as if to reassure himself that he was for real. "It's good to see you for real my friend. Come on everyone, let's go and get dressed."

In a battleframe, it would take only a few seconds to leap off the edge off the edge of the cliff, kick in your jets and gently manoeuvre down to the courtyard below. Without their battleframes, it took Whizzbang's squad close to half an hour to clamber down the mountain and that was with Tiny's assistance. The good thing was the exercise managed to help clear everyone's heads of the after effects of the TransWarp.

Running down the steps into the courtyard Whizzbang heard, "Commander! Commander Whizzbang!"

Whizzbang knew that voice and smiled as he slowed and walked up to a familiar Eagle-claw battleframe, "Group Leader Selfia."

"Commander, you're really here now aren't you?"

"Yes, I'm actual, Self."

Before she could stop herself from the impulsive action Selfia bent down and picked Whizzbang up in as light a hug as she could manage in her battleframe. "I knew you'd make the decision to come here!"

"Hey Self! Careful of the bones, they're brittle you know," Whizzbang said as she released her hug. "It's good to see you again as well. I feel like it's been an age since I was last here, not just a little over a day. By the way I never got a chance to congratulate you and Acheron."

"What for?"

"You just got married, right?"

"Oh that! We've been so busy rescuing you I completely forgot!"

Whizzbang chuckled. "And thank you for all those times. At the end of this you two are going to have to take a honeymoon."

Selfia slowly closed her eyes in a blissful thought before opening them again. "Now you're talking Commander."

"Self, you know I'm not a Commander."

Selfia laughed, "You are if I say you are."

Whizzbang let the comment slide and asked, "So where's Acheron?"

"I sent him out patrolling the north to ensure that Gardner's Digging crews aren't harassed while they mine resources."

"Good decision to get the crews back out. By the way, you and Acheron aren't from London are you?"

Selfia stared at the ground in embarrassment. "I'm really sorry Whizz. It was supposed to be our cover story. When you first materialised, on the evening of the attack, Concord Central tasked both Acheron and I to have your back. They had their eye on you from the moment you started playing the Scourge Wars simulation game about six months ago."

Whizzbang held up his hand to stop Selfia's explanations, "Self, you don't have to explain yourself any further. You were just following orders."

"But I need to explain…"

"No you don't." While they had been speaking, Bosk and the rest of the squad from Earth arrived in the courtyard and came over to where Whizzbang was talking with Selfia.

"Hey Self, it's great to see you again!" Bosk exclaimed.

"You too Bosk," Selfia said in a subdued tone.

Whizzbang turned to the Earthmen and with mock seriousness said, "I have something important to tell you all. Selfia has just informed me that she and Acheron aren't from London and that she's actually from the Concord. Selfia's a little embarrassed because she had orders to tell us a lie."

Pyro started laughing and this spread amongst the others until everyone was gasping to get oxygen into their lungs. "Dad, you've got to be kidding me!" Pyro said what everyone else was laughing about, "Self, do you honestly believe you have an English accent? We knew that you were from the Concord the minute you opened your mouth."

Bosk looked Selfia in the eye and said, "Selfia, all I know is that you saved my rear end twice now and for that, I'm eternally grateful. Each one of us owes you a debt and we will be there for you."

Between smiles and another bout of laughter, the Earthmen lifted Selfia in her frame and all upon their shoulders and marched around the Freedom Torch singing her praises. Not surprisingly, most of the songs sounded strangely like they should be sung back home in a pub with a beer or two. Whizzbang looked on at the procession and clapped his hands to the beat in the joy of meeting old friends once again. It was not long before several hundred technicians, mechanics and even a few battleframe pilots that were not on duty joined the Earthmen. Selfia was a hero and if the Concord was to survive, they needed more heroes like her.

The squad finally put Selfia down and she quickly wiped her cheeks clear of a few tears. Embarrassed by her emotional display she walked over to Whizzbang and said, "I was so worried I wasn't doing a good job Whizz, and that lie just built up in my mind into a huge issue."

"Selfia, I said don't worry. You're a hero"

Then in a loud voice so that everyone in the plaza could hear Whizzbang yelled, "It's time for me to repay a promise I made before the recent battle to save Freehold. Spread the word, tonight we party at Folly's and the drinks are on me!"

A loud cheer greeted his announcement of a party at Folly's, and below it all, Tiny's rumbling voice could be heard saying, "Now this is what I'm talking about! Time for a new cigar!" At which point he deftly tossed his old stub into a garbage receptacle. Within half a second, a fresh, lit cigar seemed to materialise between his crooked teeth.

Kheldar turned to Pyro, "It's amazing! I think my head has just cleared up with the simple mention of a party!"

With a whoop, Pyro yelled back over the cheers, "Time for us to show them all how Earthmen can dance!"

While those assembled headed towards Folly's, Whizzbang leaned across to Selfia and said, "Let it go Self. It's time to relax before the next big push. We didn't come here to mess around. We came to order a main course of major payback."

Selfia smiled and replied, "I knew you'd really come here Commander."

Whizzbang rolled his eyes at her use of the rank and then laughed as Pyro grabbed his arm to drag him up the steps leading to Folly's. They all headed to the bar for the celebration and left their battleframes for the following day. Now was the time to be grateful with friends and for those that were still standing by your side.

Despite the party going on into the early hours of the morning, Whizzbang found himself sitting on the top step of the stairs leading down to the Freedom Torch. He watched as the first rays of sunrise sparkled off both the Barrier and sea creating a magnificent blue shimmering effect all along the horizon. Holding his hand up to shade his eyes, he made out a lone sea gull gliding down on the air currents to the beach far below. Just before landing, it squawked a welcome to its friends at the edge of the water. Whizzbang took a few deep breaths to help clear out the morning cobwebs. He absently noted that the few percent extra oxygen in the atmosphere made it feel fresher and purer than on Earth.

It was a stunning view that reminded him of watching Balinese sunsets with Esther during a recent vacation. Bali was now light years away and he was missing her already. She was his rock, his closest friend and his lover. He knew he was here for the greater good but he longed to hold her in his arms. Why did the greater good have to include greater sacrifice?

Bosk, looking a little worse for the night's festivities, sidled up and sat down on the step next to his friend. They were both silent for a time as they enjoyed each other's company and gazed at the sun as it pushed its way above the horizon. "It's beautiful," he said softly.

Still staring at the view Whizzbang said, "It's a prison. You know we have to do something about the Barrier."

"I know. Any ideas?"

"Not at the moment. Interested in walking the perimeter?"

"I thought you'd never ask."

Both men stretched aching muscles as the stood and headed down the steps to their battleframes. Each of the Earthmen's frames had been carefully lined up next to each other along the wall in the main courtyard in anticipation of their return to Alpha Three. Selfia had refused to convert them back into tellurite at the battleframe console, as she steadfastly believed you were going to return. She needed a symbol of her faith and the battleframes fulfilled that role.

Whizzbang inspected the fist-sized tech that allowed his consciousness to be in control of the frame. "Bosk, not much to it is there?"

"I can't believe that this little thing transported our consciousness all the way here."

Whizzbang carefully unplugged the device and said, "I think that there is more to it than just this." He then placed it on the ground next to his Raven. "We're not going to need it again."

"I suppose your right," Bosk replied as he hefted the device in his hand.

Whizzbang turned his back to the battleframe and stepped backwards into his open Raven harness. Like a living creature, the grey suit instantly reacted to his feet in the boots and automatically enclosed itself around his body. Holding out his arms the suit's gloves moved and slid over his hands as the nanites latched the flexible armour onto his wrists. The frame then automatically tightened some areas and loosened others to ensure that it was like an extension of his body and ready to provide instant power and flexibility at a moment's notice. Actually wearing his battleframe for the first time felt so real, so beautiful and so deadly.

He barely felt the pinprick of the frame's nanomed needle as it breached his skin and tapped a vein in his inner thigh. A sudden gush of Nanomeds flooded across the gap from his battleframe and into his body so that they would be ready to heal any wound he received in combat.

Like a key sliding into a lock, the faultlessly engineered nanomeds blended with his fifty thousand years of genetic breeding. They reacted like the perfectly orchestrated machines that Altavia had designed them to be. Rather than slowing down their rush into his body Whizzbang's genetic make-up demanded more and then even more! Like an onrushing train, nanomeds flooded across the link between the battleframe and his body. The reaction was so swift and so sudden that a wave of blackness engulfed him and not knowing what else to do Whizzbang passed out.

Looking down into the courtyard from next to the Freehold scanning tower, three unlikely technicians stared with brilliant blue eyes at Whizzbang and Bosk as they stepped into their battleframe harnesses.

"And so it begins," Intellect said as he casually thumbed through a book on the inner workings of a tellurite reactor. "Should we do anything to assist them?"

Creativity bent down and pulled her violin out of its case before saying, "We've done everything that we can to prepare them. The only reason why they survived the TransWarp was due to our genetic engineering. As Wisdom said, if we do anything now we could disrupt their development and render them incapable of fulfilling their destiny."

Intellect looked up again from his book at his two companions. "We've given them the labour of our entire race in the gift of the nanomeds and nanites. Combined with their genetic predisposition the perfect blending of man and technology has just taken place."

As was his habit, Wisdom thoughtfully stroked his neatly cropped beard with his left hand and said, "It will be difficult for them, but I have faith that they will survive and even one day surpass us. It's not just the genetics or the technology Intellect, but who they are that allows the blending to take place. Without the essence of their character, either man or machine would devour the other.

Intellect nodded in agreement at Wisdom's words.

Looking towards both his companions Wisdom continued, "It's what they do with this gift that will set them apart from others."

Plucking her violin strings to see if they were still in tune Creativity said, "Wisdom, I have faith in them."

Smiling in his grandfatherly manner Wisdom replied, "So do I. So do I."

Intellect paused from reading his book and looked up. "Have we had any word that the enemy knows of our plans?"

"We have heard nothing but in times like this silence is often good news," Wisdom replied.

"So I will ask the question that Creativity has asked in the past. When should we reveal ourselves?" asked Intellect.

Wisdom gave a little laugh, "I can't believe that I'm saying this but it appears that you're both getting a little impatient." He materialised his favourite walking stick in his hand and leaned heavily upon it. The posture emphasised his thousands of years of age. "I think we can delay a little longer. There is still a little time."

Now that she was satisfied that the violin was in tune, Creativity playfully plucked at the strings with the notes from a recent orchestration. "They will need that time to discover their new abilities. I would make a guess that this will prove interesting...," she trailed off thoughtfully.

Her two companions nodded their heads solemnly in agreement.

"The plans of eons are now set fully in motion," Wisdom murmured.

Chapter 7
Transformation

Charged particles coursed through Russell's body leaving him in a catatonic state staring wide eyed at the heavens above. Trillions of infinitely complex sub-atomic machines latched onto the comparable number of neurons in his brain and flayed them wide open. Burning agony seared its way into every corner of his mind as the miniature machines went about their purpose and locked onto the double helix of his DNA. Once in place they stretched, strengthened and augmented the nucleic bonds and cleared the parallel pathways within the mind so that thought would flow more freely.

The agony felt like fire incinerating his very being from the inside out as it threatened to consume him. Doggedly, Russell held onto the true essence of his unique humanity. An intense pain enveloped his entire being. The nanomeds assaulted every muscle, bone and sinew as they went about their work of blending man and machine. Images of events in his life flashed by, faster and faster, one after another. With increasing regularity, the image of Esther appeared and he hung onto her with all that he could. Her concerned loving eyes seemed to help brace him for the multiple waves of agony that were transforming him into something more than human.

He did not know it at the time but no weapon formed or even power of mind could break his indomitable will and leave him alive. His was an incorruptible mind that would not then or ever be able to be broken. Russell was truly reborn as Whizzbang.

Beside him, his lifelong friend Mihaly lay in a comparable state of disrepair as he too experienced what it was like to have his mind wrenched away from him and then handed back in an almost unrecognisable form. Stars seemed to explode in front of his eyes, one after another, and then slowly gaining in speed, the flashing stars reached a cacophony of visual noise that was almost unbearable. He cried out in pain but no noise issued from his lips as he hung onto the essence of what made Mihaly, Mihaly. A fervent desire to see wrongs made right, compassion for those in need and a strength of will to see things done. Like Russell, at the core of Mihaly was a strength of character that was stronger than the toughest steel. He would die before any torture or inducement could break him. That was when was Mihaly was truly reborn as Bosk.

Slowly but surely both Whizzbang and Bosk struggled through the torment as their minds instantly accelerated through thousands of years of development and expanded to encompass their true genetically pure humanity. As suddenly as it began the pain ceased and they both discovered they were lying on their backs gasping for breath. What had seemed like years were actually only moments, with the sun only a fingers breadth above the horizon.

"*Oh frap! What was that?*" Bosk asked his friend as he struggled to sit up.

"*How in the frap should I know?*" Whizzbang answered as he groggily sat up. "*I feel like I've been through a meat grinder and then pieced back together by being dragged through a pasta machine!*"

"*My head is killing me, but heh.....what the?*" Bosk tilted his head on the side as he really began to think.

Whizzbang was a millisecond ahead of him and thought, "*Bosk I feel like my mind has just had an overhaul and it's a million times bigger.*"

"*Me too!*"

Whizzbang continued, "*Every memory, every experience and every idea is instantly at my beck and call. Can you remember that time we got into trouble with the teacher in grade eight?*"

"*You mean the teacher with the big black beard and glasses?*"

"*Yes, now ask yourself how many whiskers he had?*" Whizzbang said excitedly.

"*Oh frap, oh frap, oh frap! Eleven thousand, two hundred and twenty eight.*"

"*I can instantly recall, replay and inspect every aspect of anything that I've ever done!*"

Whizzbang looked back at Bosk with a startled expression on his face and said, "*Bosk, how can I hear you when your lips aren't moving?*"

"*What do you mean? I am talking and I can hear you plain as day.*"

Just then, Bosk realised what Whizzbang was referring to. They both were not moving their lips! "*Whizz is this telepathy? Somehow, we just got telepathy! What just happened?*"

"*I have no idea but let's test this out.*" Whizzbang carefully stood to his feet, turned his back on his friend and then sent a thought in Bosk's direction, "*What colour am I thinking?*"

"*Ouch! Go easy Whizz! That really hurt! It's blue by the way.*"

This time it was Whizzbang's turn to give a little yelp. Then tempering his thought down he conversationally said, "*Where are we?*"

"*Alpha Three.*"

Whizzbang turned back to look at his friend and thought, "*Bosk, we just became telepathic.*"

"*Whizz, how did that happen? What happened? What's going on?*"

"*Think about it Bosk. This is the first time that we've actually put on our battleframes for real. In the past, it's been in the game or according to Blue Sky we've had our consciousness translated here. We've never actually stepped into a physical battleframe until now.*"

"When I first put on my frame I thought I was being torn open Whiz. Did you go through the same thing?"

"Sure did. I could almost feel the nanomeds bonding with me. I wonder if all battleframe pilots are telepathic?"

"They can't be, otherwise they wouldn't need the local and extended comnet."

This time it was Bosk's turn to shake his head from side to side to test that everything was working just fine. *"That's true but why us?"*

"I have no idea, but I'm at the point that nothing's going to surprise me anymore. Bosk, we're sitting on a planet four point three light years from Earth discussing what is and what's not possible. Only a few days ago we were playing a game on our computers at home. I was more worried about the next client than saving the whole of humanity."

"Point well made. Marie always said that I spent too much of my time on my PC. She kept on saying that I should go for a walk and get some fresh air. I don't think this is what she quite had in mind."

"What I would like to know is what else we can do? Has anything else been changed?"

Bosk looked back at his friend and said, *"I wouldn't be surprised if a whole lot of things have been altered and we've become some sort of cyborg or something."*

"I'm not sure I agree with you there. I feel great. In fact, I would say that I can't remember the last time I felt this good."

"Come to think of it, I agree with you. I feel wonderful! I remember dragging myself out of bed this morning after last night's festivities but now I feel like I could run a marathon."

"So physically we feel fine and mentally we've somehow been hyper-charged as well. Let's test this telepathy a little." Whizzbang thought of his study back home and while he did this he thought to Bosk, *"What am I thinking of right now?"*

"I've got nothing," Bosk sent to Whizzbang.

"Hmmmm......interesting. It appears that we can keep thoughts private even as I think at you. By the way, I was imagining my study back home. Let's try something else. Why don't you try and find out what I'm thinking and I'll try and stop you?"

"Sort of like when we first spoke? It hurt when you sent your thought. I'm willing to try but don't complain if you end up with a headache."

Whizzbang mentally braced himself for Bosk's thought by imagining there was a wall between his friend and his mind.

Bosk spoke audibly, "Are you ready?"

Whizzbang nodded and braced his feet. He did not know what to expect so he naturally tried to expect everything. Bosk mentally balled up his will inside of himself and then pushed it almost tentatively at his friend. He watched in amazement as a pulsing golden beam of mental force that only they could both see slowly extended from himself towards his friend. Suddenly it stopped about a foot away from Whizzbang. It was like hitting a brick wall. His mental energy seemed to claw and grab at an unseen barrier until it finally dissipated.

Bosk stopped the mental attack and said audibly, "OK, that was interesting. I've never seen colours come out of my head before. What was it like from your side?"

With a bit of relief, Whizzbang relaxed his shield and mentally said, *"I felt like someone was knocking on the door. It wasn't that difficult to stop but it could get pretty annoying. Let me try with you."*

"I only pushed out a little so be gentle. You have a tendency to get excited at times and that might give me one heck of a hangover."

"Bosk, trust me," Whizzbang said as he smiled, *"You know what I'm like."*

Bosk rolled his eyes, *"Exactly what I'm worried about."* He steeled himself for the attack that Whizzbang would throw at him and mentally created a wall. Finally, he said, "OK, I'm ready."

Whizzbang mentally pushed his will towards Bosk, not too hard at first but he steadily stepped up the pressure way above Bosk's first test. He watched as a brilliant blue beam of energy launched itself at his friend and hammered at the mental shield. Sparks splattered across the surface of the invisible barrier as his mental force began to squeeze down. It was like the irresistible force meeting the immovable object. Bosk's barrier pushed back even as Whizzbang increased the attack and then as suddenly as it began, Whizzbang stopped.

"Hey Whizz, I thought you were really going to hammer me?"

"I did," Whizzbang replied thoughtfully and then continued, *"While I was bearing down on your shield I got a sense of who you actually are, Bosk. I've always loved you as a friend but this was like nothing I've ever experienced before."*

"What do you mean?"

Whizzbang paused before sending, *"I don't know how else to explain it but that I got a sense of your internal mental fortitude, the steel of your soul if you will. You would have died before you would surrender to any attack. For want of a better word, you're incorruptible."*

Bosk, mentally blushed and said, *"Err, ahhh….thanks for that, I've never been told that before.*

"I mean it. It was incredible!"

Bosk replied, *"Enough about me. When you really poured it onto my shield, I never realised half of what your willpower and drive was capable. I now know that you will never give up and never surrender no matter what. Whatever the situation you have a way of thinking that means you will either succeed or die trying."*

"I wouldn't go as far as that."

"I would now. After knowing you for over thirty five years I now finally understand that about you."

Both friends looked at each other with a renewed sense of respect just as the sun rose a hands breadth into the sky. A number of mechanics and technicians chatted amicably as they made their way to the various repair stations around the main courtyard. A few glanced at the two men in their battleframes that appeared to be staring at each other, shrugged their shoulders and went about their duties. You had to have a very particular mindset to be a battleframe pilot and it was clear that these two had seen too much combat.

Whizzbang raised his arms above his head and gave an almighty stretch. *"I don't know about you but all this work is making me hungry. Let's go find the others and tell them what we've discovered."*

"I'm with you. Do you think they'll have steaks for breakfast? I'm starved!"

Mentally laughing Whizzbang said, "*To answer that question all we've got to do is find Pyro and Elzetro.*"

Up next to the scanning tower Wisdom, Creativity and Intellect smiled to one another as an important stage in the multi-millennium long plan had just slipped into place. After eons of patiently waiting, like a supernova, key events seemed to be suddenly exploding outwards.

Creativity said with reverence in her voice, "Did you hear how loud they were?"

"Yes, it was incredible," stated Wisdom. Turning to Intellect he asked, "I assumed that you shielded them?"

"Of course. We couldn't have them announcing their presence to half the galaxy."

Creativity said, "They're already learning but they will need some time to fully understand their potential."

"They have some time still," Wisdom said thoughtfully.

Chapter 8
Breakfast

Whizzbang and Bosk did not see their sons in the mess hall so they headed Pyro and Elzetro's sleeping quarters. Whizzbang noiselessly pushed the door open, revealing their sons mess of clothes strewn across the floor and the two comatose bodies asleep in their beds. The dual reverberating snores sounding more like caged animals rather than a couple of young men who had altogether too much fun at Folly's the previous night. Despite being light years from home, it was clear that both their sons still knew how to have a good time.

Whizzbang caught Bosk's attention and touched his finger to his lips to suggest being quiet. Smiling, he then thought towards his friend, "*I forgot that I could be quiet by talking telepathically. I was just wondering if we can see what their dreaming about?*"

"*Do you think it's even possible?*"

"*Only one way to find out…*"

Whizzbang focused a soft faint wafting thought towards Pyro while Bosk did the same for Elzetro. They would later laugh at their clumsy attempt to insinuate themselves into another mind but at this stage in their development this was as good as it was going to get. The questing mental probe tapped lightly at the edge of Pyro's consciousness and skirted around to try to find a way in. It was like picking a highly complex lock. Whizzbang concentrated harder; there was something there, something almost visible but not quite tangible. If he just prodded a little more…

Like twin alarm bells, Pyro's eyes flew open and stared straight into his father's eyes with a momentary confused look on his face. "What the?" which was quickly followed by, "Dad, what are you doing here?"

"I'll explain later son."

After the initial surprise, Pyro let out a huge yawn, "Until you interrupted, I was having the best dream. I was just about to get to know that gorgeous blonde Bio frame pilot. You know…"

Elzetro let out a sudden "Yelp" as he leapt out of his bed, interrupting Pyro's description of his dream. Looking bleary eyed and a little confused Elzetro asked, "Dad? Whizz? What are you doing here?"

"I think I may have pushed a little too hard," Bosk thought towards Whizzbang a little sheepishly.

"You think? I thought that he was going to dislocate his shoulder leaping out of bed like that," Whizzbang laughingly thought back.

Whizzbang stated flatly, "As your commanding officers and fathers we thought that it was about time you both got your lazy backsides out of bed."

Pyro let out a groan as he swung his legs over the side of the bed and sat up.

Whizzbang continued, "After breakfast we'd like you to put on your battleframes and get used to them for real. It won't be long before we're in combat and we don't want to be sloppy in a life and death situation. So go and get cleaned up and we'll meet you in the mess hall in fifteen minutes."

Whizzbang and Bosk, still attired in their Raven battleframes, left their sons and headed to the mess hall for breakfast.

"You're not going to say anything?" Bosk asked.

"*Say what? We don't know whether they will be impacted by their frames or not.*"

"*That's true.*"

"*Bosk, without those battleframes the boys will be sitting ducks for any Scourge attack. They have to try them on. It's quite literally a matter of life or death.*"

"*I suppose your right. I just don't want to see them go through the process we went through.*"

"*I understand. Besides, could you imagine if we told them that they couldn't come to Central and that they weren't allowed to wear their battleframes?*"

Bosk gave a little mental chuckle, "*They'd be in their frames following us as soon as our backs were turned.*"

"*You bet they would, and if we were them, we'd be doing exactly the same thing. We also can't risk telling them anything.*"

"*What do you mean?*"

"*We seem to have come through the process intact. It could be because we didn't know anything. If we told them about what might happen then it could mess the whole thing up.*"

"*I never thought of that.*"

So on the way to breakfast Whizzbang and Bosk decided to do nothing and trust fate to look after their sons when they tried their battleframes on for the very first time.

When they reached the mess hall, Whizzbang and Bosk spotted Kheldar and DG who were both already working their way through a plate of scrambled eggs and a pile of bacon. After helping themselves to a generous portion from the servery, they joined two other men from Earth.

"What are you grumbling about Bosk?" asked DG.

Letting out a deep sight Bosk replied, "They didn't have any steaks ready."

Kheldar laughed as he said, "Steak for breakfast? I thought you Australians would have brought your own supply of vegemite or something."

"And what's wrong with vegemite?" Whizzbang interjected.

To the laughs of the others around him Kheldar screwed up his face as he pantomimed scrubbing his tongue while he said, "Look

Whizz, no offense but I've had that stuff and it's like eating salty axle grease."

Whizzbang acted as if he was mortally offend. "I have no idea why you Americans throw away the best part of the beer fermentation process."

DG's head shot up at the mention of beer, "Did someone say beer?"

The friendly banter continued back and forth across the table and a few minutes later the boys joined the table with plates precariously balancing a tower of food.

Bosk thought sheepishly to Whizzbang, *"I loved those days when I didn't have to worry about the calories?"*

"You got that right!" came the instant reply.

Breakfast finished and after cleaning up the six Earthmen headed down to the courtyard for the "undressed" men to don their battleframes.

Whizzbang and Bosk looked on as DG and Kheldar stepped into their boots and held out their arms as the nanites automatically wrapped their battleframe snuggly around their bodies. Both pilots kept on talking as if nothing was out of the ordinary.

Unlike Kheldar and DG, Pyro and Elzetro exuberantly let out a little "whoop!" of joy as they clipped into their oversized battleframe boots that also housed their jump jets. They held their arms out and let the frame go to work securing the bindings into position for maximum effectiveness. Both young men continued to talk excitedly to each other with their fathers looking on and then abruptly, they stopped and keeled over as the nanomed injection sunk home.

Bosk thought to Whizzbang, *"Why them and not DG and Kheldar?"*

"I have no idea but I imagine there will be some reason."

Both young men bore the torment of the microscopic machines melding with their DNA. Like their fathers, they crashed through the barrier that separated them from becoming fully alive and developed. After coming to their senses, they embraced their new

292

world not as boys but as fully mature men who are secure in their strengths and weaknesses. It was the day that Pyro and Elzetro grew up and became men.

Chapter 9
Central

The glide and jet-walk westward to Concord Central Command did not take very long to complete but it was enough time to discuss what had and had not happened to each of them. Both DG and Kheldar were ambivalent about not having gained the ability to broadcast their thoughts, especially when they discovered that if one of the other four instigated a communication, then they were able to talk via telepathy just fine. The two young men were initially a bit miffed that their fathers did not say anything prior to them donning their battleframes, but after their fathers explained their decision, they came to terms with it. With the good grace of sons who loved their fathers, they let the issue go.

Before leaving, Whizzbang left orders with Selfia to continue patrols and a recommendation to send Acheron and a squad southward to see if there were any survivors since the invasion began. She suggested that Gardner's teams recommence Digging for tellurite to the north and he agreed it was a good idea.

A long tunnel that could fit two large trucks side by side facilitated the journey to Central. Years earlier, Concord engineers had drilled through the mountain range that created a natural barrier between Freehold and Central Command. As they travelled, Whizzbang marvelled at the size of the regularly spaced giant plasteel beams that supported the roof above. The tunnel sloped gently downwards and exited at the base of a sheltered valley that housed Central. It was sloped at an ideal angle for squads to rapidly jet-slip their way a few feet off the floor on flaming jump jets until they exited the end of the tunnel.

Concord Central Command was a huge complex that had grown around the superstructure of a half-built space cruiser. It did not take long before the base expanded around the cruiser to house the necessary facilities to keep the Concord's presence on Alpha Three intact. Shielding his eyes with his hand against the midday sun, Whizzbang looked upwards towards the bridge and a giant topside gun emplacement mounted on the upper deck of the half-completed cruiser. Pointing upwards, he said aloud to the others, "We're headed way up there. I've only been there a couple of times before in the game, but that's where Franky and the other big chiefs make all of the decisions for Alpha's defence. By the way, did any of you notice if your reflexes have improved? I've never balanced on my jets while shooting down a slope so well in my life." He suddenly started laughing at himself, "Not that I've done it for real before!"

It was not long before all of them realized the craziness of the situation and they joined in with the laughter. It was so natural to think that they had done everything before but in reality, this was the first time any of them had actually done anything. They'd played a computer game, learned the basic concepts and then had their consciousness transported to Alpha Three but never had they jet-slipped or done any of this before. It was exhilarating!

After recovering from his fit of laughing at the irony, Bosk replied, "I did notice that we all seemed to be able to skim a lot better. Hang on, give me a second will you." Looking around, Bosk bent down, picked up a broken tree branch off the ground, and said, "Let me test something out."

Walking over to Elzetro, Bosk held the stick up and said, "I'm going to drop the stick and I want to see how fast you can grab it."

"When will you drop it?"

"I'm not going to tell…" Bosk smiled just as he let go the branch.

Almost instantaneously, Elzetro closed his hand and held the stick. It had only moved a fraction of millimetre downwards. Bosk performed the same test on Whizzbang and Pyro and then had Elzetro drop the stick for him. All of the tests were nearly identical. He then conducted the same experiment on DG and Kheldar and was pleasantly surprised to find that they too had super-enhanced reflexes, although not quite as quick as the other four.

"Whoa! It seems that we haven't been left out after all DG!" yelped Kheldar.

"As long as it allows me to kill Scourge faster then I'm in!" DG replied.

Whizzbang thought to Bosk, *"Could it be our genetics? There's something special about all of us because we're from Earth but the particular genetic code of our ancestry has provided further enhancements."*

"Who knows Whizz? As long as it helps to keep us alive I'm happy."

Whizzbang mentally nodded and then said aloud, "I couldn't agree with you more DG. The Scourge are on our doorstep and we'll need every advantage we can get to stop them. We're nearly there so let's get moving and see what Concord Central Command has to say about the state of affairs."

As they jump-jetted closer to Central there was evidence of the recent battle. Laser scorch marks and plasma burns pockmarked the barricade surrounding the base and even along the foot of the cruiser. Purple Scourge blood lay in congealed pools around the wide gateway where the fighting had been most intense. A number of obviously weary battleframe pilots patrolled the top of the wall but were still ready to repel additional assaults.

"Oh frap, look at that," said Pyro.

Everyone looked up at what was left of the huge gates. Plasteel full of bullet holes hung loosely in strips from the top. Slabs of molten metal had solidified further down the structure revealing a great gaping hole. The gate hinges were almost non-existent and hastily constructed cables and pulleys were holding up the makeshift gates themselves.

"It seems that we weren't the only ones to see some action," Kheldar commented.

Pyro pointed through the open gate and said, "Check out the crossbar. It looks like a pretzel! I didn't think that plasteel could bend like that!"

The crossbar was a beam of pure polished silver plasteel with a cross section of one foot by six inches and a length of just under twenty feet. It previously held the gates closed in the event of an attack but now it lay in a twisted heap of metal forty feet away inside the compound.

Whizzbang replied, "By the looks of it, the gates took a direct artillery shell that obliterated the couplings on the other side."

Bosk let out a slow whistle, "Frap I'm glad you took out that artillery on the hill Whizz."

After having their battleframe sub-carrier credentials scanned and authorised at a number of checkpoints, Whizzbang's squad exited their frames and entered a large cargo elevator that whisked them to the top of the cruiser.

"*Can you all still hear me?*" Whizzbang thought to his squad.

A jumble of thoughts from the five Earthmen impinged onto his consciousness that indicated that they had not lost any of their new abilities after stepping out of their battleframes. The change in each of them appeared to be at least semi-permanent.

The doors slid open and revealed a control room filled with officers scurrying back and forth with messages and monitors that were constantly being updated with information from around Alpha Three. Headset wearing console operators were speaking with battleframe pilots to collect intelligence and issue orders. The main screen currently displayed a large map of the various regions all the way from the farthest north mining settlements to the fishing villages down in the south reaches. It was like a larger and more detailed version of the battleframe wrist-comp map. Surprisingly, it was currently clear of Scourge activity.

The elevator was directly opposite a raised executive boardroom and through a glass wall Whizzbang could see three men and a women shouting and arguing with one another. He sent a thought to his squad, *"OK guys, it's time to disrupt this party."*

"Looks like they need a little help with decision making Whiz," Bosk thought back.

Up until now, no one had paid attention to the occupants in the elevator, but as Whizzbang's squad walked towards the boardroom a hush fell across Central Command. He stopped and turned in surprise towards the men and women who only moments ago were rushing about their duties. They now stood transfixed, as they stared up at him and the other Earthmen. Looking into their eyes, he saw hope reflected back. With a scraping of chairs on plasteel plated floors, those seated stood and as one performed the traditional salute. No member of the Concord would ever be alone. Whizzbang and the rest of the squad formally returned the salute with their two fingers held high.

"Whiz," thought Bosk, *"They're looking as if we're the ones that are going to save them!"*

"Perhaps we are Bosk. We might be the only hope they have…," Whizzbang's thoughts trailed off.

Glancing back towards the boardroom Whizzbang noticed that the argument had halted and each of the Generals were also staring through the glass at him and his squad. Rather than hope, their eyes were riddled with anxiety.

As they continued their walk across the command deck to the boardroom, the operations staff slowly returned to their consoles with what seemed was a fresh sense of vigour to resume their work.

Standing in the doorway to greet them was a familiar old grizzled face with a thick bristled silver moustache and short, severe, military haircut that matched. Despite being in his early seventies, there was not an ounce of fat on General Frank McLeod's muscular body. "Whizzbang, is it really you? Are you really here?" he asked rhetorically.

Whizzbang nodded and said, "In the flesh General."

"Please, Franky to you Whiz. I still can't believe you really came to help us."

Smiling Whizzbang replied, "Trust me Franky; I sometimes can't believe it either. I'm sorry for the delay in getting to Central. We were held up due to some pretty exceptional circumstances…"

Franky held up his hand to stop Whizzbang from speaking further, "Don't worry about it Whizz, I've received a full report from Selfia and as far as I'm concerned it's a miracle you made it through at all. I've heard that the new interstellar TransWarp can be a bit rough."

Whizzbang raised an eyebrow at that last comment and said, "That's got to be the understatement of the year. Before the port, we just had a little disagreement with a few Scourge friends over a hill and house." As they talked, Franky ushered them into the boardroom and indicated they should all take a seat around the large central table. A jug of water rested on the table and each of the Generals had a glass in front of them that they had been drinking. Once seated, Whizzbang introduced his squad to Franky and the three Concord Generals seated opposite.

Franky said, "Thanks for the intros Whizz, you six are becoming quite famous in the Concord. But I'm forgetting my manners; this is Generals, Alban, Felesh and Bardon."

"We're pleased to meet you Generals," Whizzbang said. He then sent a thought to the rest of the squad, *"There's something not right here. Keep your wits about you!"*

Bosk replied, *"I can feel the tension in the air but there's something else…"*

Whizzbang broadcast to the squad, *"Attention Pyro, Elzetro! Bosk and I will be focusing our attention on talking. I want you two to see if you can pick up any extraneous thoughts. We're new at this sort of thing but see what you can make out. Kheldar, DG get ready for action!"*

The four responded almost instantaneously, *"CT Whizz"*

Chapter 10
Dissention

General Felesh had a short-cropped standard military haircut and an impeccably pressed jet-black uniform with a short-collared jacket buttoned to the neck. Gold braiding adorned both his shoulders and cuffs to signify his rank and a silver embroidered jumping fox emblazoned his left jacket pocket indicating that he was in the intelligence service. A number of coloured medals above the fox sparkled whenever they caught the overhead lights.

With a surprisingly soft voice Felesh said, "At long last we have a chance to meet Whizzbang. What is it that the Scourge calls you?" Pausing in thought for a second, he continued, "That's right, the StarBlade. From your recent exploits it's a title well deserved I hear."

"Thank you General. I'm only doing my duty sir."

"Of course you are. It's the job of every battleframe pilot to defend the Concord."

Other than a different array of medals and an insignia in the shape of eagle's wings on her jacket pocket General Alban was dressed in a similar fashion to General Felesh. Her ponytail swung back and forth, as she studied each of the Earthmen with her dark green eyes. Whizzbang estimated that she was in her mid-thirties, although he had always found it hard to judge a woman's age. Putting down her glass she said, "Gentlemen, it is good to see you all. Like Franky said, I can hardly believe that you're actually here."

Whizzbang thought to his squad, *"Pyro, Elzetro, any update?"*

"Nothing. Continuing scans."

"Thank you General, your welcome is well received."

The notable difference between General Bardon and his colleagues was his deep sun tanned skin, furrowed brow and neatly clipped moustache. It was clear that he was a man of action and the quintessential infantryman. With a deep booming voice he said, "I've heard of your exploits Whizzbang and Bosk. It's a pleasure to meet your sons and friends as well." Still speaking to Whizzbang but pointing at Bosk his voice rapidly increased in volume, "What I also know is that hundreds died in the attack on Freehold while you were off searching for him. Frap, with your abilities you could have saved those people!"

Franky cut across the General, interrupting him and said, "I think what the General is trying to say is that he was impressed with your squad's recent performance and that it's good to have you with us."

Whizzbang ignored Franky's attempt at being a peacemaker, sometimes things needed to be voiced. "General Bardon, I believe you were speaking about the time that the Concord had wrenched me unknowingly into Alpha Three. Is that correct?"

General Bardon smiled, took a long drink from his glass and in a completely calm voice said, "Well done Whizz. I needed to see if you would stand up for yourself. It's one thing to read a report it's quite another to see how someone responds to a bit of combat, even if it's only verbal." The General blinked his eyes rapidly a number of times as if to clear his head. "I'm also deeply sorry for pulling you in to this mess without your permission." Looking across at the other Generals he continued, "We should have been better than that."

Whizzbang's steely blue eyes locked onto General Bardon, assessing the General's intentions and he finally nodded in acceptance of the apology.

Bosk casually rested his arms on the table and leaned forward as he said, "I'm glad that's settled. So what's going on Generals? You seemed to be having some sort of argument when we first arrived." In his, typically Bosk understated manner he added, "Just for the record, yelling at each other in front of subordinates probably isn't a really good idea."

General Felesh's soft voice still had the ability to sound like a cracked whip. "Who are you to lecture us?"

"Hey, I'm just trying to pass on some friendly advice."

Pyro's thought broke through the verbal exchange, *"Dad, the Generals are wound up like tight springs and are on the point of breaking. I'm picking up a few thoughts but it's like cracking a safe. I just need a few minutes more..."*

Whizzbang afforded a glance across to the two young men and was not surprised when he saw a trickle of sweat run off his son's temple. It looked like they were really going at it and thankfully they were not being too obvious. An incredibly difficult task considering they had no idea what they were actually doing. *"Nothing like learning on the job,"* he thought to himself.

"We never asked for your advice!" retorted General Felesh, "I voted against bringing you here. It was a mistake and should never have been done!"

General Alban rubbed her forehead with her fingertips and took another sip of her water. Finally, she said with a sigh, "Felesh, we've been through this a hundred times before and we all know your position on the matter. We took a vote and the results of the vote sit before us."

"The vote was wrong," Felesh spat back petulantly.

The tension continued to rise in the room as the Generals bickered back and forth about past decisions. An invisible hand seemed to be driving them towards the brink of a cliff and goading them along the last few inches. Whizzbang could feel that there was going to be violence and nothing, it would seem, was going to stop it.

General Bardon was now yelling at Franky. His deep reverberating voice sounded more like a battering ram. "You're pathetic! You were the one that was supposed to be in charge of Freehold and it very nearly fell. What a disaster!"

Franky uncharacteristically snarled back, "And where were you and your forces General! Mine were dying while yours were protecting your penthouse!"

"Why you little scum! At last I know what you're really thinking."

"Shut up you two!" General Alban yelled.

General Bardon smacked her verbally down with his best parade ground voice, "Who do you think you are? Lord high lady! For fraps sake, your drop ships have been an absolute waste of resources and you continue to miss crucial supply shipment deadlines while my men and women die."

General Alban leaped to her feet slamming the chair to the floor in her haste, "How dare you! My pilots are being slaughtered as they bring in your supplies and you call them a waste!"

All the Generals were now standing and completely ignoring the Earthmen as they screamed and yelled at each other. Recriminations, accusations and vitriol poured forth with a level of hate and disdain that was shocking to behold.

"We're not going to abandon Alpha Three!" Franky angrily said to General Felesh.

With a deadly calm voice Felesh replied, "But now is the ideal time to escape this death trap while we still can."

General Bardon grabbed Felesh's arm and bellowed, "Over my dead body! Alpha Three's our only hope!"

General Alban slammed her glass of water on the table so hard it nearly shattered. "General McLeod, I'm sick of seeing my crews dying while you're safe and secure in your towers. Do you have any idea what a magnet a drop ship is to Scourge fire?"

"I don't give a frap about your drop ships. I'd rather glide anyway. We all suffer losses so get over it," Franky retorted.

"She's too weak to be a Concord General," tipped in General Felesh.

"Who are you calling weak you snivelling incompetent wretch?" General Alban retorted.

General Bardon boomed in, "Felesh may be right. Never did trust a woman doing a man's job."

There was a mental click as Pyro cracked the safe, *"Oh frap! It's in the water! Don't drink the water, there's a drug in it that's driving them all crazy."*

The Earthmen were now on their feet and Kheldar and DG were moving around the other side of the large table to put a stop to any physical violence. Whizzbang watched in alarm as each of the Generals hands began to drift towards their belt holsters. Thinking only to interrupt their remonstrations he said, "Generals! Please stop this bickering. This is exactly what the Scourge would want us to be doing."

Four sets of eyes swung around to his, three faces looked tormented, twisted and seethed with anger. The fourth face only smiled and in a flash Whizzbang knew what he was dealing with.

Pyro's thought cut across the exchange, *"Dad, I can see everything now! It's Felesh! I know his every thought and deed. You have to see this! This General is one bad dude."*

Elzetro was the first to see it and mentally yelled, *"He's a Scourge spy!"*

Chapter 11
Water, Poison and the Barrier

Whizzbang instantly broadcast, *"DG, Kheldar now!"*

That is when all hell broke loose. As if in slow motion, Whizzbang watched as Franky, Alban and Bardon pulled their blaster pistols from their holsters and rather than pointing at someone raised the barrel and pushed it under their own chins.

General Felesh drew his own weapon while screaming, "The StarBlade must die…"

With his finger moving towards the firing stud, General Felesh suddenly stopped yelling and moving. He froze in space, unable to move a single muscle even down to the slight movement necessary to blow a hole the size of a deck of cards through Whizzbang's chest.

Pyro thought grimly, *"Dad, I've got him."*

At the same time, DG and Kheldar moved faster than humanly possible and knocked the blasters out of the hands of Alban and Bardon. When he first saw the Generals going for their weapons, like DG and Kheldar, Bosk moved blindingly fast, grabbed the nearest thing to hand, and hurled it at Franky. It just so happened that the nearest thing was the glass jug of drugged water. His nano-enhanced muscles and coordination sent the jug straight into Franky's chest. Water sprayed in all directions as it struck home and with a crash shattered against the metal plasteel floor. This gave Whizzbang the time to leap over the table and knock Franky's blaster from his hand.

DG quickly gathered up the weapons as Kheldar manhandled the Generals into their seats. The crashing of the jug on the floor seemed to have brought some semblance of sanity back into the situation.

Whizzbang thought towards his son so that all the Earthmen could hear, "*OK Pyro, show me what you've got.*"

Pyro showed his father, Bosk and Elzetro how he had managed to "hack" General Felesh's mind. Now that they witnessed the technique each of them were confident that they could apply it to any individual.

"Stroke of genius son. We all need to be careful with this sort of ultimate power over people. Now let's see what our General Felesh knows…"

For the next ten minutes, the General was subject to the most thorough interrogation ever applied in the history of the Concord. Felesh tried to resist a number of times but four of the most powerful minds in the galaxy battered his feeble defences aside, demanded and received answers. They went over every thought, experience and idea that the General had in his entire life.

General Felesh was not actually the General at all but a clever facsimile. The Scourge had killed the real General Felesh two years earlier and substituted him with a Scourge spy. The science of that time allowed the alteration of facial features of a person whose job it was to remain inconspicuous. As head of the Concord intelligence operations on the planet, Felesh had been able to block any significant advances against the Scourge by cleverly relaying the positions of Concord forces at critical times to his Scourge handler.

The first time that he had met with his handler was about a year ago, while on a solo reconnaissance mission to the west. It was during this meeting that the idea surfaced for him to disable the

Concord defence grid so that command centre screens would not show the movement of Scourge troops. The timing had to be right after recent secret reinforcements arrived at the Scourge command dome on the other side of Alpha Three. He used a subspace communicator hidden behind a secret panel in his personal quarters to receive his orders and time the attack.

While the interrogation was taking place, Kheldar called for medics and within minutes, he ushered them into the room where they inspected the other Generals to make ensure that there were no after effects of the drugged water. The water had traces of thalapozime in it, a drug that wildly exaggerate emotions and induce extreme paranoia. As they drank the water, the General's behaviour would become more and more erratic.

Each of the Generals received a counteragent to nullify the effects of the drug and a thorough examination to make sure that there were no lasting side effects. It was not long before the counteragent had completed its job and the Generals were well on their way to being back to themselves, although a little embarrassed by the experience.

"Pyro, you can release General Felesh now," Whizzbang ordered.

Felesh slumped forward in his chair as soon as Pyro released the mental constraints. Regaining his composure, he glared at Whizzbang and growled, "Granfaq aldag iet StarBlade."

Although Whizzbang's ears picked up the sound of Scourge speech, his mind was still in tune with Felesh's and automatically translated, "You will die StarBlade."

Whizzbang look Felesh directly in the eye and answered, "Gred a valqa gled ie vana pred."

When Whizzbang spoke the Scourge language, a surprised Kheldar looked across to Bosk for the translation. "Whizzbang said, 'Yes I will but not today.'"

"Good answer," Kheldar replied.

Felesh's eyes registered surprise and shock at Whizzbang's reply in the Scourge language. Reverting to the Concord standard he said, "You don't stand a chance you know. Our forces are overwhelming."

Whizzbang's eyes never left Felesh's, "That may be true but you underestimate our resolve. In my world there have been many people that have thought the way you do and each of them has been defeated by those that cherish life."

Felesh spat in Whizzbang's face and screamed, "Your race is a blight on the galaxy! You will be erased from history as we are the Scourge!"

Whizzbang calmly wiped the spittle from his face with the back of his arm. "I've had about enough of you. Time for a sleep. Pyro, if you'd please."

Pyro flicked a mental switch and General Felesh's head flopped forward in deep sleep.

"Pyro, how long do you think he'll be out for?"

"I just reset his internal body clock so that he felt like he hadn't had any sleep for about a week. My guess is that he'll be out for about twelve hours."

Whizzbang smiled at Pyro. "You did good son, really good." He then pressed the intercom and ordered security to come and haul Felesh away. By the time security arrived, the three remaining Generals were no longer feeling any effects from thalapozime and had regained their seats around the table.

Bosk slumped into a chair and looked forlornly at the fresh jug of water in the middle of the table. "Please excuse me for saying this but I never did trust anything that I could see right through. Is there any chance we could get a beer and some food up here? I'm starved after all of that action."

Franky laughed and everyone around the table quickly joined in. It was the laughter of relieved tensions and the simple joy of being alive to fight another day. Finally, Franky said, "Bosk, you have a way about you don't you? My friend, you're right. An army fights on the strength of its last meal." Still chuckling to himself, he pushed an intercom button and ordered a veritable feast brought to the boardroom.

For the next fifteen minutes, there was some small talk, as both parties began to get to know one another. General Bardon's brow was not nearly as furrowed without the drug in his body and he voiced what the other Generals were thinking, "Who would have thought it was Felesh? I've known the man for over fifteen years!"

Whizzbang said, "It's not your fault General. The spy was a facsimile of Felesh planted by the Scourge to disrupt the Concord's command structure at a crucial moment. That moment was just before we arrived. The real Felesh was captured a couple of years ago."

There was a polite knock at the boardroom door and the jug of water made way for the food and a selection of non-clear beverages. Whizzbang reflected that a possible downside to using some of their new abilities was they seemed to consume a large amount of energy. This theory certainly explained why they all seemed to feel so hungry.

Between mouthfuls of a chicken sandwich, Pyro broke the silence, "Generals you need to know what we've found out."

"What's that son?" General Bardon replied.

"Felesh reported directly to a General Grendig who resides in a command dome around the other side of Alpha Three. Felesh coordinated the recent Scourge attacks against the Concord for maximum impact. He was the one that scrambled the Concord's defence grid that allowed Scourge troops to be positioned throughout Alpha Three without them being detected. What he didn't anticipate was us," Pyro indicated the Earthmen. "After their recent defeats, the Scourge are at their weakest for quite some time and have retreated back to their dome while they await additional off-world reinforcements."

It was at this point that Whizzbang jumped in and said, "It's from the fortress that the Barrier that's keeping the Concord locked into this tiny part of the planet is generated. Generals, in my opinion, right now we have an opportunity to retake Alpha Three but we need to act quickly and decisively."

"How did you get all this information?" Franky asked.

"And here I was seriously considering Felesh's idea of evacuation," General Alban mumbled half to himself.

Whizzbang sent a thought to the squad, "*Should I tell them?*"

Bosk replied, "*I don't think we have any choice.*"

The others gave a mental nod of agreement.

Whizzbang took a deep breath and said, "Generals we've got to tell you something…"

Whizzbang and the team explained what happened to them when they put on their battleframes and some of the new abilities that they had discovered. General Alban was sceptical at first but her eyes widened in surprise and understanding after Whizzbang sent a thought directly to her. A person can never lie to another when they are in direct mental rapport with each other and therefore she knew that Whizzbang was telling the truth.

Franky took a long swig of his beer and said, "What else can you guys do?"

Whizzbang said, "We don't actually know. We think that something happened when our physiology encountered the nanomeds. Has anyone experienced anything like this before?"

Franky looked to the other Generals who were both shaking their heads, "Not that we're aware of. As you know from the computer game, Altavia and Professor Zeinberg developed the nanomeds as a way to heal infantry and keep them in the field as long as possible. Other than telepathy can you do anything else, anything at all?"

"We really haven't had a chance to find out or do any real experimentation and by the sounds of the new Scourge intelligence we're not going to get a chance any time too soon."

"What do you mean?" Bardon asked.

"The Concord has a real opportunity to take back Alpha Three and I think we need to seize it with both hands."

"Whizz, I know you guys are good and your new abilities are amazing but the Barrier will kill you as fast as me."

"I wonder…," Whizzbang paused mid-sentence and then turning to his squad he asked, "Did any of you drink the drugged water?"

Bosk said, "Come to think of it after the journey from Free I was a little thirsty so we probably all did." The other members of the squad nodded their heads in agreement.

Whizzbang pondered aloud, "Why didn't it affect us like the Generals then?"

Elzetro replied, "It could be that our biological machines have a slightly different genetic make-up so we are immune?"

"That could be the answer but I bet we're immune to a lot of things now. General Alban, is there any cyanide on this base?"

"Of course, it's used in the manufacturing of some specific electronic components."

"Can you please ask for some to be brought up?"

"Yes but why?"

"I have a hunch about something."

A few minutes later, an aid placed a glass bottle of deadly cyanide on the table and then exited the room. Bosk wrinkled his nose when Whizzbang poured a glass of water from the jug that had been pushed aside earlier.

"I'll just put enough cyanide into the glass to make me sick but hopefully not kill me."

Bosk exclaimed, "What the?"

"Trust me Bosk."

Everyone looked on with astonishment as Whizzbang took a few sips of the water and then downed a full mouthful.

Whizzbang looked back at his son and friends and said, "Well, I'm waiting for the poison to take effect."

Still nothing happened so he then drank the whole glass.

Bosk said, "Do you feel anything?"

"Other than having drunk the water a little too fast I feel fine."

"Dad, seriously, don't ever do this again. What was the point?"

"I think we can survive in the Barrier."

"The Barrier! You've got to be joking!" Franky exclaimed.

Thirty minutes later the Generals and the Earthmen found themselves in their battleframes standing next to the enigmatic sparkling purple tinged impenetrable wall known as the Barrier. Many battleframe pilots had tried to see what was on the other side of the Barrier and some had paid with their lives for the experience. The massive Concord repulsor beams were the only power that affected the Barrier by shielding the current Concord area on the planet. Nothing else had managed to do anything against the Barrier.

Whizzbang tied a rope around his waist and said to Bosk, "Give me thirty seconds and no matter what pull me back."

"CT Whizz"

Without further fuss, Whizzbang stepped through the Barrier and was pleasantly surprised to see that he felt normal. For the first ten seconds or so tiny purple sparks moved up and down his arms and legs but that was all.

Whizzbang sent a questing thought towards his son, *"Do you hear me?"*

"Loud and clear Dad. Is everything OK?"

"All is good. Hang on, let me try something."

Whizzbang looked at the Barrier and "pushed" at it with his will power. The Barrier seemed to respond by creating a bubble of free normal space around him. Whizzbang pushed a little harder, focusing ever-increasing levels of his will into the task. Slowly but surely the Barrier retreated away from him until he could clearly see Bosk holding his end of the rope.

"OK, show-off, that seemed to work. How'd you do it?" Bosk asked.

Whizzbang smiled and said, "It's actually quite easy. In fact, we can survive in the Barrier quite fine and other than a purple haze to everything, it's quite normal. All I did was focus my will to push it back."

All the Earthmen headed into the Barrier and even DG and Kheldar did not have any problems other than they could not push anything away with their will power. After returning to Franky and the others Whizzbang said, "Generals, we need your help."

General Alban said, "There's something that we need to clean up first Whizzbang."

"Sir?"

Franky said in a very formal voice, "By the power invested in me by the Concord and my fellow Generals I now announce to those present as witnesses that Whizzbang is to be promoted to the rank of Commander."

General Alban gave a wink and said, "We thought that we'd better make it official seeing that we've heard that the whole of Freehold refer to you as Commander anyway."

The accolades and ranks did not finish with Whizzbang. Each member of the squad of Earthmen gained a rank in the Concord. Bosk became Sub-Commander, Elzetro and Pyro Lieutenants and DG and Kheldar Captains.

Despite standing next to the Barrier, it was a moving moment for each member of the squad to receive their rank and commission. If it is one thing that Generals know how to do and that is to bestow honours.

At the end of the ceremony Franky asked, "So, what do you need of us three Generals Commander?"

To speed things up Whizzbang went into mental rapport with the three of them as well as linking in his squad, "*I plan on taking my squad of Earthmen into the Barrier to attack and destroy the Scourge fortress and Barrier towers.*"

It did not take the Generals long to get accustomed to telepathy and General Bardon thought to the group, "*That's an ambitious plan Commander.*"

"*Yes it is, but after Felesh's interrogation we have a window of opportunity now.*"

"*What else do you need?*" General McCleod asked.

"*I need all the drop ships in Alpha Three and pilots crazy enough to fly above the Barrier to this point here.*" He then mentally sent a position on the map of Alpha Three on the other side of the world.

General Alban mentally said, "*I have just the person to lead that sort of crazy job.*"

"*Who?*"

"Why me of course!"

General Bardon mentally spoke to Alban via Whizzbang, *"It's good to see that you still get messy in affairs General."*

"I've been known to indulge from time to time. Just like you General Bardon," Alban said with a smirk on her face.

Franky cut across the good-natured banter. *"You need anything else Whizz? Anything all?"*

Whizzbang thought for a moment, *"Yes, there is one more thing General. Can the Concord fix up my bar tab at Folley's? I didn't realise how expensive drinks were in Alpha Three and the men and women at Freehold can really drink!"*

All three Generals laughed heartily and Franky mentally said, *"Consider it done."*

Whizzbang sent a thought to Bosk, *"It's good to see the Generals laughing."*

"Yes. We arrived with them at each other's throats and now they're beginning to function as a team once again."

"It's what we do Bosk. We fix things."

"Now we just need to fix this Scourge base."

"I wish we'd had more time to experiment with our new capabilities."

"I just wish I had a drink," Bosk replied quirkily.

Now it was time for Whizzbang to laugh, *"Bosk, I think it's time to see if these Generals have any of the 'good stuff' ferretted away somewhere."*

Bosk's face split into a grin and Franky asked, *"What's the joke Bosk?"*

"General, I was wondering if you happen to have…"

Chapter 12
Attack!

The purple hued clouds far below slowly slid by as the drop ship made its way to the other side Alpha Three. The Barrier sparkled through the gaps in the clouds and tinged the landscape with a purple hue. It looked like they were now traveling over a vast forest while twenty minutes earlier they had been flying above snow-capped mountains.

Their aircraft was the lead drop ship in a squadron that comprised every vessel that could fly on the planet. Each craft was jam packed full of battleframe pilots that were all eager to get on with the mission. As soon as Whizzbang's squad had infiltrated the Scourge base, they were to destroy the Barrier towers so that the rest of the pilots could join in. Newly appointed as strike leaders, Gardner, Acheron, Happy and Tiny coordinated three squads each. After hearing of Selfia's respect amongst the other pilots the Generals promoted Selfia to the rank of group strike leader to help in the coordination of the entire assault. Their orders were to wait up top for Whizzbang's signal that the Barrier was clear before entering the battle.

Tearing his eyes away from the window Whizzbang said a few words of encouragement to the Earthmen and headed up the short ladder to talk with the pilot. Due to a shortage of pilots, the dual seat cockpit was currently only occupied by one. There was nothing to see in the cockpit. It was completely devoid of instruments and surrounded by reinforced armour with no glass visible whatsoever. Covered in sensors, the pilot's flight suit linked directly into the flight control systems of the dropship. The helmet provided an unobstructed virtual view of everywhere around the ship as well as relevant instrumentation and weapons status. It was very different to the flight decks that Whizzbang had experienced when he did his pilot's training back on Earth.

"General, is there much further to go?" he asked.

Whizzbang watched as General Alban twitched her hand and reached up to adjust an invisible dial before she replied, "We're nearly at the drop point. You'd better let the others know."

"Thank you for flying us out here."

"Not a problem, it's great to get behind the controls of a bird again. I've spent way too much time being a desk jockey these past years."

"All the same, it's good to have you here. How much time do we have?"

"We should all be able to circle for a couple of hours before low fuel forces us to return. It's not much time but it's all we can give you. Do you have the tellurite explosives to take those Barrier towers out?"

Whizzbang nodded, "I think we've got enough to bring them down, anymore and we'll be too heavy to glide. General, if we're longer than a couple of hours then we most likely haven't succeeded. Promise me that you'll bug out and see to the defence of the colony.

"I promise Commander. By the way, remember that when you set the fuses you've only twenty minutes to get clear. Once set, nothing can shut off the detonators so there won't be any fancy count-down timers for you."

Whizzbang laughed nervously and said, "General, we'll do our best." He then grew serious and placed a number of envelopes on the vacant co-pilot's seat. "I was wondering, if we don't make it could you arrange this to be sent through to my wife and Pyro's mother. There's also one envelope for each of the others."

General Alban looked at the envelopes as if they were poisonous snakes and said, "I've given messages like them to wives and children too many times over the years. Whizzbang, you're going to make it through this."

"All the same, we'd all appreciate it if you could forward them on."

"It would be an honour Commander. Let the others know that the messages will be sent through." Glancing up at an instrument she said, "OK, we're coming up to the drop point. You'd better get back there. I'll look for the explosions and see you in a couple of hours."

"Good bye General."

"Good luck Commander." Then awkwardly swinging around in her seat General Alban saluted Whizzbang with her two fingers to the chest and then to the sky. "You won't ever be alone."

Whizzbang smiled, "Thank you General," and then left to head down to the launch bay and the rest of his squad.

Coming down the steps from the cockpit Whizzbang looked across at his son who was now a Lieutenant in the Concord. He had already seen and won more battles than most people had ever dreamed. Bosk and Elzetro were talking quietly together while DG and Kheldar were being their normal selves, cracking a few jokes with Pyro. Whizzbang was proud of these friends, and he prayed that nothing would happen to any of them.

He cleared his throat and then chuckled at it being unnecessary. He thought, "*Gentlemen, it's time.*"

Five sets of eyes turned to meet his.

"*I just want to say that I'm proud to be leading you and…*"

"*Would you shut up,*" Bosk replied. "*It sounds to me like you were about to give one of those movie speeches before a big battle where half the people don't come back and the hero dies.*"

Everyone, including Whizzbang laughed, "*Bosk, where would we be without you? You've known me way too long. Remember that we're going to be stretching the glide so keep your height and follow my lead. What I would like to do is say a few words of prayer though, anything that will give us an edge.*"

Pyro thought, "*Let me Dad.*"

Whizzbang nodded.

"*God, keep us safe, may we destroy the Barrier and take out this base. Amen.*"

"*Well, that was short and sweet,*" said Elzetro.

Pyro replied defensively, "*If I was God, I'd want prayers to be like battlespeak. So that makes it short and to the point.*"

"*It was a good prayer son. We couldn't want any more than that.*"

Everyone nodded in agreement. Just then the light indicating the jump point changed from red to green and Whizzbang went into rapport with the General, "*We're ready here, open the back door General and see you in a couple of hours if not sooner.*"

"*CT Commander, good luck,*" Alban replied.

The back door to the drop ship slowly descended and the airframe shuddered a few times until the control surfaces compensated for the sudden disruption in the aerodynamics. Whizzbang and the squad reached up to the handholds dangling from the roof until the door had fully descended.

Looking out the open back ramp-way, Whizzbang could see the squadron of drop ships following their lead. He sent out a questing thought to the other strike leaders, "*Look after yourself and when we call, come down in speed.*"

Selfia answered on behalf of them all, "*We'll be there Commander. Take care of yourselves.*"

"*Will do Self. See you on Alpha Three!*"

Whizzbang turned to his squad and thought, "*Ready?*"

"*G2G,*" came five replies.

Whizzbang had jumped off mountains and had even searched out the highest points on Alpha Three to extend his time in the air. Jumping out of a drop ship at thirty five thousand feet was like nothing he had experienced before. Once clear of the aircraft the jet stream, over this part of the world, slammed into him and tossed him about like a leaf hurtling down a flooded stream. When he finally energised his glider wings, the sudden deceleration threatened to squish him against his battleframe.

He sent a thought to the squad, *"All wings deployed?"*

"G2G" came five replies followed by Pyro saying, *"Remind me to put some cushions in my battleframe the next time we do this Dad."*

"Good advice Pyro," Elzetro chimed in.

"OK guys, on my six. We've got a long glide ahead." Whizzbang ordered

The six battleframes swung into a "V" formation and Whizzbang referred to his wrist-comp to ensure that they remained on course. The General had dropped them a long way out so that she would not be detected and a Scourge party be arranged in their honour upon arrival.

Peering through his Charge riflescope Whizzbang could see an enormous wall surrounding a structure that would have been at least three times bigger than Central Command. Two massive towers stood on the far side of a domed structure in the centre of the compound. Enormous purple lightning bolts crackled up and down the towers in great pulsing waves of energy. Whizzbang thought to himself, *"Those towers are big. Really big!"*

Whizzbang subconsciously tweaked his glide angle upwards to slow his descent and reduce the airspeed. He knew that behind him the rest of the squad would be doing likewise. If possible, it would be better to have a little bit of extra height when they made their final approach. The reduced speed would also give him additional time to survey the structure.

"Bosk, you seeing this?"

"I'm just looking at it now. It's big isn't it?"

"Yep" Whizzbang thought back. *"Do you think we can clear the wall in the glide?"*

"We should be fine. I think the right hand side is a little lower as the terrain dips down there."

Whizzbang glanced over his shoulder at the sinking sun. *"That's probably a good direction to come in from. Any Scourge sentries will be looking into the sun as we approach."*

Whizzbang adjusted his direction slightly to the right and thought to the squad, *"Gentlemen, we're about to penetrate the Barrier. Stay on me."*

Pyro could not resists sending back, *"Locking X-foils into attack position."*

Elzetro immediately replied, *"Look at the size of that thing!"*

Kheldar laughed across the mental link at the movie parody and said, *"Cut the chatter Elzetro. Remember to stay on target."*

There were a few laughs as the tension gave way to comradery. *"They are the best,"* Whizzbang thought to himself. What the Scourge did not realise was 'The StarBlade' was not one but six and they were on their way.

Hitting the Barrier at fifteen thousand feet did nothing to their glide slope. The now familiar tiny purple sparks fired off the length of their bodies for ten seconds and then everything was normal with a tinge of purple. Whizzbang turned off his local comnet as the Scourge jamming static became too distracting. Besides, with telepathy he did not need his headset anymore. Bringing his Charge riflescope up to his eye, he could just make out two sniper class Scourge sentries walking the top of the wall. Dropping into battlespeak he ordered, *"Bosk, Sniper left, I'm right. On my mark."*

"CT Whizz, Sniper left mine."

Coming in with the sun behind them, they would be almost invisible to the sentries on the wall but Whizzbang left nothing to chance and waited until the last possible moment before revealing themselves with a blue Charge rifle beam. Broadcasting to Bosk he said, *"Three, two, one, mark."*

On the word "mark" the two sentries quite literally lost their heads as both their skulls were punctured by two intense blue beams of energy. Whizzbang ignored the Snipers bodies and the squad silently glided over the wall into the compound below. Once landed they all scurried behind the cover of a huge industrial sized waste bin against the side of a building. Luckily, there did not appear to be any enemy in the huge compound.

"Pyro, Elzetro, Bosk identify targets," Whizzbang ordered.

DG and Kheldar readied their weapons to guard the four telepaths as they went to work. During the skirmish in the boardroom, the Earthmen discovered that telepaths could sense thoughts and the physical location they came from. Whizzbang and the other telepaths sent a blanket of questing mental energy out from their position and together they began to build a picture of all of the living entities within the fortress.

Whizzbang marked the three long structures to the east as barracks and he thought they could house around four thousand Scourge warriors. Presently they contained only several hundred different thought patterns. Thankfully, the expected reinforcements had not arrived yet, that was a relief. Along the wall, were around twenty sentries and another one hundred thought patterns were within the central command dome. A smattering of other thoughts emanated from the various other buildings and a group of eight distinct patterns were coming from within a building between the two Barrier towers.

Whizzbang focused on the tower building to confirm there were still only eight thought patterns within it. He then suddenly received a surprise. By focusing his thoughts, he was able see exactly what was inside each structure. He swung his newfound perception around to each of the other buildings. With a little effort, he received a complete mental picture of exactly what was within each of them.

"Dad, how did you do that?"

In his excitement at having perfect intelligence, he had forgotten he had been in rapport with the squad. *"I wish we had more time to work out what we can do now. Try this."* He excitedly instructed them on how to tap into their new perception.

"This is incredible," Bosk, answered in awe, *"It's like an enhanced way of seeing whatever we want. Check this out, we can even look around as*

if it's broad daylight, even though the sun is just about set behind the mountains. Having ultra-vision like this means we can literally see around walls. It's a completely new ballgame!

In a few minutes, each of them tested out what Bosk was talking about and it was not long before ultra-vision became as natural to them as seeing with their own eyes.

Whizzbang ordered, *"Pyro, keep a mental eye on the barracks, Elzetro, the out buildings and wall, Bosk, you concentrate on the central dome. I'll broadcast what's happening in the building between the towers. As soon as you notice a change let us all know. Make sure you're sharing this squad wide and that DG and Kheldar are kept in the loop."*

"CT" came three mental responses.

Whizzbang mentally mapped out the plan to the squad, *"Our first objective is to take out the Barrier towers so that the cavalry up top can swoop in. This means that we'll have to remove the threats in the control room."* He marked the control room off on the mental picture. *"We then need to place the explosives at the base of each tower and to be doubly sure, inside the control room as well."* Once again, he indicated the precise locations for each explosive. *"If we take out these columns at the base of the towers then the towers should fall to either side of the command dome. If we can create any more mayhem that's well and good but let's not get the ant nest too excited until we're long gone and we can call in additional support."*

From his crouched position, Whizzbang watched the shadows lengthen and deepen as the sun finally set behind the wall over which they had just glided. They would leave in a few minutes and with any luck, the two bodies on top of the wall would not be discovered before the mission was completed.

Elzetro sent a thought towards the squad, *"I think we have a problem."*

"What do you mean?" Whizzbang asked.

"Take a look at that dish over there," Elzetro mentally pointed out a communications array on the other side of the command dome.

"What about it Elzetro?"

"I can be corrected but I believe that the big one is an interstellar dish which means that this base is in communication with someone else."

Chapter 13
More to do

Whizzbang let out a mental expletive and thought, *"Thanks for the heads up Elzetro."* After a brief pause to think through the ramifications of Elzetro's intelligence he continued, *"Guys, this isn't going to be a smash and grab after all. We need to know where and whom this command dome is speaking. If we don't take this opportunity here and now then we'll never be able to truly free Earth and the Concord."*

"What do we have to do?" DG asked.

"We need to continue with the mission to take out the Barrier towers but we also need to find out who's pulling the strings here. Let's get the explosives set by first taking out the team in the control room. Once that's completed we'll tackle the command dome itself."

Bosk thought to the group, *"Let me understand this Whizz. We take out the control room, plant the explosives at the base of the towers and then quietly sneak up on the hundred Scourge in the command dome. We do all this while the Scourge in the barracks sit all nice and tucked into their beds, no one notices the dead sentries on top of the wall or hears us take out the eight Scourge in the control room."*

"As usual Bosk, you've summarised the situation nicely."

"Whizz, just one thing." Bosk said.

"What's that?"

"How in the frap are we going to do all of this and get out of here?"

Whizzbang smiled at his friend and thought, *"I've no idea but let's take one step at a time. First, the control room."*

It was a testimonial to the strength of resolve in the Earthmen to see a task fulfilled and the confidence they had in each other that they quickly encompassed this new objective. With their new capabilities, Whizzbang's squad was actually the best of the best and they simply went about the business of actioning what needed doing.

"OK, it's time to go," Whizzbang thought to his squad.

Leaving the temporary security of their position behind the industrial waste bin the squad darted from one shadow to another in the direction of the Barrier tower control room. There was a collective mental sigh from the group as a Scourge technician exited a building across from where they were hiding, walked by their position and around a corner. Finally, the squad reached the shadowed side of the control room. Their luck held and no alarm had sounded.

"OK, ready? Remember what we'd planned. We can't risk sounding the alarm."

While DG and Kheldar stood watch in the shadows, the four telepathic humans did what only a few days previously would have been impossible. They began unpicking the mental locks of four of the Scourge in the control room. After the experience in the boardroom with General Felesh those locks quickly sprung open revealing the Scourge intellect within. There was nothing particularly special or insightful about what those minds revealed. Their sole and singular purpose was to keep the Barrier towers operational.

What each of those Scourge technicians did have at their waist was a pistol and as one, they pulled them out of their holsters and shot their four comrades other comrades in the back of the head. They then turned their weapons on each other and again pressed the firing stud. Eight bodies with neatly drilled holes in their heads slumped across consoles or lying sprawled along the plascrete floor. It was clean; it was efficient; and graphically displayed the power of psionic battleframe pilots.

"*All still clear?*" Whizzbang asked.

"*Barracks, clear,*" Pyro answered.

"*Outbuildings and wall normal,*" Elzetro followed.

"No *activity from the command dome,*" Bosk replied.

Whizzbang lead the way into the Barrier tower control room. He wrinkled his nose as the smell of charred flesh greeted him. "*Quickly, we've got to set the technicians up and get out of here,*" he thought to the squad.

While Bosk laid an explosive charge under a console, the rest of the squad cleaned up the Scourge corpses as best they could and sat them in various positions at their workstations. It was not likely to fool a close inspection but it may buy time if a guard was just flipping through security screens. In just under thirty seconds, the squad was in and out of the Barrier control room. Whizzbang then sent Bosk, Elzetro, and DG to the first tower while Kheldar, Pyro and he moved to the second.

Up close, the towers were immense structures with super-charged purple Barrier lightning crackling and snapping as it sprung between the two buildings. Each time a huge bolt of energy leapt from one tower to the other the hairs on the back of Whizzbang's arms stood on end and small Barrier sparks would run up and down the length of his body. Miraculously, none of them felt any adverse effects from being so close to the source of the Concord's prison on Alpha Three.

"*How the Barrier works is another mystery to solve,*" Whizzbang thought to himself as the three of them began laying charges around the massive plasteel pillars that supported the towers above.

General Grendig sat irritably on his raised commander's throne in the centre of the command dome. He knew that something was wrong. Years of climbing the Scourge ranks by betraying superiors and eliminating ambitious underlings taught him when something was wrong. Even when he could not put his claw on the reason, he knew better than to ignore his instincts. Lord Zechlan's warning, as crazy as it sounded, added to the fact that an inaudible alarm bell was ringing in his mind!

The General had obeyed Lord Zechlan and recalled all the Scourge forces that remained on Alpha Three back to the fortress. The promised reinforcements arriving via troop transport were still a little over a week away. Until then, he busied himself with making his impregnable fortress even more impossible to assault.

The General had personally inspected the backup systems that ensured the Barrier would pulse its waves of human killing energy across the world. Despite the implausibility of humans breaching the Barrier, he ordered pairs of sentries to patrol the outer wall and to ensure the command dome fully staffed at all times. From sun up until sun down Scourge warriors practiced their various disciplines in the training yard. It was a relief when the noise of beam and blaster fire ceased as the sun began to set and the warriors prepared for their rest cycle.

Even with all of his preparations, General Grendig was in a foul mood as he absently flipped from one security camera to another on the giant screen positioned opposite him. The fortress had hundreds of cameras and it was going to take at least ten minutes to cycle through them all.

General Felesh had been the ultimate spy and a resource that had proved most useful in the Scourge's Alpha Three campaign. To replace the actual General with an Ogzmat facsimile had taken years of careful planning. Unfortunately, just when he needed the intelligence the most the General had gone mysteriously silent. "All was going to plan until the 'StarBlade' arrived and delayed the inevitable conquest!" the General fumed.

Grendig slammed his fist against his arm-wrest and let out a low growl. A few of the officer's close by turned their heads nervously towards him. They had good cause to be nervous. In the past, outbursts like this usually resulted in a disintegration as the General looked for a scapegoat upon which to unleash his foul temper. Thankfully, Grendig returned to watching the security footage, giving the officers a reprieve from his wrath.

The image of the Barrier control room flashed up onto the monitor. The technicians were all staring at the screens attached to their workstations. Grendig had seen the picture a thousand times before, skipped to the next image and then paused. The last picture that did not look quite right. Dismissing the thought, he shrugged and moved on. He was secure in his command dome, in the middle of the fortress and surrounded by the Barrier. No human could reach him here. Lord Zechlan was wrong.

For five tedious minutes images flashed by until one of the outer western wall instantly grabbed the General's attention. Purple blood had sprayed across the camera's lens and through the haze, Grendig could see two headless Scourge Sniper sentries sprawled across the top of the walkway. Completely incredulous, it took Grendig several seconds to comprehend what he was looking at. A millisecond later, his claw had punched the alarm stud. The impossible Concord attack had begun!

Whizzbang looked up from placing the last tellurite explosive at the base of the last huge pillar supporting the Barrier tower. The whiplash like snap of Barrier lightning intermittently illuminated his position and he silently prayed, even as he worked, that any Scourge from one of the outbuildings would not spot them. Across from him, his son, Pyro, feverishly worked at securing his final explosive in place. Like a well-oiled machine, the four telepaths kept the squad up to date with the latest Scourge positions on their mental map.

"*You finished Kheldar?*" Whizzbang thought to his friend.

"*All's done Whizz,*" Kheldar replied as he came into view from around the pillar he had been working on.

"*Good. Bosk, how's it going over there?*"

"*Everything's in place Whizz.*"

"*I'll set the remote timer to synchronize the explosives from here. Get your squad over to us.*"

"We'll be with you in a minute."

"CT," Whizzbang replied as he watched Bosk, Elzetro and DG scurry from the Barrier tower opposite and stop behind the control building before running to his position. They did not want to risk the Scourge seeing them blast their jump jets and so they resorted to moving as silently as possible on their servo-powered legs. Flicking open his wrist-comp Whizzbang patched into the charges on each of the pillars and simultaneously set the timer to start the countdown.

As Bosk reached his position Whizzbang thought to the squad, *"It's done. Nothing can stop the explosions now. In twenty minutes the Barrier towers should be down and the pilots up top on their way. Now for the command dome..."*

Just as Whizzbang sent his last thought the entire fortress was instantly flooded in light and a blaring siren began its high-pitched wail. Rather than being hidden in deep shadows the six Earthmen now stood out like ducks in a row against the northern most Barrier tower.

The mental map of the positions of every Scourge began to swarm with activity. In particular, it was clear that the warriors in the barracks were rushing to mobilise for battle.

"That does it! Follow my lead, we need to head to the command dome before this place becomes flooded with Scourge!" Whizzbang thought urgently to his squad.

Now that the Scourge were aware of the attack, Whizzbang kicked in his jump jets and blasted over a number of outbuildings and directly towards the command dome. Bosk and the others followed closely behind. While soaring past the barracks entrance he thought across to DG and Elzetro, *"Any chance you could leave a surprise for the troops leaving the barracks?"*

DG and Elzetro mentally smiled, as they both dropped a full complement of anti-personnel turrets pointing towards the still closed barracks doorway. The nanite packets took a second to fall the fifty feet to the ground and another couple of seconds to energise the turrets. With choreographed precision, ten barrels mounted on squat tripod frames swung around and aimed towards the barracks doorway.

"*That won't hold them for long,*" Whizzbang thought to himself but it would cause them to think there could be more around every corner.

Whizzbang landed with a gentle crunch of his battleframe boots just as a low hum started, underpinning the noise of the blaring siren. Looking upwards, he watched a shimmering green dome begin to take shape above the entire fortress. It did not appear to affect the Barrier towers or their deadly crackling lightning.

"*Elzetro, is that what I think it is?*"

"*It looks to me like some sort of shield Whizz.*"

"*We've got some problems then.*" Whizzbang glanced at his wrist-comp. "*The Barrier towers are coming down in about sixteen minutes and yet with that shield the cavalry up top isn't going to be able to help us out. Suggestions?*"

Bosk replied, "*You can get what you need from the command dome while I take Elzetro and DG to find the shield generators and take them out.*"

"*No, that won't work. We have no idea where they are and even with our new perception, it could take quite some time. Any other suggestions?*"

Kheldar said, "*Can't we just take out a couple of the emitters to break a hole?*"

"*I don't know. I've never seen a shield emitter before. Elzetro is this possible?*"

"*We could do that but my guess is they have literally hundreds of them mounted along the top of the outer wall. It could take a while to knock out enough of them to make a break in the shield.*"

Pyro thought, "*I just had an idea. Why don't we find the shield operator, take over their mind and get him to turn the thing off? He's likely to be in the command dome and it will keep the squad together.*"

Everyone turned towards Pyro, in the pressure of the moment they had all forgotten their new abilities. The low hum of the shield wall underpinned the blare of the alarm siren. In the distance, Whizzbang could just make out the staccato firing of DG and Elzetro's turrets adding themselves to the overall noise.

Smiling at his son Whizzbang replied, "*Pyro, sometimes you come up with some crazy good ideas. OK everyone, we need to find that shield operator in the command dome and we need to find him fast!*"

Pyro placed his armoured hand against the dark metallic side of the giant dome that soared above him. He then sent a thought through the wall to search for anyone that could possibly be a shield operator. With his current skill level, he could identify Scourge technicians, officers and a couple of guards but not much else. From his distance outside the dome, picking the lock of a mind's natural defences was, if possible, a time consuming process. Even with the four of them, they did not have the time to work through each and every control operator to find the one they were after.

Whizzbang on the other hand took an entirely different approach from his son to solving the problem. Rather than using brute mental force, he decided to watch the ego in the centre of the dome. It was clear that this was a person of some importance and after a few seconds, he was able to assemble both an audible and visual picture of his enemy with his new heightened perception.

Despite the typical language barrier associated with audible communication, by using his mind Whizzbang automatically translated everything said into English. He learned that the entity in the centre of the dome was the one and only General Grendig. For the first time ever his spying also resulted in the Concord getting the first glimpse at how a Scourge command structure functioned.

Rather than a willing devotion to a higher ideal like the Concord, Scourge officers perpetually functioned in an atmosphere of fear. Fear that those above may exterminate them and fear that those below may assassinate them to better their own opportunity for promotion. This meant that any middle ranked officers were perpetually looking behind and in front of themselves for the attack on their lives that would inevitably come.

General Grendig roared at a subordinate sitting at a console in front of him, "Reinforce the guards on the outer wall with additional warriors!"

The General's thoughts were in turmoil, "*To be attacked inside his own fortress was unthinkable and yet it was happening! It was clear that his officers had failed him!*"

Clicking his fangs together in anticipation he pointed at a senior staff officer, "Come here!"

The officer knew better than to ignore such an order and almost ran towards the General.

The General's eyes were aflame with blood lust as he said, "Captain Eldark, you command the troops that patrol the outer wall. Is that correct?"

Captain Eldark looked all around himself for a way to escape Grendig's stare as he said, "Yes General!"

"How is it that the perimeter was breached without you knowing?"

"I am uncertain my General but I will find out as soon as the event is finished," the Captain's voice quavered.

General Grendig casually pulled a broad jagged foot long tellurite dagger from its sheathe strapped to his muscular thigh and began fingering the blade. "Captain, is it not your responsibility to ensure the integrity of the wall defence?"

By now, Captain Eldark was on the verge of panicking. His pale face sweated profusely while his beady pink eyes darted back and forth for a way to escape the situation. "Yes my General. I will ensure that those that failed will be punished most severely."

"That will be unnecessary as they have already been dealt with, Captain…"

The Captain sighed in relief. Maybe he would live after all.

The General looked up from his blade at the Captain and growled menacingly, "I have found the two sentries that have failed their duty and they have received their punishments at the hand of the Concord. There is just one other matter…"

With a flick of his wrist, General Grendig sent the twelve inches of tellurite flying through the air to embed in the centre of the Captain's neck. The razor sharp blade sliced through skin, muscle and bone as if they were paper. A great gush of purple blood blossomed and sprayed from the Captain's severed major artery while his body collapsed in a pathetic heap at the General's feet.

Grendig rose out of his throne, bent down and savagely pulled his jagged blade from the former Captain's neck spraying the backs of the officers at their consoles with another fountain of blood. Looking at the purple blood coating his dagger with annoyance he carefully licked the sharp edge clean with his rough black tongue. His bloodlust sated, he re-sheathed his weapon, sat back comfortably on his throne and continued as if nothing was amiss.

"Increase the power to the shield wall," the General ordered an officer sitting at the console to his far right.

Esther carefully pulled out the tiny slip of paper from her pocket and re-read the message for the hundredth time. In plain black on white, there were three characters, "G2G". Mark was not joking when he said that they could only afford to transmit a few bytes of data for messages.

Those three letters encompassed a world of feelings. Russell, James and the others were safe and well on Alpha Three. They were all "Good to Go". A number of days earlier Esther had shared the message with Marie and their girls. They were all so relieved that their men were safe. Coming out of her reverie Esther's attention returned to the three girls working at their bench.

Rose said irritably, "That's not how you insert the plasma injector into the lightning inducer. Can't you two remember anything?"

Mihaly and Marie's daughter Kathryn bit back a retort but there was no such luck with Michelle. "We listened just like you did

Rose! I'm sure that Crystal said we needed to attach the matrix coil first."

Rose looked across at what Michelle was indicating and replied a bit sheepishly, "I think that you may be right."

Kathryn's brown shoulder length locks seemed to shimmer in the brightly lit workroom light as she suddenly smiled triumphantly. "After that I think that we need to screw in the infusers and then we can insert the plasma injector."

Marie looked across at Esther and gave a little grin before she returned to her book on the history of the Concord. Esther rolled her eyes at Marie in the direction of their children. Since the men had left, the five of them had been studying everything they could get their hands on that related to the Scourge, the Concord and technology. They had a lot of learning to do and the Blue Sky Team had been exceptional teachers.

With a wistful sigh, she folded the tiny message and placed it back in her pocket before returning to her book on the basics of nano-technology.

Chapter 14
The Battle in the Dome

Outside the dome, Whizzbang felt revolted by Captain Eldark's execution but satisfied that he now knew which officer controlled the green shield wall. He marked the officer's position on the squad's mental map and said, *"Here's our man. We've got to get close enough to him to invade his mind or shut off the shield ourselves."*

"CT," came five mental replies.

Whizzbang took out a block of chocolate from his battleframe pocket and handed pieces to his fellow telepaths while he munched on a square himself. "I'm sure you've realised that whenever we use our mental powers we consume a lot energy so make sure that each of you keep your levels up."

Pyro quipped, "If it's chocolate, I'm in!"

Elzetro laughed and said, "Bring on the whole block Commander!"

Bosk rolled his eyes at their sons, "Boys will be boys. Whizz, do you have another piece?"

At this stage in their development, the Earthmen were clumsy at best with their new mental abilities. They were using sledgehammers where scalpels would have sufficed and the levels of energy expended were far beyond what they actually needed to accomplish their tasks.

Cocking his head to the side to better listen Whizzbang said, "It looks like DG and Elzetro's welcoming presents have been overcome by the troops in the barracks. Can either of you hear them?"

DG replied, "I can't, all's silent Whizz."

Elzetro said, "Neither can I. Should we drop a few more now?"

Whizzbang estimated that it would only be ten or twenty seconds before the Scourge warriors in the barracks came around the corner. "Not yet," he said aloud and then swapping to telepathy he said, *"Can any of you reach and crack Grendig or the officer in responsible for the shield wall from here?"*

Pyro conveyed what the others were thinking, *"Already tried, it's too far."*

Whizzbang thought for a few precious seconds and then scoped the beginnings of an idea with the rest of the squad. *"Ready?"*

"G2G," came the classic battlespeak response from each of them.

They ran on battleframe servo assisted legs around to the eastern entrance of the command dome. The two Scourge shock troopers guarding the entrance died courtesy of Whizzbang and Bosk's Charge rifle shots. The twin brilliant intense blue beams reached out and skewered the Scourge, one in the chest and the other through the neck. The superheated blast of energy left nothing but smoking remains.

Whizzbang looked at the dual sliding doors of the command dome entrance. They were about ten feet across and of similar height. With his perception, he could see that the six inches of reinforced plasteel was not something that they could penetrate with their current weapons.

"Elzetro, you're the mechanic, any ideas?"

"I don't think we're going to do much good here. There isn't even a locking mechanism to pick on this side Whizz."

336

"OK, *option one is ruled out then.*" Whizzbang reached out with his perception and felt two Scourge minds immediately on the other side of the door. "*There are a couple of guards really close to the door. Let me see if I can crack one of them and get them to open the door from their side. The rest of you do your best to divert the roving Scourge squads around us.*"

Mentally Whizzbang zeroed in on one of the two Slayer guards and began the process of unlocking its mind. Luckily, the Slayer was a relatively simple creature, considerably easier to 'crack' than General Felesh. Even still, it was taking precious seconds to unravel its natural mental defences.

While Whizzbang worked on the Slayer, DG and Kheldar stood guard. Bosk, Pyro and Elzetro applied their skills at mentally nudging Scourge fist leaders away from the direction of the command dome entrance. With so many Scourge, they could not afford to attempt to take over any minds so they planted suggestions that the fist leaders thought were their own. Officers suddenly believed that they heard a sound from the opposite direction to the Earthmen or thought they saw figures running away between buildings. Some were even convinced that the Concord agents were along the outer wall.

The mental map teamed with Scourge running this way and that. Despite their best efforts, a Scourge officer inadvertently turned in their direction. Elzetro thought Pyro was dealing with the fist-leader and Pyro thought Bosk was. It really did not matter who was at fault as a squad of three Slayers, two Engineers and four Shock troopers came running around from the side of a building to stare straight at them.

Bosk thought to the squad, "*We've got company!*"

A bead of sweat trickled down Whizzbang's temple. "*I just need a few more seconds Bosk!*"

"*We'll do our best Whizz.*"

DG and Elzetro instantly sprang into action and dropped a number of anti-personnel turrets from their recharged nanite packets. Snarling Slayers came charging forward with eighteen-inch blades in their hands. Behind them, the Scourge Engineers materialised a couple of golden drones while the Shock troopers dropped to their knees and opened fire. Whizzbang's squad were exposed against the doorway and for the Scourge it was like shooting fish in a barrel. Bullets pinged off armour as the Earthmen gathered around Whizzbang, their bodies providing cover so that he was not distracted from his task.

At last, Whizzbang felt a mental click and he instantly invaded the Slayers mind. Looking through his captive's eyes Whizzbang began taking in his surroundings. He stood in a small empty antechamber with a door at either end leading into the main dome complex. Conveniently, his companion Slayer stood with its back to him only a few feet away, distracted by the faint noise of the attacking squad on the other side of the door.

Whizzbang walked his Slayer over to his companion, silently drew his blade and plunged it up to the hilt into its back. He then guided the body to the floor so as not to make too large a noise. Turning to the door Whizzbang's Slayer entered the access code on the control interface and stepped back as the doorway parted in the middle. The Earthmen streamed into the antechamber to the sounds of ricocheting bullets.

Whizzbang ordered the Slayer outside before slamming his open palm against the emergency close button. A hail of gunfire previously aimed at the Earthmen shredded the Slayer and sent a shock rippling through his still linked mind. He quickly extricated himself from being in rapport with the doomed Scourge, just as he felt it drop to the ground outside, dead.

The zing and bang of gunfire from outside penetrated the antechamber and reverberated off the huge concave roof of the command dome. Scourge officers immediately abandoned their consoles and leapt to their feet in battle readiness. As quickly as the noise started, it vanished when the outside door slammed shut. Officers looked questioningly from one to another and within the centre of dome, General Grendig let out a low growl.

The Scourge command centre was immense. The dome rested on thirty pillars regularly interspersed around the circumference that raised the dome a further fifty feet off the floor. The reinforced plascrete pillars each had a girth of six people holding hands in a circle. The command centre was over three hundred feet across and from the middle of the floor to the domes peak was at least two hundred feet. The dome was fashioned from solid plasteel and rested on each of the immense pillars. A series of mounted automated gun emplacements looked down from where the pillars joined the dome.

Radiating out from the central throne, like spokes on a wheel, were places for almost a hundred officers to man consoles. Some of the officers were still standing while others had regained their seats. All of them had headsets in place that allowed them to communicate with strike leaders. General Grendig sat in the hub of the wheel on a raised dais and stared up at the three massive screens attached to girders high up in the dome.

As soon as the Earthmen walked from the antechamber into the command centre pandemonium broke loose. Scourge officers reached for non-existent weapons and screamed curses at their predicament instead.

"*No weapons?*" Bosk asked.

Whizzbang replied, "*When you're running an organisational structure based on fear you can't afford to have lessors with guns around you. It's likely they'll be turned on you. The guy we've got to watch is…*"

Just as Whizzbang completed his sentence, the command throne swivelled and General Grendig turned to face them. The General's mouth split into an evil sharp-toothed smile and with a flick of his clawed hand, he pressed a red stud on the top of his right armrest.

Instantly the automated cannons mounted on top of each pillar swung around and started firing balls of superheated plasma at Whizzbang's squad. Nano-heightened reflexes were all that saved them from annihilation as the squad split into six different directions on a blaze of jump jets.

As he shot upwards, DG dropped a number of small turrets and a health station in case any of the others required emergency meds. Elzetro followed suit and scattered additional turrets so that they deployed half way up the dome walls.

The blast of the Scourge auto-cannons, the turrets, jump jets and the squad's returning fire reverberated off the metallic silver dome high overhead. The concave shape focused the sound down into the middle of the command centre in a deafening roar. General Grendig screamed a series of curses as he flicked a claw at another switch that powered a personal shield around his throne. The shield deadened the noise to a more bearable level and provided him protection from stray gunfire as he looked up at the spectacle taking place above him. Those officers closest to the throne lay sprawled comatose in their seats or writhing in pain beneath their consoles with blood pouring out of their ears.

While hurtling through the air Bosk and Whizzbang brought their Charge rifles to bear on a number of the cannons and silenced them in a pyrotechnic explosion of molten metal fragments. Scourge officers dove under tables and consoles in an effort to avoid the falling debris. Here and there, fires burst forth and belched black acrid smoke as reports, equipment and even flesh caught afire. Screams of the wounded and dying echoed off the dome above even as the automated cannons attempted to track and extinguish the Earthmen's lives.

Pyro levelled his huge chain gun at a number of the cannons and sprayed them with depleted tellurite slugs as he shot towards the domes apex. Sparks and spent shells rained down onto those below in a torrent of metal and fire.

Bosk looked up as Elzetro blasted an auto-cannon and mentally cried out, "*Elzetro left! Left, Left!*"

Elzetro instantly pivoted in the air and blasted his jets at maximum just in time to dodge multiple plasma launches from three cannons. In the process of turning, he looked directly up at Pyro and yelled a thought, "*Pyro! Dance right now!*"

Without even thinking, Pyro sideslipped right through the air and used the concussive force of his massive chain gun to propel him faster than normal. Flecks of rapidly cooling plasma splashed harmlessly across his left side while the bulk of the super-hot liquid slammed into the plasteel dome, eating great chunks of the hybrid plastic metal before dissipating. Down below in the command centre, molten slag dropped from the roof, instantly incinerating desks, consoles and several Scourge officers.

Kheldar sent a barrage of fire towards the General's chair but soon discovered that Grendig's shield easily dissipated any direct attack. He then turned his attention to the auto-cannons and the health of his squad mates as he sent waves of nanomeds to bolster damaged frames.

It was mayhem above and below as bolt after bolt of energy sought the deaths of the Earthmen and yet each time they managed to dodge out of the way in the nick of time. The devastation below was immense. Bodies littered the floor and purple blood sprayed the walls in a multi-coloured display of the devastation wrought from the battle above. Still sitting on his command throne in the centre of the complex the General was immune to the carnage and ignored the cries and screams of his officers as they died.

Whizzbang sent a thought to the squad, "Bosk, c*over me! I'm going to try and drop the outer shield.*" Glancing at his wrist chronometer, he thought to himself, "*Any second now.*"

Bosk replied, "*CT Whizz!*"

Sitting on desks and equipment Elzetro's and DG's turrets extracted their deadly toll. Any sensible Scourge officer kept their head down with their hands firmly over their ears to dull the noise of the gunfire.

Outside the command dome, Strike Leader Aldarg struggled to bring some sense of order to the chaos. The surprise assault on the fortress from within the Barrier shook him to his core. *"How could this be?"* he thought to himself.

It was clear that the three times accursed StarBlade was leading the attack and that he was now inside the command dome itself. How the Concord pilots managed to breach the outer plasteel doorway would be a matter for later investigation. As soon as he had assessed the situation, he ordered the mobile cannons from the barracks brought up so that they could blast their way in.

"Squad Leader Barrav," Strike Leader Aldarg barked.

"Yes sir!"

"Take your squad and find out what's taking those cannon's so long!"

Squad Leader Barrav slung his sniper rifle onto his back, ordered his squad to fall in behind him and raced off in the direction of the barracks. Messengers from the outer wall reported no activity and the Barrier was still clear of all hostiles. At least that is good news Aldarg thought to himself.

Six massive explosions, each one quickly after the other, rocked the ground under Strike Leader Aldarg's feet. The shockwaves flowed out from the direction of the Barrier towers flattening temporary structures like a rampaging deranged Spyderlynx. Bolts, nuts and plasteel sheeting whizzed and zinged like bullets outward from the epicentre of the explosions, cutting warriors in half or riddling them full of holes. Scourge soared through the air like flotsam on the surface of the sea and Aldarg watched as Squad Leader Barrav pin wheeled end over end past him. It was only by instinctively reaching out and grabbing the command dome's entrance support beam that the Strike Leader did not find himself in similar circumstances.

Aldarg screamed in agony as the explosive pressure wave passed over him, rupturing his inner ear drum in its destructive journey. Purple blood seeped out of each ear canal and his knees collapsed beneath him as the intensity of the pain continued to increase. Finally, after what seemed minutes but was only seconds he gained some semblance of control over himself and unsteadily stood to his feet.

As he rested one hand against the support beam, he gingerly tested his balance as he said to himself, "*What was that?*"

Through the dust and smoke, Strike Leader Aldarg looked up in horror as he watched the enormous twenty story high Barrier towers, sway back and forth like two trees in a strange dance, waiting for the final bow at the end of a song only they could hear. In a wrenching scream of plasteel reinforced plascrete, the outer pylons that supported the tower's superstructure finally crumbled and gave way. Even while the Barrier lightning continued to flow up and down their height the two towers parted company for the last time.

Both structures teetered and gained momentum as they fell towards the ground below. Finally, with a crash and a roar like a wounded animal, both buildings collapsed along the north and south sides of the command dome and shattered into their component parts. The resulting concussive impact of thousands of tons of structure slamming into the ground sent multiple waves of destruction across the fortress. Windows shattered in outbuildings, buildings blew apart and the outer wall breeched in two places. Scourge that were once alive and well, were now nothing but a memory, buried under fifty feet of rubble.

As the Barrier towers collapsed, dust and smoke jetted out of portals and cooling vents, forming a great billowing grey cloud. With a final crash, torrents of fine particulates flooded the area, gushing around the still intact command dome and covering the entire fortress in an eerie white powder.

Coughing violently from the quantity of dust he had inhaled, Strike Leader Aldarg wretched violently and gasped for breath in between each tumultuous heave of his stomach.

"I am still alive! I am truly a Scourge!" Aldarg thought to himself.

Ripping off a section of his uniform, he tied it around his mouth and eyes to afford at least some ability to both see and breathe. That was when he noticed that the purple haze of the Barrier was gone.

High up in the stratosphere Selfia looked out a portal in the side of her drop ship at the landscape far below. Even though it was dark, she could see Barrier lightning crackling its purple haze back and forth, illuminating the mountains like some strange strobe light.

Tilting her head to her side, she spoke into her comnet, "Selfia niner, three, one, four to General Alban"

"Alban three six four eight copy Selfia."

"Any news General?"

"Nothing as yet. We're almost at bingo fuel and we'll have to turn back within the next fifteen minutes."

"I'm sure that Commander Whizzbang and his squad will come through."

"We can only hope Selfia. Hang on a second…"

Selfia could hear the General furiously tapping at instruments in the cockpit of the lead drop ship before she said, "Self, can you check if you can see the Barrier?"

"I was just looking at…..hang on. It's gone! They've done it!"

General Alban switched from Selfia to broadcasting across the entire local comnet. "General Alban to all drop ships the Barrier is down, I repeat, the Barrier is down! Drop all cargo in thirty seconds."

Selfia could not hide her smile as she thumped Tiny on the back, "Time to smash Tiny!"

Tiny smiled his trademark shattered teeth grin, spat out his old cigar and in the blink of an eye, a newly lit one materialised in his mouth. "I've been waiting a long time for this moment. I knew those Earthmen were built of tough stuff."

Selfia squeezed Acheron's hand and whispered, "I love you Ach."

"I love you too Self."

"You keep yourself safe down there."

"I will, if you will Self."

Tilting her head again to the comnet Selfia said, "Selfia niner, three, one, four to Gardner and Happy."

"Gardner, five, five, five, five here."

"Happy, niner, three, two, seven here."

One of these days, she was going to have to ask Gardner about his unusual number designator. "Gentlemen we leave in fifteen seconds. I wish you and your squads all the best as we finally rid Alpha Three of the Scourge."

"CT Selfia," came Gardner's drawl reply, "It will be a time well remembered."

"Tonight's drinks are on me Self," Happy replied.

Selfia watched as the large launch door at the back of the drop ship opened, revealing the sight of a dozen vessels behind them. A similar number were ahead and filled every operational battleframe the Concord could muster. The roar of the wind drowned out conversations that were not via the ear pieces built into each battleframe's comnet.

General Alban's voice crackled, "Battleframe pilots ready to deploy on my mark. May God be with us all. Five, four three, two, one, mark."

In an orderly fashion, the battleframes exited the ramp, energised their gliding wings and formed up around their individual Squad Leaders. As designated Group Strike Leader, Selfia was at the apex of the "V" formation, leading the way for the nearly one hundred pilots.

Whizzbang spun wildly in the air, dodging Scourge auto-cannon fire while the rest of the squad played their own game of chicken with the cannons that were tracking them. As luck would have it, he gained a moments respite as the cannons targeting systems tried to predict the movements of the darting, wheeling and dashing figures of the rest of the squad. He had to work out how to shut off the shield generators. Hanging onto a huge girder attached to one of the giant monitors in the domed roof Whizzbang took a quick breather to assess the situation

Fires continued to burn around the command centre, consoles sparked and spewed choking dark black smoke. The good news was the smoke seemed to disrupt the auto cannons tracking systems so that they were not as accurate.

Gunfire continued to reverberate off the domed roof in brief controlled bursts. The deafening noise of each expended bullet sounded like a herd of stampeding cattle. Whizzbang watched his squad mates darting in and out of the smoke and slowly but surely getting the best of the auto cannons. It looked like DG had received a blast to his right side. It would take a long time before the nanites could repair a hole that size in his armour. He must be feeling it Whizzbang thought.

Suddenly, it felt like the whole dome lurched into the air and then dropped back in place. Desks, chairs, monitors and consoles shot upwards and came crashing down. Whizzbang used a quick blast of his jump jets to maintain his position holding onto the girder.

"*Looks like the Barrier towers have just come down.*"

"*Is that was that was,*" Pyro telepathically replied.

Elzetro yelled jubilantly, "*Yeeeehaaaa!*"

Amongst the excitement, DG knew he was in trouble. He had lost count of the number of plasma bursts that he had dodged while he continuously lashed out with his Tesla lightning gun. He had already disabled a number of auto-cannons but it appeared that the remaining guns were taking their revenge by tracking and firing at him continuously.

"*Hey guys, I think I've got a problem here.*"

Pyro answered, "*Drop straight down and get out of there DG. I can see that you're frame has already suffered a hit on the right. See if you can give it some time to repair.*"

"*Sorry guys, I'm…*"

For a second time, burning hot plasma engulfed DG's right side and he felt himself tossed like a leaf on the wind across towards the centre of the dome. Even a battleframe is no match for the super-heated elements that normally reside in the centre of a star. The pain in his side was unbearable and thankfully, his body did the only thing that it could do. He passed out. The problem was that he was still over a hundred feet above the command dome floor when his jump jets failed.

As if in a dream, Whizzbang watched DG take a second hit. Plasma greedily ate at his battleframe armour and the force of the impact blasted his friend into the centre of the dome. Whizzbang cried out as DG's unconscious body crashed to the floor at the foot of General Grendig's dais. There would be no emergency porting from this side of Alpha Three.

"Man down, man down! Kheldar, can you heal DG?" Whizzbang screamed his thoughts as he lined up his Charge rifle on the General.

In a panicked thought Kheldar replied, *"I'm all out! I need some time to recharge!"*

Whizzbang pressed the firing stud just as the General's throne detached itself from the dais and hovered towards DG's body. The beam splattered against the General's shields and Whizzbang watched through his scope as Grendig looked directly up at him then smiled, with the full force of his sharpened teeth. It was grotesque; macabre; the look of pure evil. He was safe in the knowledge that no weapon that the hated StarBlade possessed could penetrate his shield.

General Grendig slowly pulled his jagged blade out of its sheath and leaning forward from his throne he bent over the prone and unconscious DG. He then roughly grabbed DG's helmet and pulled up his head to see his victim's face more easily.

Whizzbang began to panic. Not DG. He was so much fun and full of life. Not him! His mind was a chaotic tumble of emotions that seemed to block him from focusing on how to save DG. Everything was happening so fast. He could not bring his thoughts to bear on how to save his friend.

What felt like minutes were actually seconds and Whizzbang finally managed to gather his will together to assault Grendig's mind. It was going to take too long! A Scourge General by nature has a huge ego and natural defences against such an attack. Whizzbang could crack the mind but it was going to take too long.

Grendig drew back his dagger and rammed it home into DGs neck. Red, not purple blood, flowed in great gushes from DG's torn and ripped throat. Grendig then began to hack away at the battleframe pilot until DG's head adorned the tip of his long dagger point.

Whizzbang watched appalled as General Grendig laughed holding up DG's head and yelled, "This is what will become of you all!" With a flick of his blade, he tossed DG's head halfway across the command centre. He let out a loud half mad laugh as DG's head bounced off a console and onto the hard stone floor.

Whizzbang's mental assault disintegrated in the shock of seeing his friend slaughtered like a pig. The desecration of DG's body in such a manner only contributed to Whizzbang's devastation. Even while perched in his position high up amongst the girders, Whizzbang could not help himself and began wretching. The others had been too busy with the cannons to notice what was happening down below. By the sounds of it, the last of the cannons had just been permanently decommissioned.

Whizzbang wiped his mouth with the back of his hand and began to pull himself together. He jump-jetted down from his perch and on flaming jets took up a position a few feet off the command centre floor directly opposite the General. His steel blue eyes bored into the pink staring blankly back at him and then in a cold flat voice he said, "That was my friend you just butchered."

Grendig finished cleaning his blade on his black tongue and gave a low chuckle. "Do you think that I care? You will all die and we will triumph."

Still firing his jump jets Whizzbang slowly maneuvered himself towards the shield console while never taking his eyes off the General. A quick glance suggested that the console was still operational. In that split second, Grendig realised Whizzbang's intentions and jumped back into his seat so that he could guard the shield console with his personal throne shield.

Although Grendig was fast, Whizzbang's nanite infused reflexes were far faster. In a split second, he reached the console and flicked the "fortress shield off" switch. Even though the writing in the Scourge language, he found that he could clearly read it as if it was in English. The shield level meter immediately began displaying a steadily falling level of energy.

In front of him, like a caged animal Grendig let out a low growl.

As Selfia glided towards the Scourge fortress, she brought her sniper riflescope up to her eye to better survey the scene with its light enhancing capabilities. The Barrier towers had collapsed in a pile of rubble to either side of the command dome, one of them completely crushing the barracks. The outer wall had been breached in several places and through the rapidly settling dust, she could still make out a few Scourge warriors crawling amongst the rubble. What really concerned her was the green tinge that everything appeared to have.

"Gardner, do you notice the green colour across everything?"

"I was just looking at that Selfia."

"Any ideas?"

"I would swear that it's some type of force field and it's going to be bad news if we fly into it."

Selfia peered through her scope again. "The green tinge is gone now."

Selfia could hear the surprise in his tone as Gardner said, "Looks like someone's shut down the force field Self."

Using the broadcast channel on the comnet Selfia said, "To all battleframes. The Earthmen have rolled out the welcoming mat and dropped the Scourge shields. Let's make sure that we clean the mat of any unwelcome dirt on the way in. Form up on my wing."

The battleframes moved into a tight bunch around Selfia and those with long range weapons began sighting and firing at any Scourge that stuck their heads up. Selfia took her command high over the fortress to drop grenades like an aerial bombardment over any Scourge that remained alive. Not surprisingly, after the two Barrier towers had collapsed there were not that many targets left. Those that were alive, quickly died at the hands of the battleframe snipers and grenade launchers, as they glided within range. Selfia spiralled the Concord battleframes down and landed near the command dome entrance.

Strike Leader Aldarg tightened the cloth protecting his eyes and mouth from the dust permeating the atmosphere. Using his rifle as a crutch, he coughed violently a number of times to help remove the particles from the back of his throat.

"How could this have happened?" he thought to himself. "We were invincible within our fortress!"

Stumbling over broken plascrete in the half-light, Aldarg left the temporary safety of the command dome entranceway. With any luck, some warriors survived the disaster that he could regroup into a fighting force.

The crunch of metal shod boots on broken stone alerted him that a number of warriors were approaching from the far end of the street that ran alongside the command dome. The deep gloom prevented him from seeing whom had managed to reach him.

A lone battleframe pilot stepped through the haze and looked directly at Aldarg as he leant on his rifle. Aldarg knew that he was dead but why did it have to be at the hands of a human female? He had always believed that they were the weaker enemies. Looking into the eyes of the Concord pilot immediately told him that he was wrong. Male and female, they were both just as deadly.

In a single fluid motion, Selfia raised her rifle, pressed the firing stud and then continued to lead the squad of pilots behind her forward. That was how Strike Leader Aldarg died.

Chapter 15
It is Finished

Behind him, the General gave a growl and spat out, "StarBlade, it makes no difference. We will win because it is our destiny. You will become a head ornament for my ceremonial spear and I will show the galaxy just how weak you really are."

The other members of the squad descended on blasted jets and it was only then that they saw DG's mutilated body. Whizzbang felt a steely resolve transmitted across the mental rapport he had with the others.

"*We will look after DG later,*" Bosk stated flatly.

Kheldar thought, "*Can you get to Grendig or do I have to drop this whole building on his head?*"

Whizzbang thought, "*Kheldar, we can get him.*"

"*Good, don't take too long about it. We need to look after our friend.*"

"*CT Kheldar,*" Whizzbang thought, "*this won't take long.*"

The four telepaths surrounded General Grendig and other than the crackle of a few fires, the dome was deathly quiet. A desk moved off to the left. Pyro swung around and let loose a blast of his chain gun. The desk evaporated into a spray of wooden splinters and what had caused the movement parted in two.

Whizzbang looked the General in his pink eyes and asked, "General Grendig, are you sure you are safe within your shield?"

"Nothing you have can harm me and it's only a matter of time before my warriors will come to my aid."

"That's where you're wrong General."

At this range, the four Earthmen mentally punched through the shield as if it were tissue paper and began hacking at the lock that was the essence of General Grendig. They were not gentle with the General and the pain that they inflicted in the process of unlocking the General's mind was considerable.

At first, the Scourge General wondered what was happening and began swatting at invisible flies but when he finally realised his danger it was his turn to panic. He tried to put up mental barriers to block the four from cracking him open like an egg. In the end, he could do nothing against four of the most powerful minds in the galaxy. What questions they asked, they received answers and the four of them had many questions that needed answers.

The General's feeble mental defences finally completely collapsed and his mind was splayed open like a gutted fish for each one of them to examine in detail. His position in the command structure only related to Alpha Three and he reported to a person known as Lord Zechlan. Within a few minutes, they had absorbed the entirety of General Grendig's knowledge and had come to some startling conclusions.

The first thing they had learned was that this was a war without quarter. No mercy would be asked for and no mercy would be given. It was kill or be killed. There were no Earth concepts of the rules of war set by a Geneva Convention. This war did not have parallels on Earth and would only end in the complete extermination of either side.

The second thing they learned was that Alpha Three was a small part of something much, much larger. General Grendig had the impression that he was one of many Generals that reported to Lord Zechlan and there were many worlds enslaved by the

Scourge. What was unclear was whether Zechlan was actually a Scourge himself or something else altogether.

The intelligence they had gained in a few minutes was more than the Concord had been able to secure since the war began. There was a lot to contemplate and they would need the help of the generals and their friends to understand it all.

As Kheldar reverently brought DG back together, the other members of the squad moved through the command dome looking for survivors. Upon finding any officers alive, they invaded their mind, stripped them of their knowledge and then executed them. No quarter was asked for and no quarter given.

By the time, they completed their grizzly but necessary task they were all exhausted and ravenous.

"*Bosk, we need to find Zechlan,*" Whizzbang thought to the squad so everyone could hear.

"*I agree. Grendig didn't know how to contact him so we'll have to wait for an inbound call.*"

"*Elzetro, is there a way we can track a signal so we know where it's coming from?*" Whizzbang asked.

"*Hang on, let me look around. One of these guys I scanned knew how to do it; hopefully the right equipment is still intact.*"

Behind him, Whizzbang heard Elzetro and Pyro rummaging around for the equipment they needed. While they searched Bosk asked Whizzbang, "*What do we do with it?*" indicating Grendig who was still sitting in his command chair with the shield now turned off. His eyes stared vacantly into space and his breathing was quick and shallow in his induced mental coma.

"*Let Kheldar deal with it.*"

Despite his devastation at what had happened to his friend, Kheldar provided General Grendig with a quick painless death and then walked away. He needed some time to himself and wanted nothing more to do with the monstrosity.

"*Found it! Just give me a second to patch it in,*" Elzetro thought. "*We're good to go now. If Zechlan calls I'll know exactly where he's calling from.*"

"*All we have to do now is wait for him,*" Whizzbang said tiredly.

"What do you think is going on outside?" Bosk asked Whizzbang.

"I've got no idea. Let's hope that Selfia and the others have made it. Hang on, give me a sec will you." Whizzbang was so tired he could not get even a squeak of power out of his perception to see outside. After glancing at the General's body below the dais to make sure he really was dead, Whizzbang sat on the command throne. After they had stripped Grendig's mind bare they all knew every one of its functions as well as the General did. Flicking a number of switches Whizzbang brought up a screen of what was happening outside the command dome entranceway.

Bosk looked up at the cracked and damaged screen and thought, *"Isn't that the prettiest sight you've ever seen."* The image on the monitor showed that the entrance to the command dome surrounded not by Scourge but by Concord battleframes.

"We did it Bosk. Alpha Three's been won!"

"We did at that."

The victory seemed hollow without DG. There would not be any impromptu dance parties, turrets materialising to save the day or his quirky smile and wit. Yes, the Scourge were vanquished but this was the first time that Whizzbang's squad had been impacted by a loss personally. In the past, it had always been a stranger that had suffered or died, not one of their own.

DG's death crystallised the reality of the evil that they were struggling to fight. This was not a game where you get multiple lives, this was for real and for keeps. When you died here, you really died and forever.

Slowly standing to his feet Whizzbang thought to the squad, *"We need to look after our friend."*

There were grunts of agreements from the other four. They were all exhausted but some things needed finishing. A collapsed tabletop provided a stretcher and Bosk with Elzetro's help carefully lifted DG's body and head onto it. Kheldar found a covering from another table that improvised as a shroud to provide DG with some dignity.

Pyro reached into a pocket in his battleframe and pulled out a picture of all of them during a party. He placed it on DG's chest and with tears welling up in his eyes whispered, "We will never forget the good times DG."

Whizzbang led the way out of the dome while the four others carried their friend's body. He keyed in the pass code and the door slid open revealing a bright sunny day. *"The world goes on,"* he thought to himself.

Once they recognised who was exiting the command dome the Concord battleframe pilots lowered their weapons. As they watched, the Earthmen emerge from the command dome carrying DG's body sorry replaced their jubilation of victory.

Selfia, Tiny and Acheron were at the far end of what remained of the street outside the entrance, and upon seeing Whizzbang, they rushed up to him with smiles on their faces. "Commander Whizzbang, you Earthmen did it!" Selfia exclaimed excitedly. She then saw the other four carrying DG's shrouded body. "Oh no!" She looked up at the others and said, "DG?"

Pyro nodded and Selfia could see the tears still streaming down his face and those of the other Earthmen.

Tiny removed his cigar from his mouth and butted it out. This time a new lit one didn't magically appear. In his gravelly voice he said, "DG you were my friend. We had a lot of good times together that I will never forget." A single tear rolled down his rough battle scarred cheek. Dropping to one knee, Tiny bowed his head and gave the Concord salute that said DG would never be alone.

All up and down the street outside the dome entrance, battleframes dropped to one knee and with bowed heads, they repeated the salute as a mark of respect for the fallen.

Finally, Acheron stood up, walked over to the shroud, and pulled out of a pocket in his battleframe a drinks umbrella. With a broken voice he loudly said, "DG taught me that a drink always taste better with umbrellas in them." He then placed the umbrella carefully on DG's covered body.

Selfia moved forward and said for all to hear, "DG taught me that life was precious." She then placed a photo of her and DG on the shroud.

And so it went on for the next thirty minutes pilot after pilot came forward, stated a lesson that DG had taught them and left a small token of their friendship. Like the man, some were humorous, while others embodied his spirit of living life to the fullest. All were respectful and honouring of the pilot who was their friend.

Whizzbang was surprised that DG had such an impact on so many people within such a short time. While he had been making the command decisions, DG had been bolstering everyone's morale with a few kind words or sharing a drink. He went about the job of ensuring that people could still smile in the midst of a terrifying war.

Finally, Whizzbang stepped forward and fell to both his knees before his friend's body. Sadly, he said, "DG taught me the cost of leadership and the privilege of leading men such as him."

Out of a pocket in his battleframe, he pulled the tourist brochure that he had picked up in the taxi back in Los Angeles. It said in big letters on the front, "Hollywood Tourist Sites". He did not know why he had kept the brochure or why he had it with him, but it seemed appropriate that DG have a bit of his hometown with him on this world, light years away from Earth. He placed the brochure on the shroud, wiped his moist eyes and stood to his feet.

Looking across at the gathered battleframes before him Whizzbang felt a sense of pride rising up against his grief. He was proud at being part of something bigger, more noble and good. Speaking loudly so that those in the back could hear he said, "DG's passing is a terrible loss. From what we have just witnessed, many of us counted him a friend. He would not want us to be sad on a day like today, he'd want a celebration!"

Whizzbang watched as downcast faces turned upwards towards him. "Together we have achieved an incredible victory over the Scourge. We have claimed Alpha Three for the Concord and the dreaded Barrier that has kept us penned into a small area of the planet is no more!"

Smiles now adorned the faces of the pilots all around him and a few had begun to cheer at Whizzbang's last comment. Bosk leaned closer to Pyro and whispered, "Your Dad certainly has a way with words."

Despite his fatigue, Pyro straightened up in pride and whispered back, "That's my Dad alright."

Whizzbang now had the undivided attention of every pilot in the area. "Although we have won this planet the Concord and my home planet of Earth are still under threat. Even now, we are tracking inbound signals from a Scourge central base to this one. Together, as one we will stand and continue the fight for freedom!" The pilots began yelling words of agreement and loudly cheering.

"What makes humanity special is that we fully appreciate life." Whizzbang looked down at DG's body, "and death." Breaking out of his brief reverie, he continued, "But right now we have an important task to perform. We need to celebrate life by throwing a party for the great victory!"

A loud cheer went up from all of the battleframe pilots, as the pent up emotions of years of near captivity were suddenly unleashed. From somewhere a violin began playing a jig and pilots began dancing together on servo-assisted legs. Frames smashed against frames and laughter echoed off the surrounding mountains. This was going to be a celebration remembered for decades to come.

Sitting on an unbroken part of the wall Intellect looked down at Creativity playing her violin for the battleframes. She had energized a Raven battleframe to blend in with the other pilots. No one could play the violin like her and as he watched, the music seemed to encourage the pilots into greater and greater feats of dancing. Some even ignited their jets and began swirling and weaving about each other in the air.

"She really knows how to play," said a voice beside him.

Without looking Intellect answered Wisdom's statement, "She certainly does. So what do we do now?"

Wisdom removed his spectacles and began to clean them on a cloth from his jacket pocket. "We really can't interfere as yet. They need to become accustomed to their new abilities before we can introduce the next level of training."

Intellect nodded in agreement. "I just hope that they have time."

"Stop worrying Intellect. They'll have time."

"Have they detected the Scourge reinforcements as yet?"

Wisdom patted the younger man's shoulder affectionately "No they haven't but I have confidence that they'll overcome them. In the meantime, let's enjoy Creativity's moment."

"But...."

"No buts Intellect," Wisdom interrupted. "Whizzbang and the other Earthmen need time to recover from DG's loss."

"I wish there was some way he could have been saved."

"You looked at every causality and it was clear that the Earthmen needed to experience real loss before they could develop further."

"I know that Wisdom but he was so...," Intellect drifted off.

"Alive?"

"Yes, that's the word. He was so alive. I wish we could have intervened."

Wisdom nodded as he placed the now clean round spectacles back on the bridge of his nose. Thought of DG's death caused his blue eyes to briefly well with moisture before he banished it. Sighing deeply Wisdom said more to himself then to Intellect by his side, "I will miss him."

"I will miss him too," Intellect echoed.

Below them, Creativity played notes so quickly that they seemed to merge into one another. Around her pilots were completely caught up in the reckless abandon of celebrating their victory. Finally, with horsehair hanging from her bow and sweat beading her forehead she reached a crescendo in the music. After a brief pause, while the pilots cheered and clapped she struck up another tune.

Wisdom said in wonder, "She really is very, very good."

"Just like they are." Intellect indicated Whizzbang and Bosk as they quietly left the celebration. "Are they going to be able to pull them all together? The fate of the galaxy is on their shoulders."

"I really don't know but both their lines are as pure as we could make them. They are the galaxy's only hope."

An hour later Whizzbang found himself sitting on a rocky ledge overlooking the Scourge fortress far below. From his vantage point, he could see why there was little resistance after the two Barrier towers had collapsed to either side of the command dome. The devastation they had caused as they fell was complete. Where once there were buildings, barracks and training yards, nothing recognisable remained other than the huge command dome itself. *"The same dome DG had died within,"* he thought sadly.

The sudden gust the wind whistled through the rocky outcrops around him. In the distance, he could make out a new tune played by the violinist and could not help tapping his foot in time to the music. *"She could really play,"* he thought to himself.

The wind shifted and again he could hear the violin but this time it seemed to be tugging at his heart. The melody echoed his own mourning at DG's death while simultaneously healing and washing away much of the pain from the loss.

Looking down at the celebrations below Whizzbang felt so alone, he desperately needed Esther. He needed her love, her support and more than ever he needed her to tell him that everything was going to be OK. After holding them back for so long, tears poured unbidden down his cheeks as he shifted his gaze to the mountain ranges opposite. The snow-capped rugged peaks dropped away into green valleys and in a few places, he could see a river winding its way between them. It hurt to cry but letting go his emotions on the privacy of the ledge made him feel a lot better for it.

"I thought I'd find you up here," Bosk's familiar voice said behind him.

Whizzbang did not bother wiping his eyes in front of Bosk. He simple answered, "Where else would I be?"

Bosk settled in next to his best friend and together they enjoyed each other's company in silence as they stared off into the distance. Finally he said, "I don't know who's playing the violin but they're really good."

Whizzbang nodded absently. "They seem to be playing what my heart feels."

"I know what you mean." Then gathering up some courage Bosk continued, "You couldn't have done anything. None of us could."

"I know. It still hurts though. I don't know what I would do if it happened to you or the boys."

"Well it hasn't and as long as we stick together it won't"

Whizzbang sighed. "Do you miss the girls?"

"More than ever."

"So what are we going to do next?

"I'm not really sure but…"

Behind them two, all familiar voices yelled out to them both, "Dad!"

With flaming jets Pyro was first to reach his father and was quickly followed by Elzetro. Stumbling over his words in an effort to get them out Pyro said, "Dad, we've just had an inbound signal!"

Bosk turned to Whizzbang. "So it looks like we know what's next."

End of Battleframe
Book One of The Mindwars
Register at michaelgilmour.com

Receive exclusive access to
Maps of Alpha Three and key locations
Character profiles
Future book news
Discussion forums.

Glossary

Acheron	Acheron is Selfia's husband and they were both sent by General Frank McCleod to protect Whizzbang in his journey southwards. Acheron often goes into a berserkers rage when fighting Scourge in his Anvil battleframe.
Alban	General Alban oversees the air forces on Alpha Three.
Alex	The human name of Elzetro.
Altavia	Research assistant to Professor Steinberg.
Alpha Three	The third planet in the Alpha Centauri star system.
Anvil	The Anvil is a close quarter's combat battleframe that is armed with a light-weight mini-gun that fires a rapid stream of tiny tellurite slugs. It has considerable amounts of armour that protects the pilot during hand-to-hand combat. Acheron enjoys this battleframe as it provides him with a large amount of firepower and a high level of armour if he gets into a difficult situation.
Bardon	General Bardon oversees all of the ground forces on Alpha Three.

Barrier	A field of force generated by the Scourge that is death to any humans caught within it. Prior to the barrier being fully deployed the Concord managed to build a series of repulsor cannons that push it back from a small area of the planet.
Battle-pod	A Scourge device that allows the warping in of a fist (normally five) warriors to a location every five minutes. Battle-pods are black and shaped like an upright pyramid with an energy orb at the apex.
Bosk	Bosk is Whizzbang's best friend since childhood and is a specialist Raven sniper.
Comnet	The comnet is the wider communications network used by the Concord. The local or localnet is the communications network that battleframe squad members talk to one another over short distances.
Creativity	A member of the elder race.
DG	DG is also known as digital gangster and is one of the earthmen in Whizzbang's squad. He typically fights in a Rook battleframe.
Dreadnaught	The largest Concord battleframe that has ever been developed. It has a massive level of armour and is armed with a super-heavy chain gun. Pyro is one of the few battleframe pilots that can effectively manage the weight of the Dreadnaught.
Eagle-claw	A specialist recon battleframe that has stealth capabilities while being lightly armoured. Pilots of this frame typically use a bolt-action long-barrelled rifle that shoots a depleted tellurite slug at high velocities. Selfia enjoys the freedom of this battleframe as it allows her to survey an entire battlefield and fire at targets where it can be of the most use.
eport	An emergency teleport or eport occurs when a battleframe determines that a pilot is on the verge of death. The pilot and battleframe are instantly teleported to the nearest Concord stronghold for

emergency services. The potential downside to eporting is that it can be psychologically traumatic, leaving some pilots in a vegetative state.

Elzetro	Elzetro is Bosk's son and the best friend of Pyro. His preferred battleframe is a Rook.
Engie	Concord slang for a Scourge Engineer. These warriors can hack into Concord systems and launch probes for scouting enemy locations.
Esther	Esther is Russell's wife and a former nurse. She is the mother of her son Pyro and daughters Michelle and Rose.
Evkon 316	Developed a number of years ago Evkon 316 is the best pain blocker that the Concord has ever developed. Evkon 316 blocks the majority of the pain that a traumatised wounded pilot with otherwise experience.
Felesh	General Felesh overseas all Concord intelligence operations on Alpha Three.
Freehold	The second largest Concord base on Alpha Three. Situated on the side a hill, it overlooks the ocean and pristine beaches. Built like a resort, the base even has thatched huts and bars for providing rest and recreation for pilots.
Gardner	Gardner prefers to be guarding tellurite mining Diggers but is known as one of the most stealthy pilots in the Concord.
Grendig	General Grendig commands all Scourge forces on Alpha Three from the security of his command dome.
Happy	Whizzbang's friend that warns Concord Central on Alpha Three of the impending Scourge attack. Happy is a close friend of Whizzbang and pilots a Rook battleframe.
Intellect	A member of the elder race.
James	The human name of Pyro.

Jug	Concord slang for a Scourge Juggernaut. They are a heavily armoured battleframe that carries a portable plasma cannon for offensive armament.
Kaladon IV	The fourth planet out from the sun of Kaladon and the birthplace of the Concord.
Kheldar	Kheldar is one of Whizzbang's squad members and fights using a bio-battleframe.
McLeod	Franky, Frank McLeod is a General in the Concord armed forces and coordinates all activities on Alpha Three.
Mihaly	The human name of Bosk.
Nanites	Tiny programmable machines that manipulate tellurite to build battleframes and other structures. If a battleframe receives damage during a battle then like a living organism, nanites will work at repairing damage.
Nanomeds	Nanomeds are microscopic machines that are automatically injected into a wounded pilot's body by their battleframe. Nanomeds heal the pilot at the cellular level so that they are always at their peak level of health.
Ogzmat	A Scourge facsimile of a human used for infiltrating and spying on an enemy.
Plasteel	A blending of hi-tensile steel and polymer plastic. It is one of the most versatile materials developed by the Concord for off-world colonization.
Pyro	Pyro or Pyromaniac is Whizzbang's son and best friends with Elzetro. He prefers using the largest and most powerful Concord assault battleframe known as the Dreadnaught.
Raven	A type of reconnaissance battleframe that is preferred by both Whizzbang and Bosk. It is lightweight, low armoured and highly stealthy. The typical weapon used by Raven pilots is the Charge sniper rifle that fires a concentrated high intensity energy beam.

Ray	Story name of Whizzbang.
Rex	The Rex is one of the most powerful Concord heavy assault battleframes and is only second to the Dreadnaught. As well as being hugely armoured the Rex fires a heavy chain-gun that packs an enormous recoil. This is Tiny's preferred battleframe.
Rook	A popular battleframe that has a medium level of armour and a lightning gun for offensive purposes. The unique feature of the Rook is that it can deploy a number of anti-personnel turrets. The Rook is the preferred battleframe of Happy, DG and Elzetro.
Russell	The human name of Whizzbang
Scourge	The Scourge are a race of pale skinned, pink-eyed humanoids that are completely ruthless and never take prisoners. Like Concord pilots, Scourge infantry have a number of different battleframes that empower them in a variety of ways.
Selfia	Selfia recently married Acheron and is the brains of the two of them. She pilot's an Eagle-claw battleframe and quickly rises through the Concord ranks to become a squad group leader.
Shock	Concord slang for a Scourge Shock Trooper. They have medium armour and fire the equivalent of an assault rifle.
Slayer	A Scourge Slayer is often armed with a light machine pistol but typically uses a tellurite crystal dagger in close combat.
Snipe	Concord slang for a Scourge Sniper that is similar to a Concord Raven other than they fire a ruby coloured laser.
Starblade	Almost mythical nemesis of the Scourge.
Steinberg	The father of nanite and nanomed technology that allowed the development of the modern battleframe.

Tellurite	A crystal that can be converted to malleable energy and then back into crystalline form. Malleable energy is manipulated by nanites to build almost any structure and is the basis of Concord technology. All battleframes are built and powered from tellurite.
Thomas	Story name for Bosk.
Tiny	After an initial confrontation with Whizzbang at Freehold, Tiny has become one of Whizzbang's staunchest allies. He's known for smoking acrid cigars and has an almost toothless grin. Tiny, pilot's an Anvil battleframe.
TransWarp	TransWarp's are similar to larger portable battle-pods. When deployed they can warp in up to twenty Scourge warriors at a time.
Whizzbang	A battleframe pilot that was initially the concept of the Concord Blue Sky research program. After losing his parents to a Scourge attack Whizzbang focused his life on becoming the best sniper in the Concord. It is later discovered that Russell truly brought Whizzbang to life.
Wisdom	A member of the elder race.
Wrist-comp	Built into every battleframe, a wrist-comp allows the pilot to connect to Concord control interfaces.

About Michael Gilmour

Born in Melbourne, Australia Michael founded his first business when he was just 16 years old. After completing his BSc in electronics and computer science, he continue his entrepreneurial career and has founded many Internet startups over the past 25 years.

In 1998, Michael completed his MBA and served as a director of the prestigious Australian Internet Industry Association, the last two of which he was elected to the position of vice-chairman. As a member of the board, he contributed to forming industry policies for, cyber-crime, copyright and chaired the committee for establishing the online advertising standards for Australia.

For the past 8 years, Michael has been growing his domain management company, ParkLogic, and now has clients the world over. He is a regular industry commentator via his blog and is a highly sought after speaker at global industry events.

Michael has always had a desire to write his own novel. In his early teens, he would arrive home from school and head straight to his bedroom to enter the fantastic worlds created by authors like Tolkien, and Herbert. He would often get engrossed in the adventures long after his official bedtime and read by the hallway light, much to his mother's displeasure.

Given his Internet career, Michael took his first tentative steps towards his goal when he wrote a series of episodes for a gaming website he was developing. Two years later, he completed his debut novel, Battleframe, which is the first book in The Mindwars series. He is currently working on book two in The Mindwars and is looking forward to the adventures that lie ahead.

Michael is married to Roselyn and she has become hist first port of call for editorial advice. His three children are also reading his novels and have been an enormous support on the journey.

Michael regularly blogs on michaelgilmour.com and has provided a host of material on his books that is freely available to registered readers.